DEDICATION

For Tristan David Drake

The previous four generations of the family
have read voraciously, so I hope he'll
carry on the tradition.

THE FAR SIDE OF THE STARS

DAVID DRAKE

THE FAR SIDE OF THE STARS

This is a work of fiction. All the characters and events portrayed in this book are fictional, and any resemblance to real people or incidents is purely coincidental.

A Baen Books Original

Baen Publishing Enterprises
P.O. Box 1403
Riverdale, NY 10471
www.baen.com

ISBN: 0-7434-8864-4

Cover art by Stephen Hickman

First printing, December, 2004

Library of Congress Cataloging-in-Publication Number 2003014259

Distributed by Simon & Schuster
1230 Avenue of the Americas
New York, NY 10020

Production by Windhaven Press, Auburn, NH
Printed in the United States of America

ACKNOWLEDGEMENTS

Dan Breen continues as my first reader, making my prose better than it would be without him.

Dorothy Day and Evan Ladouceur have been addressing specialized continuity problems in this one, and my webmaster Karen Zimmerman not only helpfully read my drafts but also archived them. (After you've killed as many computers in the middle of projects as I have, you learn not to take chances.)

Speaking of which, my son Jonathan got me going again when I did kill a computer. I can't claim to have consciously raised my own techie, but it seems to work very well if you have the time. I'm reminded of the Neolithic hunters who set their axeheads in split living branches, so that when the wood regrew it gripped the stone perfectly.

Clyde Howard helped research bits of information that I knew I had but couldn't put my finger on till he'd provided them.

My friend Mark Van Name made an observation that allowed me to write this book (and I expect future books) in a greater state of contentment than ever before. I don't think it makes the prose better, but it's certainly an improvement for me.

Writers aren't easy to live with, and I may be more difficult than most. My wife Jo manages, and she feeds me very well besides.

My thanks to all of you.
Dave Drake
david-drake.com

AUTHOR'S NOTE

One of the problems when you're writing of either the past or the future is "How much should I translate?" I don't mean simply language: there's a whole complex of things that people within any society take for granted but which vary between societies. (But language too: I had somebody complain that the Arthurian soldiers in *The Dragon Lord* talked like modern soldiers. My reaction to this was that I could write the soldiers' dialogue in Latin, but the complainant couldn't read it; and if I'm going to translate into English, why on Earth wouldn't I translate into the *type* of English the same sort of men speak today?)

Weights and measures are a particular problem. I don't assume that the world of the far future will use the weights and measures of today, but I'm quite certain that my inventing new systems will do nothing desirable for my story. (There are people who're really happier for a glossary of made-up or foreign words. I'm not, though I'll admit I still occasionally murmur to myself, *"Tarzan bundolo!"*)

In the RCN series Cinnabar is on the English system and the Alliance uses Metric, simply to suggest the enormous complexity I expect will exist after Mankind spreads among the stars. (Well, I certainly hope we'll spread among the stars, but I won't pretend I'm sanguine about our chances at the moment.)

Communications protocols are very roughly based on those of the 2nd Squadron, 11th ACR, during the period it was—I was—under the command of LTC Grayle Brookshier. There were a lot of stories about squadron and regimental commanding officers. The stories about Battle Six were all positive.

I think I should comment on the background of this novel also. Today physical travel is easier than ever before, and television takes us literally anywhere. The world is generally accessible to most people, and as a result it's becoming homogenized. I don't insist that this is a bad thing, but it's a major change from the situation of a generation ago, let alone that of a hundred years in the past.

In the late 19th century a party of Russian nobles bought a South Seas trading schooner from its owner/captain, hired as captain the former mate (a man named Robert Quinton), and for several years sailed the Pacific from Alaska to New Zealand, from Kamchatka to Diamond Head. They hunted, bought curios, visited ancient ruins, and viewed native rites in a score of localities.

This sort of experience was available only first-hand and only to the exceptionally wealthy (or their associates like Quinton, who wrote a memoir of the voyage). Today anybody who watches PBS and the Discovery Channel can see everything those aristocrats saw, or at any rate as many of those things as survive.

I've tried as one of the themes of *The Far Side of the Stars* to give the feel of that former time, when travel was a risky adventure possible only for the few. While I'm glad that many—myself included—can share the world's wonders today, I do regret the passing of the romance of former times and the fact that maps no longer have splotches marked *Terra Incognita*.

Dave Drake
david-drake.com

CHAPTER 1

Adele Mundy wore for the first time her white Republic of Cinnabar Navy dress uniform. The sleeves had the chevrons of a warrant officer, the lightning bolt of the Signals Branch, and a black ribbon of mourning. She paused to check herself in the mirror in the entryway of her townhouse.

Three generations of Mundys had lived in Chatsworth Minor, ever since the family became so politically prominent that Adele's grandfather replaced their previous townhouse in Xenos with these imposing four stories of brick, stone, and ornate carvings. Adele had grown up here, but she'd been off-planet continuing her education as an archivist the night sixteen years ago when the Three Circles Conspiracy unraveled and gangs arrived to carry off the remainder of her family for execution.

She'd never expected to see Chatsworth Minor—or Cinnabar—again. When she learned that the heads of not only her parents but also her 10-year-old sister Agatha had been displayed on the Speaker's Rock, she hadn't wanted to *see* any relic of her previous life.

She smiled faintly into the mirror. Times change, but people change as well. The stern-looking naval officer with splashes of medal ribbons on the bosom of her tunic wasn't the reserved girl who'd left Cinnabar for the Academic Collections on Bryce just in time to save her life. They shared facial features and a trim build, that was all.

Or almost all; because both the officer and the girl lived with the bone-deep certainty that they were Mundys of Chatsworth. Adele's parents had been egalitarians and members of the People's Party, but there'd never been any doubt in their minds that the Mundys were first among equals . . . and no doubt in their daughter's mind that whether she was a scholar or a street-cleaner, she was a Mundy. There'd been times after her parents were killed and their property confiscated for treason that Adele believed a street-cleaner probably lived better; but that didn't change anything that *really* mattered.

Adele's servant Tovera—if servant was the right word—glanced at her mistress briefly in the mirror; her eyes flicked on, never resting anywhere very long. If Adele was prim, then Tovera was so colorless that casual observers generally paid her less attention than they did the wallpaper. For the funeral she wore a gray dress suit of good quality, also with a mourning ribbon. Her only other ornamentation was a blue-and-silver collar flash that proclaimed her a retainer—the sole retainer at the present time—of the Mundys of Chatsworth.

Tovera missed little but cared about even less; perhaps she cared about nothing except whatever task she'd been set or had set herself. Having Tovera around was much like carrying a pistol with a trigger as light as thistledown.

The pistol in the sidepocket of Adele's tunic was so

flat it didn't bulge even a dress uniform. Its trigger was indeed light.

Smiling again Adele said, "I didn't have to check myself, did I, Tovera? You'd have told me if something was wrong."

Tovera shrugged. "If you wanted me to, mistress," she said. "I don't imagine we'll attract much attention at this affair."

Adele adjusted the set of her own black ribbon. "No," she said, "I don't suppose we will. But Daniel loved his Uncle Stacey, and I wouldn't care to fail Daniel."

I'd rather die than fail Daniel . . . But she didn't say that aloud, and Tovera wouldn't have cared anyway.

Adele glanced at the footmen, waiting patiently as she'd known they would be, and then to the doorman. The house servants wore Mundy livery, but unlike Tovera they were employed by the bank which on paper leased the townhouse. That was one of the perquisites which had fallen to Adele by virtue of her friendship with Lieutenant Daniel Leary, RCN; the son of Corder Leary, Speaker Leary to his associates even though he'd given up the speakership of the Assembly years before.

"I believe we're ready, then," she said. The doorman bowed and swung open the front door of softly gleaming beewood cut on what had been the Mundy country estate of Chatsworth Major. With the four footmen ahead of her and Tovera trailing a polite pace behind, Adele stepped into the court.

Times indeed change. Speaker Leary had been primarily responsible for crushing the Three Circles Conspiracy—and Adele's family—into a smear of blood . . . but it was his influence acting through the agency of Daniel's elder sister Deirdre which had returned the townhouse to Adele's ownership when she decided she wanted it after all. Ligier Rolfe, the distant cousin who'd taken possession of the truncated estate after the Proscriptions, probably didn't to this day know what had happened to end his ownership.

The tram stop was at the mouth of the court, now quiet, which had acted as an assembly room when Lucius Mundy addressed his supporters from the fourth floor balcony of Chatsworth Minor. Political power had never meant anything to Adele; indeed, so long as she had enough to feed her and the freedom of a large archive in which to indulge her passion for knowledge in the abstract, she didn't care about money. Even so it pleased her to think of how furious her cousin's wife, Marina Casaubon Rolfe, must have been when she was evicted from a house to which the mere wealth of her merchant family would never have entitled her.

Tovera must have noticed her expression. "Mistress?" she asked mildly.

"Do you remember Mistress Rolfe?" Adele said.

"Yes," Tovera said. "A fat worm."

"I was recalling," Adele explained, "that she saw fit to insult a Mundy of Chatsworth."

Tovera didn't comment. Perhaps she smiled.

Servants lounging at the entrances of other houses fronting on the court rose and doffed their caps, standing with their heads bowed as Adele passed by. In Lucius Mundy's day, all these houses had been owned by supporters of the People's Party. They'd suffered accordingly, but those who bought the properties in the aftermath of the Proscriptions were generally social climbers like Marina Rolfe. To them Adele's return gave the neighborhood the cachet of a real aristocrat's presence; they'd made very sure that their servants were properly obsequious.

Adele couldn't imagine what her neighbors made of the fact that Mundy of Chatsworth was a naval officer;

and a warrant officer besides, a mere technician instead of a dashing commissioned officer like her tenant, Daniel Leary. Aristocrats were allowed to be eccentric, of course.

"Mistress?" Tovera said again.

"Am I eccentric, Tovera?" Adele asked, glancing over her shoulder.

"I wouldn't know, mistress," Tovera said. "You'd have to ask someone who understands what 'normal' means."

Adele grimaced. "I'm sorry, Tovera," she said. "It's not something I should joke about."

As Adele and her entourage approached the stop, an east-bound tram pulled onto the siding. Another monorail car clattered past on the main line, heading west toward the great roundabout in the center of Xenos. By law only the Militia, the national police, could fly aircars within the municipal limits of the capital; the likelihood that a touchy rival aristocrat would shoot down a private aircar passing overhead made the law more effective than merely legal sanctions could have done.

Many of the great houses had their own tramcars which teams of servants set on the rail when their master or mistress chose to go out. Adele had a respectable nest egg in the form of prize money gathered while under the command of Lieutenant Leary, but she couldn't have afforded such an establishment even if she'd seen any use for it.

She'd gotten used to taking care of herself; she preferred it that way now. She had Tovera, of course, but it was easy to forget that Tovera was human.

A footman ran ahead to engage the tram that'd just stopped, saving Adele the delay before another car arrived in answer to the call button in the kiosk. At this time of day that might be as much as half an hour. The funeral was being held at a chapel near Harbor

Three, the great naval base on the northern outskirts of Xenos. Adele had allowed enough time—of course—but she preferred to be a trifle early than to miss the start of the rites because of a run of bad luck.

Adele Mundy had seen a great deal of luck in her 32 years. Quite a lot of it had been bad.

The man who got off the tram wore a hard-used, one might almost say ragged, RCN 2nd class uniform, gray with black piping. It was the minimum standard of dress required for off-duty officers in public, though given its condition—there were oil stains on the left cuff and a mended tear on the right pants leg—the powers that be in the Navy Office might have been better served had the fellow donned clean fatigues instead.

The recent armistice between Cinnabar and the Alliance of Free Stars had led to the decommissioning of many ships and the consequent relegation of officers to half-pay status. For those who didn't have private means, half-pay was a sentence of destitution. This was obviously an unfortunate who couldn't afford to maintain his wardrobe—

"That's Lieutenant Mon," Tovera murmured in her ear.

"*Good God, it is,*" Adele blurted under her breath. She'd unconsciously averted her eyes in embarrassment; poor herself for most of her adult life, she had no desire to wallow in the poverty of others.

Such concerns didn't touch Tovera any more than love or hate did. The man coming toward them was a potential enemy—everyone was a potential enemy to Tovera—so she'd looked carefully and thus recognized Daniel's first lieutenant.

"Good afternoon, Mon!" Adele called, stepping through the line of footmen who'd deliberately placed themselves between her and the disreputable-looking stranger. "What are you doing here? Have you completed the *Princess Cecile*'s repairs already?"

"Mundy?" said Lieutenant Mon. "Thank God I found you. Is Captain Leary here as well? I need to see him soonest. I *must* see him!"

Mon was a dark, close-coupled, morose officer in his early thirties. His technical skills were above the high average of RCN officers, and his doggedness made up for his lack of brilliance. Mon had neither family wealth nor the interest of senior officers to aid him, so his advancement in the service had been embitteringly slow.

Adele respected Mon but she didn't particularly like him. She doubted that many people regarded him as a friend.

Mon's saving grace was the way he'd reacted when Daniel Leary gave him his first taste of honor and prize money. There were officers—many officers—who'd have been envious of the lucky younger superior who swept from success to success while they plodded in his wake. Mon by contrast had shown only gratitude and utter loyalty.

"Daniel's at the Stanislas Chapel," Adele said. "Commander Bergen died, and Daniel's in charge of the arrangements. We're headed there now, but, ah . . ."

The tramcar began to chime in mindless irritation at being held at the stop. Adele glanced at the vehicle but held her tongue; her frustration was with the situation, not one more noise in a city that was full of them.

Mon glanced down at his uniform. "Oh, this?" he said, flicking the stained cuff. "Oh, that's all right. I've got my Whites in storage at Fastinelli's. I'll pick them up and go straight to the chapel—it's only a stop or two away from Stanislas."

He started back into the tram; the footman

holding it in place stepped across the doorway to block him. "No, no, that's all right Morris!" Adele said. "My colleague Lieutenant Mon and I will travel together to the chapel. He'll change when he gets there."

They all boarded, the footmen first to clear space for their mistress—though the only others in the car were a disconsolate couple wearing shapeless blue robes. They cowered at the far end. Xenos was the capital not only of Cinnabar but of the empire which Cinnabar ruled. The city drew tourists, workers, and beggars from more worlds than even an information specialist like Adele Mundy could determine without checking the handheld data unit in a discreet thigh pocket on all of her uniforms, even these Dress Whites.

Adele smiled wryly. She'd be less uncomfortable stark naked but holding her data unit than fully clothed without the unit. Yes, she supposed she was eccentric. . . .

The monorail whined away from the stop, then jolted onto the main line. They'd switch to a north-bound line three stops on instead of going west to the main transfer point at the Pentacrest.

She wondered if the foreign couple had a real destination or if they were simply riding the cars for want of other occupation. They didn't look the sort to bury themselves in study as Adele Mundy had done when she was a lonely orphan in a foreign land.

"Ah, Mon?" she said, voicing another awkward topic that thought of poverty had brought to mind. Fastinelli's was the large-volume naval clothier's located near Harbor Three. Strictly speaking the firm didn't have a storage facility, but it did loan money against items of uniform which were surplus to the requirements of temporarily embarrassed officers. "Since you've just landed and won't have collected your pay yet, can I offer you a small loan for your storage fees?"

"What?" said Mon, obviously surprised. Whatever he

was furrowing his brows over, it didn't seem to involve settling with the pawnbroker at the end of the tram ride. "*Oh*. Oh. Thank you, Mundy, quite decent of you, but I'm all right. Count Klimov gave me a drawing account to arrange stores."

Adele's eyes narrowed minusculely. "You did just land, didn't you, then?" she said, knowing that her tone was thin with a justified hint of displeasure. The lieutenant was obviously concerned about something, but that didn't justify what by now amounted to rudeness in ignoring her initial polite question. "You brought the *Princess Cecile* back to Cinnabar, that is?"

Mon stiffened, then scrunched his face with embarrassment. "Yes, mistress," he said. "Your pardon, please, for being distracted. Yes, we completed repairs to the *Princess Cecile* four weeks back. I brought her directly from Strymon in accordance to the orders that reached me while she was still in dry-dock. We landed at Harbor One a few hours ago, and I came to see Lieutenant Leary as soon as I'd rendered my accounts to the harbormaster."

"Harbor One?" said Adele, puzzled at mention of the lake northwest of Xenos where the first human colony ship landed. Early in Cinnabar's history Harbor One had sufficed for both her commercial and naval traffic, but those days were long past. Commercial transport had shifted to Harbor Two on the coast a hundred and twenty miles from the capital, while the RCN had built the vast artificial basin of Harbor Three for its operations at the close of the First Alliance War seventy-five years before.

"Why yes, mistress," Mon said. "The *Princess Cecile* is being sold out of service. I assumed that you—that Lieutenant Leary, at least—had been informed of that?"

"No," Adele said. "Daniel doesn't know that. I'm quite sure he'd have said something."

She sat back on the tram's bench, staring in the direction of the scratched windows while her mind grappled with what Mon had said. She felt the same disbelieving emptiness as she had when she learned that her family had died during the Proscriptions.

The words were simple, the concept quite understandable. The *Princess Cecile* was a foreign-built corvette, badly damaged in battle off Tanais in the Strymon system. You could never trust a ship after structural repairs, and there were many conservative RCN officers who didn't believe you could really trust a hull built on Kostroma in the first place. Now that Cinnabar and the Alliance were at peace, it made better sense to dispose of the *Princess Cecile* rather than bear the expense of maintaining her in ordinary.

Oh, yes, Adele could understand the reasoning. The analytical portion of her mind also understood why the heads of the Mundy family and their associates were displayed on Speaker's Rock when their conspiracy came unravelled.

But in both cases, Adele's stomach dropped into a frozen limbo while her mind spun pointlessly around the words and their implications.

The *Princess Cecile* was simply a small warship. Adele had first seen her less than a year ago, when she was a Kostroman corvette overflying a banal national parade. The *Sissie* was cramped and uncomfortable even at the best of occasions, and much of the time Adele had spent aboard her had involved danger and discomfort well beyond anything she'd previously experienced in a life with more than its share of squalid poverty.

And yet. . . .

A year ago Adele Mundy had been a lonely orphan eking out an exile's existence in a third-rate court whose ruler affected to be an intellectual. Her title was Court

Librarian, but her duties were those of a performing seal. Now she had her nation and even her childhood home back. She had the whole RCN for a family, and in Daniel Leary she had a friend who would stand with her to death.

None of these things were the *Princess Cecile*; but they had all come about through the *Princess Cecile*.

"Mundy?" Lieutenant Mon said in a worried tone. "Are you all right?"

Adele opened her eyes—she didn't recall having closed them—and gave Mon a crisp smile. "Yes indeed, Mon," she said. "A little sad, perhaps, but I'm on my way to a funeral, after all."

Mon nodded solemnly, looking out at the six- to eight-story buildings along the tram route. The top floors were luxury suites with roof gardens; the ground level was given over to shops, often with the owners' apartments on the floor above. In between lived ordinary people, bureaucrats and lieutenants with families larger than their incomes; librarians and mechanics and off-planet beggars jammed a dozen to a room. Lived and in their times died, because everything died.

Rest in peace, Princess Cecile. *You too were a friend.*

"*Retired Rear Admiral Aussarenes and wife,*" said the buzzy whisper in Daniel Leary's left ear. A member of the staff of Williams and Son, Undertakers, sat in the back of a discreet van parked across from the Stanislas Chapel. She checked everyone in the receiving line against a database and passed along the information over a radio link. "*He commanded the* Bourgiba *when your uncle was its third lieutenant.*"

Not its *third lieutenant*, Daniel corrected mentally. Her *third lieutenant*. A ship was female, even when she was a cranky heavy cruiser with a penchant for blowing her High Drive motors—as Daniel remembered well from the stories Uncle Stacey and his cronies told in the office of the repair yard while his sister's young son listened agog. Williams and Son specialized in society funerals, but the RCN was a very specialized society.

"Good morning, Admiral Aussarenes," he said aloud. "Uncle Stacey would've been honored to know that you and your good lady have come to pay your respects. May I present you with a ring in remembrance of the occasion?"

He offered the velvet-covered tray. The bezel of each silver ring was a grinning skull surrounded by a banner reading COMMANDER STACEY HARMSWORTH BERGEN, RCN.

Aussarenes took a ring and tried it for size on the little finger of his left hand. He walked stiffly, apparently as the result of back trouble. "I don't need a ring to remember Lieutenant Bergen," he said in a rasping, belligerent voice. "A damned troublesome officer, I don't mind telling you. Apt as not to be up on a mast truck when he was supposed to be on the bridge!"

"Darling," his wife muttered in the tone of exasperated familiarity. *"Not* here."

"Well, he was!" the admiral snapped. He looked up and met Daniel's eyes. "But he was the best astrogator I ever knew. When Bergen conned us, even the *Bitchgiba* could show her legs to a well-manned battleship if the course was long enough."

"Thank you, Admiral," Daniel said with a broad smile. "My uncle knew his limitations, but he appreciated praise when he was due it."

"Aye," said Aussarenes as Lady Aussarenes surreptitiously tugged his arm. "I hear you learned astrogation from him, boy. That's well and good, but mind that you stand your watches too!"

They passed into the chapel. Daniel continued to smile as he offered thanks and a remembrance ring to the next person in the receiving line, a man whose firm supplied antennas and yards to Bergen and Company. Perhaps a smile wasn't the proper expression for a funeral, but it was more natural to Daniel's ruddy face than a solemn frown.

Besides, the turn-out for the event was remarkable both for the number and the rank of the attendees. Commander Stacey Bergen was the greatest pathfinder and explorer in Cinnabar history. He hadn't gotten the recognition he deserved during his life, but the splendor of his funeral made up for that—at least for his nephew.

"*Senator Pakenham and her husband, Lord William Pakenham,*" Daniel's earpiece whispered. Daniel wouldn't have recognized the hatchet-faced woman with a rotund, very subdued man in tow, but he recognized her name as that of the chair of the Senate's committee on external relations. Pakenham wouldn't have known Uncle Stacey from Noah's bosun, but she was here paying her respects in company with quite a number of the Republic's other top political figures—because they wanted to please Corder Leary.

Speaker Leary hadn't attended the funeral of a man he'd always treated as a poor relation—which Uncle Stacey was, truthfully enough, for all that their partnership Bergen and Associates ran at a profit. Perhaps he was avoiding the awkwardness of meeting the son who hadn't spoken to him in the seven years since their violent argument ended with Daniel enlisting as a midshipman in the RCN. Nevertheless, he'd used his influence to add luster to the funeral of the brother-in-law he'd despised in life; and for that Daniel would thank him if they chanced ever to meet again.

"*Captain-of-Space Oliver Semmes,*" said the undertaker's woman over the radio link. "*Naval aide to Legislator Jarre's delegation.*"

For a moment Daniel's mind failed to grasp the

implications of the unfamiliar rank and the green-and-gold uniform of the trim little man bowing to him. His first thought was: *Some wealthy landowner wearing the comic-opera uniform of the company of fencibles he commanded by virtue of his rank in his borough*.

No, not comic at all: this was the dress uniform of the Fleet of the Alliance of Free Stars. Daniel didn't know his enemies' honors well enough to identify most of the medals on Semmes' tunic, but he recognized the lavaliere dangling from a white and silver ribbon as the Cross of Freedom, which was neither a trivial award nor a political one.

"Captain Semmes, it's a pleasure to see a distinguished member of your service," Daniel said. "Commander Bergen would have been deeply cognizant of the honor."

He cleared his throat while his mind groped for the correct words. It wasn't a situation he'd envisaged dealing with. Uncle Stacey had indeed viewed all Mankind as a single family striving together to rediscover and populate the universe . . . but that wasn't the official position of the RCN, nor the personal opinion of Lieutenant Daniel Leary; and it *certainly* wasn't the viewpoint of Guarantor Porra, who ruled the so-called Alliance of Free Stars with an iron fist and a security apparatus of legendary brutality.

"Ah . . . may I offer you a ring in remembrance of Commander Bergen?"

Semmes picked up a ring between thumb and forefinger, moving with the precise delicacy of an automaton. "I was privileged to meet your uncle once, Lieutenant," he said, cocking his head sideways to see how Daniel took the revelation. "On Alicia that was. My brother and I were aides to Frigate-Captain Lorenz, and Commander Bergen was surveying routes from Cinnabar to the Commonwealth."

"Ah!" said Daniel. Lorenz was a man whose reputation had spread well beyond the Alliance, a swashbuckling officer as renowned for feats of exploration as he was notorious for greed and utter amorality whenever he wasn't under the direct eye of his superiors. "Yes, that would have been almost thirty standard years ago, would it not?"

"Twenty-seven," Semmes agreed with a nod, fitting the ring he'd chosen onto his finger and holding it out to examine it critically. "We were most impressed by Commander Bergen's skill—as an astrogator."

He met Daniel's eyes squarely. "He was not a fighting officer, though, was he?" Semmes went on. Daniel might have been imagining the sneer beneath the bland assessment. "Your uncle?"

Daniel nodded crisply. "No sir, my uncle was *not* much of a fighter," he said. "Fortunately, the RCN has never lacked for officers to supply that particular deficiency."

He gestured the Alliance officer on into the chapel; not quite a dismissal, but an unmistakable hint. "Perhaps we'll meet again, Captain Semmes," he added.

"He's the sort who'd try to swim off with fifty feet of log chain back in Bantry," Hogg muttered into Daniel's ear from behind. "Thinking about it, something along those lines might happen right here in Xenos, young master. Eh?"

The voice from Williams and Son was identifying the next man in line as the recording secretary to the Senate committee on finance—quite an important fellow as Daniel well knew. Daniel had other business that was more important yet.

"Hogg," he said, turning to fix his servant with a baleful eye, "there'll be none of that, even in jest! An officer of the RCN cannot—and I will not—have a servant who acts like a street thug!"

"Begging your pardon, master," said Hogg. He sounded at least vaguely contrite, for all that he met Daniel's glare with level eyes. "It shan't happen again, I'm sure. I was a mite put out by the fellow's disrespect for Master Stacey, is all."

Daniel nodded, forced up the corner of his lips in a smile, and returned to the receiving line. "A pleasure to see you, Major Hattersly," he said. The recording secretary had a commission in the Trained Bands. "May I offer you a ring in remembrance of Commander Bergen?"

The trouble in dealing with Hogg was that he wasn't so much of a servant as the tough older brother who'd raised Daniel in the country while Corder Leary busied himself with money and politics in Xenos. Daniel had a countryman's instinctive love for Bantry, the family estate. Money was useful only to spend, generally on friends, and as for politics— well, young Daniel had spent days watching the colony of rock cavies on the banks of Tule Creek. So far as he was concerned, they were not only far more interesting than his father's associates, they were on average a good deal smarter.

Corder Leary didn't think often about his son. Deirdre, the elder of his two children, was stamped from the mold of her father and absorbed his tutelage with a flair of her own. Daniel's mother was a saint— everybody agreed that, even her husband, which was perhaps the reason he only saw her on the few times a year when he was in Bantry for other business. But a saint doesn't have the temperament or the skills to handle a very active, very *male*, child . . . and Hogg had both in abundance.

Mistress Leary would've been horrified to learn not only what Hogg had taught the boy but even more by the way Hogg disciplined him. She never did learn, however, because one of the things Daniel learned from Hogg was how to be a man and not go blubbering to his mommy when he got clouted for doing something stupid.

Daniel didn't want to face the task of covering for a retainer who'd misguidedly scragged a high representative of a power with whom Cinnabar was for the moment at peace. He'd deal with the situation if it arose, though, because he was a Leary and understood his duties to his retainers . . . another thing he'd learned from Hogg.

Besides, Daniel hadn't been any happier than Hogg was to hear the implied sneer at Uncle Daniel's lack of credentials as a warrior. Particularly since the gibe was justified.

"Admiral and Lady Anston," said Daniel's earpiece. *"He's head of the Navy Board, but he has no connection with Commander Bergen that I can find."*

Great God almighty! Daniel thought. He had a momentary fear that he'd blurted that aloud in the face of the head of the RCN—though Anston had heard worse and said worse in his time, there was no doubt about that.

He'd been a fighting admiral and a lucky admiral; the two in combination had made him extremely wealthy. Instead of retiring to spend the rest of his life indulging whatever whim struck his fancy—porcelain, politics, or pubescent girls—Anston had for the past eighteen years turned his very considerable talents to the organization and preservation of the Republic of Cinnabar Navy.

As head of the Navy Board he kept the RCN out of politics and kept politicians of every stripe out of the RCN. Everybody knew that naval contracts were awarded to the suppliers who best benefited the RCN and that ships and commands were allocated according to the needs and resources of the Republic—as determined by the head of Navy Board.

Anston was a florid man in his mid sixties. He ate and drank with the same enthusiasm he had fifty years earlier when he was a midshipman running up and down the rigging of his training battleship. Some day he'd die. That would be a worse blow to the RCN and the Republic than anything the Alliance had managed in the past century of off-and-on warfare.

But Anston was alive now, the most important man in the RCN and one of the most important in all Cinnabar; and he'd come to Commander Bergen's funeral.

"Good morning, Admiral Anston," Daniel said. An analytical part of his mind watched the proceedings dispassionately. It noted that Daniel's voice was pleasant and well modulated, and it marvelled at the fact. "Uncle Stacey is greatly honored to see you here."

"Is he?" said Anston, grinning grimly at Daniel— one spacer talking to another. "Well, I wouldn't know about that, boy; I leave those questions to the priests. I do know that I used the route Lieutenant Bergen charted through the Straw Pile to reach the fullerene convoy from the Webster Stars before it met its Alliance escort. The profits paid the RCN's budget for a year and didn't do me personally so badly either, eh, Maggie?"

He beamed at his wife, as near a double to him as their different sexes would allow. Her pants suit was covered with lace and ruffles—but all of them black, so from any distance she was merely a pudgy older woman instead of the clown she'd have looked in contrasting colors. "Josh, don't call me Maggie in public!" she said in a furious whisper.

Anston clapped her on the buttock. Lady Anston affected not to notice, but the admiral's aide—a lieutenant commander of aristocratic bearing—winced in social agony.

"What was Semmes saying to you?" the admiral demanded in a lowered voice. "He came calling at my office—for courtesy, he said. I was out and I'll damned well be out any other time he comes by!"

"Nothing that matters, your lordship," Daniel said. Behind him, Hogg grunted agreement with the admiral's comments. "He met Uncle Stacey on Alicia, when the Alliance expedition under Lorenz arrived just after the government had signed a treaty of friendship with the Republic."

"I guess he wouldn't forget that," Anston said with an approving guffaw. "They had no idea we were operating within ten days Transit of there—and we wouldn't have been except for your uncle's nose for a route where nobody else could see one."

"Josh, we're holding up the line," Lady Anston said, glaring at Daniel as though he and her husband were co-conspirators in a plot to embarrass her.

"Well, Commander Bergen isn't complaining, is he?" the admiral said in a testy voice. Then to Daniel he continued, "Listen, Lieutenant. The Senate doesn't want a war with the Alliance so it pretends there won't be one. I don't want a war either, but I know sure as the sun rises that war's coming. Coming whenever Guarantor Porra decides it's in his interest, and that won't be long. You needn't worry about being put on half pay—you're the sort of young officer the RCN needs even in peacetime. And when it's war, you'll have a command that'll raise you up or use you up, depending on the sort of grit you show. On my oath!"

The admiral passed on into the church, guided to the front by one of the corps of ushers provided by Willams and Son. The rhythms of his wife's harangue were intelligible even though the words themselves were not.

"*A navy warrant officer,*" said the undertaker's prompter. Then, testily, "*She should have been directed to the gallery via the back stairs!*"

"Hello, Adele," Daniel said, gripping Mundy's right hand with his and clasping his left over it. "By God, I'm glad you could see this! They've turned out for Uncle Stacey, by *God* they have! He'd be so proud to see this!"

Adele nodded with her usual neutral expression. Tovera, as pale as something poisonous from under a rock, stood just behind and to the side of her mistress. Daniel had a fleeting vision of the scene when an undertaker's functionary tried to shunt Adele to the gallery as a person of no account; he grinned broadly.

"Daniel," Adele said, "Lieutenant Mon's back with the *Princess Cecile* and seems in a desperate rush to see you. He'll be here for the service as soon as he changes into his dress uniform."

"Ah?" Daniel said, letting his left hand drop to his side. He met Adele's gaze calmly. She didn't show emotion as a general rule, but they were good enough friends that he could see when the emotion was present regardless. "I'll be glad to see him, of course—but what's wrong?"

Adele cleared her throat. "He says the *Sissie* is to be sold as excess to RCN requirements," she said. "I gather it will happen very soon. In a matter of days."

"Ah," Daniel said, nodding his understanding. "They must have a buyer, then. I regret the matter, though of course I understand the advantages to the Republic."

"Of course," Adele agreed. "I'll see you after the service, then. Back at the house, I suppose?"

Daniel nodded, though he wasn't really listening. All he could think of for the moment was the light of the firmament blazing about him as he stood on the deck of his first command—the RCS *Princess Cecile*.

"Come along, mistress," Hogg said. "I'll sit you down in front."

"I *hardly* think—" said the chief usher, a severe figure imbued with a mincing, sexless aura of disapproval.

"That's right, boyo," Hogg snapped, "you hardly do. Put a sock in it while I take the master's friend down t' the best seat in the house!"

Hogg and Mundy disappeared into the nave of the chapel; the chief usher fulminated at an underling.

"Good morning, Captain Churchill," Daniel said to the next in line, an old man wobbling in the grip of a worried younger relative. Churchill had been a midshipman with Uncle Stacey.

The fabric of the universe distorting around the gleaming prow of the Princess Cecile, *under the command of Lieutenant Daniel Leary....*

CHAPTER 2

Between wheezes for breath, the undertaker snarled at the troupe of actors wearing death masks of Stacey Bergen's famous ancestors in the rear yard of the chapel. Adele considered taking out her data unit to determine whether the large, elderly man—tall but definitely overweight besides—was Master Williams proper or the Son. The urge was wholly irrational so she suppressed it, but it would've taken her mind off the past and the future; and off death, at least for the moment, which is what it seemed to Adele that the past and future always came down to.

She smiled. She knew other people viewed life differently, though she'd always suspected that they hadn't analyzed the subject as rigorously as she had.

The undertaker had finally sorted the actors to his satisfaction. The clowns in the initial group started off down the boulevard singing, "*Stacey came from the land where they understand . . .*"

The females wore caricatures of RCN uniforms and the males were in grotesque drag. Mind, some of the prostitutes Adele had seen plying their trade successfully outside Harbor Three were scarcely less unattractive. The RCN had high standards in many respects, but she'd come to the conclusion it was any port in a storm when it came to sexual relief after a long voyage.

"... *what it means to fornicate!*" sang the clowns to the music of the flutes some of their members played.

The actor playing Commander Bergen was next in the procession, walking ahead of the discreetly motorized bier which a member of the undertaker's staff guided. Torchbearers, statuesque women in flowing garments, flanked him.

Adele had listened without comment to the discussions Daniel and the widow held as to what age the actor was to portray his uncle. They'd finally decided on the man in his prime forty years ago when he'd just returned from the first of his long exploring voyages in the *Beacon*. The actor wore mottled gray fatigues with senior lieutenant's pips on his collar; he walked with a slight limp, miming the result of a fall on a heavy-gravity planet and the spinal injuries which eventually left Stacey confined to a wheelchair.

"*Where even the dead sleep two in a bed . . .*," sang the clowns. The masked "ancestors" followed them out of the courtyard in pairs, moving at a stately walk while the clowns capered and mugged for the spectators lining both sides of the street to the crematorium. A funeral of this size was not only entertainment for the poor, it was news for all Xenos.

The Bergens were an old but not particularly distinguished house; Stacey, who had retired from the RCN as a commander, was typical of his family. Today his lineage had been improved by leading military and political figures of the past. The families involved would never have lent the death masks without pressure that could only have come from Corder Leary.

Adele'd never met Daniel's father and hoped never to meet him; that would save her the decision as to whether or not to shoot the man responsible for her parents' death. But no one had ever accused Speaker Leary of doing things halfway.

"*. . . and the babies masturbate!*" sang the clowns.

"Mistress Mundy?" murmured a voice in her ear; one of the undertaker's functionaries. "Come, please. The living family is next."

Adele followed the little man through the crowd gathered inside the courtyard gate. He was polite as befit anyone dealing with people of the rank of those waiting, but he squeezed a passage for her with the authority of a much bigger fellow indeed.

"You and Mistress Leary will follow Lieutenant Leary with the widow," the fellow said, depositing Adele, frowning in doubt, beside Deirdre Leary. Daniel's elder sister wore a tailored black suit of natural fabrics. The rosette on her beret was cream-and-rose, the Bergen colors.

"Ah, Deirdre," Adele said. "Yes, of course you'd be here."

Deirdre Leary had requested when she met Adele that they deal with one another by first names. Referring to their relationship as informal would've been stretching the word beyond its proper meaning, though. Adele respected the other woman, but she felt the two of them had as little in common as they did with the chlorine-breathing race of Charax IV. She presumed that Deirdre reciprocated her feelings.

Adele was irritated with herself for not having expected Daniel's sister to be at the funeral. Speaker Leary's two children were, after all, the deceased's closest relatives by blood. And for that matter, Adele had almost nothing in common with Daniel either—on paper.

The last of the actors passed through the gate. The undertaker spoke to Daniel, making shooing motions with rather less ceremony than Adele thought was due the man who was paying for this affair. Supporting the widow, a countrywoman who'd cooked and kept house for the retired commander and who had never said a word in Adele's hearing, Daniel stepped into the street.

Adele's eyes narrowed. How much *was* this costing, anyway? She had a scholar's disregard for money, but Daniel's attitude was more that of a drunken spacer . . . which of course he was, often enough. Lieutenant Leary'd been a lucky commander, but even the captain's share of prize money didn't overwhelm the needs of a 23-year-old officer who demonstrated the same enthusiasm for living as he did for taking his command into the heart of the enemy's fire.

The undertaker turned to Adele and her companion. His mouth, open to snap a brusque order, closed abruptly. He bowed low to Deirdre.

Adele started forward, matching her pace to Daniel and the widow. It struck her for the first time that the bill—or at least the whole bill, knowing both that Daniel was stiff-necked and that he had very little conception of what things really cost—might not be going to the nephew after all. She looked at Deirdre but said nothing; there was really nothing to say, after all.

The crowd in the street had a carnival atmosphere quite beyond the traditional life-affirming bawdy of the clowns in the lead. Adele heard spectators identifying members of the procession, herself included, to their children and companions. She couldn't imagine how they were able to do that until she heard a hawker in the near distance call, "Get your programs! Every famous personage, living or departed, listed here with their biographies!"

Deirdre glanced over with a dry smile. "Surprised?" she asked.

"Gratified, rather," Adele said. "I don't think there's anything that could have made Daniel happier. Since he got his first command, at any rate. You arranged it, I presume?"

"I was acting on instructions," said Deirdre. "My principal will be pleased that you think matters are going well."

Deirdre's principal would be her father—and Daniel's.

The three-block avenue from the Stanislas Chapel to the crematorium was through public land which had been a floodplain before the Market River was first channelized, then covered. On a normal day there'd have been people doing outdoor gymnastics and running on the tracks around both halves of the property. A maze of kiosks on the north side catered to shoppers of all varieties. The booths were dismantled every dusk, leaving commercial activities to prostitutes of both sexes. Since Harbor Three lay just the other side of the perimeter fence, trade in the hours of darkness was also brisk.

This morning everybody in sight had come to watch the funeral procession. She smiled wryly. Turning to Deirdre she said, talking over the crowd noise, "Commander Bergen actually deserves this pomp for having opened so many trade routes for the Republic . . . but his actions aren't the reason this is happening, are they?"

Deirdre shrugged. She was dark-haired and reasonably attractive in business clothing. If she'd put the effort into her looks that most women seemed to, she could look stunning. Adele doubted that Daniel's sister felt any need to bother. Money and power would bring her any men she wanted, and the likelihood was that Deirdre shared with her brother a complete disinterest in what the partner of a night chose to do the next morning.

Adele couldn't object. She herself wasn't interested in a partner at all.

"It depends what you mean by 'his actions,'" Deirdre said, meeting Adele's eyes with a level gaze. "The fact that he was a good friend and teacher to Corder Leary's son certainly has something to do with it."

"Yes, I see," Adele said, nodding crisply.

"But since we're on the subject of business . . . ," Deirdre said. "Do you know what my brother intends to do as heir to Commander Bergen's share of the shipyard? The Republic's present state of peace with her neighbors will limit the opportunities open to a young naval officer, I should think?"

Adele faced front, her expression cold. Her first reaction was shocked amazement; then the humor of it struck her and she chuckled aloud. They *had* been talking business, as Deirdre viewed the world, after all.

Everything could be refined down to business if you looked at it the right way. The cost of the most elaborate funeral in a decade was on one side of the ledger; Adele didn't know, couldn't *guess*, what Deirdre put in the other pan of the balance, but she knew there had to be something.

"I haven't discussed the future with Daniel," she said, wondering if the other woman would find her smile insulting. It wasn't meant to be; not entirely, at least. "He's been quite busy with funeral preparations, of course. Based on what he's said to me in the past, I don't imagine that he's interested in becoming a Cinnabar businessman, however."

In all truth, Adele couldn't imagine her friend as anything except an RCN officer. Perhaps she was unduly influenced by the fact she'd only known Daniel

for a year in which naval duties had absorbed him . . .
but the uniform fit him perfectly. If anyone could be
said to belong to the Republic of Cinnabar Navy in
war or peace, it was Lieutenant Daniel Leary.

Her smile quirked wryly. Perhaps the same was true
of Adele Mundy, who'd found a family which respected
her talents and which was willing to use her just as
hard as it used her friend Daniel.

"A shipyard can't simply be left to the workmen
to run," Deirdre said. Her voice was thinner than it
had been a moment before. Nobody likes to have her
nose rubbed in the fact that someone else sees no
value in what she holds dear; for all that Deirdre
must have known before she raised the subject that
Adele had no more interest in business than Daniel
did. "Unless there's a suitable manager in place very
shortly, the silent partner will demand that Bergen
and Associates be sold up. I can understand my
brother having other priorities—"

She probably couldn't understand, any more than
Daniel could have understood Deirdre's preoccupation
with wealth and political power; but it was the polite
thing to say.

"—but he's trustee for Uncle Stacey's widow during her life. That will surely affect his decision?"

The crematorium was a low, cast-concrete building,
modeled on a pre-Hiatus temple; there were Corinthian
pilasters across the front. The actor dressed as the
deceased took his place to one side of the square
bronze door flanked by the torch bearers, while the
attendant locked the bier against the opening.

The coffin was closed; the last six months had
ravaged Stacey beyond what his nephew was willing
to display to the world. A touch of a button would
roll it through the door into the gas flames.

The clowns had split to either side of the

crematorium and waited behind it, still wearing their
costumes but talking among themselves in low voices.
Their parts were played, but their dressing rooms
were trailers behind the chapel, inaccessible until the
crowd dispersed.

The troupe of ancestors seated themselves on the
triple semicircle of folding chairs, each with a pole
holding a card with the name of the character the actor
represented. An usher guided Daniel and the widowed
Mistress Bergen to their place on the left behind the
actors; another usher gestured Adele and Deirdre to
the right.

Adele looked across the lines of age-blackened death
masks to Daniel Leary, who beamed with pride and
the joy of life. Beside and behind her, ushers were
arraying the other mourners—admirals and cabinet
ministers and merchant princes.

She looked at her companion. "Deirdre," she said,
"your brother will fulfill his duties to the widow in the
fashion that seems best to him. I can't guess what that
will be; I'm not Daniel. But—"

She felt herself stiffen to even greater rigidity than
usual, and her voice honed itself to a sharp edge.

"—I would be very surprised if it crossed his mind
that he should take up the partnership that his father
used to degrade Uncle Stacey. And if Daniel did consider that, I would be merely one of his many friends
to tell him that the notion was absurd. Am I sufficiently
clear?"

Music, an instrumental version of a martial hymn,
boomed from speakers beneath the front corners of the
crematorium. The coffin began to rumble forward.

"Perfectly clear," Deirdre said. "I'll report your
thoughts to my principal."

The bronze door sprang upward and shut behind
the coffin; an instant later, Adele felt the throb of the

concealed gas flames. Deirdre leaned closer to continue in Adele's ear, "For what it's worth . . . Speaker Leary doesn't respect very many people. I believe that he'll be more pleased than not that his son is one of those few."

Attendants had opened side gates so that spectators could disperse through the park as well as going up the avenue to the chapel the way they'd come. Daniel took off his saucer hat and mopped his face and brow with a handkerchief. He could barely see for sweat and the emotions that'd been surging through him during the morning.

"It went well, Uncle Stacey," he muttered under his breath. By God it had! All Cinnabar had turned out to cheer the Republic's greatest explorer off on his final voyage.

Maryam Bergen had left on the arm of Bergen and Associates' shop foreman, an old shipmate of her husband's and, not coincidentally, her brother. A mere workman couldn't be part of the official mourning, of course, but the foreman and most of the other yard employees had been given places just outside the fence where they had an unrivaled view.

"Here you go, master," Hogg muttered, offering Daniel a silver half-pint flask. He'd already unscrewed the jigger measure that covered the stopper. He eyed the dispersing crowd, wearing an expression of the same satisfaction that Daniel felt.

"What is it?" Daniel said as he plucked out the cork.

"It's wet and you need it," Hogg said. "Just drink."

Not precisely what a gentleman's gentleman would have said, but Daniel was a *country* gentleman which was a very different thing from the citified version. He took a swig of what might have been cherry brandy and certainly was strong enough to fuel an engine.

The actors playing Stacey's ancestors had joined the clowns behind the crematorium. They'd handed the deathmasks to footmen from the families which'd provided them and were removing their costumes; attendants folded the chairs on which they'd been sitting.

The man who'd impersonated Stacey was talking to the undertaker. He was the contractor as well as the principal performer, for the undertaker handed him a purse. He weighed it in his hand and bowed.

Adele stood alone just beyond the ranks of chairs. When she caught Daniel's eye she nodded, turned, and walked away. Tovera, who must've been watching from the other side of the fence during the ceremony, trailed her mistress closely.

Daniel smiled in appreciation. Adele wouldn't intrude, but she hadn't wanted to leave without saying goodbye.

"Lieutenant Leary?" said a voice at his elbow. Daniel turned abruptly and found the principal actor beside him. "My name is Shackleford, Enzio Shackleford. I trust our performance was to your taste?"

It was disconcerting to see the fellow still in uniform but without the mask and wig, for his wild white hair was utterly unlike anything a spacer would wear. In a cramped, weightless vessel, such strands would've drifted in all directions.

Daniel swallowed the swig of brandy that'd been in his mouth when the man startled him. Part of it went down the wrong pipe; he sprayed it onto the sleeve of his Dress Whites that he got over his mouth and nose in time.

Hogg muttered and snatched the kerchief from Daniel's cuff to mop at the liquor. It would've made better sense to sneeze on the actor's utility uniform. . . .

Shackleford pretended his attention was fastened on

matters of supernal interest on the horizon. "A most gratifying house, if I may say so, Lieutenant. A turn-out that would've done honor to the most respected admiral or statesman. I was pleased to be in charge of the performance."

"Your pardon, Master Shackleford," Daniel managed through spasms; the strong brandy burned like spattering thermite on the soft inner tissues of his nose. "Yes, yes, you did splendidly."

"I like to think that the Enzio Shackleford Company gives value far above our small additional increment of cost compared to just *any* self-styled thespians," Shackleford said with an airy gesture of his hand to indicate they both were true aristocrats. "Allow me to provide you with my card, sir."

He did so with a flourish that suggested he performed card tricks when nothing more lucrative offered itself.

"You may have occasion at any moment to require similar services," Shackleford continued. "How well it has been said, 'We know not the day and hour of our passing.' In your moment of grief, sir, do not fail to call on the first name in posthumous impersonations— the Enzio Shackleford Company!"

Daniel frowned, trying to imagine who else might die for whom he'd be responsible. Adele, perhaps? Though she was at no obvious risk unless catastrophe struck the *Princess Cecile*, in which case the vessel's commander was unlikely to be in a position to arrange the funeral.

Thought of the *Princess Cecile* lowered a gray curtain over Daniel's mind; he took a long, deliberate drink from the flask, drawing its contents far down. He'd been tense throughout the day, afraid that some mistake would turn the proceedings into a farce. He'd felt no sadness, though; this had been a celebration of

Stacey's life and—as it turned out—a triumph. The flesh, frail even in life, was now ash; but the name of Commander Stacey Bergen was on the lips of everyone in Xenos.

Uncle Stacey's glorious send-off was past, and now present reality was intruding on the euphoria of the afternoon. Daniel had Admiral Anston's word that the Admiralty would find him a command; that counted for more than a signed and sealed commission from anybody else. The thought of the *Sissie* being gutted and turned into an intra-system tramp, though—that was troubling.

Gutted—or simply bought by a breaker's yard for her masts, electronics and drives. Though the boom in trade that came with peace should give all spaceworthy hulls enough value to spare the *Sissie* that final indignity for a few years further.

Daniel took another drink. When he lowered the flask empty, he saw Lieutenant Mon coming toward him against the grain of the departing crowd.

In general terms he was glad to see Mon, who'd been as satisfactory a first lieutenant as Daniel could imagine serving under him: competent, careful, and brave—though that went almost without saying in an RCN officer. No few of those who wore the uniform were pig stupid, but cowards were as rare as saints. Besides those professional virtues, Mon was loyal to Daniel beyond what could be expected of a human being.

On the other hand, if Mon was coming to moan about having to feed his large family on half-pay when the *Sissie* went out of commission, well—Daniel would sympathize, but at another time. For now his grief was for the corvette herself.

"Sir!" Mon said, clasping Daniel's hand. "Thank God you're on Cinnabar. I had nightmares of you being off on an embassy to Kostroma or the Devil only knew where!"

Mon's dress uniform fit poorly—he'd lost weight since he last wore it, which might have been five or more years in the past—and he hadn't taken time to update his medal ribbons. Daniel let a smile of satisfaction touch his lips: the citations Mon had won in the brief time he'd served under Lieutenant Leary would have made the cabbage patch on his tunic much more impressive.

Quite apart from the fit of his uniform, Mon looked dreadful. At the end of the brutal run to Sexburga, seventeen days in the Matrix without a break, everybody aboard the *Princess Cecile* looked like they'd been dragged through a drainpipe . . . and even then, Mon had been in better shape than Daniel saw him now.

"I'm here, right enough," Daniel said with a note of deliberate caution, "but as you can imagine, Mon, I have a good deal on my plate right at the moment. Perhaps later . . . ?"

"Sir," Mon said. His face screwed up in despair and frustration. "*Daniel*, for God's sake. I need help and I don't know where else to turn!"

"Ah," said Daniel, nodding in understanding. "Well, I hope I always have a few florins for an old shipmate."

He reached for the wallet that'd be attached to the equipment belt of the 2nd Class uniform he usually wore on the ground. His Whites used a cummerbund rather than a belt and had no provision for carrying money or anything else of practical value.

"Hogg?" he said, trying to hide his irritation in forgetting the situation. "Do you have ten—that is, twenty florins you can let me have until I'm back in my rooms?"

"Sir, it's not *money* . . . ," Mon said. He straightened and looked around, suddenly a man again and an

RCN officer. "Look, can we go somewhere and talk? This is . . ."

He shrugged; Daniel nodded agreement. Standing in the open among attendants sweeping up the debris of a funeral simply wasn't the way to discuss anything except the weather.

"Right," Daniel said. "The last time I looked there were bars just down the street. We'll find a booth and see how I can help you."

He gave Mon his arm and they started up the avenue, by now almost empty of mourners. Though there was no lack of bars this close to Harbor Three, they weren't the sort of places that an officer usually entered wearing his dress uniform.

Still, if Daniel kept his intake to only a few drinks— or anyway, a moderate amount—then he shouldn't have to replace his Whites because they were dirty; or they were bloody; or they'd been torn completely off his back in a brawl that'd started the Lord knew how. And if he did have to replace his uniform, well, an officer of the RCN was always ready to make sacrifices for his fellows.

CHAPTER 3

Buelow's, only three doors down from the Stanislas Chapel, catered to warrant officers looking for a place to have a drink rather than common spacers intending to get falling-down drunk as quickly and cheaply as possible. Daniel eased himself into a booth, realizing as he did so that it was the first time since dawn that he'd taken the weight off his feet.

The three-dimensional photographs on the walls were of landscapes rather than sexual acrobatics. Daniel couldn't identify any of the scenes, but the three-legged creature clinging to the face of a basalt cliff certainly wasn't native to Cinnabar. The dark, pitted wood of the bar came from off-planet also; Daniel noted with interest that its vascular tissue seemed to curl in helixes around the bole, rising and sinking through the slab's planed surface like sections of a dolphin's track.

Hogg seated himself beside the cash register where he would unobtrusively take care of the charges; a woman in uniform, an engineer by her collar flashes, was drinking a boilermaker at the end of the bar. Other than them and the tapster who walked over to the booth, Daniel and Mon had the tavern to themselves.

Daniel glanced at the tapster and said, "So, Mon? I believe yours is whiskey and water?"

"No, no, Leary," Mon said, shaking his head violently. "Thanks, I mean, but I've sworn off for, for the time. I'll have—"

He looked at the solid, balding bartender and grimaced. "A shandy, I suppose," he said. "Yes, a shandy."

"And for me as well, sir," Daniel said brightly, wondering if Mon had gone out of his mind. Aloud he continued, "Well, Mon. What d'ye need to see me about?"

Mon set his hands firmly on the table with his palms down and the fingers spread, stared at them as he organized his thoughts, and then lifted his weary eyes to Daniel. "Look sir, it's like this," he said. "While the *Sissie* was rebuilding on Tanais, we got a message through the High Commissioner to the Strymon system that we were to bring her home to Harbor One for disposal. I guess you'd heard that?"

"Yes," Daniel said, "I had."

He didn't add that he'd heard it from Adele less than two hours ago. Strictly speaking nobody'd been required to tell him, since he'd turned over command of the *Princess Cecile* to his first lieutenant while she was in dock.

The fact that he hadn't heard a whisper about the sale out of service of the corvette he'd captured and commanded in actions that thrilled all Cinnabar, let alone the RCN, had to have been conscious concealment rather than mere oversight. Anston, or more likely the captain heading the Board of Materiel, must have thought that the famous Lieutenant Leary could raise enough of a public outcry to reverse the Board's reasoned decision.

And so he could've done; but he wouldn't have. The needs of the service came first with Daniel Leary, as they should do with every officer of the RCN.

"Well, you can imagine I wasn't happy about that," Mon said, stating the facts baldly as though the situation had no emotional weight for Daniel. "But then a couple nobles from Novy Sverdlovsk arrived with a letter of introduction from the High Commissioner. Count Klimov and wife Valentina, their names were, and they wanted passage to Cinnabar."

He shrugged. "No problem there, of course," he went on. "We weren't on a fighting cruise, and you'd drafted forty crewmen to the Strymon dispatch vessel you sailed home on. It was just a matter of the passengers providing a share of rations to the officer's mess—and I don't mind telling you, captain, that I've never had better rations anywhere in my life, on shipboard or land. They've got more money than God, the Klimovs do."

The tapster returned with the shandies, thumping them down on the table. "Thank you, sir!" Daniel said, but the fellow turned with only a grunt and walked back behind the bar.

Daniel eyed the muddy brown fluid in his glass, a mixture of draft beer and ginger ale or whatever else the bar kept for a mixer. The tapster looked as though he were disgusted to've served something so debased. Daniel didn't blame him.

"Well, it turned out that the Count and his wife were coming to Cinnabar to hire a ship so they could tour the Galactic North," Mon said, raising his glass. "Rather than use a Novy Sverdlovsk crew and vessel, they wanted the best. Besides, they knew Cinnabar'd opened the shortest routes to the North. Your Uncle Stacey had."

He drank, made a sour face, and set the shandy down again. He started to speak but paused to wipe his lips with the back of his left hand.

"Touring the North?" Daniel said, pursing his lips

in concentration as he stared at his glass. "You mean, visiting the Commonwealth of God? I suppose people from Novy Sverdlovsk might find it interesting, though I recall one of Stacey's old shipmates saying he'd seen pig sties he thought were prettier than Radiance, and the rest of the Commonwealth wasn't up to that standard."

"I don't think they care much about the capital," Mon said, rolling his palms upward. "The Count says he wants to do some hunting, and his wife studies people that never got back into space after the Hiatus. The relict societies, she calls them. You know, wogs with bones through their noses who'll cut out your heart and eat it because the Great God Goo tells them to. It's her life, I guess."

"Scholars, then," Daniel said. "I don't think the Commonwealth controls a tenth of the worlds that'd been settled in the North before the Hiatus, and 'control' is stretching it to describe the government anyway. The planets pretty much run their own business, and the Commonwealth fleet supports itself by extortion when it isn't straight piracy."

By a combination of treaty and threat the ships of Cinnabar and her allies were exempt from the abuses, at least in cases where there might be survivors to bring back word of what had happened. But all vessels trading into the Galactic North went armed, even though guns and missiles reduced their cargo capacity.

"Yeah, well, it's still a damned fool way to waste time and money," Mon said. "But they've got money, the Lord knows they have. And that's the rub, Leary. When they learned the *Sissie*'d be going on the block, they decided to buy her themselves for their tour. And they want me to captain her, at a lieutenant commander's salary!"

"Why Mon, that's wonderful news!" Daniel said,

rising in his seat to reach over the table and grasp
Mon's shoulder. "And they couldn't have a better man
and ship for the job! Why, good God, man, you had
me thinking there was something wrong!"

If the Klimovs could afford to crew the corvette, she
was an ideal choice for a long voyage into a region
which was unexplored where it wasn't actively hostile.
The *Princess Cecile* was a fast, handy vessel. Though
light for a warship in a major fleet, she was far more
powerful than the pirates and Commonwealth
naval units (where there was a difference) she'd meet
in the North.

Mon would have to resign his commission, but under
the circumstances the Admiralty would grant him a
waiver so that he could rejoin at some future date at
the same rank. All he'd lose was seniority on a day-
for-day basis—and his half-pay, just under a quarter
of what the Klimovs were offering for his services.

As for the *Sissie*—well, she wouldn't be a warship
any longer, but she wouldn't be a scow running bulk
supplies to asteroid miners either. Good news for the
ship, good news for her acting captain—and good news
for Daniel Leary, two recent weights off his back!

"There *is* something wrong!" Mon said miserably.
"Sir, what am I going to do for a crew? With the
peace treaty signed, all the trading houses will be
hiring spacers. I'll have nothing but drunks and gutter-
sweepings—for a voyage to the North, and not to the
major ports either."

While Daniel thought over what Mon had just said,
he sipped his shandy. Good grief! it was dreadful. He
supposed he'd drunk worse . . . well, realistically, he
knew he'd drunk worse; but he certainly hadn't been
sober while he was doing it.

"Well Mon . . . ," he said, resisting the urge to swab
his mouth and tongue with something clean or at any

rate different. "I should think based on what the Klimovs offered you, they'd pay something better than going wages for seasoned spacers. In fact, I'd expect most of the *Sissie*'s current crew would sign on with you. She was always a happy ship—and lucky in her officers, if I may say so."

A middle-aged man came in with a younger woman, moderately attractive but respectably dressed—a second wife, perhaps, but not a whore. "Hey Bert," the man said to the barman as they headed for the end booth. "The usual for me and Mamie."

"Coming up, Lon," the tapster said as he set a pair of glasses on the bar.

"Luck!" Mon said bitterly into his empty glass. "That's the problem. On the voyage home we had a dozen breakdowns. Mostly the damned High Drive— Pasternak finally figured out that the gauges they'd replaced in Tanais were off, so we were feeding eight percent more antimatter to the motors than he thought. We had half the motors go out, eaten through by the excess. Plus two of the masts carried away in the Matrix. We didn't lose a rigger, but we would've if Woetjans hadn't grabbed him without a safety line and then caught a shroud with her free hand."

Woetjans, the bosun, and Pasternak, the engineer— Chief of Rig and Chief of Ship respectively—were both officers who did credit to the RCN. Woetjans in particular, a big raw-boned woman, was worth a squad of almost anybody else when she entered a brawl with a length of high-pressure tubing.

"Well, that's the sort of thing that happens with a major rebuild," Daniel said reasonably. "That's what shakedown cruises are for, after all. Are the Klimovs upset?"

"Them?" Mon said scornfully. "Good God, Leary, they're used to Sverdlovsk ships. They'd be happy enough if the hull didn't split open and *all* the antennas fall off!"

He shook his head, miserable again. "No, no, it's the crew," he said. "They think I'm a hard-luck officer. I heard Barnes say that opening his suit in a vacuum'd be quicker than going to the back of beyond with the *Sissie* now, and the other riggers on his watch agreed. And word'll get around the docks, of course. Hell and damnation, it already has!"

"Ah," said Daniel, understanding completely but unable to think of a useful remark to make. "Ah."

It was quite unfair, of course, but spacers were a superstitious lot. There were ships—well-found according to any assayer—which had reputations as killers; and there were captains who, whatever their technical qualifications, were known as Jonahs. No spacer shipped with either, not if there was a choice; and now, with the merchant fleets hiring, all spacers who could stand more or less upright had a choice.

"God damn all spacers to Hell!" Mon said. "God damn *life* to Hell!"

He turned on his bench and said, "I'll take a whiskey and water. A double, dammit, and keep the bottle out!"

He looked at Daniel and said in a despairing voice, "I know, I don't need my wife to tell me that I put down maybe more than's good for me. But liquor never affected me on duty, you know that sir?"

"I never had a complaint about you, Mon," Daniel said still-faced. He could use a drink himself, but it didn't seem that ordering one was going to make the situation better.

"I thought with everything going wrong, you know . . . ," Mon said, squeezing his face with his spread hands. "That, you know, if I went on the wagon, that the trouble would let up. That God'd take his thumb off me, you know what I mean?"

"Yes, I know," said Daniel. Spacers are superstitious by nature; they're too close to random death on every working day to be otherwise. That was no less true of acting captains than it was of the riggers under their command.

"And the next watch the Port One antenna carried away and took the spars and sails from Two and Three besides," Mon concluded bitterly.

The tapster came with his drink, setting it down on the table and watching Mon sidelong as he walked back behind the bar. Hogg was watching also. Daniel wasn't concerned, but Mon was obviously closer to the edge than Daniel would've wanted on the bridge during action.

"Daniel," Mon said, holding the drink in both hands but not raising it. "Sir. The men will listen to you, you know they will. Will you come to the mustering-out parade tomorrow and talk to them? Sir, I've got *five* brats now, my wife delivered while I was on Tanais. I can't make it on half-pay, I *can't*, and if I have to take a crew of fag-ends to the Galactic North, well—"

He smiled with a wry sort of humor. "Well, then, I'd say Barnes'd be right. I'd do better to open my suit in a vacuum."

"I . . . will consider our options tonight, Mon," Daniel said, rising deliberately so that it wouldn't look as though he were fleeing his old shipmate; which was what he was doing, near enough. "And I'll be at the mustering-out parade, I promise you. That's ten hundred hours?"

"Aye, ten hundred," Mon said, rising also with a radiant smile and gripping Daniel's hand. "Thank God. Thank *you*, sir. If I can just keep a stiffening of trained men we'll be all right, I swear we will!"

Daniel nodded without amplifying his earlier statement. He needed to be at the pay parade to thank the crew which had followed him to Hell, not once but several times; and who'd brought the *Princess Cecile* and her commander back as well. But as for what he was going to say to them—

He owed Mon the respect due a loyal and competent officer; but he owed a great deal to every soul who'd served on the *Sissie* with him. He wasn't going to tell them to throw their lives away; and despite what he'd said to soothe Mon, the corvette's troubles on the voyage home would convince *anybody* that he was a hard-luck officer. He wasn't a man Daniel would willingly follow to the North, nor one to whom Daniel would pledge his honor to encourage others to follow.

There was a buzzing. Hogg, preparing to leave, reached into his breast pocket for the phone he carried while in Xenos. He listened for a moment, then said to Daniel, "We need to get back to the house, master. *Now.*"

They headed for the door together, the servant leading his master by virtue of starting a double step ahead. As they burst back into the sunlight, Hogg added in a low voice, "That was the major domo, sir. Mistress Mundy had some trouble. Bad trouble."

The tramcar on which Adele and her entourage returned also carried fourteen home-bound office workers, filling it to the legal limit. Adele's footmen—well, the footmen accompanying her and Tovera; the Merchants and Shippers Treasury paid their salaries, though they wore Mundy livery—would've barred the strangers if it had been left to them, but Adele's parents had prided themselves on their concern for the lower orders. Adele, who'd spent most of her life in those lower orders and knew a great deal more about them than her parents had, nonetheless restrained her servants in their memory.

On the other hand, she hadn't felt she needed to allow the car to be loaded *above* the legal limit. At this time of day there'd normally have been forty people per tram; as passenger number twenty boarded at the Pentacrest Circle, Adele's footmen blocked the door and used their ivory batons on the knuckles of anybody trying to pry it open before the car started. Adele preferred to think of that as self-help in enforcing the law rather than a noble trampling on the rights of the people.

She smiled. Though she could live with the other characterization. She'd been trampled on often enough herself.

The car pulled into the siding at the head of her court, rocking slightly on the single overhead rail. No one waited to board on the eastbound platform; the office workers poised expectantly to spread out farther when Adele's party disembarked. They knew how lucky they'd been to have so much room as they rode to their high-rise apartments in the eastern suburbs of Xenos.

As Adele followed her footmen onto the platform, a tram pulled into the westbound siding behind her. She sensed Tovera turning her head, holding her flat attaché case with both hands. A young naval officer in his 2nd Class uniform got off, a stranger to her. Probably someone coming to see Daniel, a friend or perhaps a messenger from the Navy Office.

The seven houses on the court were as quiet as usual on a summer evening. Half a dozen men wearing varied livery squatted on the doorstep of the end house on the left side, next to Chatsworth Minor. They rose, pocketing the dice and the money, when they saw Adele arriving home.

One of the group was her doorman; he walked quickly back to his post without looking sideways to acknowledge her presence. Unexpectedly two other men followed him.

"Mistress Mundy?" called the RCN officer behind her. She turned, then halted to let him join them. The footmen were unconcerned, but Tovera's right hand was inside the attaché case she held in the crook of the other arm.

"Yes?" Adele said; not hostile but certainly not welcoming either. She didn't like being accosted by strangers, especially strangers who knew her name. This lieutenant—she could see the rank tabs on his soft gray collar now—was clean-cut and obviously a gentleman before the Republic granted him a commission, but he was still a stranger.

"Your friend Captain Carnolets hopes you'll be able to dine with him tonight at his house in Portsmouth," the lieutenant said, stopping a polite six feet back. That put him just beyond arm's length of Tovera, toward whom he glanced appraisingly. "He apologizes for the short notice, but he says he's really quite anxious to renew your acquaintance."

I don't know any Captain Carnolets, Adele thought. And of course she didn't; but she knew Mistress Sand, who controlled the Republic's foreign intelligence operations with the same unobtrusive efficiency as Admiral Anston displayed within the RCN.

If Adele had needed confirmation, the way the messenger reacted to Tovera provided it. He wasn't afraid of her, exactly; but he was as careful as he'd have been to keep outside the reach of a chained watchdog—and he'd recognized instantly that the colorless "secretary" *was* a watchdog.

"Yes, all right," Adele said. "But I'll change clothes first."

She turned and motioned the footmen on. Having servants was a constant irritation, complicating even a business as simple as walking down the street. On the other hand, the fact that she'd made the journey home in reasonable comfort instead of being squeezed into less space than steerage on an immigrant ship was an undeniable benefit. . . .

"My name's Wilsing, by the way," said the lieutenant as he fell into step with her. "There's no need to change for the captain, mistress. He was most particular about his wish to see you as soon as possible."

"Which will be as soon as I've changed into civilian clothes, Lieutenant Wilsing," Adele said, letting her tone suggest the irritation that she felt. The only association her dress uniform had for her was the funeral of a man she'd respected and whom her friend Daniel had loved.

It wasn't Mistress Sand's fault that this funeral had reminded Adele that her own parents and sister had been buried without ceremony in a mass grave—all but their heads, of course, which had probably been thrown in the river after birds pecked them clean on the Speaker's Rock. It was true nonetheless. Adele felt the meeting would go better if she got out of her Whites.

When Adele was within twenty feet of Chatsworth Minor's recessed entrance, the doorman turned and said something to the men who'd followed him. They were burly fellows; though they were dressed as footmen, their livery didn't fit well.

One pulled a blackjack from inside his jacket and clubbed the doorman over the head; the doorman staggered into the pilaster, then fell forward on his face. The thug's companion drew a pistol and pointed it in the air.

Adele glanced behind her. Eight men, mostly holding lengths of pipe and similar bludgeons, had entered the court and were walking toward her purposefully. One of them had a pistol. *They must've been in concealment in the pavement-level light wells of one of the houses across the boulevard. . . .*

Lieutenant Wilsing pulled a flat phone out of his breast pocket. "Don't!" Adele said under her breath.

The gunman at the front of Chatsworth Minor aimed his pistol at Wilsing. "Drop it, buddy!" he snarled. "I won't warn you again!"

"Drop it!" Adele repeated. She edged behind one of the footmen so that her left hand could reach into the side-pocket of her tunic without the gunman seeing her.

Wilsing let his little phone clack to the ground. His face had no expression.

"Now the rest of you step away and you won't be hurt!" the gunman said. "We're just going to teach your mistress not to steal houses from her betters!"

"I have the ones behind," Tovera murmured.

"You men!" Adele said to the terrified footmen. They were trying to look back at her and to watch the gunman also. "Get out of the way at once. This isn't your affair."

"But mistress—" said the senior man, a fellow who could—and probably did—pass as a gentleman when he was off-duty and looking for recreation among the female servants from other districts.

"Get out of the way or I'll take a switch to you, my man!" Adele shouted. She sounded on the verge of panic; the part of her mind that dealt with ordinary things like servants had been disconnected from her higher faculties. Her intellect was focused on the developing situation.

The footmen scrambled off to the left. One started to go right, then sprinted to follow the others when he realized he was about to be left alone.

The eight thugs from the head of the court must be very close now. The gunman in front laughed and sauntered forward, accompanied by the man with the blackjack.

Adele shot the gunman in the left cheekbone with

her pocket pistol. *The light was from the west; she hadn't allowed enough for the low sun.* She shot him a second time through the temple as he spun away with a cry, then put a third pellet into the back of his skull while he was still falling. She heard Tovera's submachine gun firing quick, short bursts like the crackling of an extended lightning bolt.

The Mundys were a pugnacious house, quite apart from their political endeavors. Her parents had believed that the best protection they and their offspring had was to be deadly marksmen—not to win duels, but to make it clear to any outraged enemy that challenging a Mundy was tantamount to suicide.

The thug who'd knocked out the Chatsworth doorman dropped his blackjack and fell to his knees screaming. The servants who'd been dicing at the next house had frozen when the first man pulled his gun; now they collided with one another in their haste to open the door and run inside.

Mother would be proud of me, Adele thought as she turned. *Those hours in the basement target range hadn't been wasted. It's good to learn skills at leisure so that they're available when circumstances force a career change. . . .*

The eight men who'd been behind Adele's entourage were all on the pavement now. Several were thrashing violently, but those were their death throes. At least one had started to run.

The barrel shroud of Tovera's weapon was white hot. Like Adele's pistol, the sub-machine gun accelerated projectiles down its bore with electromagnetic pulses. The pellets' aluminum driving bands vaporized in the flux, so sustained shooting created a good deal of waste heat. The muzzle of Adele's own pistol shimmered and would char the cloth if she dropped it back into her pocket.

Tovera turned and shot the thug who was praying on his knees. He sprang backward, a tetanic convulsion rather than the impact of the light pellets directly. Three holes at the base of his throat spouted blood.

Adele grimaced. "Sorry, mistress," Tovera said as she slid a fresh magazine into her weapon's loading tube. "But we didn't need a prisoner. We already know who was behind it."

Adele had a sudden vision of Marina Rolfe herself kicking on the pavement, spraying blood. Of course knowing Tovera, it might not be anything that quick for the lady who believed the Casaubon family money insulated her from retribution when her thugs crippled the rival who'd ousted her from the status she thought she'd purchased.

"Don't kill her!" Adele shouted. "Don't kill her, Tovera, or I'll hunt you down myself. On my honor as a Mundy!"

Tovera dipped her head in acquiescence. "I understand, mistress," she said.

A stain was spreading across the trousers of the gunman Adele had killed; his bowels had spasmed when he died. She went down on one knee, still holding the pistol in her left hand. It'd cooled enough that she could put it back in her pocket now, but she was too dizzy to do anything so complex at the moment.

Tovera fitted her sub-machine gun back into the attaché case she'd dropped when she began shooting. Wilsing had picked up his phone and was speaking into it in urgent tones. He didn't seem affected by what he'd just watched, until you noticed that as he spoke his eyes flicked across building fronts. They always stayed on the second story or above. He wasn't taking any chance of seeing the carnage surrounding him.

Wilsing hadn't done anything but stand where he was; none of these deaths were on his conscience. But only a sociopath like Tovera could watch such slaughter and not be affected by it.

The senior footman said, "Mistress, what should we do?" Adele tried to speak but the words caught in her throat. He grabbed her shoulder and shook her. "Mistress, what do we do?"

Adele rose to her feet, putting the pistol away. She hadn't reloaded, but it had a 20-round magazine. *I don't think I'll need to kill more than seventeen additional people tonight*, she thought. *Of course it took me three shots to put the first one down. . . .*

Aloud she said, "Get into the house and call the Militia. I'm sure somebody else has done so already, but make sure there's been a call from Chatsworth."

"Mistress Mundy?" Wilsing said as he lowered the phone. "We need to get to, to Captain Carnolets as soon as possible. Quickly, now!"

"We can't leave—" Adele began.

The young lieutenant waved his hand at the sprawled bodies. "This has all been taken care of!" he said angrily. "Come! It's really most important!"

"We'd best do as he says, mistress," Tovera said with a smile as cold as a cobra's. "Mistress Sand isn't a person who likes to be kept waiting."

Adele nodded curtly. "All right," she said. "I don't suppose I need to change after all."

Wilsing pulled out an oddly-shaped key as he led the way back to the tram stop. Adele avoided all the outstretched limbs, but despite her care her right half-boot came down on a trickle of blood. The sole was tacky, at least in her mind, with every step she took thereafter.

CHAPTER 4

Militia aircars were parked across both the east- and westbound monorail sidings at the head of the court. The slowing tramcar sensed that the stop was blocked and began to accelerate again. The half-dozen other passengers in the car with Hogg and Daniel gaped and chattered about what was going on.

Daniel grabbed the emergency stop cord and pulled hard, cutting the current to the magnets that levitated the car above the rail. They slid to a screeching, sparkling halt between the two police vehicles. A heavy-set passenger lost his balance and slammed into the front of the car with an angry shout.

Hogg stepped out and held the door open. Daniel let go of the cord and followed his servant. He was aware of the gabbling of his bruised fellow passengers only as he might have noticed the twittering of birds when he walked past a hedge on important business.

There were a dozen Militia personnel in riot gear in the court, but they were in a tight, frustrated-looking group under the eyes of a civilian woman with the red-and-gold Leary rosette on her collar and a man in the uniform of the RCN's Shore Police with a stylized gorget. Two aircars had landed in the court proper. One was an enclosed van with SHORE POLICE/REPUBLIC OF CINNABAR NAVY on the sides.

The other vehicle wore Militia markings but was of much higher quality than those the Republic bought for its national police. Daniel didn't recognize that particular aircar, but he'd seen earlier versions of it before his break with his father. Speaker Leary kept a small fleet of them for his use and that of his personal security detachment.

"Stop right where you are!" said the maybe-Shore Policeman, pointing his left index finger at Daniel while his right hand hovered over his holster. "You've got no business here!"

"I'm a resident," said Daniel, continuing to walk forward. "And besides, I'm Lieutenant Daniel Leary."

"I don't care if you're—" said the cop; he was certainly a cop, whatever his precise affiliation. Daniel drove a straight left into the man's solar plexus, doubling him up as suddenly as a thrown brick.

"When the man tells you he's a Leary, you'd *better* care, buddy," said Hogg said as he sauntered past at Daniel's heel, putting on a pair of mesh-covered gloves. He kicked the fellow's knees out from under him.

A Militiaman laughed. Speaker Leary's official looked at him; she didn't frown or even raise an eyebrow, but he fell silent anyway.

Daniel walked around the van. The other side was hinged down; four men in nondescript coveralls were loading sheet-covered bodies into it. There were several in the vehicle already, stacked on the floor like cordwood.

"Who—?" Daniel said. He had no particular emotion at this moment, just a need to gather information.

He snatched back the sheet from the face of the corpse being lifted into the van. It was a man with a sunburst tattoo on his right cheek: nobody Daniel knew, and anyway a *man*.

"You there!" a man in the utility uniform of an on-duty RCN commander. "Lieutenant! Stop where you are. You have no business here."

Four footmen from Chatsworth Minor stood in a tight circle, surrounded by SPs and Leary retainers. Another Mundy servant was on a stretcher by the front door, his head bandaged. Daniel wasn't sure, but the fellow looked like the day-shift doorman.

"I have every business here," he said, his voice ringing from the facades to either side. "I was told that my shipmate Adele Mundy was in difficulty. Where is she, if you please?"

Eyes peered out from the drawn blinds of the silent houses. None of the residents or servants showed themselves openly, but Daniel knew every soul in the court was watching unless they were in a sick bed or drunken stupor.

There were half a dozen uniformed SPs and an equal number of folk in coveralls; workmen, Daniel supposed. Garbage collectors, one might say. Corder Leary's personnel amounted to six or seven besides the woman watching the Militia.

The RCN commander—who was no more a part of the RCN Daniel served than he was a priest—held a phone. He looked hard at Daniel; Daniel stared back, giving him no change. The phone came up toward the commander's face, then lowered again.

"Lieutenant," he said, "you may go into your dwelling if you like, but you're to stay there until the street is reopened in a few minutes."

"Where is Adele?" Daniel demanded. He wasn't shouting, exactly, but he was speaking very distinctly

in a voice that could've been heard on the bridge of
a warship during action.

Good *God*, how many bodies were there? A couple
more lay behind the footmen and guards nearer the
house, and the pavement Daniel crossed toward the
commander looked like it'd been painted red.

"Lieutenant, that's none of your concern!" said the
commander. He looked toward the heavy-set man
beside him. The latter wore a midshipman's hollow
pips, but he was muscle pure and simple.

"The *Hell* it's none of my—" Daniel said, and this
time he was shouting.

"Sir, she's all right!" cried one of the footmen. "She
and that snake of hers—"

A Shore Policeman grabbed the servant by the throat
and raised his riot baton. He shouted, "You were
warned, boyo!"

"Hogg," Daniel said, but he didn't need to give the
order. A four-ounce deep-sea sinker had already spun
out of Hogg's hand, trailing a shimmer of monocrystal fishing line.

The weight *toonk*ed into the SP's skull, just behind
the right ear. Hogg recovered it neatly into the gloved
hand which held the sinker on the other end of the
line. A bullet couldn't have dropped the fellow more
neatly.

The "midshipman" reached for his belt holster. Daniel
caught his right thumb. "Don't!" he said, and as the
heavy's knee came up Daniel shifted his hip, took the
jolt on bone, and felt the scrunch of cartilage tearing
as he dislocated the fellow's thumb, he'd *told* him. . . .

There were guns out, SPs or whoever they were but
Speaker Leary's retainers were armed also. There'd
been a bloodbath an hour ago in this quiet court and
there was about to be another because some flunky had
lashed out when Daniel Leary asked about a friend.

"Stop!" shouted the leader of SPs "For God's sake, put your weapons away, now! *Now!*"

Nobody moved for a moment, not even Hogg—though his two sinkers continued to spin in opposite directions. His long folding knife was out in his left hand.

"This is Speaker Leary's son," said a well-groomed man in civilian clothes with a Leary flash. He might have been a lawyer or an accountant, one who was abnormally careful to stay fit. "Sir."

The "sir" was perfunctory.

Daniel stepped back. He was trembling with surges of the adrenaline he hadn't burned off in the past few seconds.

"Yes, I take your point," the commander said, grimacing in disgust at the situation. "Look, we're all on the same side."

His glance took in Daniel. Daniel was glad of it, but he could only manage a nod as he twisted his hands together to work out the incipient cramps.

The burly midshipman was holding his right hand in his left. The shock wore off; he muttered in delayed pain.

"Will you shut *up*, for God's sake?" the commander shouted, letting off his own stress. Calmly to Daniel and the head of the Speaker's detachment he continued, "Lieutenant Leary, your friend's safe. She was called off on business that had nothing to do with this. I give you my word on that."

Daniel straightened and took a deep breath. "Very good, Commander," he said, his voice almost under control. "I'm glad to hear it."

"And now . . . ," the commander said. "Just go inside and let us clean up the mess, all right? There'll be a firetruck along to wash the pavement as soon as we've got the debris out of the way. Just a few more minutes."

Daniel took a deep breath. "Yes, all right," he said. "I need to change clothes."

He saw the footmen standing silently terrified in the midst of strangers holding guns. Two of them were talking in low voices to Hogg, who ignored the SP on one side of him and the blocky civilian with a sub-machine gun on the other. Hogg's line and sinkers were in the palm of his right hand, and he'd folded the knife away wherever it was he kept it.

"I'll take my people with me," Daniel said, keeping his tone mild. There'd be time enough to shout if the need arose. He nodded toward the footmen. "Of course."

Since Adele wasn't present, the four were his responsibility. They straightened, looking expectant and desperately hopeful.

"Yes, take them, then," said the commander. He turned to the footmen and said, his voice suddenly harsh, "I won't tell you lot not to talk. But I'll point out the obvious—getting too public is going to bring you to the attention of whoever sent these fellows the first time. Understand?"

Three of the footmen nodded agreement. The fourth stood with his mouth open in abject fear.

"Let's go," said Daniel, deliberately walking through the guards and carrying the footmen with him out the other side on the way toward the house. They had to step between the two sprawled corpses. Daniel managed to do that without looking down; he wasn't sure how the servants managed.

"I've been talking to the boys, master," Hogg said when they were out of earshot of the security people. "Seems this was because of the former owners, the Rolfes, getting stroppy about the way they lost their freehold."

"Ah?" said Daniel. "Yes, that would explain it."

The injured doorman was sitting up, supported by one of Speaker Leary's people. He tried to stand as Daniel approached with the other servants.

"You men," Daniel said, looking over his shoulder at the footmen. "Bring your colleague inside, if you will. I'll send for a doctor."

"He's likely all right," said the civilian who'd been tending the doorman, handing his charge over to the footmen. "Keep checking him during the night for concussion, that's all."

The major domo himself opened the door. The household staff was gathered in the lower hall, watching intently.

"I was thinking, master . . . ," Hogg said. The court shook with the thrum of fans lifting a heavy aircar; the vanload of bodies was on its way off to somewhere suitable. Having waited for the vibration to subside, Hogg continued, "I was thinking that if you didn't need me yourself tonight, I'd go tend to some business of my own?"

Daniel looked at his man. "Yes, I'll be all right, Hogg," he said. "Unless there's something I can do to help you?"

"No need you getting involved, master," Hogg said, walking off down the hall through the gaggle of house servants. "I'll get some gear from my room."

He looked back over his shoulder. Hogg was balding and a little overweight. His clothes, from heavy ankle boots to the kerchief around his neck, were scruffy and decidedly rural: a perfect Sam Bumpkin disguise for a man who was smart and just as ruthless as a weasel. "Tovera 'n me'll be plenty for this business, never fear."

"I'm not afraid," Daniel said quietly to Hogg's back. He looked at the house servants. "Get on to your duties," he said in feigned exasperation. "And if you don't have duties, at least don't hang about in the hall here."

Daniel started up the stairs. "Sir?" called the major domo. "Is there something, ah, in particular you'd like us to do?"

Daniel looked back over his shoulder. "No, just keep things ready for Officer Mundy's return." He paused, then continued, "I'll be going out myself shortly. My former command's docked at Harbor One. I think I'd like to see her before she's sold."

The tram rattled off the main line onto a spur; trees with long, dangling branches framed the entrance to the route. *Daniel would know what they were*, Adele mused. She found the thought so comforting that she brought her data unit out of its thigh pocket and switched it on.

"Mistress?" said Lieutenant Wilsing, raising an eyebrow.

"I wondered what the trees were," Adele said. She slid her control wands from their pocket in the case. For a trained user, the wands gave much greater speed and precision than any other interface. "I decided it'd be a good test to look them up for myself, since Lieutenant Leary isn't here to identify them for me."

"Here in the entrance corridor, you mean?" Wilsing said. "They're Maranham cypresses, brought back by Captain St. Regis when he opened Maranham three hundred and fifty years ago. This is quite a famous grove, as a matter of fact."

"Thank you," said Adele, dryly. *Well, that was another way of getting the information. . . .*

They entered a broad commons encircled by a ring of neat brick houses set well back from the tramway. It was late evening; the sky remained bright but the ground was in deep shadow.

"The fourth house . . . ," Wilsing said. "There."

The tram moaned to a halt; on this lightly used byway there was no need for sidings. Wilsing removed the special key he'd thrust into the control panel, sending the car directly to the destination he'd programmed instead of halting for additional passengers that the central transportation computer had determined it could carry efficiently.

"The service has aircars, of course," Wilsing said as he snapped the key onto his belt pouch, then bowed Adele off the car ahead of him. "But Mistress Sand prefers that we remain as unobtrusive as possible."

Adele smiled faintly. She agreed with the policy, but she rather suspected that Wilsing and the others of his type whom Mistress Sand used as flunkies would rather cut a wide, flashy swath through Cinnabar society. The need for quiet competence was at least one of the reasons that Sand came to people like Warrant Officer Adele Mundy when she needed real work done. . . .

Wilsing paused on the brick pavement as the tramcar purred away, gesturing toward the open space within the monorail track. Pieces of naval paraphernalia were displayed there. Near at hand was a plasma cannon, its muzzle raggedly eroded. Farther around the circle was the lump of a High Drive motor, and in the center rose a starship's antenna.

Wilsing pointed to the antenna. "Commander Stacey Bergen conned the *Excellence* to Alexandreios from the truck of that mast," he explained. "I've heard that described as the most amazing feat of astrogation since Cinnabar returned to the stars."

"Lieutenant Leary believes his Uncle Stacey was a uniquely skilled astrogator," Adele said as she surveyed the small park. It was really an outdoor museum, the sort of exhibit that retired RCN officers would create

for their own sort. The fact they'd given Commander
Bergen pride of place would mean a great deal to
Daniel . . . which was almost certainly why Wilsing
mentioned it. Perhaps the young man had virtues
beyond those of good breeding after all. "I don't know
of anybody better qualified to judge than Daniel."

Wilsing led Adele up the path to one of the houses
nestled back among the trees. Bands of light marked
the edges of the crazy-pavement ahead of them,
advancing as they did; a porch light shone over the
door in dim sufficiency.

The servant who opened the door was too senior
to wear livery. He bowed low and said, "Lieutenant
Wilsing, I believe you know the way to the red drawing
room. The Captain left a decanter and glass on the
table for you. Mistress Mundy, you're awaited in the
library. Will you please follow me?"

The servant—the only person visible apart from
Wilsing, who absented himself into a side chamber with
a nod—led the way through a pair of rooms whose
furnishings were as simple as they were exotic. All the
furniture was hand-crafted from strikingly-patterned
wood, though the pieces in the first room were as
different from those of the second as either was from
anything native to Cinnabar.

The house had a hallway along the side; doors of
a simpler pattern than the ones Adele passed through
nested in the left-hand wall of each room. The hall was
for servants, not the owner and his guests.

The door of the third room was open; Adele saw
glass-fronted bookcases within. "Please go through,
mistress," the servant said, bowing again. As Adele
entered the library, he closed the door behind her.

Bernis Sand rose from a banquette in a corner and
gestured Adele to the other end of its upholstered
curve. "Good of you to come, Mundy," she said. "Here,

sit down. Can I offer you refreshment? My friend Carnolets keeps an impressive cellar."

"Nothing, thank you," Adele said. "Well—water, if that's possible? My throat's dry, I find. Very dry."

"Yes, of course," Sand said, touching a call-plate set into the table in the center of the banquette. She was a stocky woman of indeterminate age, almost sexless in the library's muted light. She wore a pants suit of brown herringbone twill, nondescript from any distance but of natural fabric and the best workmanship. "I hear you had some trouble this evening. Is there anything I should know about it?"

Adele shook her head curtly. She sat on the banquette, concentrating on her action so that she didn't have to meet the spymaster's eyes. "It was a private matter," she said. "It's been resolved, or it shortly will be."

Her left hand, the hand she'd killed with again tonight, twitched with an incipient cramp. She massaged the palm with her right thumb and fingers, staring at the rich honey-on-bronze grain of the table and seeing instead the face of the gunman as her first pellet blew two teeth out through his left cheek.

The servant set a carafe and glasses on the table and silently vanished again. "Mundy?" said Mistress Sand. "Are you sure you wouldn't like something stronger?"

"Very sure indeed," Adele said in a steady voice. She poured herself a glass of water and drank, pleased to note that her hand barely trembled.

Sand seated herself on the other end of the banquette; she and Adele weren't quite facing one another across the small table. She glanced at the tantalus in an alcove near the door, but instead of getting a drink she took a tortoiseshell snuffbox from her waistcoat and poured a dose into the cup of her left thumb.

"Do you know anything about the Commonwealth

of God, Mundy?" she asked conversationally, then lifted the snuff to her nose.

"I know very little about any part of the Galactic North," Adele said. She'd brought out her data unit and its control wands without conscious consideration. "My family had no business interests in the region. I've sometimes considered—"

She looked at Sand with a wry grin.

"—that there might be interesting pre-Hiatus volumes in what passes for the libraries of various local rulers, but I'm not going to live long enough to catalog a fraction of what I could find in attics here in Xenos."

In the center of the room stood a globe whose continents were set in seas of contrasting semi-precious stone. The planet wasn't Cinnabar or any other world Adele recognized.

Sand blocked one nostril with her index finger, snorted, then sneezed violently into the handkerchief she'd taken from her right sleeve. She looked up, her expression shrewd.

"The Commonwealth isn't very prepossessing for a fact," she said. "Half the local captains are pirates if you turn your back on them, and the central government makes up with brutality for what it lacks in competence. But it's big—loose as it is, the total trade out of the Commonwealth supports a good tenth of the merchant houses in Cinnabar and our allies. For generations the Commonwealth's been more or less friendly to us. If it should side openly with the Alliance, there'd be serious effects for our relations with the smaller states which depend on trade with the North."

Adele found what she'd been searching for in the holographic display hanging above her data unit. She leaned back against the cushion and smiled coldly at

Sand. The mere cite was enough to bring the episode of family history vividly to her mind.

"In the aftermath of the Three Circles Conspiracy," she said, her tone dryly precise, "an RCN battleship under Admiral O'Quinn fled to the Commonwealth. I would have thought that the Commonwealth's refusal to return the vessel and its crew of mutineers would have seriously soured relations."

"Yes, the *Aristoxenos*," Sand said, nodding. "Most of her officers turned out to have been members of the Popular Party. A cousin of yours was the first lieutenant, I believe?"

"Yes," Adele said. Her smile was as cold as the winter moon. "Commander Adrian Purvis. My closest *living* relative as a result of his having successfully fled."

"In fact the *Aristoxenos* is part of the problem," Sand explained, rising and walking over to the tantalus. "But you see, the Commonwealth of God has its own internal divisions, rather worse than those which beset the Republic sixteen years ago. O'Quinn made his first planetfall on Todos Santos in the Ten Star Cluster where Governor Sakama had already been pursuing a policy independent of the government on Radiance."

Without turning, Sand held to the light a glass of liquor the color of sun-struck brass. "With a modern battleship and an RCN crew to support him," she continued, "Sakama took an even stronger line. The *Aristoxenos* practically annihilated a Commonwealth fleet six months later, guaranteeing that the central government would be content with lip service from the Cluster."

"I see," said Adele. She poured more water, but she didn't feel the need to drink it. Having a real question to deal with had jerked her mind out of the blood-drenched groove it'd been running in ever since she shot the gunman this afternoon.

*She'd had no choice. He'd attacked and she'd
defended herself. She'd had every legal and moral right
to shoot the man. . . .*

But only sociopaths like Tovera killed without regret,
because they had no consciences and no souls. That
wasn't Adele Mundy. Not yet.

"Warships degrade without maintenance," she said
aloud, meeting Sand's eyes as she turned. "Ships do
and crews do as well. Has the Cluster been able to
maintain the *Aristoxenos*? Because if not, I doubt it's
an effective fighting unit by this time."

"'Effective' is a relative concept, Mundy," Mistress
Sand said. "Given the sort of small, indifferently-crewed
ships that make up the Commonwealth naval forces,
yes—the *Aristoxenos* is still effective, at least as a
deterrent. And the drubbing she doled out to the
central government fleet created a legend that fifteen
years doesn't erase."

Adele turned up her left palm. "Go on," she said
quietly. The quickest way to learn what Sand wanted
from her was to sit and listen.

"The Ten Star Cluster lies on the shortest routes
from Cinnabar to the Galactic North," Sand continued.
"The Republic had more serious concerns at the time
than the defection of one battleship—"

Adele nodded curtly. The Alliance had massed naval
forces to threaten several Cinnabar dependencies. Had
the conspirators successfully gained power in Xenos,
Alliance squadrons would almost certainly have swept
in to support them. The actual fighting didn't go
beyond isolated single-ship actions, but there'd been
no certainty of that before the fact. Speaker Leary
hadn't been about to order the RCN to send to the
back of beyond a powerful force which might be
needed to defend Cinnabar itself.

"—and later, capturing or destroying the *Aristoxenos*

at the cost of permanent hostility from whoever ruled the Ten Star Cluster looked like a very poor bargain. Besides—after tempers had cooled, there was very little stomach for executing a thousand or so mutineers."

Adele thought of the pair of soldiers cutting off the head of her little sister Agatha, who'd managed to avoid capture for several weeks before she was caught. The act had shocked the consciences even of those who'd ordered the Proscriptions.

"Yes," she said without emotion. "I can imagine that would be a problem. A practical politician might decide to live and let live."

Sand seated herself again across from Adele. She sipped from her crystalline drink tumbler, but her movements appeared to have been less a matter of thirst than an excuse to turn her back while she spoke difficult truths.

"The situation was—is—satisfactory from Cinnabar's point of view," Sand said. She shrugged. "Politics is the art of the possible, after all. It remains a serious thorn in the flesh of the authorities in Radiance, however. Quite apart from the insult, tribute from the Ten Star Cluster had provided a third of the central government's revenues. After the *Aristoxenos* arrived, that of course ended. And now . . ."

She drank, her eyes holding Adele's over the glittering crystal arc. She set the tumbler down and continued, "I have reports that Alliance personnel are building a modern naval base on Gehenna, the only satellite of Radiance. If the Commonwealth government were to reconquer the Ten Star Cluster with Alliance support, the ramifications for the Republic would be very serious."

"I can see that," Adele said carefully. "What I don't see . . ."

As she chose her words, she let her eyes rove

slowly over the ranks of glass-fronted bookshelves. She couldn't read the spine stampings from where she sat, but it was obvious that this was a real collection rather than yea-many books by the yard that one often found in households whose noble residents chose to affect erudition instead of sporting prowess or a taste for the graphic arts.

A space captain with a real affection for literature had ample time and opportunity to pursue his hobby. Carnolets was apparently one of those captains. Adele felt a surge of warmth toward a man—or woman; she had no way of knowing—whom she'd never met.

" . . . is why you sent for me," she continued, locking her gaze with the spymaster's. "If there's a naval base on Gehenna, then it's a matter for the whole RCN. Not for me."

"The Senate doesn't want a war," Sand said bluntly. "And the shipping firms, from the largest to captain-owned tramps, *really* don't want a resumption of hostilities. The Cinnabar ambassador to the Commonwealth, Train of Lakeside, believes the base on Gehenna is still years from completion. If he's correct, then there's no need for precipitate action on our part."

Sand drank. Lowering the tumbler she went on, "I can't prove Train is wrong, but I will say that if that good gentleman said the sun would rise in the east I'd want a second opinion. I want you to determine the actual progress on the base."

Information cascaded across Adele's holographic display under the direction of her control wands. Gehenna was fully a third the diameter of its primary, Radiance, but it was uninhabited, cold at the core, and lacking a significant atmosphere. A great deal of water was trapped within the mantle, though, offering reaction mass for the plasma thrusters that lifted starships into hard vacuum where they could use their antimatter High Drive motors.

Gehenna would make a very suitable naval base for someone who was willing to trade a degree of discomfort for nearly complete secrecy.

"Are you going to send a ship to the Radiance system?" Adele said. She'd almost said, "—send the *Princess Cecile*?" but that would never happen again.

She continued to scroll through data. The best way to learn what you needed to know was simply to study what had been published, correlating the bits in your mind and noting the anomalies. When things didn't fit it meant that somebody was lying, and the mere fact of the lie would often show you the truth behind it.

"The Commonwealth embargoed Radiance to foreign naval vessels three years ago," Sand said, her tone bleak with suppressed anger. "Ambassador Train was quite angry about it, because he'd been intriguing to have his private yacht declared an RCN warship so that its crew and maintenance would come out of the naval appropriation. It didn't cross his mind to report the matter through official channels, however."

"How, then?" Adele said, looking up from her display for the first time in minutes. Had some Commonwealth magnate expressed a desire for a trained librarian?

"Count Klimov and his wife Valentina from Novy Sverdlovsk plan a private expedition to the Galactic North," Sand said. "They're quite real—they have no connection with either me or Cinnabar more generally. But they're buying the *Princess Cecile* and have hired Lieutenant Mon as her captain. I want you to go with them as signals officer."

"Ah," Adele said. She shut down her data unit and crossed her hands on the table. Her eyes were unfocused; her mind spun as she dealt with the implications of the spymaster's simple statement. *A plum job like that made it obvious why Mon had been so excited when he came looking for Daniel . . . but that was the only part of the business which* was *obvious.*

"You of course know Lieutenant Mon," Sand said quietly, setting down the empty tumbler. "Are your relations with him good?"

"Yes, certainly," Adele said with a flash of irritation. "He has my confidence, of course. But. . . ."

She rose to her feet and slid the data unit away in its pocket. "Mistress Sand," she said. "I understand the importance of the matter to, to the Republic. But I don't wish to give you an answer immediately, because if I must my answer will be no."

Sand nodded calmly. "I appreciate your concerns, mistress," she said. "I'll expect your answer when you're able to provide it."

Adele turned to the door as the servant silently opened it. She wondered how long it would take to get a tram out here to Portsmouth. . . .

"Mundy?" the spymaster asked. Adele turned. "Would your decision become easier if the Klimovs hired Lieutenant Leary instead of Mon as their captain?"

Adele smiled, though only someone who knew her well would recognize the humor in the expression. "Yes," she said, "it would. But the likelihood of Daniel maneuvering a fellow officer out of a position he desperately needs is something less than the chance that Daniel will decide to join a celibate religious order."

She was still grinning as the servant led her to the front door where Lieutenant Wilsing waited for her.

CHAPTER 5

The tram ran only to the gate of Harbor One. Three
drunks sprawled against the side of the kiosk. One of
them straightened as Daniel dismounted and called,
"Begging your pardon, lieutenant, but could you spare
an old spacer the price of a drink? I was gunner's
mate aboard the *Burke* oncet, till I lost me arm at
Xerxes Two."

Only one strip light in the kiosk's interior still
worked; the speaker was in shadow, his voice so rusty
that Daniel was scarcely willing to swear he was male.
He was missing his left arm, true enough, though that
could've been the result of a drunken accident as
probably as an incident of Admiral Cawdrey's great
victory over the Alliance a generation ago.

"Yes, of course, my man," Daniel said, fumbling in
his purse for a one-florin coin. He found a five
instead—and tossed it to the fellow. "Can you perhaps
tell me where the *Princess Cecile* is berthed? She
arrived from—"

"Slip Seventeen, that's the third on the right as you
go in the gate," said another of the drunks. His voice

was muffled because he'd pulled his woven cap down over his face. "Arrived oh-eight-one-seven hours this morning from the Strymon system, scheduled for immediate disposal."

"Ah?" said Daniel. "Indeed, thank you sir."

He reached for another coin. The first drunk raised the five-florin piece in his only hand and said, "Bless you, lieutenant, but this is as much as we can drink in a night. Any more'd only be stolen, and our throats slit besides like enough. God speed your course, sir."

The guard at the gate was chatting with several civilians; he merely threw a casual salute to the lieutenant's badge on the saucer hat Daniel wore tonight with his 2nd Class uniform. Daniel walked into the enclosure.

Harbor One was historic in the sense that it had launched the ships by which Cinnabar returned to the stars after the thousand-year Hiatus which ended Mankind's first ventures into the wider universe. For several centuries the harbor had remained the main starport of the expanding Republic, but it'd continued to be used after it lost importance. By now the site was a nautical jumble shop from which every piece of its evocative past had been razed to make room for something newer—or simply something else. Uncle Stacey had remembered when a rank of pre-Hiatus brick barracks stood on the eastern edge of the compound, but woven-wire cages of salvaged High Drive motors were there now.

Ships, generally several to a slip, filled the basin. For the most part they were berthed too close together for one to lift off without damaging others; they'd have to be towed into the center of the pool for that. Many of them weren't in condition to lift, of course. The vessels in Harbor One sometimes had a past, but there was no future for them, at least in the RCN.

The *Princess Cecile* stood out like a jewel on a mudbank. Other ships made do with a single area light at bow or stern, but the corvette's auxiliary power unit was still live. Not only were her running lights on, open ports flooded the slip with illumination from her cabins. The harbor water winked, and the indirect glow cast a memory of romance over the scarred concrete quay.

Music sounded from a bow compartment—*"Ize the bye that builds the boat and Ize the bye that sails her. . . ."* It was a song from the East Capes, the region where the Leary estates lay. A trio of male voices were singing to the accompaniment of a flute.

Daniel hadn't expected more than a minimal anchor watch—and those spacers very likely drunk, as their fellows were drunk in the taverns nearest the harbor, spending the advances crimps had provided at steep discounts against the pay parade in the morning. Instead at least a dozen crewmen in their glittering, beribboned shore-going uniforms sat or stood in the entrance hold, talking quietly.

A catwalk led from the quay to the main hatch. Daniel walked toward it. Woetjans—the big bosun was unmistakable; her leave cap sported a ribbon for every port she'd called in during thirty years in the RCN— saw him approaching and straightened. She keyed the rubidium-plated control stub hanging from her neck on a chain, her badge of office, and the corvette's public address system piped CAPTAIN COMING ABOARD. The singing forward stopped and everyone in the entrance hatch came to attention.

Daniel felt a shiver of delight at the bosun's call. He didn't expect he'd ever lose that feeling, even if they were carrying him on a litter to die aboard the ship he commanded.

"Stand easy!" he said as his boots thumped the narrow, quivering catwalk. He walked as straight as a rigger, never looking down. The RCN trained its midshipmen to do every job the common crewmen did. Officers who couldn't walk the yards while the sails billowed to the thrust of Casimir radiation, or replace a scale-clogged thruster feed while a vessel was under weigh, didn't deserve to command spacers who could.

He smiled at the group as he stepped onto the *Princess Cecile*'s nickel-steel C Deck. The armored companionway up to B and A Decks was to the right, forward; the down tube to the Power Room and bulk storage was on the left. Even floating in harbor the ship felt shiveringly alive. There was nothing quite like being aboard a starship; and for a spacer like Daniel Leary, there was nothing better.

"I'm not the captain, you know, men," Daniel said. "I thought I'd come aboard the old girl once more as a private citizen."

"Right," said Woetjans. "You're not captain and I'm not a rigger. In your ear!"

Sun, the gunner's mate—acting gunner on a corvette, which didn't rate a senior warrant in that slot—held out a squat, long-necked bottle; in place of a label, a medallion was cast into the dark ruby glass. "Here you go, sir," he said. "Ah . . . ? It's all right. Barnes and Dasi have the duty and they're sober."

"It'd be all right regardless, Sun," Daniel said. "Tonight."

They were *all* sober or the next thing to it, though some had probably put down more liquor than a landsman who intended to walk away would've done. Vesey, one of the pair of midshipmen from the Strymon cruise, was among them; initially Daniel'd missed her slight form between Barnes and Dasi, who'd returned to Cinnabar with Daniel aboard a requisitioned Strymonian cutter. Those riggers—and several other crewmen in the immediate group—had come to the *Princess*

Cecile tonight for the same reason Daniel had: to say goodbye.

Daniel swigged from the bottle. It was excellent brandy, though he couldn't identify it closer than that. He offered it to Sun, but the gunner's mate said, "I've had mine, sir," and gestured toward the four machinists who'd appeared down the forward corridor. One had stuck a short flute into a pocket of her coveralls. Daniel gave her the brandy instead.

"Midshipman Dorst will be back shortly, sir," Vesey said. She was trim and blond, scarcely half the size of her male shipmate; and lover, though Daniel didn't carry his duty of standing *in loco parentis* to his midshipmen to the extent of involving himself in that sort of private business. "He went to see his mother as soon as we docked, is all."

Vesey had showed herself an able astrogator, not just by computation but with at least a touch of the *feel* for the Matrix that had made Stacey Bergen and to a considerable degree his nephew Daniel legends in the RCN. Dorst wasn't either as smart or as clever as Vesey, but he was as solid as bedrock; that too was a virtue the RCN prized in her officers.

"So, Woetjans . . . ," Daniel said, trying not to be completely obvious. "Lieutenant Mon said you had your share of trouble on the voyage back from Strymon?"

The bosun made a sour face. "I've had worse, I guess, sir," she muttered, refusing to meet Daniel's eyes.

"Well, if you have," said Sun forcefully, "then you've been harder places than I have, thank the Almighty." He turned to Daniel and went on, "Sir, you wrung the *Hell* out of us when you ran us to Sexburga in seventeen days straight in the Matrix, I swear you did, and we had less trouble with the ship than I'd expect in dockyard. Mon brought us back and, well, I'm bloody glad to have solid ground under my feet. *Bloody* glad."

"Amen to that," muttered Chief Engineer Pasternak, who'd just come up from the Power Room. A third of the *Sissie's* crew must be aboard her tonight, a remarkable percentage for a ship returned to her home port for the first time after a long cruise. The entrance hold was becoming crowded, but there was no larger compartment aboard the corvette until the stores were off-loaded.

"Tush!" said Daniel. "I don't regret pushing her the way I did, but you all know as well as I do that half the trouble you had on the return voyage was because of the strain I laid on her outbound."

The machinist who'd just emptied the brandy bottle snorted. Perhaps the liquor had gotten up his nose.

"Mon said you had passengers, too," Daniel went on. "What were they like?"

The spacers looked at one another. After a moment Vesey said, "Well, the Klimovs aren't bad, sir. For foreigners, you know. Quite open-handed folk, the both of them."

"Sober, they're all right," said Woetjans, her eyes on Daniel. "When the Count's got a drop or two in him, which is most times, he's apt to forget he's not back on Novy Sverdlovsk with his house slaves. He threw a bottle at the spacer doing for him—and got decked for it."

"That was me, sir," said Timmons, a short, good-humored technician whom Daniel had never known to show any more temperament than the paint on the bulkhead did. He looked at his feet in embarrassment. "Sorry, sir."

"Sorry for bloody what?" demanded Woetjans. "The day some wog gets away with hitting a Cinnabar spacer is the day I defect to the Alliance. But—"

Her eyes hardened on Daniel again.

"—if Klimov had been captain instead of a passenger,

then hitting him would've been mutiny and an open hatch for the fellow who did it. That's so, isn't it, sir?"

"I've known RCN officers who did as much, Woetjans!" Daniel said sharply. "So have you, I dare say."

"Aye, and worse," Sun said with a chuckle. "Cap'n Reecee fired a shot at the sailing master when we came out of the Matrix four light-days from where her reckoning had put us. He wasn't any better a shot than she was an astrogator, mind."

"Reecee was an RCN officer, Sun," Woetjans said. "Not a wog!"

"Amen to that," Pasternak said, offering around a retort of clear fluid; industrial alcohol from the hydraulic system, very likely. That was the standard Power Room drink.

"I haven't met Klimov . . . ," Daniel said. Vesey drank and handed the retort to him. "If he likes the *Sissie* well enough to buy her, as Mon says he does, then he and I share one taste, at least."

He drank, a careful sip followed by a deeper draft when he was sure the fluid had been cut with water. Drunk straight, industrial alcohol dried the mouth and throat as badly as swallowing live coals, but the mechanics and engineers didn't always bother to dilute it.

"And Mon says Klimov plans to pay top wages as well," Daniel said, keeping his eyes on Woetjans as he passed the retort to the machinist at his side. They all knew what he was talking about, that Mon was a shipmate and an officer he respected. . . .

"Well, he won't be paying them to me," Sun said bluntly. "I've got a machinist's rating, besides which there's plenty merchant skippers sailing routes where they'd feel better to have Lieutenant Leary's gunner aboard."

"Wages're fine, sir," Woetjans said, apologetic but

clearly coming from the same place as Sun. "The thing is, though—"

She gestured with her left hand.

"—there's never been a spacer yet who lifted ship with anything still in her pocket. Some leave most of their pay with their families, sure—"

Woetjans might mean the plural literally. It wasn't just a music-hall joke that spacers kept separate households at each planetfall of a regular route.

"—and some of us spend it in bars; but we all *spend* it. Another florin a week doesn't mean very much, especially if we don't come back."

Well, that was blunt enough; even without Pasternak repeating, "Amen to that!"

"Sir?" said Dasi. He and his mate Barnes were big men and utterly dependable. They weren't the quickest minds in the RCN, but they were experienced enough that either would make a good bosun's mate the next time Daniel had an opening to fill.

"Aye?" said Daniel. He'd heard the tram stop outside the gate. He didn't turn his head, but from the way Vesey brightened as she looked past him, the fellow trotting toward the *Princess Cecile* was Midshipman Dorst.

"What should we do, sir?" Dasi said, his face screwed up with concern. Timmons offered him a bottle; he was too perturbed to notice it. "Should we sign on with this wog and Mr. Mon? Do *you* want us to?"

Daniel sighed, waving away the return of Mr. Pasternak's retort. "Dasi," he said. He let his eyes trail across the faces crowding the entrance hold; all of them familiar, all of them troubled. "All of you. When we served together aboard the *Princess Cecile*, I never doubted that you'd obey whatever order I gave."

He stiffened into a formal Parade Rest, the posture

he'd have taken if he were addressing them from a reviewing stand. He continued, "I have neither the right nor the will to give you orders now. You and I both have decisions to make, but we make them as individuals because we're no longer captain and crew."

"Too bad about Mon," said Woetjans, shaking her head in summation. "But I guess he'll find a berth somewhere."

Daniel cleared his throat. "I'll be getting back to my quarters," he said. "I . . ."

His throat clogged and his eyes began to sting. That damned hydraulic fluid!

"I'll be at the paying off ceremony tomorrow," he said, forcing the words out in a rush. "Fellow spacers, there was never a ship luckier in her crew than the *Princess Cecile*!"

Daniel turned and strode back toward the tram stop, almost colliding with Mr. Dorst whom his blurring vision missed. The cheers of the *Sissie*'s crew followed him all the way to the gate.

Adele heard the front door close and the murmur of voices. She opened her study and stepped into the hallway just as Daniel started up the stairs.

"Please join me, Daniel," she said; which was foolish since obviously he was coming to her quarters on the second floor already. She'd asked the doorman to send him up as soon as he arrived, no matter what time it was. "Some matters have arisen that I'd like your advice on."

"You're all right, Adele?" Daniel said. He'd taken off his billed hat when he entered the house; his face, lighted from above the stairwell, had the hard, controlled expression that she'd seen on the bridge of the *Princess Cecile* in action but very rarely otherwise. "I'm sorry not to have been here when you, ah, returned."

"Oh, there's nothing wrong," Adele said, frowning in puzzlement. "I just had some questions about my plans that I—oh. Oh, I see what you mean."

She ushered him into her study, realizing as she did so that it was messy by ordinary standards. Books and paper were stacked on most of the flat surfaces; she was researching the Commonwealth of God, and some documents were available only as hardcopy. She'd cleared a second chair in expectation of Daniel's arrival, though.

"The business when I came home?" she said. She shrugged. "The doorman'll be off work for several days, I believe. Apart from that, everything is, well, normal. I'd expected questioning by the authorities, but apparently it's all been swept under the rug."

Adele had reloaded the pistol as soon as she got home. It was in her pocket now, not against real need but for the security its slight weight afforded her subconscious. The little weapon had become an addictive drug. It was the thing that best kept the nightmares at bay, though it was the cause of those leering nightmares as well.

"Yes," said Daniel. "Hogg and I arrived during the clean-up. The people involved appeared to be able."

Adele closed the door and motioned to the upholstered seat across the leather-topped desk from her own straight chair. A wine bottle and two glasses waited on the tray a servant had brought earlier in the evening.

"Hogg isn't here, by the way," she said. "He left a message for Tovera, and they're still out."

Daniel grimaced as he sat down; he looked suddenly tired. "Adele?" he said. He lifted his head and met her eyes with a determined expression. "I gave Hogg free rein on dealing with what happened here this afternoon. Whatever comes of it is on my head; I want you to be very clear on that."

Adele smiled faintly. "Have some wine," she said, uncorking the bottle. "It's from what used to be Chatsworth Major. The new owners renamed the estate Skyland, but the grapes are the same."

She poured, one glass and then the other. The wine was a dark honey color; not a famous vintage, but a comfortable one and a familiar taste that brought her childhood and its security a little closer.

"As for anything that happens to the Rolfes, Daniel . . . ," she went on. "I'd say that's on the head of the person who sent thugs to knock our doorman around. But for what it's worth, I told Tovera not to kill anyone. She's quite trustworthy that way."

She quirked a grin at Daniel as she handed him his wine. "Emotion doesn't get in the way with her, you see," she said. "She doesn't lose control."

Daniel drank and nodded approvingly before lowering the glass again. "You said you had questions?" he said, raising an eyebrow.

"Mon will have told you that aristocrats from Novy Sverdlovsk are buying the *Princess Cecile* for a voyage to the Galactic North," Adele said, continuing to smile faintly. One of the few personality traits she and Daniel shared was a dislike for circumlocution. "An acquaintance, probably the person who had our court cleaned after the incident this afternoon, wants me to accompany them in order to get an impression of Alliance activity on Radiance and its satellite."

She didn't go into detail or use Mistress Sand's name, knowing that the whole business would make Daniel uncomfortable. He was by no means a blunt, unsophisticated naval officer—he was Speaker Leary's son, for God's sake!—but in Daniel's ideal world actions would be open and transparent. He believed that if he did his own job openly and very well, he could leave other aspects to those who found them more congenial. Leave them to people like his friend Adele, it might be. . . .

"I see," said Daniel. He seemed calm, but he tossed down the wine instead of remembering to sip it. She reached for the bottle, but he waved her away brusquely with his free hand as he frowned in concentration.

He *did* see, of course. Adele had never met anyone who more quickly integrated disparate data than did her friend Daniel. It had gained him a deserved reputation as a combat commander, and probably equal envy from acquaintances marveling at Leary's success with women.

"Lieutenant Mon's as good a technical officer as you'll find," Daniel said, his eyes on the corner of a bookshelf. It was vanishingly improbable that the works filed there—pre-Hiatus fiction, a collection which Adele had chosen to recreate though she didn't share her mother's taste—was of any interest to him. "Nothing else appearing, I'd wish you Godspeed."

He looked up, his face again uncommonly hard. "However, the *Sissie's* crew have decided that he's an unlucky captain," Daniel continued. "They may well be right. Mon won't be able to hire a trustworthy crew, I'm afraid, and the risks on a voyage to Radiance will be very great. Unacceptably great, I would say, unless your need were also very great."

He raised an eyebrow.

Adele nodded, turning the stem of her wineglass between thumb and forefinger. "That's my judgment as well," she said dispassionately. "My acquaintance made clear her opinion that the matter *is* of weight comparable to the risk."

"With all respect to your acquaintance," Daniel said, his voice very much that of his father's son, "I doubt she has a proper grasp of the danger involved under these precise circumstances. Uncle Stacey opened most of the present routes to Radiance. Lieutenant Mon for all his undoubted virtues is neither Stacey Bergen nor a man who's ever made the run to the North himself."

Adele sipped her wine, letting the remembered flavors recall for her a simpler, sunnier childhood. "I'm inclined to agree with you, Daniel," she said, "but I'm sure beyond question that some colleague of mine will be aboard the *Princess Cecile* on this voyage. I have no idea who it would be, but I'm confident that there's no one more familiar with the *Sissie* and her capabilities than I am. And I'm afraid—"

She smiled wryly across the table.

"—that the Mundy family's involvement in the Three Circles Conspiracy leaves me under more of an obligation to the Republic than an ordinary citizen would be."

Daniel rose to his feet. "I'll give the matter some thought," he said. He sounded suddenly nonchalant. "There may be a way out."

He smiled broadly at her. "For now," he said, "I'm going to bed. I need to be at the mustering-out ceremony for the *Sissie*'s crew in the morning. You'll be joining me, I hope?"

"Yes, of course," Adele said as she stood to show him to the door. She, like Daniel himself, had been on half-pay since they'd returned to Cinnabar six weeks earlier; they had no official connection with the *Princess Cecile*. If he wanted her present, that was a good enough reason to be there, however.

"Good," he said, skirting a stack of books on the floor. Each was marked with the name of the person who'd loaned it because Mundy of Chatsworth was collecting information on the Galactic North. Adele's family connections had become useful again.

"There's usually an answer if folk of good will get together to find one," Daniel said, grinning as he stepped through the door she'd opened for him.

Despite what Adele could only think of as the puerile silliness of the comment, she found herself grinning back. The Daniel Learys of this world somehow made childhood homilies not only seem true but, based on her own experience, *come* true.

CHAPTER 6

A dozen spacers from the *Princess Cecile* and the civilians of both sexes attached to them shared the tramcar with Adele and Daniel as it slowed to the siding at Harbor One. She frowned again at her civilian clothes and said in a quietly tart voice in Daniel's ear, "I really could have worn my dress uniform too, you know!"

Daniel looked down at his own resplendent Whites. Instead of medal ribbons, he was wearing the awards themselves. That meant a startling amount of glitter—in particular the Order of Strymon in Diamonds, an aiguillette of gold and silver cords fastened at his breast and epaulette with clasps whose stones were the size of a child's teeth.

"Oh, that's not called for," he said in a tone of mild satisfaction. "I'd never look like this at a real RCN affair, but to impress civilians—and civilians from Novy Sverdlovsk besides—I thought it was the thing."

He met her eyes; his smile had just the least professional crispness. "That's *my* job," he added. "You'll want to stay inconspicuous, I believe."

The tram rocked to a halt. Without thinking about

it, Daniel stepped through the mass of spacers standing closer to the door; they were squeezing against the sides to let the officers by. Adele followed, realizing wryly that she was the only person on the car who didn't take it for granted that the captain and signals officer would get out first. Her parents would have understood perfectly—not that they'd ever have ridden in a public conveyance—but Adele herself had lived in poverty for long enough to have lost the instincts of privilege.

Two more cars pulled up behind the one they'd ridden. Both were full of spacers and the same assortment of civilians as the ones who'd accompanied Daniel and Adele. The remainder of the *Princess Cecile*'s crew already stood in four loose ranks on the quay in front of the corvette.

An officer in grays was seated behind a portable table with an enlisted clerk, flanked by a pair of Shore Police with sub-machine guns. The pay chest, still locked, waited on the table.

"Daniel, the civilians?" Adele whispered.

"Some are wives," Daniel murmured in her ear. "Well, spouses. The others are crimps or their agents, making sure that their advances are covered before the rest of the pay is drunk up. If there's any remaining, of course."

Lieutenant Mon, wearing his dress uniform like Daniel, stood at a little distance from both the paymaster and the crew. He brightened noticeably when he saw Daniel approaching, but he still looked haggard.

"Mr. Mon, might I have a word with you please?" Daniel called. In an aside he added, "This concerns you in a way also, Adele, so I'd appreciate it if you joined us."

Mon threw a glance over his shoulder, then came toward them at a quickstep; the newly-arrived spacers passed him in the opposite direction to fall in with their fellows.

Adele judged Mon had been looking at the strangers who were watching from the open hatches of the *Princess Cecile*'s bridge, forward on A Deck—the uppermost of the corvette's four levels. Several wore RCN uniforms, but two were civilians. The woman was dressed in a medley of garish colors; the man's black-and-white suit was cut to slant toward his left shoulder, making him look as though he were about to fall over.

"The Klimovs are aboard with the dockyard representative and a survey party from the Navy Office," Mon muttered, making explicit what Adele had already assumed. He wrung Daniel's hand. "Sir, I . . . I'd be very grateful for anything you can bring yourself to say to the crew."

"Before I address the crew, Mon . . . ," Daniel said. "I have a proposition for you."

It seemed to Adele that he was being unusually formal with his old shipmate. Daniel hadn't been the sort of captain who maintained a psychic distance between himself and those whom he commanded.

"Sir?" said Mon, straightening instinctively. His expression was too blank to be described as puzzled.

"You may know that I've become heir to my uncle's controlling interest in Bergen and Associates," Daniel continued with the same smooth formality. "I'll need a yard manager, as I myself will be off-planet much of the time even if the present state of peace lasts. Which is unlikely unless the Almighty shows Guarantor Porra the path of righteousness before the RCN has to do it again."

His smile was that of a senior taking a junior into his confidence to the extent of a mild joke. Adele marveled straight-faced to watch her friend become a kindlier version of his own father. At this moment the two lieutenants had ceased to be fellow officers: they were patron and client, and she saw exactly where the interview—it wasn't a discussion—was going.

"I want you for my yard manager, Mon," Daniel said. "I can't tell you precisely what the conditions of employment will be—I made a brief call to my sister Deirdre this morning and she's working out the details—but there'll be profit participation. I told her to set the percentages so that the manager is initially paid at the level of a full commander. If the yard flourishes, so of course will the manager. Uncle Stacey wasn't healthy enough for the past several years to keep things going at their best."

"Good God, captain," Mon said. "Good *God!*"

"Will you accept, Mon?" Daniel said, raising his eyebrows. "I can't think of a man I'd rather have in the position."

"Sir," Mon said. He stepped forward and wrung Daniel's hand hard. "Oh, bless you, sir, I.... You won't regret this, I swear!"

He sobered and started to look over his shoulder, then caught himself. "Ah, what about the Klimovs, sir?" he said quietly. "I haven't signed the articles, I couldn't until the ship passed to their ownership, of course. But they're expecting me, you know, to ..."

Daniel clapped Mon on the shoulder. "Well, Mon," he said, "the RCN has always stood by its commitments. But while the crew is being paid, why don't you introduce me to the Count and his wife? Since you're taking a knotty problem off my shoulders, it's only right that I should solve a relatively minor one for you."

There were seven people already on the bridge. Daniel ducked through the hatch and stepped aside so that Mon could enter to introduce him. The quarters weren't exactly cramped, but when Daniel stood in this familiar space he was always mentally prepared to control a warship . . . which would be very difficult with so many supernumeraries crowding him.

The RCN personnel were a yard superintendent named Blaisdell with the rank of Lieutenant Commander—a red-faced man whom Daniel knew slightly; he was indifferently competent and must by now have given up all hope of promotion before he was forcibly retired—and four nattily-uniformed personnel from the Navy Office: a commander, two lieutenants (Daniel had expected one), and a senior clerk with warrant officer's pips. All were strangers to him.

In addition there were the two civilians, a trim little man with a moustache and square-cut beard, both gray-speckled, and a tall woman who'd looked like a walking jumble sale when Daniel'd glimpsed her from the quay. Close up he could see that the swatches of bright-colored fabric had been donned with care and taste—albeit flamboyant taste. She'd fit in well with the spacers on the quay in their shore-going costumes and the civilians who'd battened onto them in more-or-less formal arrangements.

"Count Klimov," said Mon, commencing the series of presentations, "allow me to present my colleague and former commanding officer, Lieutenant Daniel Leary."

Klimov extended his right hand, palm down. Daniel wondered if the fellow expected him to kiss it. If so, he was due for a disappointment. . . .

Daniel touched fingertips with the Count, saying, "Your highness, it's a pleasure to meet you. Mon and the crewmen I've spoken with describe you and your wife as gracious companions on the voyage from Strymon."

"And we've been hearing about you from Lieutenant Wilsing and the others," said the strikingly-dressed woman. "The Hero of Kostroma *and* the Hero of Strymon. And so young and handsome!"

She embraced Daniel, offering her cheek imperiously. Daniel gave her the peck she demanded and disengaged himself. Valentina Klimovna was younger than her husband but not young. To be sure, she was attractive enough to provide real competition for some of the professionals watching the pay parade.

Wilsing—the male lieutenant—nodded minusculely at the mention of his name. The fellow was still a total stranger to Daniel.

"Civilians are impressed by the sweep and color of battle, of course," Wilsing said, offering his hand. "Though it's your skill as an astrogator that particularly impresses me, Leary. An honor to meet you at last."

Daniel shook the man's hand, feeling a trifle dazed. Part of his mind was trying to remember sweep and color in any of the battles he'd participated in. All *his* memories of battle seemed to be in black and white, dots on a Plot Position Indicator and people without faces running across landscapes whose features remained schematic while the action was going on. There'd never been time for anything else.

"Mr. Wilsing . . . ," Daniel said, returning the fellow's firm handshake. He had a reputation in the RCN, he knew that well, but the most common effect of it on his peers—his rivals for promotion—was grudging respect when it wasn't unconcealed envy. This was the sort of fulsome praise an ignorant civilian would offer.

Daniel faced the commander—his name tape read QUERIMAN—and saluted as crisply as he could manage. It wouldn't have done for an admiral's aide, but drill and ceremony had never been Daniel's strong suit. "Sir!" he said sharply.

The commander nodded, waving a negligent hand in an informally sufficient acknowledgement of the salute. "Pleased to meet the ship's commander, Lieutenant," he said. "For a foreign-built corvette, you managed to keep her in respectable order."

Daniel gave Queriman a professional smile. The *Sissie* had faced an Alliance battleship at pistol range, so she wasn't going to be hurt by casual insults from a bureaucrat in uniform. Biting off the several further comments that crossed his mind, he said, "I'm pleased that you think so, sir."

The Klimovna tugged her husband against the bulkhead between the gunnery and signals consoles. They whispered to one another in rapid, husky voices—in some language other than Universal as best Daniel could tell, though he was deliberately trying not to overhear.

He glanced out the open service hatch, wide enough to pass a navigation console. Adele was sitting beside Woetjans as the line of spacers wound its way past the paymaster to fall into new ranks on the other side. When the whole crew had been paid, Mon as their acting captain would dismiss them from the RCN in accordance with his orders from the Navy Office.

"Count Klimov?" Queriman said with a touch of asperity. "I believe if you're ready, we can proceed now with the sale of the vessel. That's correct, isn't it, Blaisdell?"

"Yessir, it surely is," the dockyard representative said. "Nothing for me to do but sign the forms. The sale's as-is, no warranties whatever."

"I will be with you shortly, gentlemen," the Count said sharply. *As if he was talking to a servant*, Daniel thought, and then suppressed a smile. *No, if Queriman was a servant, the Count would've backhanded him instead of speaking*.

"Lieutenant Leary," Klimov continued, "join my wife and me in private, if you will. The room next door—"

The captain's watch cabin.

"—will do."

The Klimovs stepped off the bridge, obviously expecting Daniel to follow them; which of course he did. Matters were developing even better than he'd hoped they would.

The watch cabin was little more than a fold-down bunk which doubled as a desk when reversed, and a chair which could be cantilevered from the opposite side. The flat-plate communicator above the stowed bunk could access the navigational system, but the exiguous display meant the captain would use it only for cursory checks on the officer with the conn. Some captains would've curtained off the head beside the hatch—the ship's plumbing ran through the interior bulkheads—but the same bare functionality as the crew facilities sufficed for Daniel.

A prison cell on a civilized planet would generally have more room and amenities, but the symbolism thrilled Daniel every time he entered it. It was the *captain's* watch cabin, after all.

"Lieutenant Leary?" Klimov said before Daniel had closed the hatch behind them; he didn't latch it, but the appearance of privacy was important to Daniel if not the civilians. "The war with the Alliance is over, so many naval officers will be released with only a pittance, is that not true?"

"Yes, though of course as citizens we can only be thankful that our Republic is at peace," Daniel said sententiously. He wouldn't lie to these foreigners, but everyone would benefit if they were allowed to continue in the misapprehensions with which they'd started.

"We will pay you forty florins a week in Cinnabar money to captain the *Princess Cecile* for us to the North!" Valentina said with a theatrical gesture. It would've looked better in larger quarters; here her rings clacked the bulkhead, chipping paint. Undeterred she continued, "Lieutenant Wilsing says a lieutenant like you on half pay would get only fifteen florins, that is correct?"

"Yes it is," Daniel agreed, wondering why a functionary from the Navy Office would be at such pains to praise him to the Klimovs and at the same time convince the Klimovs that he would be available to captain the *Sissie* as a civilian. The answer of course was that a functionary from the Navy Office wouldn't; therefore Wilsing's real duties lay somewhere else. "Of course money isn't the only matter that would concern me should I consider your offer."

"More money, then!" Klimovna said, glaring at her husband. "Georgi, I told you were a fool! Captain Dannie, fifty florins a week!"

She doesn't listen very well, Daniel thought with a faint smile. *Of course that wasn't a problem limited to women or to civilians, either one.*

Aloud he continued, "Count and Countess, let me ask you a question: were you satisfied with the ship and her crew on your voyage from the Strymon system?"

"Yes, of course," Klimov said, exchanging puzzled expressions with his wife. "That is why we wish to buy her, don't you see?"

"Ah, but you're buying only the ship," Daniel explained. "You need a crew as well—and I'll tell you frankly, without a crew as good as this one the voyage you contemplate will at best be very unpleasant."

"So hire this crew," said Klimovna, shrugging expressively. "Where is the problem? Hire whoever you want—you are the captain."

"The only way I believe I can hire these spacers or others of their experience," Daniel said, "is if they come as *my* retainers. That is, you and the Count contract with me for the *Sissie*'s full wage bill, and I undertake to pay the crew out of that amount. A director of the Merchants and Shippers bank—"

He'd almost said "Deirdre." It wouldn't have been a disaster, but formality was still the better policy here.

"—is working up a detailed contract now; I don't have the precise figures."

Count Klimov guffawed with delight. He turned to his wife and said, "You see what the sly dog is doing? We pay him, and he pays the serfs—what he pleases!"

"You have the principle correct," Daniel said through a fixed smile. "Though Cinnabar spacers are *not* serfs."

Still smiling but enunciating with care he continued, "I asked you if you were satisfied during your voyage from the Strymon system. This new endeavor will be on the same terms. That is, the control and discipline of the crew will be entirely in the hands of me as captain. You will give me orders, and I will command the ship."

"What difference does it make?" said the Count.

His wife looked at Daniel with unexpected shrewdness. "Your lords of the navy make you captain on those terms," she said. "You've served them well, it seems. Georgi and I will trust you as far as they, I think."

Daniel nodded politely. "Then there's only one matter left to clear up before I accept your offer," he said. "I'll ask my colleague Lieutenant Mon to relinquish his prior right to the position. I believe he'll be willing to do so."

He set his hand on the hatch's bar handle.

"There is no need!" said Klimov. "Nothing was signed, nothing at all!"

"Perhaps not," said Daniel, his tone courteous to a fault. "But RCN officers are punctilious about their honor . . . and so are the Learys of Bantry. I hope you'll keep that in mind, because I'm looking forward to congenial relations with you during our voyage."

He cleared his throat and smiled broadly. "I believe we're ready for you to conduct your business with the Navy Office. While you're doing that, I'll address what I hope will be our crew," he said. "Yes?"

"Yes, yes of course," said the Count with a dismissive gesture.

"Yes," said Klimovna. "*Very* congenial."

Adele sat on a forty-gallon drum on the quay beside the *Princess Cecile*. The container was still part full from the way it sloshed when she shifted her weight, but she had no idea with what. Her data unit was on the similar drum in front of her, so she'd adjusted it to project its holographic display higher than she'd normally have done. Nothing that she needed to attend was happening on the dock, so she'd resumed winnowing data regarding Radiance and the Commonwealth of God more generally.

Calling the Commonwealth a government was stretching the point. The Chief Elder was the titular head of a polity of over a hundred stars, but he answered to a Council of Seventy—and the fleets, numbering anything from three to a dozen depending on politics, were semi-autonomous and elected their own admirals.

"Mistress," Woetjans said. Adele heard the bosun speak and filed the fact to be dealt with as soon as she'd shut down the volume of the *Shipping Instructions* she was reviewing.

Factions within the Commonwealth elite were at daggers-drawn—literally, often enough. If the Alliance navy was willing to expend its resources at such a distance from its nearest existing bases, it could easily find powerful backers on Radiance.

A group claiming that human beings could breathe water could find backers on Radiance; all it would take was spreading a little money around. The Commonwealth was a bizarre assemblage that seemed to cling together only because its parts couldn't even agree to separate.

"Mistress?" Woetjans repeated. The bosun touched Adele's shoulder. Adele's left hand dropped into her tunic pocket. Her eyes were blank and her mind was awash with blazing terror, the hormonal rush that short-circuited thought by screaming *"Run or kill!"* to the lizard brain.

"The captain's about to speak, mistress," Woetjans whispered. If she'd noticed Adele's hand starting to come out of her pocket holding the little pistol, she was too polite to mention it.

"Thank you, Woetjans," Adele said, her voice trembling. She got off the drum to pick up the wand she'd dropped. With it again in her hand, she shut down the data unit as Daniel faced the crew in the light of the sun edging over the corvette behind him.

"Well, shipmates, it's been a long time since I've seen you all together," he said, his cheerful voice booming. "In a moment Lieutenant Mon will give you your discharges, but he's allowed me to say a few words to you first."

Daniel stretched his left arm back, pointing toward the *Princess Cecile* without taking his eyes off the ranks of spacers. The midshipmen and warrant officers, all but Adele herself and Woetjans—who'd apparently appointed herself to look after the signals officer—stood at the left end of the common crewmen.

"You all know the *Sissie*'s being sold out of service," he said. "What you haven't known till now is that I'm leaving the RCN to become her captain. The Klimovs, the passengers who came from Strymon with you, have

hired me to take them to the Galactic North aboard
what was the finest corvette in the RCN!"

"Holy God and Her Saints!" Woetjans bellowed. The
whole crew was either chattering or standing openmouthed, a matter of how different temperaments
reacted to amazement.

Dorst and Vesey were embracing. They couldn't
afford 1st Class uniforms—neither had family money—
but their Grays sported more medal ribbons than most
officers several ranks their senior could claim.

"What about Lieutenant Mon?" Sun called, his voice
echoing from the corvette's flank with a metallic harshness that was probably unmeant. "We heard he was
going to be captain!"

"Mr. Mon has agreed to manage my late Uncle
Stacey's shipyard," Daniel said, adjusting his volume as
the crew fell silent as he resumed speaking. "He'll be
hiring in the near future, I shouldn't wonder, and any
of you who fancy staying on solid ground for a time
might look him up. But for the rest of you . . ."

Adele smiled. She could've broadcast the speech
through the Sissie's public address system, but Daniel
obviously hadn't felt he needed mechanical support; and
he'd been right, as he generally was with anything to
do with ships or spacers.

He put his hands on his hips and leaned his torso
back slightly, giving the assembled spacers a huge grin.
"You'd have to be crazy to come with me!" he said.
"You may think some foreign civilian would let you
slack off, but think again! The Sissie's crew won't be
working for Count Klimov, they'll be signing on with
me personally, Daniel Leary. They'll be under RCN
discipline same as if the Sissie were in commission."

The murmuring of the listening spacers built again
like sudden surf.

"We'll be lifting with a full crew," Daniel resumed

after a pause to let the more clever spacers explain what he'd just said to their denser fellows. "We'll be carrying missiles, though not a full magazine, and we'll have expended some of them before we come back or I badly misjudge the North."

Adele realized suddenly that her friend was addressing not only the Cinnabar citizens in front of him but also the Klimovs watching from the bridge hatch above. He was being carefully circumspect in the words he used—

Which didn't prevent Koechler from shouting to his fellow riggers Barnes and Dasi, "No, you ninnies, we *won't* be working for wogs, we'll be working for Mr. Leary!" in a voice loud enough to be heard on the street outside the compound.

"We won't be at war," Daniel went on, "but going among those cut-throats and pirates in the North will be as dangerous as war. Maybe worse!"

"We've seen pirates, sir!" Sun cried. "Seen 'em and seen 'em off, haven't we, spacers!"

"You know we bloody have!" Woetjans roared and the whole crew took up the shout.

"You'll be paid an honest spacer's wage and a little more," said Daniel, "because you're working for the Learys of Bantry now! But there'll be long watches and no loot. I'll be conning us according to my Uncle Stacey's logs, and I'll tell you God's truth that there'll be hard runs. I wouldn't trust any other ship and crew than the *Princess Cecile* and her Sissies to make them."

"If anybody else could do it, then you can do it blindfolded, sir!" Dorst cried.

For a half-heartbeat Adele wondered if Daniel had instructed a claque before he spoke . . . but he surely hadn't. The corvette's crew was speaking its collective mind, and it was with its former captain, body and soul.

"Let me give you a warning," Daniel continued, as

though he weren't noticing the chorus of cheers. "Some of you men'll 've heard that dancing girls in the Commonwealth have their cunts crosswise so they get tighter when they spread their legs. *I* don't believe it!"

He paused again, then thundered through the laughter, "Though I feel it's my duty to science and the Republic to investigate the matter fully!"

And what do the Klimovs think of that? Adele thought, smiling faintly again. She didn't recall hearing that the culture of Novy Sverdlovsk was notably prudish, however. Even if it were the Klimovs could realize from the delighted hilarity that most of the assembled spacers would follow Daniel Leary into the jaws of Hell, let alone to the Galactic North.

Daniel would doubtless be investigating dancing girls and an assortment of other women. So long as they were young enough and pretty enough and bubble-headed enough to meet his standards.

Adele had started to pull out her data unit again, to check on the sexual mores of Novy Sverdlovsk. She slipped it back into its pocket and crossed her hands firmly in her lap . . . though she doubted that at this moment she could draw the attention of the *Sissie's* crew away from Daniel even if she took off her clothes and danced on the barrel.

"I expect we'll lift from Cinnabar in seven days time," Daniel said. "For the next forty-eight hours, any spacer who served under me on the *Princess Cecile* in the past has a guaranteed berth on her. After that I may start filling places with folk I don't know and trust so well."

"By God, I'll sign the articles right now!" Barnes said. "Dasi and me both! Where's the book, captain?"

The formation started to break up as spacers edged forward. Adele stepped from the barrel; in a moment, there was likely to be a rush that shoved Daniel off the quay into the filthy water of the pool on which the *Princess Cecile* floated.

"Fellow spacers!" he shouted, holding his arms straight up in the air for attention. The crowd quieted.

"In a moment," Daniel continued, "I'll go back onto the *Sissie's* bridge. There I'll sign aboard every soul of you who wants to join me. But before I do that—"

He raised his arms again. "No, wait!" he said. "Hear me out!"

The crowd quieted again. "Fellow spacers," Daniel said. "I've joked with you this morning, but I say this in all truth, the truth I owe you as my shipmates in hard places. The voyage I intend will be a hard one and dangerous. When we return, *if* we return, we'll have nothing to show for it but the memory of a job well done. That is *all* I promise you."

"They'll have the right to say to the whole world," Adele shouted, surprising no one more than herself, "that they were with Captain Leary in the North. Every real spacer who hears that will envy us—and they'll envy the money we come back with!"

This time Daniel couldn't have silenced the cheers if he'd wanted to. Instead he turned grinning and walked up the catwalk into the *Princess Cecile*. The crew, all but a handful, jostled to follow him to the bridge and the muster book.

CHAPTER 7

Adele had expected to reinstall the special equipment in the Signals console; she'd removed it herself, after all, when she left the *Princess Cecile* in dock on Tanais and returned to Cinnabar aboard a Strymonian cutter. It'd been unlikely that anybody would even notice the non-standard modules, let alone be able to use their sorting and cryptographic capabilities, but a librarian who isn't obsessive probably isn't a good librarian, and Adele Mundy was a very good librarian indeed.

As it turned out, three technicians and Lieutenant Wilsing—wearing coveralls and looking as incongruous as Adele would in a brothel—were doing the refit. There was neither need nor for that matter room for her involvement. She could've found a place to sit and work either aboard the corvette or elsewhere, but she decided to simply step out onto the quay and view what was going on from enough distance to get a grasp of the whole of it.

The two companionways—the only internal connection among the corvette's four levels—were armored

like the decks themselves. The spacers went up and
down the helical treads in long jumps; Adele wasn't
especially sure-footed, nor was she in a hurry. She was
halfway down the stage from B to C deck when she
heard someone enter the tube at the top, but she'd
scarcely gotten clear of the hatchway when Sun crashed
into the entrance hold behind her.

"Oh, sorry, mistress!" the gunner's mate said. He gestured her ahead of him out the main hatch and onto
the catwalk; Adele didn't have any real destination, so
she walked along. "I didn't hear you with all the racket.
Do you know how many missiles they'll leave behind
for us?"

Adele deliberately stepped onto the concrete quay
before she turned to follow Sun's gesture. A lowboy
with three cradles, two of them already holding missiles, waited to receive the third long cylinder clanking gear-tooth by gear-tooth down the conveyor from
the magazine on B Deck.

"One moment," Adele said, setting her data unit on
the barrel where she'd sat earlier in the morning to
listen to Daniel's speech. It was already linked to the
Sissie's computer; she brought up the proposed manifest and said, "We're to carry ten."

She heard Daniel's voice from above, modulated by
the faint breeze; she glanced up. Daniel and Woetjans
were on the top, the truck, of an antenna extended to
its full 90-foot height above the corvette's dorsal spine.

Adele grimaced and looked back at her display; she
was mildly afraid of heights. Besides, she didn't see
what Daniel and the bosun could learn in that fashion that they couldn't learn by looking at the tubes
while they were nested together and lying flat against
the hull. Still, it was their job; she wouldn't thank
anyone who tried to tell her how to do hers.

Though Adele's attention was deliberately on her

display, it was a moment before the words she read penetrated her disquiet over what might happen to her friends if a freak gust of wind struck or the *Sissie* for some reason rolled; then she frowned. Sun peered over her shoulder—uselessly, because the air-formed holograms were only a shimmer anywhere except at the focal point of Adele's own eyes.

"This says that the missiles are single-converter units captured with the vessel when it was in Kostroman service," Adele said. "But surely that's wrong? Daniel acquired RCN standard missiles before we even left Kostroma."

Sun cleared his throat in something like a chuckle. "Well, mistress," he said, "if there was any deal like that, it was done off-book. A fighting captain like Mr. Leary—and a captain with as much to trade as Mr. Leary had—wouldn't have lifted with wog missiles no matter what the manifest showed."

Missiles, a warship's primary armament, were miniature spaceships driven by High Drive motors. If they were allowed to run to burnout they reached .6 C. The projectiles were solids, because even fusion warheads would've added nothing significant to their kinetic energy at such speeds.

For shorter-range engagements, acceleration was a significant factor. Twin-motor missiles, each with its own antimatter converter, had the same terminal velocity as single-motor units, but they reached it in half the time though at nearly double the cost. Cinnabar and the Alliance considered the expense justifiable; most of the lesser navies didn't or couldn't spend the extra money.

The lowboy's pair of lifting arms locked around the missile, fore and aft. A man from the Logistics Service stood at the control panel at the vehicle's rear; his female partner was in the articulated cab. Chief

Betts, the *Princess Cecile*'s missileer, watched from the open bay.

"Wish we were keeping them all," Sun said wistfully. "Though I guess we'll be well-armed compared to most freighters—*and* the Chief knows how to use 'em."

"The Klimovs needed the space for their stateroom," Adele explained. "A warship doesn't ordinarily have room for an extra pair of socks, in my experience."

Sun laughed. "Well, mistress," he said. "I never heard about anybody trying to smuggle a pair of socks. But most everything else at one time or another's found its way into frame spaces or spar cavities."

He looked at Adele and grinned. "*And* into the bores of plasma cannons, some folk say. Though I wouldn't know anything about that myself."

Adele chuckled because it was expected of her. Looking past Sun's shoulder toward the compound's gate she saw one of the half-ton powered carts the Logistics Service used for light deliveries. Tovera was driving and the man beside her was Hogg.

"Pardon me, Sun," Adele said, shutting down her data unit and stowing it with the same easy reflex as she breathed. "My servant's arrived, and I need to check some matters with her."

"God speed you, mistress!" Sun called back over his shoulder as he started for the gate. He was carrying a well-stuffed ditty bag. As he passed the cart going the other way he began to sing, *"I don't want your millions, mister, I don't want your diamond ring. . . ."*

Adele wondered what you'd want to smuggle from Strymon to Cinnabar that fit within the 4-inch bore of a plasma cannon. She didn't know, but she was pretty sure that the gunner's mate did.

The cart stopped directly in front of Adele. Hogg hopped out, stepped around the blunt prow of the vehicle, and helped Tovera down from the driver's seat. Both of them stank of smoke, and Tovera in particular looked as though she'd had to crawl through a sewer pipe.

"We figured you'd want to hear it from us," Hogg said belligerently. His voice rasped, his eyes were bloodshot, and the hair on the backs of his hands had been singed. At that, he looked much better than Tovera did. "There was a fire in a townhouse in West Valley where the new money lives. Folks named Rolfe had been in the house this past six months or so."

"I see," said Adele. "And yourselves? You look as though you should have medical attention."

"Tovera's going to take a session with the *Sissie*'s Medicomp," Hogg said. "Rather'n, you know, do anything official. All right?"

"Yes, of course!" Adele said. "Tovera, do you need help to—"

"No, mistress," Tovera said. She held her attaché case in both hands as though it were a lifebuoy as she floated on a shoreless sea. "No one died in the fire. No one at all."

"Good," said Adele. "Now get into the Medicomp."

Hogg watched the slight figure walk up the boarding bridge without wobbling. From the back she looked even worse. Her hair was crinkled, and sparks had burned holes in her tunic.

"Get some of the soot sluiced out of her lungs and some burn cream, she'll be right as rain," Hogg said. That was a reasonable assessment—the corvette's automated medical system was capable of tackling much more serious injuries than Tovera's appeared to be—but Adele thought she heard an element of prayer in Hogg's voice as well.

"I'm a little surprised," she said, trying to keep her tone non-judgmental, "that the flames spread so quickly that you were caught in them."

"Mistress, I swear to God!" Hogg snarled in frustration. "Look, I'm not trying to cover my screwup, not to you and the master, but there wouldn't have been any problem at all if that woman had the sense God gave a goose!"

The lowboy was pulling away from the quay with the deliberation imposed by its load of multi-ton missiles. A similar vehicle waited to take the single extra round remaining in the *Princess Cecile*'s magazines. Up the roadway from the tram stop walked the Klimovs and a Navy Office functionary whose gray uniform made him look like a tree-branch fallen between his florally-arrayed companions.

"An electrical fire broke out in the walls, you see," Hogg said, pursing his lips with the memory. "Anyhow, that's what it looks like. All the walls at once, though. There was plenty of warning, alarms going off all over the house, and the stupid bitch stays to get her jewelry before she runs!"

"Marina Rolfe," Adele said. She remembered the face screaming, its features distorted by rage and fear but not, Adele was sure, attractive on their best day. "Marina Casaubon Rolfe."

"Right, and she could roast like a chicken for anything I cared," Hogg said, "but damned if Tovera didn't go in after her. Said she mustn't die."

The second lowboy whirred and clanked into place. The tractor ran on caterpillar treads, but the trailer was supported by four full-width pneumatic tires like bolsters. The Klimovs started to walk across where the lowboy was about to back into position, but the naval official stopped them in time.

"Well, hell," Hogg said. "She's just a little thing, Tovera is—"

Adele managed not to blink at the description. It was accurate enough in the sense that viruses are small, weasels are small, and the pistol in Adele's pocket was quite a small one. . . .

"—and I went in to fetch them both." He brushed his fingertips over the back of his left wrist with a sour expression.

"Are *you* all right, Hogg?" Adele said, irritated that she hadn't said something sooner. While he didn't look or sound as bad as Tovera, he'd obviously had a harrowing time himself.

He chuckled. "Bless you, mistress," he said. "I've looked worse than this plenty mornings after an oyster roast back at Bantry. *And* been hung over."

Reaching in a baggy countryman's side-pocket, he brought up a sparkling handful. The settings were ugly, but some of the gems were very fine indeed. "Besides, there were compensations," Hogg said.

He sobered suddenly. "But I want you to know that Tovera didn't do anything wrong," he went on. "She's the only reason that woman's alive. Left to her own devices, they'd be combing her bones outa the rubble when it cools enough tomorrow or the next day."

"Didn't do anything wrong," was a matter of definition, of course; but in this particular case, Hogg's definition and Adele's own were quite similar.

"Thank you, Hogg," she said. "I'll keep that in mind."

She looked at the short, stocky man; middle-aged and no more prepossessing than the fellow who'd just maneuvered the lowboy into position. "And thank you for your services to the Mundys of Chatsworth as well. I won't forget that."

Hogg laughed. "Oh, mistress, you're as much a Leary now as I am," he said, "for all my name's Hogg. But this one, well, let's just say I take it personally when somebody litters the master's street the way that lot did."

He sauntered up the catwalk, whistling a jig. The

powered cart remained where it was, abandoned rather than parked, Adele supposed.

"Count Klimov!" Daniel called as he started down the shrouds bracing the antenna. He wore riggers' gloves, but even so he must be risking tearing his forearms as he swung and slid. "Countess! I'll meet you on the bridge and we'll go over the route!"

Adele smiled at a memory. If Hogg said she was a Leary now, who was she to argue?

Daniel signed the articles—*Daniel Leary, son of Corder, of Bantry; Lt (Res) RCN*—and handed them to Count Klimov with a flourish. "Well sir," he said, "you've hired the finest crew a vessel this size ever shipped; and you've hired me as well."

Diamond saws and the snarl of arc welders vibrated through the *Princess Cecile* as yard workmen converted her into a yacht with quarters suitable for a pair of aristocrats. Star travel couldn't be made comfortable, but a stateroom in place of half the missile magazine would give the Klimovs more personal volume than an admiral could boast.

The question of comfort aside, star travel couldn't even be made *safe* when it involved the sort of destinations the Klimovs fancied. Well, again the *Sissie* and her crew should suit them as well as they could be suited.

"That your crew should be excellent is no coincidence, Captain," the Countess said. "We've been talking with the guest-friends we're staying with here in Xenos, the Collesios, and hearing what a great hero you are. They're impressed that we were able to hire you. You are a coup for us, you see?"

She and the Count had changed clothes since he saw them at the pay parade this morning, but the style was the same. Daniel wondered if the Countess intended to wear bulky outfits throughout the voyage. The *Princess Cecile*'s corridors and spaces—and those of any other warship, even an 80,000-ton battleship—were tight to allow the greatest possible quantity of equipment and stores to be packed aboard.

"With all respect to your friends, Countess . . . ," Daniel said, seating himself at the command console to bring the navigational display live in the center of the bridge. "They're civilians and don't appreciate how much luck and the professionalism expected of every RCN officer went into the stories they heard. Besides which there was—"

He grinned through the pearly blur that was coalescing into a star chart.

"—quite a lot of media fabulation, to be frank."

The Collesios weren't a family familiar to Daniel. In all likelihood they were a merchant house with interests on Novy Sverdlovsk, whose members had stayed with Count Klimov or his ancestor while visiting that planet. The Collesios were now returning the hospitality.

The Countess patted his cheek. "I am Valentina, yes? Georgi can be the Count all he likes . . . ," she gave her husband a look that Daniel classed as "appraising" in the same sense that one appraises a suite one may rent. "But my father was a duke, and the title doesn't have the same ring in my ears."

"Your father, the duke with thirteen daughters on the *right* side of the blanket," Klimov said. The words had the sound of familiarity; if there'd ever been passion in the exchange, time had cooled it. "You did well to get me, and you know it."

He stepped back so that he could see Daniel without looking through the air-formed hologram. "Now, Captain Leary, what do you propose for our itinerary?"

Spacers were passing up and down the A-Deck

corridor with a frequency that duty didn't explain, but so long as they didn't intrude on the bridge Daniel was happy with them getting a look at the *Sissie*'s new owners. Most of the crew was at liberty for the next five days anyway, though Pasternak and Woetjans had teams making bloody sure that the series of aggravating failures in both rig and powerplant ended before the ship lifted from Cinnabar.

"Well, sir," Daniel said, cueing the first of the presets he'd loaded into the computer this morning before joining the bosun aloft on the replaced antenna, "the red pip is the Sverdlovsk system, green is Strymon, and blue here is Cinnabar, that's just for scale."

He gestured. A fourth dot, this one orange, appeared at a considerable angle to the others among the milky dusting of stars too small to see as individuals. "And here is Todos Santos, the capital of the Ten Star Cluster and the entry point to the North for vessels sailing from Cinnabar. You know, of course, that distance—time, really—within the Matrix doesn't precisely equate with that of sidereal space, but it gives you a feeling for what's involved strictly as a matter of astrogation."

"Yes, yes, of course it is very far," Klimov said, his tone marginally short of sounding irritated. "Thus we buy a fine ship and hire you, not so? Why are you telling us this when I ask you what planets we will stop at on our course through the North?"

"Very good, sir," Daniel said mildly. He'd listened to what the Count was saying instead of simply flying hot . . . and Count Klimov was quite right. He'd meant what he said, not what Daniel had assumed he meant.

"The short answer . . . ," Daniel continued, touching the control panel; Novy Sverdlovsk and Strymon sank into the sparkling mass, leaving only Cinnabar and Todos Santos highlighted. "Is that we'll put in at Todos Santos, both to refit the *Sissie* after a long run and to gather better information about the region. Through me and my Signals Officer, Mistress Mundy, you have access to the best information available in the Republic about the North; but that's none too good. Besides Todos Santos, I expect we'll put into Radiance at the other end of the Commonwealth of God. By then we'll probably be ready for a further refit."

"Yes, but the *purpose* of our voyage . . . ?" Klimov said, no longer peevish but clearly unsatisfied. "The things we have come to see?"

"Yes," said Daniel. "You want to go hunting, Count, and Countess—Valentina—"

Catching himself before her slim, beringed finger waggled in his face.

"—you are a student of ethnology. While you share an interest in pre-Hiatus artifacts."

"Yes, exactly," said the Count. "What of those things?"

"He doesn't know yet, but he'll learn," the Countess said. "That is correct, is it not, Captain Dannie?"

Daniel shrank the starfield so that he could meet the Klimovna's eyes without a milky holographic veil between them. "Countess," he said, "I will promise to call you Valentina henceforth if you promise *not* to call me Captain Dannie. Are we agreed?"

"Agreed, Daniel," she said and stretched her hand out over the astrogation tank. He touched fingertips with her and withdrew his hand.

"And of course your wife is quite right, Count," Daniel continued with a smile. "I don't have enough information yet to give you our intermediary planetfalls; but I will before we lift in seven days. I'm going through my Uncle Stacey's logs. For the most part they deal with sailing directions, but there are notes regarding the planets where he put in for air and reaction mass. More important, I've asked Mistress Mundy to use her resources. She's Mundy of Chatsworth, by the way; one of the most noble houses in the Republic, as your friends the Collesios will tell you."

"But she is your signals officer?" Klimovna said. "The sort of populations which interest me will not have radios, let alone starships."

"She's acting as my signals officer," Daniel explained, "but her training in the Academic Collections on Bryce was as a librarian—an information specialist. Mistress Mundy will learn whatever can be learned on Cinnabar about suitable planetfalls. When we reach Todos Santos, she will learn more. You will not be disappointed, sir and madam."

The Klimovs exchanged a long glance. She nodded and the Count stepped to the hatch and swung it to before returning to face Daniel.

It was the wife who spoke, however, saying, "There is one further matter, Daniel. Eighty years ago our planet was ruled by a man named John Tsetzes."

"He was a mercenary soldier who made himself emperor," Klimov put in. "He called himself Emperor Ivan the First. Twenty years later he was overthrown and fled on an armed yacht."

"I see," said Daniel, a placeholder limited to the very little bit that he *did* understand thus far. Keeping his mouth shut seemed to be the best way to learn more.

"Tsetzes took the national collection with him," Valentina said. "Items of great sentimental value to the nation and sometimes more. In particular he took the Earth Diamond. You have heard of it?"

"No ma'am," Daniel said, "I have not."

But in thirty seconds Adele could tell you more than you know yourself, he thought, *or I miss my bet.*

"Regardless, it is very famous," Valentina said with a dismissive gesture. "It is a perfect diamond, the size of a man's head; spherical and hollowed out."

"That's indeed impressive," said Daniel. Jewels had value, but no jewel could truly be said to be unique given that all the universe was open to human acquisitiveness. The labor of hollowing out a huge diamond, however, invested it with a value beyond that of the material itself.

"It is more than that," said Klimov. "The name, the Earth Diamond, is not just words. On the inside of this diamond sphere is carved a map of the continents of Old Earth before the Hiatus, a thing that could never be duplicated in the past two thousand years. Now do you see?"

"Yes," said Daniel. He blinked with the weight of what he'd just been told. "I do."

The Hiatus in human civilization occurred when the first tier of star systems colonized from Earth revolted against the home world. The war was fought with asteroids accelerated to slam into planets, distorting the crust and killing all but a few percent of those living on those worlds before the war started.

It was a millennium before mankind returned to the stars, and the return came from second- and third-tier colonies, worlds like Cinnabar and Pleasaunce which had been too minor for either side to bother destroying. No one today could tell what the Earth looked like before the Hiatus, because the continents had died along with those who lived on them.

"We know—" Valentina said.

"We believe!" said her husband.

"We *know*," Valentina repeated, "that John Tsetzes fled toward the Galactic North. Deserters from his ship said as much. No sign of him or the treasures he took has ever appeared. We thought, Georgi and I, that if we could perhaps trace Tsetzes, it would be very important for us at home."

Daniel pursed his lips. "I can see that, yes," he said.

"But I must emphasize that ships vanish in the Matrix, and ships crash while trying to land on planets that no one else ever visits. The chance of our finding a vessel that disappeared sixty years ago isn't very great."

He didn't know enough about the political structure of Novy Sverdlovsk to be sure what "very important" meant in the present context, but the Countess might well be suggesting the return of such an heirloom could be parlayed into leadership of the planet. That was none of Daniel's business, of course.

"No one has been searching," Valentina said. "Not really."

"In any case," said the Count, "we will hunt and collect artifacts. And if more eventuates—who knows? Eh?"

"Indeed, who knows?" said his wife. With a smile that emphasized her unusually wide mouth, she again reached over the astrogation tank.

Daniel smiled back; but instead of touching hands, he brought up the display. "Sir and madam!" he said, "Mistress Mundy and I will do our best to accommodate you."

CHAPTER 8

A barge with two powerful hydraulic winches pulled the *Princess Cecile* slowly from her slip by cables attached to ringbolts on her outriggers. A tensioning capstan on the quay paid out a third wire cable, attached to the corvette's stern to keep her from sliding into the barge once she started moving.

By splitting her display, Adele could watch both; but in fact she didn't really understand what was going on, so watching the affair would be a pointless exercise. She'd switched instead to an analysis of Harbor One's message traffic. That had nothing to do with her either, but at least she understood it.

The noise was quite remarkable. Adele's helmet protected her eardrums, but the cacophonous shrieks and roars and bangs through the hull made her body vibrate.

Most of the *Sissie*'s hatches were closed, but the bridge access port was still hinged down. Daniel stood on the lip, steadying himself with one hand while he called orders to his own crew and the yard personnel through his commo helmet. He'd clipped a safety line

to his equipment belt, but if he slipped from the transom he'd strike hard against the lower curve of the hull
before snubbing up.

Adele grimaced. Daniel didn't expect to slip, and
having seen him in the *Sissie's* rigging she didn't
expect him to slip either. Besides, nobody was asking
her to do it.

"*Daniel, what is going on?*" Countess Klimov asked
over what she'd been told was the command channel.
"*Is everything all right?*"

During undocking and any other time the captain's
full attention ought to be on his work, the Klimovs'
messages were routed to Adele's console—and stopped
there. The only signals going directly to Daniel were
those of the Chiefs of Rig and Ship, First Lieutenant
Chewning at his station in the Battle Direction Center astern, and the ground staff controlling the winches.

Acting by the polite reflex of handling something for
a friend while he was busy, Adele reverted to the split
view and exported it to the Klimovs display. Because
the icon at the top of the screen wouldn't mean anything to them, she added a realtime image of her
face . . . and a grim, glowering person she looked, she
realized.

She attempted a smile without much improvement
and said over the private channel she'd just opened,
"Sir and madam, Captain Leary directed me to keep
you fully informed while he's immersed in preparations
for liftoff. Do you have any questions about what's
going on?"

"*What is going on?*" Klimov demanded. "*These
pictures? What are they?*"

There wasn't room on the corvette's bridge for two
additional consoles, but neither was there any practical way to keep the ship's owners off the bridge.
Daniel's answer had been to turn his watch cabin into

an annex by removing the bulkhead. He'd placed two acceleration couches in the space. Armored conduits welded to the deck connected the Klimovs' jury-rigged displays to the main computer, but their controls worked only to access data unless Adele released the lockout she'd imposed.

"A tugboat's pulling us into the center of the pool so that we can lift off without damaging other vessels," Adele said calmly. "The images are of our bow and stern."

The bow pickup was at the base of Antenna Dorsal One; she could see a tiny image of Daniel's head and torso, his right arm gesticulating. You had to know what you were looking at for it to make any sense, of course; which was generally true of life. Context was everything. . . .

"There's not really much to see," she continued aloud. She chuckled. "Though rather more than there will be as we lift off, since then we'll be in a cocoon of steam and then hydrogen ions. I wonder—would you care to see what I suggested to, ah, Captain Leary for our first planetfall?"

Adele turned her head to look into the annex, past Sun reclining at the gunnery console. She'd have gotten a better view of the Klimovs by putting their images on her display, but she hoped looking directly at them would seem reassuring. Even as a child she'd been more interested in her privacy than she was in other people, but her present task required that she appear to be social. She supposed she could manage it, at least for the time being.

"There is a planetfall?" said the Count. "But I have not been told!"

"She's telling you now, Georgi," his wife said sharply. Adele wasn't sure they realized they were speaking, even to each other, through the communications system

rather by ordinary voice. The helmets they wore projected cancellation waves to save their hearing. She went
on, "*Yes, all right, mistress. Show us the planet. It can
only be better than machines and dirty water, yes?*"

"Cuvier Catalogue 4795-C has a sufficiency of dirty
water also," Adele said dryly, her wands weaving a set
of images from the corvette's computer onto the
Klimovs' displays. When Adele had leisure, she slaved
whatever computer she was accessing to her personal
data unit and used the familiar system as her controls.
Occasionally this cost her a few microseconds of
machine time, but that was a cheap price to pay for
the reflexive assurance she gained. "There are compensations, however."

The Austines were one-time allies of the Mundy
family, though distantly enough that the house had been
merely decimated after the Three Circles Conspiracy
instead of facing near extermination. They'd provided
family documents at Adele's request.

Ninety years earlier, an Austine had been associated
with a colonial survey endeavor. No official reports of
the expedition survived so far as Adele could find, but
Surveyor Austine's handwritten journal did. With it was
a holocube which projected six separate images depending on which face was pressed.

"It's a little farther out than Captain Leary had
intended for our first planetfall," Adele continued.
"Eighteen days, he estimates. There are no major ports
between Cinnabar and the Ten Star Cluster anyway,
and 4795-C at least will supply us with reaction mass."

The first image was of a rolling, misty landscape in
which trees dangled serpentine branches. Occasional
highlights gleamed above the fog's monochrome blur,
but they were too far away to have shapes.

Surveyor Austine hadn't used standard notation in
her private journal. Adele by herself could no more

have identified the planet than she could have flown—but of course she hadn't been by herself. She'd explained the situation to Daniel, and after only a few minutes at the astrogation computer he'd found the world and begun plotting their course. They made a good team.

"The dominant predator . . . ," she said, cueing the next image. "Ranges up to thirty-five feet in length."

"Ho!" said the Count. *"Yes, a fine trophy! Yes!"*

Austine had called the animal a dragon. For her amusement Adele had checked a zoological database for Cinnabar and its client worlds; she'd found over three thousand species called "dragon" alone or in combination. For all that, the name fit well in this case.

The pictured creature rested on a point of rock, its head turned toward the camera—which must have been at a considerable distance, judging from the lack of image resolution. Its body was snakelike but it had a pair of strong clawed legs at the point of balance and, barely visible, a pair of slender arms folded against the upper body. The eyes were faceted, set to either side of a great hooked beak.

"The creatures, the dragons . . . ," Adele said, switching to the next image. "Fly. You can't see it very well, but the source says that the animal extends translucent plates, she calls them feathers, out more than a yard along its midline all along its body."

The dragon in flight was little more than a twisting shimmer in the sky with a dark line running down the middle of it. Adele had allowed her software to sharpen the image somewhat, but going farther than this would've been invention rather than improvement. Mist, distance, and the creature's movement conspired against clear imaging.

"Flying?" Klimov said. He turned to his wife. *"This is wonderful! Our captain has done well, little dove."*

Adele blinked at the affectionate diminutive—
Klimovna certainly wasn't little nor could Adele imagine
her as a dove, but that was between the couple. Nor
was Adele particularly offended by the Count giving
Daniel credit for what she had done; she'd read enough
to know that Novy Sverdlovsk society was straitjacketed
by preconceptions of rank and gender.

But it was also true that it didn't make her like
Klimov better.

A warning whistle blew; red icons pulsed on the displays of those within cancellation fields. The *Princess
Cecile* lurched sideways, then steadied with a slap/slap/
slap of waves reflected between the outriggers.

Because in an atmosphere starships used plasma
thrusters, whenever possible they landed on enclosed
bodies of water. That made it easy to take on reaction
mass, and in addition a lake or lagoon absorbed the
jets of charged ions harmlessly. A few liftoffs and landings would begin to crater any solid surface, even
bedrock or reinforced concrete.

The *Princess Cecile* was a long cigar balanced by
the outriggers which were now extended; after liftoff
they'd be drawn up against the hull so as not to
interfere with the antennas and sails. She wasn't a boat,
though, but rather a floating solid with no more
ability to maneuver than a bobbing cork. All things considered, the yard personnel were doing a competent
job of towing the corvette's 1200 deadweight tons from
the narrow slip to the center of the pool where her
liftoff wouldn't damage the other vessels in the harbor,
but it was still an awkward task.

"Good," Adele said with brusque enthusiasm. She
wasn't exactly faking her reaction in order to calm her
audience, but in this case the approval she voiced was
more intellectual than emotional. She didn't like
being sloshed sideways any better than the Klimovs'

expressions showed that they did. "There'll be a few final adjustments; then I believe we can expect to lift off."

She cleared her throat, projected the next two images as a pair, and resumed, "Most of the animals on 4795-C—no one bothered to name the place, of course—are plant eaters. The lesser ones hop—"

You could see a degree of kinship between dragons and the animal browsing sedges at the margin of a lake, but the herbivore was built more like a bipedal egg than a serpent. It showed no sign of alarm at the photographer whose shadow showed in the image.

"—whereas the large ones are nearly sessile and sweep the area around them with their tongues. I doubt you'd find them good sport, though they do get very large."

The image on the right could've been a muddy hillock except for the description Austine had left in his journal. Knowing that it was alive, Adele could see tiny eyes and realize that the curved line at the edge of the image area was the creature's thirty-foot tongue rather than a branch waggling from the trunk of a fallen tree. The photographer had kept his distance, perhaps realizing as Adele did that being caught in the tongue's sweep would be fatal even if the creature spat out your remains in disgust a few moments later.

"No, no, nothing there," Klimov agreed dismissively. *"But a dragon, now, that will make a unique trophy."*

"There are also structures on high ground," Adele said, throwing up the final image. She heard the Countess take a sharp breath.

A tetrahedral crystal pyramid shone on a hilltop. Even in this world's dim sunlight, the shimmering reflections and refractions had overwhelmed the image until Adele's software corrected for them. The pyramid's base appeared to have been cast onto the rocks rising from the slope beneath; rain had splashed mud some distance up the clear sides. In the center of the face toward the camera was an opening, a wedge whose triangular sides paralleled those of the structure itself.

"The source wasn't able to analyze them, but they're clearly artificial. There were over a thousand of them on the main land mass ninety years ago, and that was on the basis of a very cursory survey from orbit."

"*Yes, this is very interesting!*" said Klimovna. "*Who is it who built this, please?*"

The words were polite though the tone was peremptory. Adele smiled faintly; she might have done the same, so she couldn't fault the Countess.

"The source didn't have the faintest idea," she said. "The dragons, the large ones at least, appear to use the structures as their lairs, but it seems unlikely that they were the builders."

She didn't say, "impossible." As a scholar Adele had always been willing to discount travelers' tales, but since fate and the RCN snatched her from the library to the surface of distant worlds, she'd seen things with her own eyes that she found hard to explain.

Clearing her throat again she continued, "I presume more vessels have landed on 4795-C than the survey ship on which the source travelled, but they've left no record I could access in the time available. Perhaps I'll be able to learn more in the archives of Todos Santos, if you choose to delay there."

The Countess looked at her husband. "*Yes, perhaps we shall,*" she said.

The whistle blew again. Daniel stepped back into the *Princess Cecile* with a smile of satisfaction while behind him the rectangular port began to whine closed.

"*Ship, this is the captain,*" he said as he grinned at Adele. "*Prepare for liftoff!*"

❖   ❖   ❖

Daniel Leary, captain of the private yacht *Princess Cecile*, settled into the couch of his console. His tremble of fear was a new thing, something he'd noticed only since he'd become a commanding officer. Liftoffs had never bothered him before.

He checked the lockout disconnecting the console, then let his fingers caress the touchpad to gain its feel again. Everything was as it should be, the minuscule hum of a living machine waiting for him to order its next action. He switched it on.

Daniel grinned. He'd worked, he'd *fought*, very hard to rise to a position where he could fear that some freak failure of hardware or programming would flip the vessel onto her back as she started to lift off.

"Captain to Power Room," Daniel said over the command channel. "How do things look, Mr. Pasternak? Over."

"All green, Captain," said the Chief Engineer from his post in the center of D Deck. *"The flows on Port Four and Starboard Five are down ten percent, but the valves are brand new. They'll wear in, and if they don't I'll polish them with emery. Over."*

"Ninety percent is more than adequate, Mr. Pasternak," Daniel said. "Out."

Being slightly down in water flow on two of the corvette's plasma thrusters wasn't a matter of concern. The *Princess Cecile* could reach orbit with 40% total power, though Daniel'd be dumping reaction mass if he ever got into that situation. The thrusters were all in the green—literally; the icons showed across the top of Daniel's display—but it was more than a matter of courtesy that caused him to check directly with Pasternak. A good engineer had a feel for things that a computer readout couldn't equal, and Pasternak had shown himself to be good as well as dedicated.

"Mr. Chewning," Daniel said, his words cueing the channel to his new first lieutenant at the duplicate controls in the Battle Direction Center. "Are you ready for liftoff?"

Chewning was thirty-eight standard years old and still a midshipman. He was a heavy-set man, slow of speech and perhaps of thought as well. He'd applied for the vacancy created when Mon took a dirtside job; and Daniel had accepted him over the score of younger, sharper officers looking for adventure under Lieutenant Leary.

Chewning wasn't flashy, but his record showed him to be utterly dependable. He'd accepted a series of thankless, demanding duties during his service with the RCN, including twice nursing home vessels too badly damaged for repair anywhere but in a major dockyard. He'd plodded through each task successfully . . . and been handed another one in return.

The last thing the *Princess Cecile* needed was a brilliant young first lieutenant determined to show himself—or herself—to be just as dashing as Daniel Leary. Chewning was brave—he must be, to have brought the crippled *Cape Coronel* to port in seventy-two days with a six-man crew. But he didn't feel he had to prove it.

"*Sir, we're ready,*" Chewning said. He and the two midshipmen with him in the armored BDC were ready to take over if the bridge crew were lost or incapacitated. "*Over.*"

"*Captain, we've been cleared by Harbor Control,*" Adele said, her voice as emotionless as a speech synthesizer. "*Over.*"

"Ship, this is the captain," Daniel said on the general push. "All systems are green, all hatches are closed, the vessel is cleared for liftoff. We will lift in thirty seconds. Commencing sequence . . . *now.*"

He enabled the plasma thrusters, letting the control system itself light the nozzles in balanced port and starboard pairs. He could override the computer and do as good a job, but he didn't need to—either because of the ship or to prove himself.

The thrusters lit but remained at low power: Starboard Three and Port Four, Starboard Two and Port Three, working outward from the ship's center of gravity to affect her balance as little as possible.

The *Princess Cecile* trembled, as much from waves in the pool as from the minimal thrust. A shroud of steam billowed, masking the optical sensors on the hull. Daniel's external displays switched automatically to high-frequency, low-power radar to paint a picture of the vessel's immediate surroundings.

A ship could lift or set down with its ports open, but the bath of live steam and charged particles was uncomfortable for the crew as well as damaging to the vessel's interior. An assault barge landing on a hostile world had reason for such a stunt; a yacht on a pleasure cruise did not.

"Orbital control has reserved a slot for us," Adele said. Her voice, calm even when she was murderously angry, seemed particularly out of place while the ship around her strained thunderously to slip the leash of gravity. *"I've fed the course data to the navigational computer. Over."*

"Message received," Daniel said. *"Out."*

He could check the data, but there was no point in doing so. While in cis-lunar space above Cinnabar, all vessels were under dirtside control. Depending on the state of alert—and even after an armistice with the Alliance had been formally approved, Daniel suspected the state remained very high—deviating from the imposed course would bring either a guard vessel and the loss of the captain's papers . . . or simply a

ship-wrecking blast of ions from the Planetary Defense
Array that protected Cinnabar from attack.

Thruster output rose to a nominal 20% power; the
Princess Cecile skipped up and down on the waves her
own exhaust hammered into the pool. All other gauges
and readouts were at the high range of their readiness
parameters.

"Ship," Daniel said as he thumbed a roller switch
from STANDBY TO LIFTOFF, "we are commencing liftoff."

All eight feed valves opened to 70%; the thrusters
roared. The *Princess Cecile* shuddered, matching thrust
to gravity, then began to lift with the ponderous maj-
esty of a queen mounting her throne. But no queen
ever had a throne as high as the one to which the *Sissie*
would carry her captain. . . .

Icons on Daniel's display indicated the Klimovs were
both speaking; to him, he supposed, but you couldn't
expect laymen to have good sense. Adele would keep
them occupied, and perhaps they'd learn in the future.

The *Princess Cecile* rose, her initial acceleration
moderate. The bow was down three degrees, but the
computer had begun adjusting power before Daniel
could reach the control. The thruster nozzles were
aligned correctly—that could be checked on the
ground—so there must be a problem with stowage.
Perhaps one of the tanks of reaction mass had warped
during the hammering the *Sissie*'d taken in battle.
Mon should have noticed it, but he'd had other
problems to deal with—

And despite Mon's technical skill, he didn't have
quite Daniel's feel for a ship. Daniel grinned with a
pride that was surely harmless if he kept it within
himself: very few captains had *his* feel for a ship.

The *Princess Cecile* lifted suddenly out of the plume
of steam from the harbor. She was accelerating at 1.2
g, as much thrust as a sensible captain chose except

in an emergency. Starship hulls were optimized for the barely-perceptible thrust of Casimir radiation against their charged sails; high acceleration, especially within a gravity well, would strain her fabric if it didn't rupture the vessel outright.

An occasional streak of plasma drifted past the *Sissie*. From below the vessel would be a flare of coronal brilliance, dangerous to the eyes of anyone who looked directly at her; the thunder of her progress would tremble through Xenos and the surrounding countryside. Nothing like the liftoff of a battleship, of course, but still a reminder of Mankind's raw power.

The vessel's progress steadied. Daniel looked at the altimeter; they were passing through 100,000 feet. The atmosphere had become thin enough that he could engage the High Drive, if he had to and if he was willing to accept the erosion of the motors when air molecules combined violently with antimatter particles which hadn't been devoured in the normal reaction. He wouldn't switch to High Drive here until Cinnabar Control had routed him through the minefield, of course.

"Ship, this is your captain," Daniel said. No one could see his face, but he knew he was smiling like a triumphant angel. "God bless the *Princess Cecile* and those who fare upon her!"

He couldn't hear the cheering for the ship's own thunder, but he knew the cheers were there; and he was cheering himself.

CHAPTER 9

4795-C wasn't any more prepossessing from orbit than it'd seemed from Surveyor Austine's handheld photos of years before, but at least the *Princess Cecile's* new imagery gave Adele a way to distract the Klimovs while the corvette roared downward.

Daniel had said the landing would be a little tricky because they'd be setting down on land instead of in the water. 4795-C had no lack of open water—ponds, lakes, and broad meandering rivers were evident to the naked eye, despite the mist that covered the entire planet—but since there was no dock to tie up to, the *Sissie* would drift with the wind.

From the Klimovs' expressions, either the prospect worried them or they were simply uncomfortable because of the thrusters' bone-shaking snarl and the additional half their body mass weighing them down in their couches as the vessel braked. So far as Adele was concerned, she trusted Daniel's skill implicitly—and sixteen days (Daniel had shaved two days off his estimate) in the Matrix with only a few hours total taking star-sightings in sidereal space had been quite enough for her. The chance of Daniel flipping the

Princess Cecile onto her back because he'd misjudged the way exhaust would reflect from solid ground was vanishingly slim, but Adele wasn't entirely sure she'd regret death if that were the alternative to additional uninterrupted star travel.

"Captain Leary is landing *here*," Adele said calmly over the channel she'd set aside for herself and the Klimovs. Her wands drew a red cross on the gray-brown image. For an instant she showed an entire planetary hemisphere, but she quickly reduced the scale until it was a ten-by-ten kilometer square with the X still in the center.

As an afterthought, she added thin grid lines. "You'll note—"

And to make sure they did, she circled the sites in red.

"—that he's put us within three kilometers of a pair of pyramids."

"*And the dragons?*" asked the Count, proving that Adele had successfully distracted him. The Klimovna seemed altogether less flighty than her husband, though Adele wasn't ready to say she liked the woman. In fairness, neutrality was about all Adele felt regarding most human beings.

"We'll need to be on the ground to determine that," Adele said. "The source suggests that they're not uncommon, though; or at any rate, they weren't uncommon ninety years ago."

The *Princess Cecile* was a small general-purpose warship, not a dedicated reconnaissance vessel. Her equipment could probably locate some of the creatures from orbit, but that'd appeared to Adele to be a waste of time. Daniel had taken her recommendation to go straight in.

The Klimovs had taken their meals at a combined mess of the *Princess Cecile*'s officers and warrant officers. This was a change from normal RCN practice, but Daniel felt it was the better idea on a vessel as small as a corvette.

Adele smiled; her ideologically egalitarian parents would've approved, though in their hearts they'd have viewed Pasternak as a mechanic, Purser Stobart a mid-level servant, and Woetjans as a strange and possibly dangerous performing animal.

The common mess and the very strain of an unusually long run without reentering normal space had brought the Klimovs and the *Sissie*'s company together. Class aside, the Klimovs had more in common with warrant officers and even common spacers than they did with commissioned officers who were almost invariably members of the Cinnabar upper classes. The Count wasn't stupid and his wife appeared to Adele to be quite intelligent, but in terms of education and the general understanding of human civilization neither of them could match the corvette's two midshipmen.

"We have the aircar," Klimovna said, perhaps a trifle artificially bright. Planning a voyage to the untraveled parts of the universe wasn't the same as watching yourself rush down toward a foggy mudhole with the ship keening a high-frequency buzz of plasma thrusters running at high power. *"Surely in a fifty-kilometer radius you'll find something to shoot, Georgi."*

The *Princess Cecile* paused in the air. She wasn't quite hovering, but her rate of descent had slowed to a crawl. *"Ship make ready for landing,"* said the general channel. Lieutenant Chewning was speaking from the Battle Center, though Daniel had the conn. *"We will touch down in ten seconds."*

The thrusters roared anew, but the corvette was settling again. "The Captain's increased mass flow but flared the thruster nozzles," Adele said quickly, because the dichotomy of *more sound but falling faster* disturbed her every time she felt it. "If he needs to lift suddenly, it's quicker to—"

Steam billowed around the *Princess Cecile*, rocking the hull from side to side. *We should be on land!* Adele thought; but of course the bath of ions from the thrusters would vaporize the boggy soil and soft-bodied vegetation into a plume.

"—close the nozzles than to feed more reaction mass—" she continued, without a pause or even a stammer to suggest that her own heart had leapt when something unexpected occurred.

The thrusters shut off abruptly. The sudden silence was as stunning as a gunshot in a library. Adele hadn't realized they were actually *down*; the feel of the outriggers compressing their struts had been lost in thumps and shuddering as the exhaust hurled baked sod against the *Sissie's* underside.

"*Ship, this is the captain,*" Daniel said, rising from the command console to stretch his torso backward with his hands on his hips. "*We've made a good run and a clean landing. May we make many more together.*"

He turned and surveyed the bridge. Sun had already begun to unlock the dorsal turret, lowered into the forward hull to avoid serious buffeting during descent from orbit; Betts was focused on his attack board, though if he launched missiles in an atmosphere their backblast would destroy the corvette herself.

Daniel met Adele's eyes and grinned. "*Chief of Ship,*" he continued, still using the general push instead of speaking to Pasternak on the Power Room channel. "*Let's open her up and see what the landscape looks like with our own eyes. I dare say more of us than just me are looking forward to being on solid ground. Captain out.*"

The clanks and whines of hatches undogging merged with the hisses and bell-like notes of differential cooling within the vessel's hull. Daniel bent close to Adele's ear and said without going through the commo system, "Mind, I don't know just how solid what *I* see outside really is."

"Well, I've mucked out cowyards that didn't stink so much," said Hogg, sliding a pair of loading tubes for his stocked impeller down the neck of his shirt. Each tube held twenty projectiles and a capacitor charged to accelerate them down the coil-wrapped bore. "But I wouldn't say this is riper'n the *Sissie* was getting after so long recycling the same atmosphere. The filters aren't good for sixteen days."

Daniel Leary sniffed. When he shifted his weight, the baked ground crunched beneath his bootsoles.

"Part of the way this smells is that the exhaust burned everything when we set down," he said judiciously. "The mud's mostly organic. Though . . ."

He sniffed again and added, "I'll admit that the touch of sulfur is special."

Hogg chuckled grimly. "You haven't been in the crew's quarters when Lamsoe and Dasi're having a fart contest, I guess," he said. "But it's good to see the sky, again, I'll say that. Even—"

He looked around the horizon with a sour expression. "—this sky."

Count Klimov watched with great interest as a team of riggers drew his aircar from the hatch forward on C Deck. They'd hung a winch from Antenna Port B; Woetjans was riding the half-extended mast, clinging by her legs and left hand as she kept eyeball contact with the vehicle that'd been lifted from the hold on the level below. Ordinarily D Deck was underwater, so access to the bulk storage there was through the deck above.

Valentina Klimovna gave the proceedings a cursory

glance, then walked purposefully to where Daniel and Hogg stood twenty yards from the *Princess Cecile*. Leary's concern over the Countess' wardrobe had been misplaced: during the voyage she'd worn coveralls of tough, drab moleskin that seemed every bit as practical as RCN utilities. Now that they'd landed she'd changed into a loose, many-pocketed hunting outfit which again seemed functional, for all that it was probably very expensive.

The same could be said of her impeller. The stock and fore-end were of some lustrous wood with a swirling grain, and the metalwork was scrolled and inlaid with hunting scenes in gold and platinum. Daniel didn't doubt it'd hit just as hard as the pair of service weapons he and Hogg had taken from the *Sissie's* armory, though.

"So, Daniel?" she said. "You are coming with me to the pyramid, yes?"

"Yes, I thought Hogg and I should accompany you," Daniel said. "You and your husband, I believe?"

"Georgi thinks we will find a dragon for him to shoot," Klimovna said. "He likes to shoot things."

She grinned; the expression made her look a decade younger. "I like to shoot things too, but not so much."

Her eyes appraised Hogg. "Your man here can drive an aircar?"

"Sure!" said Hogg. "You bet—"

"No," Daniel said firmly. "Hogg can't drive an aircar any better than he can sing hymns, and he's got more experience singing hymns. If—"

"Well, if somebody'd give me a chance to practice, young master . . . ," Hogg muttered with a hurt look on his face.

"—necessary there are spacers aboard who can drive, though I was thinking that it's less than a mile to the pyramid there—"

He pointed to the glitter on the rise to the west. Even with the sun at zenith, the surface of 4795-C had the feel of misty twilight.

"No matter," Klimovna said, brushing aside the suggestion of walking before Daniel got the words fully out. "I will drive; I planned to anyway."

Daniel had landed the *Princess Cecile* in a maze of meandering streams rather than among separated ponds. Hiking—even a moderate distance—probably wasn't a good idea, though he was uncomfortable about being in an aircar to hunt prey that flew.

He was uncomfortable about the Klimovs, also. Until you'd seen how a person behaved with a gun in his hand, you really couldn't judge how safe they were to be around. Adding the variable of an aircar was bothersome.

Low sedge-like vegetation grew in shallow water and up the banks besides. Daniel found it difficult to be sure where the margin was until he noticed that the stalks rising from the water had a touch of gold overlaying the dark green of their fellows rooted in land.

On a settled planet, he'd have an overview from the *Sailing Directions* and perhaps detailed supplements on the local natural history. Well, when the *Princess Cecile* returned to Cinnabar, he'd copy his logs to the Publications Bureau of the Navy Office. There they'd be available to spacers who knew they'd be landing on 4795-C in the future.

If there were such folk, ever in the future history of the Republic.

At a distance from the streams, thumb-thick tubes lay awkwardly across the mud like tangles of hose. Every foot or so, the horizontal stems sent up jointed vertical shoots that got no more than six inches high. Cilia burrowed into the soil from the sides of the stems;

if there were substantial roots as well, they were lost in the surface muddle.

At intervals "trees"—bare spikes, leafless like the tubes—rose. The ones nearby were ten or a dozen feet tall, but some on the slope of the hill in the near distance were possibly double that. A few of them split into a double stalk at the midpoint, but Daniel could only conjecture whether they were simply genders or if he was seeing different species.

"Oh!" the Klimovna said. She clutched Daniel's arm to demand his attention, pointing with the gun in her other hand. "Look! It's alive!"

"It" was a ball about the size of a commo helmet, standing on two sharply-bent legs and browsing in the knot of tubes across the creek. Its head was small with long, narrow jaws; instead of eating the whole plant, it nipped off the tops of the vertical shoots with surgical precision.

Its hide was a shiny gray-green, similar to the algae-covered mud. Daniel had seen the creature and three other members of its . . . flock? herd? when he scanned the landscape on infrared from the *Sissie's* hatch, but the Klimovna hadn't noticed it till it hopped to a new location after cleaning its immediate surroundings.

"Yes, they seem quite harmless," he said, forbearing to add that the vegetation and for that matter the bacteria-rich muck on which they were standing were also alive. Differently alive, he supposed. "There's a pair of much larger animals—"

He extended his right arm, managing in doing so to detach the woman's hand. "There, in the middle of that slough?"

Klimovna snatched a monocular out of her breast pocket and focused on the pair of creatures, each the size of a brood sow, which lay half submerged in the water as they ate arcs out of the sedges along the bank. Daniel wondered if her instrument had as many modes as the RCN goggles he was using. Thermal imaging— infrared—was a great deal more useful for finding animals in this foggy landscape than straight optics were.

"Umm . . . ?" the woman said. She shook her head and put the monocular away. "Not a good trophy, I suppose."

"I shouldn't think so, no," Daniel said austerely. He grimaced, imagining the problems involved in dragging a half-ton carcass to dry ground and then caping it. That wouldn't concern the Klimovna, since she—cor- rectly—assumed it would be somebody else's problem.

"All right, release it!" Woetjans bawled. "Now, get the cargo net unwrapped so somebody can fly the bastard off it. Or—"

She turned, poised on the antenna like an extremely large ape, and looked at Daniel. "Sir, do you want us to lift the aircar off the netting 'stead of flying it off? I guess the right six people could do it, though I'll use more with this muck so slick."

"No, we will fly off now," Klimovna called, striding toward the vehicle with an enthusiasm that splashed mud onto the legs of the jodhpurs bloused into her high boots. "Come along, Daniel."

Hogg snorted and said something under his breath, but the woman's brusque order didn't bother Daniel overmuch. The RCN was a good school in which to learn the art of obedience to the whims of your superiors. Valentina was his superior, so long as she didn't interfere with the good governance of the *Princess Cecile*. He had no justifiable complaint.

"Ship, this is the captain," he said as he followed at a cautious distance from his employer's side. "Hogg and I will accompany the Klimovs in the aircar to the pyramid at a vector of 132 degrees,. Lieutenant Chewning is in charge till my return. Continue second level maintenance. Six out."

A patter of "Rogers" answered. Pasternak, standing with his head in a thruster, waved.

Klimovna slipped behind the driver's yoke as soon as she reached the open aircar. Woetjans ran out ten feet of cable, riding the hook to the ground just ahead of Daniel. The Count started to get into the front passenger side but his wife waved him away. "No, you in back with the servant, Daniel in front. For balance, Georgi."

Hogg snorted again, but this time with what Daniel suspected was appreciation. Before Hogg or the Klimovs could say anything further, Daniel said, "The lady wants us kitty-corner, Hogg. Sit behind her."

Hogg obviously thought the lady was flirting—which she hadn't done while the *Princess Cecile* was under weigh, thanks be to a benevolent God. That might well be correct, but he and Hogg were each forty pounds heavier than the Klimovs. Daniel wasn't comfortable in aircars to begin with, and he was perfectly willing to believe that a vehicle built on Novy Sverdlovsk might not adjust automatically for an unbalanced load the way it ought to.

At any rate, the Count didn't object. Klimovna glanced behind to make sure her passengers were settled, then ran up the fans and hopped the vehicle forward twice before getting enough velocity to stay airborne.

They passed low over the stream, spraying the peat-black water into tiny droplets that glittered like flung diamonds. The surface plopped as scores of animals, many more than Daniel had observed, hurled themselves into it.

In contrast, a dozen hog-sized beasts lurched out

of a marsh. They moved in disjointed hops which nonetheless covered a good deal of ground in a short time. The Count saw them and pointed.

"Later, perhaps!" his wife said, shouting over the intake rush and the thrum of the fans. "We want a dragon."

The Klimovna drove well, but the aircar seemed underpowered even though none of the four passengers was unusually heavy. Daniel frowned, wondering if he should've shipped an RCN utility vehicle. He could've wangled one, he was sure—and for that matter, the Klimovs hadn't shown themselves tightfisted—but that wouldn't have solved the problem of stowage. Finding room for this light runabout had been difficult enough.

The air a hundred feet up was noticeably clearer than at ground level. The pyramid's glittering outlines sharpened; its hilltop base floated on a cushion of mist that concealed enough of the muck below to make the landscape more attractive.

"Look, there's many more of them!" the Count said, leaning forward between his wife and Daniel. He waved his left arm. "They're all around us!"

The hills, though unimpressive in themselves, were high enough to bring many of the pyramids into the sunlight. They sparkled from horizon to horizon like sun-struck icicles on a winter morning.

That was precisely what Adele had predicted and the orbital imagery confirmed, but especially to a layman the real thing had an impact that intellectual knowledge lacked. Aloud Daniel said, "Yes sir. And I hope the dragons will be easy to find as well."

"I seen two of 'em so far already," Hogg said. "I guess when you're ready, that won't be a problem neither."

"What?" said the Count. "Where?" He and Hogg fell into a private conversation, the servant pointing across the seat with his left index and middle finger while Klimov leaned dangerously—and pointlessly—over the side.

Klimovna slowed the aircar in a broad S-curve as they approached the pyramid, giving herself time to pick a landing place. She didn't hover; perhaps the vehicle *couldn't* hover with its present load.

The best choice, virtually the only choice unless they wanted to land at the bottom of the hill and hike up the slope, was directly in front of the structure. Which *wasn't* a good choice if the dragon who lived there happened to be home.

"Hogg, watch the outside," Daniel ordered as the aircar slanted in. That was the other risk, something thirty feet long with talons and a dismembering beak diving out of the sun onto nest-robbers. But he didn't want to slither a hundred feet up slick mud either. . . .

Klimovna landed neatly, fishtailing but not hopping. Daniel'd been sitting on the edge of the cab with his left leg out. Even before the vehicle'd halted, he jumped clear with his impeller mounted on his shoulder, aiming toward the triangular opening six feet above the ground.

"How do we get inside?" the Count said, holding his weapon at the balance as he walked past Daniel. "Little heart, can you fly us—"

"Stop!" Daniel shouted. *The stench should've warned Klimov even if he didn't bother looking at his feet!* "Sir, please—there may be a dragon inside. The remains of its meals are all around us."

One of the stripped carcasses had been of what looked like the larger species they'd seen. A calf—a shoat?—no doubt, but it still had weighed as much in life as the Count himself did.

"Is it inside, then?" said Klimov. "Shall I shoot to bring it out?"

"Sir," said Daniel, his mouth dry as his mind reviewed the ways the immediate future could very quickly deteriorate. "I think if you'll just brace my right foot, I can get high enough to see into the cave. Thermal imaging will tell me if there's anything inside. If not, you and your wife can—"

"Yes," said the Klimovna. She went down on her left knee in the mud, bracing her arm against the smooth crystalline side. "But here, step on my thigh. It will hold you."

Hesitant only in his mind—an RCN officer shouldn't show doubt when he knew he had to act—Daniel set the arch of his boot on the woman's leg just back of the knee. He rose, lifting his head, shoulders, and rifle muzzle over the lip of the opening. He scanned the interior with thermal imaging, then switched to light amplification.

The passage reached straight back into the pyramid without bends or bulges. It contained nothing save scraps of previous meals—and not many of those. The resident was a messy eater, but it apparently swept its den with some care.

Daniel stepped back. "Thank you, Valentina," he said with a nod that approached a bow. Her leg trembled, but she hadn't flinched; he could've shot accurately if he'd needed to.

He leaned his impeller against the face of the pyramid, made a stirrup of his hands, and went on, "May I lift you inside in return for your greatly-appreciated help?"

"Here, you," the Count said, plucking Hogg's sleeve. "Kneel down. I'll step on your back."

"Not bloody likely," Hogg said, continuing to search the sky. "And if you jiggle me again while I'm watching for flying snakes, you'll be down on the ground yourself."

"I'll lift you in a moment, sir!" Daniel said quickly. "If the dragon isn't at home, it may be coming home."

The Klimovna smiled, stepped onto his hands, and caught herself neatly on her hands and knees at the mouth of the passage. She'd left her weapon beside Daniel's; as soon as her weight lifted, he took the impeller by the balance to hand to her. She'd gone inside instead of waiting.

"Sir," Daniel said, leaning the weapon back and interlacing his hands. "May I help you mount?"

Above them Valentina remarked something. The angled walls distorted the words beyond understanding, but she didn't seem worried.

"Yes, yes," the Count said. He wasn't angry about the rebuke. Despite the cultural overlay, Klimov seemed quite a decent fellow. "But can you get me higher? I'm not as supple as my wife."

"Certainly," Daniel said. He waited for the Count to position himself, raised him to waist height, and then pitched him up and forward as he would've done with a log he'd lifted on end.

Klimov hurtled into the cave with a startled cry, his weapon clattering on the crystal. It was only then that Daniel realized he should've checked to make sure the safety was on.

Valentina stepped into view, sidling to get around her sprawling husband. "There is nothing in here, Daniel," she said. "Do you suppose it was a tomb, or what? It certainly isn't natural, and it's all one piece."

Daniel looked up the slope of the structure. This one was just under sixty feet high. He'd used the laser rangefinder to measure all the pyramids visible from the *Princess Cecile*; they ran from a little over fifty feet high to a touch under seventy-five, all of them perfectly regular tetrahedrons which—save for the opening in one side—could've been tossed randomly onto the ground.

"Ma'am," Daniel said. "Valentina. I'm sure I don't have any idea. Except as you say, that it isn't natural."

As he spoke the words, he felt a sudden doubt. Couldn't they be natural? He'd seen regular crystals, none nearly so large but—

Realization struck him. He scuffed the ground with his bootheel, then scraped sideways at the dimple he'd kicked.

"There's an apron of the same crystal here in front," he said, loud enough for all three companions to hear. "The mud's splashed up and covered it over the years, I guess."

"Faugh, there's nothing here," said the Count, stalking to the front of the tunnel where he stood by his wife. "It is time that I shoot my trophy, yes?"

"Yes, all right," said Valentina. She sat on the edge of the opening with her legs dangling, then half-jumped, half slid to the ground. "Hogg, you will direct me," she added.

"There's one over that way about half a mile," Hogg said, pointing with his extended left arm. "He's eating something, it looks. See him?"

Daniel dialed his goggles' magnification up to x32, bringing the dragon into sharp focus against the reed-choked water beyond. It was eating beyond question— its beak dipped and rose repeatedly, each time ripping up a rag of flesh which it tossed its head to swallow. The beast's victim was hidden in the vegetation, however.

"Very good!" Daniel said with honest enthusiasm. "It has a bright red crest. Perhaps it's a male in breeding plumage?"

"A trophy," the Count said. "That is enough."

Before Daniel could offer to take his impeller, Klimov slid down the face of the pyramid. Daniel grabbed him so that he didn't pitch over on his face when his feet skidded on the mud. The weapon slanting out in front of him didn't go off—again.

They piled hastily into the aircar. Daniel and Hogg continued to scan the skies; the dragon they'd spotted might not be the one which laired in this pyramid.

Valentina spun the fans up. "Don't fly us too close, please!" Daniel said, regretting that the Klimovna wasn't wearing a commo helmet. He had to shout to be heard over the intake roar, but instinct read loud voices as anger or threat. "Three hundred yards is as close as I think—"

Valentina slid the aircar over the lip of the apron, using the drop-off to bring them up to flying speed smoothly. She drew back on the control yoke, lifting the car to its original altitude and scrubbing off velocity at the same time. Daniel doubted the little vehicle would be controllable at much over seventy or eighty mph. By God, they should've walked despite the mud!

The dragon undulated forward. For an instant Daniel thought the movement was an optical illusion. Then the creature's powerful hind legs thrust back with spray of mud, and the sinuous body lifted like a flatworm planing.

The dragon curved toward them, climbing swiftly. Daniel got a good look at the membranes extended on both sides of its body. Adele's book said they were individual "feathers" and so they might be, but from this distance they looked like seamless membranes so thin they were almost transparent.

The wings rippled in strokes driven by the muscles of the dragon's whole powerful body. Their total area was considerable, though they stretched lengthwise instead of sticking out from the torso like other wings Daniel had seen.

"Set us down!" Hogg was screaming. "Set us down!"

The Count aimed over the side. When Valentina

banked starboard, heading for the ground *fast*, her husband tried to follow the dragon; the impeller's barrel whacked Daniel's helmet.

"Not in the air, by God!" Daniel shouted, reaching back blindly and managing to grab the weapon ahead of the fore-end. If Klimov fired, the hot barrel would raise blisters across Daniel's palm and the inside of his fingers. That was still better than getting a slug through him, the driver, or the forward fan. . . .

The dragon curled away, gaining altitude rather than attacking. Its wings formed paired shimmering helixes as they rose above the mist.

Valentina pancaked in, jerking the throttle open at the last instant when she realized how hard they were going to hit. The back of the car came down in a tangle of the tube plants which hid something solid— a rock or the stump of a large tree. The rear fan disintegrated; the front, on overload power, flipped the car upside down.

Daniel bounced out over the bow, skidding through a clump of fern-like tendrils. The liquescent soil kept him from breaking ribs, but he'd had all the breath knocked out of him. He probably would've drowned except for the protection of his helmet visor.

Rolling onto his back, all he could manage for the moment, Daniel ripped his helmet off. The faceshield's static charge was supposed to keep it free from dust, but there were limits.

Where's the dragon? and there it was, arrowing down out of the sun. Daniel's impeller was still in his left hand. He sat up, ignoring the pain, and threw the gun to his shoulder. He didn't aim after all because what looked like a pound of mud was clumped over the muzzle. It filled the bore just as sure as that dragon was going to eat them all if somebody didn't have a bright idea fast.

The aircar's front fan howled and bucked, shoving its intakes down into the soggy soil. Each time it stalled and unclamped, then repeated the cycle as soon as it sucked in another gulp of air. Hogg was caught underneath, only his head and torso free. From the curses he was shouting he hadn't even had the breath knocked out of him, but he'd lost his gun.

Valentina was on the ground behind the aircar, unconscious or at least unmoving. She'd had the yoke to cling to so she hadn't come loose when Daniel did. Instead she'd been flung a good twenty yards in the opposite direction when the vehicle flipped. Where the Count himself was remained beyond immediate conjecture, but Daniel hadn't had much hope there anyway.

Which left Daniel Leary without a bright idea to his name. He stepped forward holding his impeller by the barrel and wheezing, "Come here and let me bash your head in, snake!" Creatures with compound eyes saw motion more easily than shapes, so the dragon ought to ignore the remainder of the aircar's passengers.

The dragon had been stooping on the overturned vehicle. Sure enough it twisted in the air, supple as an earthworm, and kicked out with its powerful hind legs to clutch its victim. It overshot Daniel, unused to its prey coming toward it.

The dragon's feet had three toes, two forward and one back, each armed with a glittering black talon as long as a man's hand. The left dewclaw caught the back of Daniel's tunic as he lunged into the club he was swinging. The hook jerked him into a backward somersault before the tough fabric parted.

Daniel rolled to his feet. The dragon tore great divots as it hit the ground and twisted with the supple grace of a strangler's noose. It'd folded the wings on its neck and torso, but the back portion remained fully spread; it was using its tail as an oar to brace the striking beak. *Adele was right: they're individual feathers. . . .*

Daniel swung the gun at the creature's head. It was too quick for him: the beak, a foot long and sharp as a meathook, clamped on the receiver.

The dragon gave a quick jerk, probably intended to break what it thought was the neck of the creature it'd grabbed. Daniel didn't lose his grip on the weapon's barrel, but the dragon's strength whipped his feet off the ground before slamming him down again. He continued to hold the gun, but only by instinct. The last impact had knocked all conscious will out of him.

Still with the gun in its beak, the dragon took a deliberate step forward. Its breath had the enveloping stench of anaerobic decay. Its fist-sized, multi-lensed, eyes glittered like jewels a few inches from Daniel's face as it prepared to place its other foot in the middle of his back and pull him apart.

Steel flashed in the air. The hilt of Hogg's folding knife stood out from the center of the dragon's left compound eye. The five-inch blade was buried in the bundled optic nerves.

The dragon launched itself skyward. The wing on the creature's left side flared stiffly, but feathers on the right half fluttered without strength. The dragon curved in the air and smashed down, splashing the wet soil. Its left leg was kicking and its beak gnashed the air.

The *whack!whop!* of a powerful impeller firing into a nearby target startled Daniel more than he'd thought he had the energy for right at the moment. The dragon's skull deformed; half the upper beak and a splash of brains flew off in the humid air.

Daniel turned his head. Count Klimov held his gun

to his shoulder. He fired three more times, the recoil of each round rocking him back. He was walking the slugs down the dragon's spine, breaking it into segments which trembled in separate rhythms. The creature was no longer a danger, even by accident.

Klimov lowered his impeller; waste heat from the projectiles it'd accelerated made the barrel glow dull red. He looked at Daniel. "I decided I didn't need that trophy, Captain," he said.

Daniel tried to get to his feet. He used his gun as a pole, but it folded under the stress. The dragon's beak had sheared halfway through the aluminum receiver.

"Very good shooting, sir," Daniel said. He braced himself on one knee, then lurched fully upright. Klimovna leaned on one elbow, so at least she hadn't been killed.

"Somebody want to get this fucking car off me?" Hogg demanded.

Daniel walked to the vehicle, bent, and switched off the power; the fan slowed with a peevish moan. "I'm very sorry, Hogg," he said. "I'm afraid lifting the car will have to wait for the crew I see coming toward us from the *Princess Cecile*."

He waved to indicate matters had settled down. Raising his arm sent a line of jagged pain all the way to the toes of his left foot.

Had the knife Hogg threw survived the Count's shot? Pray God it had, because you could never tell when you'll need something like that again.

"Captain Leary?" the Count said. "What is the next port on our itinerary?"

"Todos Santos, the capital of the Ten Star Cluster, sir," Daniel said. "How long would you like to remain here before we lift ship?"

"I don't want to remain here even as long as it will take me to walk back to the *Princess Cecile*," the Count said, giving Daniel a wintry smile. "That long I must wait, I know. But not much longer, all right?"

"Aye aye, sir," Daniel said. "I know exactly how you feel."

CHAPTER 10

Hanging in orbit, cooling their heels outside Todos Santos' defensive minefield, may have made everybody else aboard the *Princess Cecile* jittery and snappish, but Adele found it the ideal place to gather information—which was her job, after all. *When my job isn't shooting people*, she added mentally; and because she was in a good mood, that whimsy made her tight smile broaden by a hair's-breadth.

If she'd known how to whistle, she'd have whistled as Daniel did in similar circumstances. It probably wasn't worth the effort to learn the art now; though perhaps. . . .

She caught movement from the corner of her eye and glanced to the side. Daniel glided over to her console, his face unwontedly grim. The *Princess Cecile* had gravity or its equivalent only on a planet or under power. Todos Santos Control had assigned them an orbit which they could leave only at the risk of being treated as hostile by the planetary defenses, so they couldn't have stooged about under 1 g acceleration even if the corvette had unlimited water remaining in its

151

storage tanks to be converted into fuel for the High Drive.

"Can you get a notion of how long we'll wait for landing approval, Mundy?" Daniel asked, as usual professionally formal in public settings. The fact he'd come over to talk without going through the commo system showed how much inaction frustrated him, though.

She'd forwarded to Daniel's console the layout of the harbor at San Juan, the planetary and effectively national capital; technically the Ten Star Cluster was part of the Commonwealth and tributary to Radiance. The ship's ordinary sensors would've provided images showing the size and number of ships in the great harbor, but Adele's—the additional software and equipment from Mistress Sand—added the vessels' names, their arrival and planned departure dates, and all the other information in the files of Planetary Control.

In a few minutes, she'd have completed gathering all the data in the vessels' computers. Oh, yes, this was a *fine* environment for a skilled information specialist.

"There seem to be only two picket boats," Adele explained. She shrank the communications data she'd been working with to a sidebar so that she could project a spatial display for Daniel. Instead of echoing the image to his helmet visor, her first thought, she switched her console to project an omnidirectional view. She frowned. "According to Control Authority records there are five, but I can't find any physical sign of the others."

Daniel chuckled, returning to his normal good humor. "I'm confident that the pay and maintenance charges *do* exist—in somebody's pocket," he explained. "Well, this isn't Cinnabar, you know; and even on Cinnabar . . ."

"Ah," said Adele, nodding. She reminded herself again that records might be wrong when there were human beings in the equation. She should just factor that in as she would the chance of equipment failure, instead of feeling a surge of anger every time she learned that *somebody had deliberately corrupted her data!* "Yes, of course. In any case, one of the picket vessels cleared a Kostroman freighter forty-seven minutes ago and is on its way to the *Princess Cecile*. The other picket vessel is ..."

She frowned. "That's odd," she said, switching back to the commo screen without thinking of her guest. *This might be important.*

"Daniel," she said, "the other picket is clearing an Alliance freighter out of Pleasaunce named the *Goldenfels*, ID Number 83191-7."

"Well, that's proper," Daniel said, locking his right leg around the post of her seat as he squinted at the display. It would mean as little to him as his astrogation tank did to her. "The Alliance was never formally at war with the Commonwealth, you know. There just isn't much Alliance traffic because of distance and the risk of piracy."

"Daniel," Adele said, pursing her lips in exasperation, "that's *all* I can tell about the *Goldenfels*. I can't get into their navigation system through their communications suite. The ship's shielded too well."

"Ah!" said Daniel, his face placid and wearing a quizzical smile. "Can they get into our system, Adele?" he asked.

"Of course they can," she said tartly. "If they couldn't, it'd be a dead giveaway that we're a spy ship, wouldn't it? To anybody who had the equipment and the necessary skill, I mean."

She gave her friend what she supposed was a smile of rather prissy satisfaction. "They can't get into *my* system, however," she added. "And according to the manifest they can read, we have a much smaller crew, mostly from Novy Sverdlovsk. And no missiles."

"*The Klimovs are approaching the bridge,*" Tovera's voice whispered through the left ear of Adele's helmet.

"Captain, how long must we stay like this?" said the Count as he slid through the hatch inexpertly; though at that he was rather better at it than Adele was, she noted with a degree of irritation. The Klimovna followed her husband, bouncing from the deck to the ceiling of the passage.

They'd gone to their stateroom on C Deck after the *Princess Cecile* fell into orbit around Todos Santos, hoping to find it more comfortable than the bridge annex. Apparently they'd been disappointed in that hope.

"*Guardship* Abdul Hassan *docking with Cinnabar vessel* Princess Cecile," an edgy voice said over the ground control channel in a demand rather than an announcement. "*Prepare to receive port control officials.*"

"*Princess Cecile to Abdul Hassan,*" Daniel replied. His voice was blurred to Adele in what was now a familiar fashion, coming by radio through her helmet as well as directly from his lips to her ears. "We'll receive you at our forward dorsal hatch. *Princess Cecile* over."

Rather than "out," Adele noticed, indicating that he expected to resume transmission. The locals hadn't bothered to code their signal, either out of sloppiness or deliberate discourtesy.

Daniel turned to the Klimovs, straightening and wedging the toe of his left boot between Adele's console and the bulkhead to anchor him. "Port control will board in a few minutes, sir," he said politely. "I trust that when a few formalities are taken care of, we'll be cleared to land."

He coughed. "Ah, one of the formalities is likely to

be a tip to the officials," he added. "Otherwise we might remain in orbit for an extended period."

"Yes, of course," said Klimov. "How much?"

The Count shrugged, but he shouldn't have. The motion sent him drifting toward the ceiling again. His arms windmilled.

"The Kostroman freighter that just got clearance paid a hundred and fifty Kostroman ducats," Adele said. "If those are New Ducats, as I assume they were, that's about a hundred and ten Cinnabar florins or . . ."

Her left wand twitched, providing data she was irritated not to have prepared earlier.

"Three thousand two hundred and eighteen Sverdlovsk crowns."

The Klimovs looked startled that she'd been the one to answer. Daniel only smiled, though now that Adele thought about it she guessed he wouldn't have realized she'd amassed quite so much information so quickly.

The spacer who'd steadied Klimovna now gripped the Count, keeping himself anchored by a toe against the hatch coaming. Klimov lifted his tunic to expose a money belt, then began counting Alliance marks into the palm of his left hand.

"Captain, there's a ship approaching," said Sun, speaking loudly enough to be heard while keeping his whole attention on his Gunnery display.

"*Ship, port control is about to board us,*" Daniel said on the general push. The Klimovs listened intently; they weren't wearing the commo helmets they'd been issued, so he made a point of speaking directly to them. "*We should be splashing down in half an hour, thanks to the owners' reasonable attitude regarding port charges.*"

"*Good-oh for the Klimovs!*" somebody shouted over the PA system. It was probably Dorst, since only the bridge and the Battle Center could access the speakers at the moment. There was a general ragged cheer.

"And Sun?" Daniel said, leaning closer to the gunner. "If your turrets aren't locked fore and aft, I'll derate you right now."

Sun turned and grinned at him. "They're locked, sir," he said. "But they aren't stowed. I figure we're in the North, now, so we can take a little knocking around on descent just so we don't look like patsies to the wogs, right?"

Adele winced. When the Klimovs were safely off the bridge, she'd remind Sun that "wog" wasn't a word you used when the owners traveling with you were from Novy Sverdlovsk. . . .

"There's a customs boat docking with us, Captain," Woetjans warned over the hard-wired connection from the *Princess Cecile's* hull. As soon as the corvette dropped into orbit, the riggers had furled the sails, rotated the spars vertical, and locked them to the antennas which they telescoped and folded for landing. The bosun sent the port watch below then, but she and the starboard watch remained outside.

"Acknowledged, Woetjans," Daniel replied. "Bring them through dorsal forward and follow them aboard."

He smiled to the Klimovs, floating at angles to the deck. A rigger from the port watch held his arm out; the Klimovna gripped his wrist and held herself steady. "Our bosun announced the arrival of the guard vessel," Daniel explained. "It'll be just a few minutes."

When a vessel was in the Matrix, the thrust of Casimir radiation against her charged sails slid her between bubble universes of varying space-time constants. Even so small an input as a radio signal or the electromagnetic field of a current-carrying wire could introduce literally incalculable variables.

The problem didn't exist in sidereal space, but the

riggers used radio frequency gear sparingly nonetheless. The handsignals and semaphores by which they set the sails in the Matrix generally sufficed for other times as well.

Adele could've watched the *Abdul Hassan* sending lines to the *Sissie*, but the fine points of ship-handling wouldn't have been any of her affair even if the locals were likely to teach her something that the corvette's crew didn't know. Instead she entered the computer of the other port control vessel, the *Piri Reis*, and pirated the information the local inspectors were sending back from the *Goldenfels*.

The boarding team unreeled a fiber-optic cable to their own vessel, making the data impossible to jam or intercept—until it got to the *Piri Reis*. At that point it became Adele's at literally the speed of light. Her wands flickered as she watched the images cascade through her display.

The airlock just aft of the *Sissie's* bridge cycled, then purred open. A pair of helmeted strangers came out, followed by crewmen whose rigging suits made them look huge and clumsy compared to the others in flexible airsuits. The crystalline flex joining the first local's helmet to his ship was hair fine. Even knowing it must be there, Adele could see only a quiver in the air.

The rig was expensive and of the highest quality. The only justification for it she could imagine was that it kept the inspectors honest—in the sense that their superiors knew exactly how much the bribe had been so that those superiors could extract their proper portion.

"As I'm the owner, Count Georgi Klimov," the Count said, stepping forward with the help of the spacer behind him, "I believe it's my place to greet you. I trust you'll find our papers in order, and also that you'll honor me by accepting this little token."

He flashed a little sheaf of circuit-imprinted bills, each with the picture of Guarantor Porra, toward the inspector unreeling the optical fiber, then handed them to the other man. Adele used his helmet camera's image to see the denominations which the Count's hand hid from her: eighty-five marks, which according to the rate current in Xenos when the *Princess Cecile* lifted would be worth one hundred and twelve Cinnabar florins. She frowned at this further evidence that the Count was worthy of more respect than she'd been willing to grant him.

The inspectors huddled for a moment, taking much longer to count the money than Adele had. At last they looked up and the one with the camera shrugged. "Your papers are fine," he said. "You've got berth D-73."

The money vanished into his tool pouch. His partner added, "There'll be wharf charges too. We're just clearing you to land."

"D-73 is in the Outer Arc," Daniel said, drawing the eyes of everyone present toward him. "I notice slip A-12 is open, alongside the *Aristoxenos* where some of us might have old shipmates. I wonder if there might be a way we could land there? The causeway to the Inner Arc would save the Count and Countess from having to take a boat to shore; their aircar came to a bad end on the world we just visited."

"The A slips are for fleet only," said the inspector who'd taken the bribe; his fingers touched his tool pouch. "Or special cases."

"Anyway, the *Piri Reis* already cleared a freighter for A-12," said the man with the camera. "It'd mean squaring the *Piri*'s crew too."

"How much?" said the Klimovna bluntly.

The inspectors looked at her, then toward one another. The man with the camera shrugged. The other nodded in decision and said to the Klimovs, "For the

A slips, two hundred and fifty marks. We couldn't do it for less."

"Done," said the Count. He opened his money belt again.

Daniel pushed off from the bulkhead, sliding backward to the command console as smoothly as a seal swimming. His fingers began to dance forcefully over his touchplate, adjusting the display.

As the Count paid the additional sum into one inspector's gloved hand bill by bill, his partner closed his helmet so he could use its microphone to speak to the crew of the other guardship. He spoke with animation, finally grasping his partner's hand with the money and holding it directly in front of his helmet camera.

Nodding forcefully, he opened his visor again. "I made a mistake," he said. "Slip A-12 is open after all. We have assigned it to your fine vessel, Count Klimov. A pleasure doing business with you!"

He turned and opened the airlock's inner door, the air behind him shimmering as his communications cable wound back on its take-up spool. His partner, patting the bribe away in his tool pouch, followed.

As the airlock closed, everyone on the *Princess Cecile*'s bridge except Adele grinned with satisfaction and began to chatter. Adele was listening to the scene on the *Goldenfels'* bridge where the other team of inspectors explained to Captain Bertram that his ship wasn't cleared for slip A-12 after all.

She frowned with concern. If Bertram had been present, her hand would've been touching the pistol in her tunic pocket.

"Ship, this is the captain," Daniel said, lying back on the couch of his console with the surface of Todos Santos three thousand miles below on his display. "I'll be initiating landing sequence in two minutes and . . ." He waited for the digit to change. "Forty seconds. Prepare for landing, out."

The *Sissie's* computer would land the vessel. A sidebar listed the already-programmed thruster impulse by seconds per nozzle. If Daniel chose he could add the actual course track, a skein of red lines, which would circle the planetary image until it terminated in slip A-12 (though the harbor itself wasn't visible at the present scale). He didn't bother, but when they entered the atmosphere he'd switch to direct visuals.

Adele inset a red-outlined communications block in the upper left corner of Daniel's display. The text read LASER SIGNAL FROM *GOLDENFELS*.

"*Vessel* Princess Cecile," an unfamiliar voice said. According to the icons, Adele was routing the signal only to Daniel and the Battle Center. "*The Goldenfels has been allotted slip A-12. Don't interfere or you'll regret it.*"

A ship was lifting from the harbor, circled in yellow by the display. Daniel had caught the puff of steam as the *Princess Cecile* passed over San Juan. It was one of the country craft, ships of five or six hundred tons. They towed bulk cargoes which they picked up in orbit, carrying only high-value items within their hulls. Without external loads they were ideal for smuggling and for piracy.

Daniel began to key in new course data; his face wore a smile. His fingertips hammered the virtual touchpad, but that was from the enthusiasm with which he always typed, not out of anger. He wasn't angry. . . .

"Ship, battle stations," he said over the general push. The sidebar which showed braking impulse blurred, then sharpened to reflect the course changes. "There's an Alliance freighter which believes it can push us out of our landing site. The RCN is going to show them they're wrong this time too. Initiating landing sequence . . . *now!*"

Over the roar of the thrusters on 80% flow he added, "Six out."

Daniel was vaguely aware that he'd dropped back into naval parlance: in his mind, he was no longer the Captain but rather Ship Six. Very probably the crew had always thought of him that way.

As for the Klimovs, well, they hadn't seemed like the sort who'd take to being pushed around either. If Daniel guessed wrong, he supposed it proved he hadn't been cut out to command a civilian vessel.

"Todos Santos Control, this is Cinnabar registry vessel *Princess Cecile*," Daniel said, cueing both the ground control satellites and the *Goldenfels*. He noticed from the icons that Adele was sending the transmission by tight-beam microwave not only to the Alliance freighter but also to both orbiting guardships. "We are proceeding as directed by Todos Santos Control to slip A-12, San Juan Harbor. Please acknowledge, over."

His words slurred slightly from braking impulse and the thrusters' vibration. Things were rattling adrift even on the bridge; God knew what was happening in the main compartments. The crew had expected to circle down at 1 g; instead they were dropping at twice that.

Daniel hoped the Klimovs were strapped into their couches, but he didn't have time just now to check. An icon on the top of his display indicated they'd both have been talking to him if Adele hadn't blocked the signals. That meant at least they hadn't broken their necks.

"*Control to Princess Cecile,*" said a testy female voice. "*You're cleared to land. If you children have a problem up there, make sure you solve it before you*

*reach the ground or I swear we'll jug all of you!
Control out."*

That was what Daniel'd expected and really the best
he could hope for. The *Sissie* didn't need the locals
to sort out an Alliance ship for her, but if Todos Santos
had gotten involved it would've complicated a situation that was already complicated by the fact Cinnabar and the Alliance were at peace. . . .

"*Six, this is Six-two,*" Chief Missileer Betts reported.
"*Target acquired, courses set for first four missiles.
Over.*"

Daniel switched to the Plot Position Indicator as his
main display; the attack board, commo, gunnery, and
realtime visuals appeared at reduced scale along the
bottom. Sun had the pipper for the dorsal turret's twin
4-inch plasma cannon centered on the *Goldenfels*,
though at the present range the weapons would harm
only the sails furled to the freighter's spars. The ventral turret, offset toward the stern of D Deck, was still
aligned fore-and-aft, but Sun had unlocked it.

"*Cinnabar vessel, I'm warning you!*" the voice from
the Alliance freighter snarled. "*We're landing in slip
A-12. If you're underneath when we come down that's
just too damned bad for you! Goldenfels out!*"

The fellow was still using a laser communicator, so
the atmospheric buffeting and the haze of ions from his
plasma thrusters interfered with reception aboard the
Princess Cecile. Adele's software smoothed off the burrs
of static, but if the Alliance officer hadn't been so angry
he would've changed his mode of communication.

The *Princess Cecile* was a warship with frames and
bulkheads stressed to endure harder braking than any
freighter could match. The *Goldenfels* had started its
descent a few seconds earlier than the corvette, but
there was no possibility that the Alliance vessel would
reach the surface first.

On the other hand, the freighter weighed some eight thousand tons empty. If her captain was serious about bringing her down on top of the *Sissie*—and he certainly sounded serious—then something needed to be done quickly.

"Mr. Sun, lock the dorsal turret onto the *Goldenfels'* port quarter," Daniel ordered, expanding the gunnery screen to forty percent of his display. He was using the ship's common channel instead of the command push so that everybody aboard knew what was happening. "On the order I want you to walk your burst stern to bow along the line of her port thruster nozzles. Wait for the order! Over."

On the display the Alliance freighter was a slender dark mass above the twenty bright flares of its plasma thrusters. The *Princess Cecile* was already twelve thousand feet below and to the east—up-orbit—of the *Goldenfels*. Sun shifted his pulsing orange crosshairs back and outward from the center of her belly, saying, "Aye aye, sir."

"Adele," Daniel said as his fingers danced. "Transmit the image from our gunnery board to the *Goldenfels*. Break. *Goldenfels*, this is Daniel Leary of Bantry. If your vessel comes within a half mile of mine when we get below fifty thousand feet, I'm going to shoot away your offside thrusters. If you're very good, you'll be able to catch your pig of a ship before she turns turtle and augers in. Leary out!"

Daniel shrank the gunnery screen back to the bottom of his display and breathed deeply. He was trying to get his muscles to relax so that they wouldn't cramp if he had to move quickly . . . as he very likely would.

"Ship, this is Six," he said as red and blue tracks on the PPI marked the courses of the two descending vessels. "For those of you who don't have gunnery training—"

By which he meant particularly the Klimovs, who had a right to be both furious and terrified at the way things were going.

"—let me explain that the *Goldenfels* cannot use any ventral guns that might bear on us—"

Daniel didn't know with certainty that the Alliance freighter was armed, but it'd be a common-sense precaution for any ship trading in the Galactic North.

"—while her thrusters are in operation. Plasma from her own exhaust would distort her bolts if it didn't do worse. If the Alliance captain shuts off power this deep into his descent, he'll almost certainly crash regardless of what we do. Six out."

Daniel licked his lips. A line of sweat had gathered at the brow of his helmet. He'd have liked to wipe it away before a drop fell into his eye, but he was afraid that'd send the wrong signal to those of the crew who were watching a feed of their captain's face.

Beaded lines continued the astrogation computer's prediction of where the two ships would be in the next few minutes if one or the other didn't make a change. Both courses ended together in San Juan Harbor, though the scale was too small to identify slip A-12 precisely. The freighter's image swelled on the gunnery display, a distorted spindle half-hidden beneath an opalescent haze of charged particles.

The gunnery display went almost white as the freighter's plasma thrusters increased power. For a moment the image flared there; then it shrank, seeming to draw upward. In fact it was the *Sissie* dropping away while the *Goldenfels* braked and shifted course minusculely. The Alliance captain was heading for slip D-73, Daniel supposed. At any rate, Daniel wouldn't want to be the officer who tried to lift a ship back to orbit after so rapid a descent.

"Ship, this is Six," he said. He lifted his helmet and mopped his forehead with the sleeve of his tunic. "Prepare for touchdown, spacers. And welcome to Todos Santos!"

CHAPTER 11

Adele's taxi clanked to a halt in front of a building larger though no better kept than the rest of those on the twisting street. The driver switched off the turbine of her little tractor; it slowed with a ringing sound that might've been normal and with an unpleasant keen of rubbing metal that probably wasn't.

"The palace of Lord Purvis!" the driver said to Adele with a flourish of her arm. A dozen men and a few women squatted in the strip of shade against the front wall of the building. One of the women appeared to be a tailor with a hand stitcher; she was sewing cuffs of contrasting material on the shirt of the fellow waiting bare-chested beside her.

The location agreed with the address given for Commander Adrian Purvis in the Admiralty Records in Government House . . . to the degree that *The palace of Prince Pedro Sforza, in the Timber Merchants' Quarter* was an address. It was a better address than the Cluster's Admiralty Records were records, certainly. Good God, these people's idea of a filing system was the electronic equivalent of throwing papers in a

167

drawer! If Adele hadn't been very good at information retrieval, she'd never have been able to—

Adele slid the data unit away in its pocket as she got out of the wagon, shaking her head in self disgust. She *was* very good at information retrieval; and if she hadn't been, that would be her fault and not that of whatever passed for archivists here on Todos Santos. Besides, from what Daniel had muttered as he surveyed the Cluster fleet, the Admiralty was all of one sad piece with its records and the addresses of senior fleet officers.

"Twenty-five Cinnabar florins, gracious lady!" the driver said, getting off the bucket seat of her vehicle and bowing low. She ignored Tovera who stood at the back of the wagon, covering both traffic in the street and the idlers in front of the palace with alternate quick glances. "A pleasure to serve so great a personage as you!"

Adele hadn't seen any aircars in San Juan. Ground transport was eclectic and mostly of off-planet manufacture. The taxi she'd hired was a tractor running on continuous belts, which pulled a wooden cart whose pair of high wheels were almost certainly meant for a bicycle.

There were any number of other styles and ages of vehicles, often with a body of wood or wicker on ancient running gear. The closest thing to public conveyances were larger versions of the tractor-drawn cart Adele had ridden in, but though they followed more-or-less fixed routes, they didn't appear to keep any schedule.

"The correct charge is thirty piastres," Adele said, withdrawing a coin from the dispenser in her belt pouch. "A Cinnabar florin is worth about fifty, but I recognize that you'll have to exchange the coin for your local scrip; and there's the matter of the tip as well, so I won't require that you give me change."

When Adele called her cousin to set up the meeting, she'd asked what the proper fare from the harbor was. She'd refused his offer of an escort. While she wasn't hiding her presence in San Juan, neither did she want the sort of pomp that would convince even ordinary Alliance merchants and spacers in the city that she was more than a casual visitor. Letting people mistake her for a spy would be as damaging—and as dangerous—as if they identified her for valid reasons.

"What!" shouted the driver. "You insult me—"

She turned to engage the idlers in her harangue.

"—and you insult my planet!"

The palace was a courtyard building with three stories and a further false front along the street. The ground floor had no openings except a gate. The small windows of the second story and the larger ones of the third had iron lattices which seemed more functional than ornamental. The walls were mostly brick from which cream-colored stucco had flaked in large patches, but every six feet or so there was a tie course of pinkish stone.

One of the iron-bound gate-leaves was open. Guards lounged in the shade of the tunnel beyond, silhouetted against the bright courtyard where servants were hanging up laundry.

"Do you foreigners think you can come to Todos Santos and rob her hardworking citizens?" the driver cried.

Vehicles were moving slowly enough in the narrow street that passengers turned their heads to listen. The idlers were interested also. One man got to his feet, glowering. The woman beside him dug a stone out of the packed dust before she rose. Tovera shifted slightly.

Adele strode briskly to the half-open gate. An idler whose striped garment had been sewn from one piece of cloth shifted to block her, then saw what glinted in

Adele's hand half out of her pocket. He jumped back and muttered to his fellow without taking his eyes off Adele.

"A Mundy is threatened!" Adele called to the lounging guards. Her voice rang through the arched tunnel and into the courtyard beyond. "Will a Purvis let her be beaten at his doorstep?"

The guards jumped to their feet, their equipment clattering. There were six armed men wearing scarves in the orange-and-blue Purvis colors. A dozen others, mostly women, were either spouses or house servants relaxing with the guards. A boy cooked skewered vegetables on a miniature gas grill in the corner of the closed gate leaf and the wall.

"What's this?" demanded a man with pistols holstered on crossed bandoliers instead of a shoulder weapon like the other guards. From his accent he'd been born on Cinnabar, a crewman from the *Aristoxenos*. The rest of the guards appeared to be locals.

"I'm Mundy of Chatsworth, Commander Purvis' cousin!" Adele said. "This scum and her henchmen—"

She pointed at the taxi driver, now standing openmouthed with a blank expression. She'd backed against the saddle of her tractor.

"—have attempted to rob me!"

"Clear 'em away!" the guard commander said, drawing his pistols. "Bloody *hell*! Clear 'em away now!"

He stepped into the street but waited beside Adele against the gate leaf. His men rushed out, swinging impeller butts at anybody they could catch. The hangers-on followed, wielding belts, staves, and what looked like a pair of circular knitting needles.

The victims fled instead of trying to resist. Adele presumed that the guards would've opened fire as blithely as they clubbed their weapons if anybody'd been fool enough to object to a beating.

The driver lay sprawled in the street. Tovera had remained on the other side of the wagon, out of the way. Now she leaned over the tractor and grasped the driver by the collar. With a strength surprising in her slight form to anybody who hadn't seen it before, she dragged the woman over her saddle and left her dangling there.

Blood smudged the yellow dust; an impeller butt had smashed the driver's nose and cheekbones. Twenty-five florins—twenty-four, really—wasn't so very much, but the honor of a Mundy was worth life itself. . . .

Tovera switched on the tractor's turbine, then dropped it into gear and stepped back. The vehicle trundled awkwardly away, down a street which had emptied when the trouble started. Tovera walked over to Adele, the attaché case under her left arm and her right hand resting lightly on it.

The commander of the guard holstered his pistols, then wiped his brow with the corner of his neckscarf. His men and their entourage were trooping back into the gateway, chattering merrily. One woman was showing her companion a necklace of perforated coins and uncut stones that Adele remembered the tailor having worn.

"Sebastian!" he said to a soldier wiping the butt of his impeller clean on his shirt tail. "Take Lady Mundy to see Himself. And don't be daft enough to ask her for a tip or you'll get worse than the dogs just did."

"With me, mistress," Sebastian said, bowing low. His finger was through his impeller's trigger guard; the muzzle waggled in a broad sweep that would've included Adele's head if she hadn't ducked. He turned and swaggered into the courtyard.

"Very nicely done, mistress," Tovera murmured in Adele's ear as they followed the soldier. "If I'd dealt with them myself, they'd probably have declared us enemies of the state and had the army kill us."

She giggled. "Not that I care, of course," she added. "But you would."

"Yes," said Adele. "I suppose I would."

They crossed the courtyard. A balcony screened by a carved lattice projected from the upper—the second—floor of the wing directly opposite. Guards sat beneath the woven mat strung over the base of the outside staircase. They got up as Sebastian and his charges approached.

"The Chief says these two go to see Himself at once!" Sebastian said to another former Cinnabar spacer, this time a tired-looking woman with a chain of alternating hearts and RCN monograms tattooed around her throat.

"Yeah, well, that's for me to say, ain't it?" the woman said. She touched the communicator clipped to her epaulette.

Before she could speak into it, one of the sections of lattice pivoted up and a familiar face peered down. "Adele, is that you already?" called Adrian Purvis. "Come up, come up! We've been discussing the situation ever since you called."

And lest Adele wonder who her cousin meant by "we," another section of lattice raised. She recognized that face also, from images she'd studied in preparation for the present mission. She hadn't met Admiral O'Quinn before in the flesh.

Daniel had released the starboard watch, the riggers from the port watch, and all the officers save himself, Pasternak, and Vesey. Woetjans and the regular crewmen were gone, cutting a swathe through the nearest bars and brothels, but the other officers save Adele— on business of her own, nothing Daniel needed or wanted to know about—and the Purser, Stobart, watched solemnly from the outriggers as Daniel and the Chief Engineer inspected the thrusters. Even Stobart was gone only because he had to arrange for stores to replace those used up on the voyage out from Cinnabar.

Daniel sat in the inflatable raft which mechanics holding ropes on both outriggers steadied. Pasternak stood in front of Daniel with his head in a thruster nozzle.

After a moment he lowered the laser micrometer and said, "Down three millimeters is all, and the throat's as smooth as a baby's butt. Sir, I could turn these into a quartermaster's store as unused if I waited for Monday morning and got a clerk with a hangover!"

"By God, didn't I bloody tell you, Betts?" Sun said, clapping the Chief Missileer on the back. "There's no jinx with Mr. Leary in command. Why, when he was captain before, not even Mr. Mon could bugger our luck!"

"*Bridge watch to Six,*" Vesey called. "*Sir, there's a crowd coming this way. Maybe it's a parade, but there's soldiers at the front and what looks like a little tank or something. Over.*"

"Bridge, I'll meet them on the dock," Daniel said, frowning. "Killian, haul me over to your side; Pachey, loose your line. Lively now, we've got company coming!"

Sun got a hard expression and climbed the outrigger's telescoping strut instead of bothering with the ladder to the main hatch. He'd been a motorman working on High Drives before his rating made him the *Sissie's* acting gunner. Betts was older, heavier and probably never as active, but he mounted the ladder with similar grim haste.

"Don't do anything obvious with the weapons!" Daniel shouted as the two warrant officers disappeared into the hull. He jumped to the outrigger himself.

Instead of boarding, he trotted to the cable which moored the corvette to the quay. Over his shoulder he added, "Mr. Pasternak, check the High Drive on your own, if you will!"

Daniel hopped over the funnel-shaped rat-guard midway along the cable—they didn't stop rats either, that he'd seen—and stepped to the stone quay. He was wearing utilities—a clean pair since he wasn't going to be working on the drive units, just observing the inspection—and a billed cap. Apart from the single stars embroidered in black on his lapels, he could've passed for one of the common spacers. It wasn't the outfit in which to greet an official delegation, and that was definitely what was coming along the quay toward the *Princess Cecile*.

There were soldiers, all right, but the six in the front rank were playing instruments of orange thermoplastic extruded into trumpet shapes. The amplified music was loud, stirring, and—except for crackles of static from one of the trumpetoids—perfectly in tune.

The troops behind were armed to the teeth, generally with laser packs rather than electromagnetic impellers, but this clearly wasn't an attack. The vehicle—Vesey's "little tank or something"—was a utility tractor with steel sides welded onto the rear bin. An automatic impeller was mounted on a pintle there, but for this event the gun was aimed skyward. Patterned fabrics draped the sides.

Maybe they're coming for the Count, Daniel thought. A Novy Sverdlovsk flag, red and white silk blazoned with a red eagle, hung from the tip of the mast which was extended over the quay, but the Klimovs had gone into San Juan as soon as the slip cooled down enough for Daniel to open the hatches.

He'd sent ten crew under a petty officer as the Klimovs' escort. The assigned spacers escaped maintenance duties and might be able to relax some themselves, depending on circumstances.

Lamsoe and Tulane were on guard at the main hatch as part of the anchor watch. They joined Daniel on the quay, holding their sub-machine guns so that they were ready but not threatening. They didn't look worried, but they obviously weren't happy with the situation. *No* spacer is happy with a surprise, even if it's a fresh meal twenty days out.

The tractor stopped. The statuesque, gorgeously-dressed woman in the box glanced over the corvette and the three spacers on the quay. She settled her gaze on Daniel, and said, "Daniel Leary, son of Corder Leary, of Bantry? Governor Sakama Hideki sends his greetings and says he'll be pleased to accept your visit at once."

Three servants who'd walked behind the vehicle set the boarding ladder they carried against the side of the box. "If you'll mount," said the woman, "we'll be off immediately."

"Yes," said Daniel. There were quite a lot of things he could've said, all of which would've been a waste of time and breath. "Ship—" cueing his commo helmet "—this is Six. I'm calling on Governor Sakama. Mr. Chewning is in charge until I return. Six out."

He looked at the two spacers, then pointed to the flag hanging limp from the mast eight feet overhead. "Lamsoe?" he said. "Can you and Tulane get me that flag *now*? Don't hurt it any more than you need to."

"Roger," Lamsoe said, slinging his weapon over his neck. Tulane, a beefy man who'd won squadron trophies for all-in wrestling when he was younger, laced his fingers into a stirrup. Lamsoe settled his foot into it and said, "Go!" Tulane hurled his partner onto the mast.

Lamsoe locked his legs around the tube and snicked out the blade of his multitool. The lanyard was of woven boron monocrystal, nothing an ordinary knife would cut. Two quick strokes left the grommets still reeved to the line and the corner-cropped flag fluttering down into Daniel's hands.

Daniel tied the vivid silk as a sash around the waist of his mottled gray fatigues. The Governor probably meant to put him off-balance by not giving him time to dress for a formal reception. That was a clever move of its kind; as a tactician himself, Daniel could respect the subtlety of the mind which had devised it. But an RCN officer ought to be able to teach wogs a thing or two about field expedients!

"I'm very glad for the chance to meet his excellency the Governor," Daniel said as he strode to the boarding ladder. He mounted, glancing over his shoulder at the *Princess Cecile*.

Only someone very familiar with the corvette would have noticed the change from ten minutes earlier. The dorsal turret was still aligned with the ship's axis, but the twin plasma cannon were minusculely elevated from their locked position. In the best tradition of the RCN, Sun had his guns ready for whatever happened next.

CHAPTER 12

"Sit down, Mistress Mundy," said Admiral O'Quinn, gesturing Adele to a place that'd obviously been saved for her on a low circular bench draped with rugs. In the center was a small serving table holding glass carafes of wine and platters heaped with fruit, most of it unfamiliar. Two women and two men besides O'Quinn and Cousin Adrian were already seated. They wore RCN-style dress uniforms with the starburst of the Cluster replacing the winged sandal of Cinnabar; each had a chestful of garish, dangling, medals.

Adele's eyes took a moment to adjust to the lattice-shaded loggia. She kept her face emotionless, but the appearance of the others, the senior officers of the *Aristoxenos*, shocked her. Certainly it'd been sixteen years—and she herself was no longer the girl who'd just arrived on Bryce to study in the Academic Collections—but the officers gathered here looked not only older but unhealthy.

When Adele last saw her cousin, he'd been a noted fencer; now he was distinctly pudgy and the collar of his formal tunic pinched deep into the fat of his neck.

Broken veins spiderwebbed Admiral O'Quinn's nose; he was drinking wine from a twenty-ounce mug. The other four, the surviving members of the battleship's second through sixth lieutenants, were in comparable condition.

Servants stood at both ends of the loggia with more bottles of wine and fruit platters. They wore splashy, well-used clothes, often ill-fitting; cast-offs from their superiors, Adele realized. Adrian glanced at them and said, "Go on, get out of here! We need to talk privately!"

"But Lord Purvis?" said the servant with waxed mustachios who appeared to be the senior of those present. "If you need more—"

"Go on, damn you, get out!" Adrian snarled petulantly. "Do you think I couldn't have you bastinadoed, Aurelio?"

The servants crowded out the doors to the interior of the building, leaving them ajar. If Adrian really thought he was gaining privacy, he was a fool; but the chances were he was just salving his conscience by paying lip service to security concerns.

"Sit down," O'Quinn urged again, "and have some of this wine, mistress. It's nothing like what we had at home, but I find it palatable."

Adele stepped over the bench and seated herself carefully. The central table was low and three feet away, strictly for serving rather than dining. Two officers were eating what looked like miniature pomegranates; they spat the seeds onto the rugs layered over the floor.

Face as stiff as cast iron, Adele took the offered glass. It was a brandy snifter, but O'Quinn had poured it full of the same vintage he was drinking. She sipped. The flavor was interesting, though there was an earthy hint that she suspected would be an unpleasant companion the morning after drinking a quantity of the wine.

There was no likelihood of that, however, since

either the vintage was fortified or the sugar-converting bacteria here on Todos Santos were remarkably resistant to poisoning by the ethanol waste product. She didn't think, "You could fuel an engine with this!" because she knew full well that you couldn't; but she also knew that a mug the size of Admiral O'Quinn's would have her comatose before she reached the bottom.

"Tell us frankly, Mistress Mundy . . . ," said Bodo Williams, the Second Lieutenant. Her cheekbones stood out from tight-stretched skin. When her hands began to tremble she clasped them before her, but even that didn't completely control the shaking. "Tell us—did the Senate send you as their emissary to arrange the terms of our repatriation?"

Adele blinked. *Good God!* But it was a serious question, as serious to them as it seemed absurd to her. The six former RCN officers stared at her with a mixture of hope and desperation.

"Lieutenant Williams," Adele said carefully. "Admiral, all of you. . . ."

She set her glass on the floor beside her and took out her data unit to occupy her hands. The rugs weren't a firm surface, but obviously nobody else cared if the glass spilled.

"I'm not an envoy," Adele said bluntly, sweeping the fearful eyes with her own. She spoke with a hostile edge, an unintended but natural result of these people putting her in a ridiculous position. "Of the Senate, of anybody. I'm Adele Mundy, calling on my closest living relative—my mother's brother's son—when as a result of my private employment I found myself unexpectedly in the city where he lives."

She glared at Commander Purvis. "And Adrian?" she continued, "I'll note that I didn't expect my desire to see a relative would involve me in a conspiracy which was a demonstrably bad idea sixteen years ago!"

Adele hadn't known what she was going to say until the words came out of her mouth. She rose, sliding the data unit away. She'd taken it out to calm her as she gathered her thoughts, but now they blazed in a white fury that might require her to have her hands free. How *dare* these—

"Adele, we're not conspirators!" Adrian said, stepping toward her with his arms out. Adele jerked backward and the bench caught her knees. She toppled but Adrian grabbed her by the shoulders and held her upright.

"Adele, we're not conspirators," he repeated softly as he leaned away again, one hand still touching her arm. He was breathing hard. The others were on their feet also, all but Williams who'd fallen back to the bench and now braced herself on the serving table for another try. "We . . . when you came, we thought you might be coming for us. That's all."

Adele took a deep breath, then stepped over the bench. "I'm not leaving," she said, noticing the sudden misery on the faces of the gathered officers. "I just needed to get on the other side of this *damned* barricade."

She tapped the bench with her toe. She'd knocked over the wineglass, all right, and soaked the cuff of the one civilian suit she'd brought with her aboard the *Princess Cecile*. Not a matter of great moment, she supposed, but typical of other things.

"Forgive me for my discourtesy," Adele continued. Her reaction could have been worse: she hadn't drawn her pistol. "I understand your concern, but to the best of my knowledge—"

Which was very good knowledge indeed.

"—neither the government of Cinnabar nor the RCN more specifically have any active concern with the *Aristoxenos* and her crew. That's far in the past.

You can live your lives in as great an assurance of safety as—"

She smiled with the bleak humor that seasoned the dark parts of her life. Not long ago those parts had been almost all of her life.

"—any of us have in this existence."

"We thought . . . ," said Admiral O'Quinn, holding his big mug in both hands and staring into its empty depths. "That since you were . . . ?"

He looked up without finishing the sentence.

"Yes," said Adele crisply. "But that was coincidence. My stopover is merely because Todos Santos is a nexus for routes into the North, which my foreign employers wish to explore."

She smiled again with her usual quirky humor.

"Much the same reasons that brought you here in times past, I suppose," she added.

"But the captain of your ship is Speaker Leary's son!" said Estaing, who'd been—who probably still was—the battleship's Fourth Lieutenant. "If you're not the emissary, mistress, is he?"

"Mr. Estaing . . . ," Adele said in a cold voice. Estaing was a tall man, rangy and handsome in file imagery. He hadn't run as far to fat as some of the others, but he had the eyes of a ferret and a facial twitch as regular as a metronome. "I said you're safe. *No* one is searching for you. Not me, not Captain Leary, and not even the three women to whom you apparently promised marriage in the days leading up to the discovery of the Three Circles Conspiracy!"

That was probably more than a former RCN warrant officer, now on the beach, should have known about a man she'd never met. Still, she'd said it and had no real regrets. She'd read the files on the *Aristoxenos'* officers, not because she'd expected to meet them but because she was Adele Mundy and she

liked to know things. Politics aside, Lieutenant Estaing
was a pig.

Nobody spoke for a moment; Estaing flushed and
turned away.

"Adele," said Adrian. "Please—I think you're mis-
understanding. We aren't afraid of the Senate hunting
us down. We thought, you see, just possibly . . . that
Cinnabar was offering to let us return."

Oh good God, Adele thought, not for the first time
in this interview. She had to struggle to restrain a laugh,
instinctive protection against the horror of the situation that she'd just uncovered.

"Adrian," she said aloud, speaking as carefully as
she'd have chosen her footing across a muddy field.
"I can't speak to that, and I assure you Captain Leary
has no knowledge of the subject either. He's estranged
from his father, and he was never interested in politics anyway."

"But they allowed you back?" Adrian said. "And we
thought . . . ?"

"The Edict of Reconciliation was issued over a
decade ago," Adele said, speaking sharply so that her
words wouldn't be mistaken for agreement. "I had
occasion to read it carefully, as you might imagine.
The Edict specifically excepts certain categories of
people, in particular mutinous members of the RCN
and the Land Forces of the Republic who failed to
accept the terms of the amnesty within six months
of the offer."

"I told you!" said Tetrey, the Sixth Lieutenant; a
petite woman in old pictures, a mass of pasty flesh in
present reality. "I told you there was no way they'd take
us back, but you had to go ahead with this charade!"

"Well, what was the choice, you stupid cow?" Estaing
shouted. He raised his hand; Adele, blank-faced,
reached into her pocket.

"Mr. Estaing, sit down and be silent!" Adrian snapped. "Now, by God!"

Estaing didn't sit, but he grimaced and drew back from Tetrey. *A pig*, Adele thought, drawing another deep breath as her hand came out of her pocket empty.

"Sirs and ladies," she said, all eyes on her again. "I don't say that there's no chance of you returning to Cinnabar, just that the question has nothing to do with the arrival of the *Princess Cecile* on Todos Santos. I, ah, know some persons of influence in Xenos. When I'm next on Cinnabar, I'll make discreet inquiries if you'd like me to. But I can tell you nothing now beyond what you probably know already."

She cleared her throat. "If you'd indulge my curiosity?" she went on. "I don't understand precisely why you'd want to return. Your present situation—"

She let a sweep of her eyes take the place of a gesture.

"—appears comfortable, and at best . . . well, I'm sure you know that your property in the Republic was confiscated. In honesty, I can't imagine much of it would ever be returned; and even if it were, I doubt it would allow you to live in palaces like this one."

"Aye, Corder Leary doesn't have a palace like mine," Admiral O'Quinn said, seating himself heavily on the bench. He raised his mug reflexively, then remembered it was empty. He took the carafe by its handle, found it empty too, and glared. For a moment Adele thought the admiral was going to hurl one or the other across the room, but instead he relaxed and grinned at her sadly.

"I don't need a palace," he said. "Not here in the Cluster, anyhow. I want to go home, Mistress Mundy . . . and it doesn't look like that's going to happen. Not unless I want my head to decorate the Speaker's Rock."

"We're RCN!" Estaing said. "They won't humiliate us that way!"

"We *were* RCN," Adrian Purvis said. "Now we're pirates. And if it comes to that, I don't want to be hung at a formal ceremony in Harbor Three, either."

He turned to Adele. "Thank you for your candor, cousin," he said. "I . . . hope we'll have an opportunity to talk about old times later during your visit to Todos Santos; but not, I think, this afternoon."

"No," Adele said. "Good day, Adrian."

She nodded to include the other officers in her leave-taking, then opened the door and backed onto the stairway again. The bright sun struck her, but she was shivering as she started down toward the silent, watchful Tovera.

The officers of the *Aristoxenos* lived like princes—now. But the ruler who'd welcomed them was dead, and the battleship whose power they'd wielded was rusting away. Even if the Alliance didn't support the Commonwealth, there'd soon come a time when the wealth granted in former days was worth more to the new Governor than the support of a band of fat, aging foreigners.

"Mistress?" said Tovera, following in echelon as Adele strode for the gate.

"I don't know how we'll get transportation back to the ship," Adele murmured quietly, "but I didn't want to ask them for help. The less association we have with them, the better."

They walked through the archway. The guards rose, and the RCN spacer in charge doffed his cap to Adele.

"It was like being in a tomb," Adele said. She wasn't sure even Tovera could hear her. "It *was* a tomb. They're just not quite dead, yet."

❖   ❖   ❖

Daniel, standing on the east-facing balcony of the Governor's Palace, felt the roar of a ship lifting in the harbor behind him. The *Sissie's* Chief Engineer said over the commo helmet, *"I think Converter Three's performing below spec, sir. It's brand new or anyway was when we lifted from Tanais Base, but it's only running at 88%. Over."*

The balcony overlooked a canal; beyond a tugboat pushing a line of barges toward the harbor, the city of San Juan rose in irregular terraces. None of the buildings were very high, but three lofty aqueducts fell from the hills and marched across the city to the water plant near the palace.

"I think we'll leave it in place, Mr. Pasternak," Daniel said. "The unit doesn't seem to be failing, just low output. I wouldn't trust anything we found here to replace it. Keep an eye on things, and if necessary we'll take steps when we dock at Radiance or another major port. Out."

The ship had risen high enough above the palace that its exhaust glittered on the black water of the canal. In Xenos window glass would've been flashing also, but most of the houses here made do with lattices and louvers.

"Roger," Pasternak replied. *"Out."*

Birds no bigger than Daniel's outstretched finger fluttered about the balcony, snapping up crumbs from the snacks other loungers were eating. They had six limbs: four wings, attached at either end of the torso, and a pair of legs in the middle. It'd taken Daniel a moment to realize that the odd fluting he heard wasn't the wind in the rooftiles but rather the birds themselves; he looked forward to checking . . . well, having Adele check . . . the natural history database in the *Princess Cecile's* computer.

Daniel had expected that being rushed to the

palace meant he'd be ushered in to Governor Sakama immediately, but when he'd climbed the broad marble staircase to the Governor's public apartments, the guard at the open door of the Hall of Audience stopped him. He had the choice of standing in the huge circular anteroom which dwarfed the hundred or more military and civilian officials who lounged or strolled in small groups within, or going out onto the balcony which ran the full width of the building.

Daniel went outside and got on with the business of the *Princess Cecile*. He could oversee Mr. Pasternak as well by spread-band radio as he could looking over the engineer's shoulder, and he simply wasn't going to let this silliness bother him. If he'd been an RCN officer on active service, of course, he might have had to take steps. . . .

He felt the presence of someone approaching and turned his head. He expected it was another of the beggars who seemed to be allowed on the balcony but not the anteroom; instead a soldier with a paunch and a spreading white beard said, "Spacer Leary? The Governor will receive you now."

Daniel raised the visor of his commo helmet as he followed the soldier through the anteroom. If the Governor'd given him time to dress, he'd be wearing more formal headgear than this. Now he wondered whether he should doff it as he would the saucer hat of his Whites, or if it was better to pretend the helmet was just part of his head; which it was, pretty generally, while the *Sissie* was under weigh. He decided he'd keep the helmet on.

His guide stopped beside the guard at the door to the Hall of Audience. Daniel stopped also. "Go on!" the soldier said with an angry gesture. "The Governor's waiting!"

Daniel stepped through, smiling faintly. These foreigners got themselves into such a state. . . .

The hall's arched ceiling was a good thirty feet high in the center and covered to the clerestory windows with florid paintings. Mythology, Daniel supposed: agreeably fleshy women wearing not much, and men of a similar sort—albeit less agreeable. He could've studied the figures all day in close-up through his face-shield's magnification and they wouldn't have meant any more to him than what he'd gotten with a cursory glance.

He'd bet Adele could tell who the figures were and who painted them besides, though. Quite a remarkable woman, that. He and the RCN—and probably the other people she worked for besides—were damned lucky to have Adele Mundy on their side.

When Daniel looked into the Hall of Audience on his arrival, Governor Sakama had been sitting at the far end of the eighty-foot room, talking with half a dozen locals in uniforms or formal robes. Nothing had changed, save that Sakama and his entourage were all watching Daniel approach at a deliberate pace. Cushioned benches were built into all four sides of the room but save for that group—the Governor seated, his courtiers standing in front of him, and a scattering of servants at a discreet distance—no one else was present.

Because Sakama Hideki had succeeded his father Sakama Iyoshi a few years previous, Daniel had a mental impression of Hideki being a young man; in fact he was in his late fifties: swarthy, thin-featured, and as alert as a hawk. The courtiers were a mixed bag. The civilians, two men and a woman in lace-embroidered robes, looked sharp. One of the men held a portable data unit that from where Daniel stood could've been a duplicate of Adele's.

On the other hand, the three military officials, all male, weren't prepossessing. Daniel noticed that their pistol holsters were empty, but a sub-machine gun of Cinnabar manufacture rested on the bench beside the Governor.

Daniel marched to within six feet of where the Sakama waited, halted, and from instinct—it wasn't anything he'd planned—struck an Academy brace and saluted. "Sir!" he said. "Lieutenant Daniel Leary of Cinnabar, at your service."

When his brain took time to analyze it, Daniel decided it'd been the proper thing to do as well as the right one. The Governor almost certainly had a high military rank as well as the civil title he went by, so a reserve officer of the RCN *should* salute him on meeting. But when there isn't time for analysis, you have to go by instinct. Daniel's instinct had taken him safe through several battles, and the present situation might not be far short of another one. You couldn't tell with foreigners. . . .

"The Cluster is pleased at your visit, Captain Leary," Sakama said. His voice rasped as though his vocal cords were scarred. "Perhaps you would care for some refreshment? I can summon a boy with wine or perhaps an assortment of nuts? Terran maranha nuts grown here in the soil of Todos Santos are a great delicacy on Cinnabar, I'm told."

"Thank you, your excellency," Daniel said, then went on to the lie, "but I'd just finished eating when your invitation arrived. Your planet appears a marvelous place, and I'm looking forward to sampling its delights as soon as I've accomplished my duties to the vessel I command."

"Yes, it's your duties that my advisors and I wanted to speak with you about, Captain Leary," Sakama said. The female civilian and one of the military officers were staring at Daniel in a combination of rage and loathing, but the remainder of the courtiers kept their eyes averted.

The Governor drew on the long, amber stem of his pipe while he continued to smile at Daniel. "You are the son of Speaker Leary, are you not? It is perhaps not a coincidence that you've come to the Cluster at this time?"

Daniel pursed his lips. He dropped from his brace into Parade Rest, his hands crossed behind his back. The perfumed tobacco smoke tickled his nose, and he didn't want to sneeze.

"My father is Corder Leary, yes, your excellency," he said, keeping his tone mild and completely emotionless. "But my family relationships have nothing to do with my presence on Todos Santos at the moment. I'm in the private employ of two nobles from Novy Sverdlovsk who want to visit unfrequented corners of the Galactic North. I recommended we put into Todos Santos to refit the yacht after her run from Cinnabar."

He didn't mention their intention to put in at Radiance also, though it must be obvious to the Governor. Most of the Galactic North could be described as unfrequented, with few docks other than those of Todos Santos and Radiance capable of performing major repairs to a starship.

Sakama leaned forward. "You know that the Council of the Commonwealth is in league with the Alliance now, don't you?" he said. "That's a threat to the Cluster, certainly; but a threat to you in Cinnabar as well. Not so?"

"Your excellency . . . ," Daniel said, speaking with the careful sincerity of truth. "I don't know anything about such a league. If such a thing is true—"

"It is true!" said the official holding the data unit.

"They have a base on Gehenna and will send a huge fleet there shortly. Battleships and many other ships!"

"Do you think we don't know what goes on in Radiance?" the female official said harshly. "But how are we to stop it? This is your fault, your war with the Alliance, but we're the ones who'll pay for your failure to act!"

"Madam," said Daniel, deliberately turning his head and lifting it slightly to look down his nose at her. "If there's information which the Republic needs to know, then I'm sure that the proper parties know it. You'll have to direct your questions elsewhere, however, because I'm not one of those people myself."

But Adele is, unless I'm very badly mistaken.

He fixed Governor Sakama with his gaze. Daniel knew perfectly well that the fellow could have him taken out and shot, or perhaps shoot him personally with that sub-machine gun; it was a working weapon, not a gilded and engraved toy.

Daniel said in a firm voice, "So, your excellency— I'm honored that you requested my presence to clear up that little misconception. If you have questions that I *can* answer, I'd be more than happy to. Otherwise, I won't impose on your time. Eh?"

It didn't do to show weakness, except with the girls who thought weakness was the same as sensitivity. In Daniel's experience weakness was usually the same as self-absorption, but he was willing to wear any suitable camouflage on a hunt. Which he'd be doing as soon as he got back to the *Princess Cecile* and made sure she was settled to a degree that allowed her captain to take some liberty himself . . . if he got back alive.

"We didn't request Mr. Leary's presence in order to hector him, Ayesha," the Governor said with a frown. The catch in his throat made the words sound harsher than perhaps they were meant, but Sakama's look wasn't one that Daniel would want an autocrat directing at him.

The woman, Ayesha, must have felt the same way. She fell to her knees and prostrated herself, catching Daniel's ankles before he could jump back. "Your pardon, gracious lord!" she said, speaking into the rug-covered floor. "My life is yours to command."

"Get up, please!" Daniel said, shocked and disgusted. The woman was twice his age, powerful, and—judging from the words if not the tone of her complaint—obviously intelligent. *She shouldn't be abasing herself!*

To the Governor he added, "Really, your excellency, we in the Republic of Cinnabar pride ourselves on a frank exchange of views. I took no offense."

Neither part of that disclaimer was wholly true. Had the woman as ambassador to Cinnabar used that tone on Speaker Leary, he'd have had her flogged on the Senate floor while his fellow Senators applauded. But Ayesha's fear seemed to be of worse than a flogging, and *that* was uncalled for.

You could never tell what wogs would do. They might even decided to murder the son of a powerful Cinnabar politician. . . .

Sakama leaned forward slightly, his eyes fixed on Daniel. "Captain Leary?" he said in a whisper that made Daniel think of a cat playing with something alive. "You say you're sure that proper persons are dealing with the matter of the Alliance building a naval base on Gehenna. *How* are you sure?"

"Your excellency," Daniel said, "I know as little as you do about the workings of the Republic's high political levels. Less, perhaps, because it was never a matter of interest to me even when I was on polite terms with my father. Which I have not been for these past seven years."

He paused for effect. He'd let his voice rise slightly as he fell into the rhythms of a speech to the *Sissie's* crew, convincing his listeners of the importance of what he was saying and his utter sincerity in saying it.

"But I do know that the Republic of Cinnabar has for a thousand years supported her friends and defeated her enemies," Daniel continued. *Sometimes those enemies were the friends of the past who'd found the burdens of friendship with the Republic too onerous; but this was a stump speech, not a lecture.* "If there's something that the rulers of the Republic should know, they know it. I have no idea how that's accomplished, but I trust the system that has risen from strength to strength for a millennium!"

If the Governor and his advisors decided Daniel Leary was a rabid Cinnabar patriot with nothing in his head but the formless assurance that his country would triumph, they would send him back to his proper business . . . as Daniel intended they should. If Sakama recognized that Daniel had been speaking cold, rational truth as well—that wasn't a bad thing either.

Sakama leaned back on his cushions with a sigh and a grimace. "You may leave, Captain," he said. He waved a hand in dismissal. "Perhaps another will come from Xenos, who knows more and can say more."

As Daniel turned to return to the door with the same measured stride that brought him to the Governor, he heard the counselor with the data unit say morosely, "Perhaps. But even if it's very soon, it may be too late!"

CHAPTER 13

The alley was too narrow for even the three-wheeled cyclo which'd brought Hogg and Daniel to the produce market where they'd lounged by the well curb, taking in the sights and waiting. Latticed wooden balconies built out from the upper stories almost met overhead. The passage kinked to the left some thirty feet from where they stood at its junction with the road to the harbor.

"Can't say I like it," Hogg muttered. In his loose garments and broad-brimmed hat he could've passed for a local man, at least after the shadows got a little longer. "Could be six guys waiting right round that corner to teach you not to fool with the local women."

"That's why you're with me, Hogg," Daniel said equably, shrugging in the gray cape he'd donned over his 1st Class uniform when they left the market. His Whites and glittering medals were the lure with which he'd trolled the market. He'd smiled faintly but he hadn't spoken except to murmur apologies when bumped, and he'd avoided eye contact, particularly with women.

After one pass through the market, he and Hogg settled to wait. They hadn't needed to wait very long.

Daniel glanced around. There was traffic on the main road, but nobody paid special attention to the two of them. Whistling a snatch from "Abel Brown the Spacer," he stepped into the alley. *I'll drink your wine and eat your pies, I'll screw you blue and black your eyes. . . ."*

"*And* her husband may be home waiting for her and her not knowing it," Hogg said.

"Quite true, Hogg," Daniel agreed, pausing to listen before stepping under the first of the louvered balconies. He heard muted voices from within the house, but there was nothing of concern to him.

Shopping was women's work on Todos Santos, but there were many men in the produce market: stallkeepers, servants, and the bodyguards accompanying women of high station. There were also a few young men who, like Daniel, avoided contact with both the crowd of shoppers and with one another. Those fellows were all well got up, but none of them had a costume as vivid as RCN Dress Whites. A billet with written instructions had dropped from a puffed sleeve into Daniel's lap before he'd been half an hour in the market.

"You know, master," Hogg continued, "there's professionals here in San Juan too. They're a whole lot cheaper than having your dick sewed back on might be."

Daniel passed an inset doorway on the left. He heard the balcony above him creak as someone's weight shifted, but nobody spoke. He and Hogg were past the bend in the alley now.

"Tell me, Hogg," Daniel said in a low voice as they proceeded. *The third doorway*, the note said. That would be the one to the right, beneath a second-story balcony. "When you were growing up on Bantry, did your family buy meat at the Servants' Store?"

Hogg snorted. "Not unless Pap was too hung over to walk his snares," he said. "And after I turned six or so, not even then. Who'd want to eat chicken when the tree hoppers were fat on nuts?"

He chuckled and added, "And aye, I understand. Who knows? The maid what passed you the note didn't look half bad herself."

Daniel stopped at the third doorway. It *ought* to be the right one, but . . . The note didn't say, *Knock*, or *Whistle* or whatever, and there wasn't an eyeslit in the heavy panel. Which was odd unless—

He looked up. There was a giggle from the balcony; a trap door in the balcony floor opened inward. Daniel caught a glimpse of lace, then a bundle of sticks dropped down unraveling as it fell. It was a ladder of battens hung on cords.

"Keep an eye on things if you please, Hogg," Daniel said in a low voice. He gave the ladder a practice tug. Then, with a quick glance around, he started up. He'd have swung wildly if Hogg hadn't belayed the bottom of the ladder, but the silk-and-bamboo construction was certainly strong enough.

The trap door wasn't meant for anybody quite so bulky as Daniel Leary wearing his dress uniform under a cloak. He squirmed, angling his torso into the enclosed balcony. Light entered through lattices, softening everything into a world apart from the street outside. Perfume clung to the wood, and more giggles sounded from the dim interior of the house proper.

Daniel and every other member of the *Sissie*'s crew carried an emergency communicator while on liberty. The plate now buzzed. For a moment Daniel fought the urge to ignore it, but they'd only call him in a real emergency.

"Are you coming, Mr. Officer?" breathed a voice from just out of sight inside the house.

Daniel sighed and slid the flat communicator from his sash. "Six here," he said. "Go ahead."

Adele sat at her console, her data unit on her lap. Her wands twitched across information she'd collected through the *Princess Cecile*'s antennas and had processed with a navigational computer which in minutes or less could calculate courses across the universes of the Matrix. She smiled as she worked, as happy as she was capable of being. Certainly she was content, which was all she'd ever asked from life.

"*General quarters!*" ordered Woetjans, the watch officer. "*There's an aircar approaching, a big one! Over!*"

Adele switched her display to an optical pickup on the corvette's hull. If she could just find the vehicle identification code, she could search for the owner through the mass of data she'd collected. . . .

Crewmen ran down the corridors to their action stations. "Bessing!" somebody shouted on B Deck, his voice echoing up the companionway. "Get the arms locker open! Where's Bessing?"

Bessing, a rigger who was striking for an armorer's rating under Sun—now on liberty—was already sprinting down the corridor to the locker adjacent to the Battle Center. The electronic key was in his hand.

"*Everybody return to duty!*" Woetjans said. "*It's the Countess and there's nobody with her. Bridge out.*"

Adele didn't understand why the Klimovna was returning alone, but it was no cause for concern; least of all to Adele Mundy. She went back to her own affairs, downloading the files involving the Cluster Naval Self-Defense Force. Nobody'd asked her for the information, but at some future date Daniel or Mistress

Sand—or someone at present unknown—*might* ask about the Cluster's navy. Because Adele was who she was, she gathered the information now.

Also there was the matter of the *Goldenfels*. The Alliance freighter was sealed against Adele's devices, so she was methodically searching all the Cluster files involved with the vessel. The bureaucrats' records, official and otherwise, would provide a good start on the data she wanted.

"Good afternoon, Countess," Tovera said in a loud voice.

Adele jumped internally, suddenly aware that someone—that the Klimovna—stood beside the signals console. Adele compressed her display, though it was only a blur of light from any angle but that to her own eyes, and looked up.

The Countess smiled down at her. "You appear to concentrate, Mistress Mundy," she said.

"Yes," said Adele. "It's the only way I know to accomplish anything."

The Countess sat sideways on the couch of the gunnery console, continuing to smile. Adele noticed that she hadn't responded to Tovera's greeting. Granted, Tovera had been warning Adele of the foreigner's presence, but she still deserved a response.

"You work very hard," the Klimovna said, ignoring what Adele had meant for a blunt warning that she was busy. "You've only been off this tiny boat one time since we've landed, have you?"

Adele's eyes narrowed. The short answer would've been, "Yes," though the fact hadn't occurred to Adele until the other woman mentioned it.

Still, Adele's duties to Mistress Sand required at least the passive cooperation of the *Princess Cecile*'s new owners. Aloud she said, "Countess, some of the most beautiful and historic buildings in the human universe are libraries, and I've been privileged to work in the best of them. While I'm working, though, I'm aware of nothing but data and the means by which I access it."

She gestured, then continued, "My console provides me with that in a more readily accessible form than I could find anywhere else on this planet."

Except just possibly at a similar installation on the *Goldenfels*.

"Countess, you say countess!" the Klimovna said with a moue and a shake of her head. "Please, call me Valentina. I should like that we be friends."

She paused, staring intently at Adele, then continued, "You are not the jealous sort, I think? Are you, Adele?"

"What?" said Adele in puzzlement. Light dawned, bringing a broad—perhaps tactless—smile to her face. "Ah, I understand. Ah, Valentina, at the risk of mistaking where this conversation is headed, let me assure you that I have no physical relationship with Lieutenant Leary—with Daniel. I've never had such a relationship."

"But . . . ?" said the Klimovna. "You seem . . . ?"

"We're friends," said Adele. "Daniel happens to be a tenant of the house I own in Xenos. But to be more frank with you than our slight acquaintance warrants—"

And to cut short a conversation that Adele found extremely distasteful.

"—I've never been interested in a man—or woman— in that fashion. Whereas Daniel, so far as I've seen, has never been interested in a woman as old as I am. That's thirty-two standard years, Valentina."

She paused, holding the other woman's eyes, then added, "I'm only seventeen years younger than you are."

The Klimovna jerked back as though struck. In fact

a slap probably wouldn't have shocked her as badly as that bit of precise knowledge did. Well, she'd forced Adele into an unpleasant conversation, so she could take the consequences of it.

"Piffle!" the Klimovna said after a long moment, rubbing her hands hard on the thighs of her pants suit. "Men are fools, some of them. What can some young bubblehead offer them, compared to an experienced woman of the world, eh?"

"I'm sure I don't know," Adele said dryly. Then, because it was an aspect of the matter that had irritated her too—though improperly—during her friendship with Daniel, she added, "Though it appears that the bubbleheadedness is at least part of the attraction. I won't even speculate why."

"Piffle," the Klimovna repeated, staring at the outer bulkhead with a disgusted expression. She rose to her feet, her hands interlaced behind her back. She didn't leave, though, as Adele first thought—and hoped—but simply looked away.

She turned back to Adele abruptly. "I suppose my husband's still out?" she said.

"So far as I know," Adele agreed, "though you should check with the watch officer to be sure. I thought the two of you were together."

"Faugh!" said the Klimovna. "Georgi likes to drink and gamble and who knows what? Why would I want to watch that? I bought an aircar to replace the other one."

She waved her hand. *To replace the one you crashed*, Adele amended, but silently.

"Daniel's man Hogg arranged it," the Klimovna continued. "A very clever fellow, Hogg. I wonder if he would care to serve me in place of his present master?"

"I doubt it," said Adele dryly.

"I don't think Hogg would cut your throat for asking," said Tovera unexpectedly. It was like having the chair itself speak. "But he might. Hogg's quite an interesting fellow—as servants go."

"I take Tovera's point," Adele said, raising her voice to speak through any chance that the Klimovna was going to say the wrong thing. "It would be unwise to raise the question with Hogg. Old family loyalties, you know. I suppose you have the same thing on Novy Sverdlovsk?"

The Klimovna sniffed. "At home, servants know their place," she said, but she wasn't looking at either Tovera or Adele when she said it. "Anyway, I bought this car from a store of unclaimed goods. Hogg introduced me to the warehouse manager."

Did he indeed? Adele thought, struggling to keep a straight face. Well, it was no business of hers. Knowing Hogg, the *Princess Cecile* would have left Todos Santos long before any owner returned to claim his property.

Because Adele had reduced her display, a small red asterisk appeared in the air over the data unit. She closed her lips over the polite fluff she'd been creating to offer Klimovna—small talk must be easier for other people—and brought the display up to full size.

Oh. Oh! That must mean—

"Ship, this is Loppy, I'm with the Count only he's upstairs," said a voice. *"We got a situation here and we're going to need help bloody damned quick. Over."*

Because the call was on an emergency channel, it got a priority routing to the bridge and the Battle Center as well as to Adele's console. The call plates every spacer on liberty carried were meant for recall by the ship. The plates' outgoing transmissions generally carried only a half mile or so.

Adele had directed the ship's technicians to adjust

the plates' programming to use the relay system that carried messages for the Governor's Guard, giving them full two-way capability. For ordinary crewmen that didn't matter a great deal—the establishments serving their needs were generally well within a half mile of the harbor. The detachment escorting Count Klimov would've been out of touch without the modification, though, as would Captain Leary himself.

"*Loppy, this is Woetjans,*" said the bosun. As watch officer she was using the command console, but the couch was adjusted to Daniel's height. It made a clumsy match for Woetjans' raw-boned frame. "*Go ahead.*"

"*Top, we're in a fancy club, dunno what the name of it is,*" Rigger Loppinger said. "*It's not just a bar and a knock shop, the Count's upstairs in the card room playing with the captain of the* Goldenfels. *You remember—*"

"*I remember,*" the bosun said grimly. "*Spit it out, spacer!*"

Adele's wands flickered. She'd already queued a recall signal; now she called up the triangulated location of Loppy's call and superimposed it on files from San Juan's chief of police. The establishment was the Anyo Nuevo; and judging from the amount it paid in bribes each week, it was a very upscale place indeed.

"*Top, the Count's cleaning out the bastard from Pleasaunce,*" the rigger said. "*He'll own his back teeth in a little bit. They wouldn't let us in the card room, but I could hear it through the doorway. Thing is, there's twenty spacers from the Goldenfels drinking down in the bar here, and I don't think their captain's going to let the Count go home with his money. Can you get us some help? Over.*"

The Klimovna was speaking, had been speaking for some while. Adele was only vaguely aware of her, the way she heard the hum of the corvette's fusion bottle on D Deck. Tovera had backed the older woman away so that she wouldn't brush Adele with a sweep of her arms.

Woetjans turned awkwardly on the couch. Her face was anguished. "Mistress?" she called across the bridge to Adele. In an emergency riggers like her didn't think about radio communication. "Can you raise the captain, because—"

"Six here," Daniel said, answering the summons Adele had sent as soon as Loppinger mentioned the *Goldenfels*. *"Go ahead."*

"Woetjans, I'll take this," Adele said, bringing a look of relief to the bosun's face. "Daniel, Count Klimov is playing cards with Captain Bertram of the *Goldenfels* in the Anyo Nuevo, whose coordinates I've downloaded to you. The game will shortly result in violence. Bertram has twenty spacers with him and his ship has a total crew of three hundred and fifty-six, according to the amount the port medical inspector just paid into his private account to clear the ship from quarantine. Ah, over."

She was sure how many crew the *Goldenfels* carried because she'd compared the payment to that made for the hundred and twenty-seven passengers and crew aboard the *Princess Cecile*. Cheating a government was one thing. Cheating an official personally by shorting his bribe was something else, and much more dangerous.

Daniel whistled, a sound which the recall plate only partially transmitted. *"That's no freighter!"* he said. *"The* Goldenfels *must be an auxiliary cruiser."*

In a different tone but with almost the same breath he continued, *"Very well, sound recall."*

Adele acted as she heard the words, nodding assent to the bosun.

"Woetjans, how many men are aboard the Sissie *now? Over."*

"Twenty-four either on watch," Woetjans said, *"or back from liberty early. But those're in bad shape some of 'em, over."*

"Very good," said Daniel. "Can you lay on transport? Because if we have to run a mile and a half to this bar, we're none of us going to be in good shape. Over."

"The aircar," said Adele.

"Right, the lady's back with an aircar!" Woetjans said. *"I shouldn't wonder we could fit twelve in her—she's a big sucker. Over."*

"Yes," said Daniel. "Woetjans, take nine and yourself. Stop to pick me up at—"

"Daniel, I've downloaded the coordinates," Adele said hastily.

"Roger, me and Hogg," Daniel resumed. *"No guns. Adele, take charge until Mr. Chewning reports back. Six out."*

Woetjans was on her feet bellowing, gathering personnel both with her raw voice and over the ship's PA system. "Daniel!" said Adele before he broke the connection. "Do you want me and Tovera—or just Tovera?"

"Good God no!" Daniel replied, his voice strained as if he were doing something physically demanding while still holding the call plate in one hand. *"Adele, if there's shooting in this city, you can depend on it that the Governor's troops will execute everybody they catch. Just don't let anybody from the* Goldenfels *aboard the* Sissie, *and make* damned *sure the guns're manned. Over."*

"Over, Daniel," Adele said. "Out."

She leaned back in her couch and closed her eyes, feeling suddenly empty. There was a good deal happening, but she herself had nothing to do except wait.

The Klimovna's voice penetrated the mental barriers Adele had set up when she had no time to deal with trivia. Adele opened her eyes. "Madam," she said.

"Your husband is in trouble over a card game. Captain Leary and some of the crew are on their way to extricate him. Ah, they'll be taking your aircar."

Bessing was seated at the gunnery display. Nobody was at the command console or the missile board, but the three senior ratings in the Battle Direction Center could handle anything up through lifting ship, Adele supposed.

"Georgi *will* play," the Klimovna said. She made a moue. "So clever, he thinks himself."

She looked sharply at Adele. "He will be all right?" she said. "Tell me the truth."

Adele met the older woman's eyes, her face expressionless. "Yes," she said at last. "I think the Count will be all right. Daniel—Captain Leary—will send him back in the aircar, I expect."

But will Daniel be all right with hundreds of Alliance spacers baying for his blood? Adele thought.

Oh. Yes, of course. There *was* an answer.

Adele's wands flickered as she entered the maze of local communications systems. There were six simply for the San Juan district, two of them surprisingly sophisticated. There was no common system even for the military. The army, the navy, and the Governor's Guard were all separate.

The Klimovna was speaking again somewhere close by in the background. Adele found the node she needed and entered it, bypassing the firewall. She took a deep breath and began to speak.

Barnes, swearing like the spacer he'd been for the past twenty years, deliberately slammed the aircar hard on the street. The overloaded vehicle bounced upward on a combination of momentum and air compressed by the fans in surface effect. The huge cloud of dust looked like a bomb blast, but they cleared the furniture van whose driver had kept right on coming out of the sidestreet when he saw the aircar hurtling down the boulevard a bare seven feet above the rutted surface.

Daniel'd braced himself against the dashboard, but the weight of husky spacers behind him slammed him hard anyway. His ribs didn't crack, so it was cheap at the price.

Barnes wasn't a good driver in the conventional sense, but his very ham-fistedness made him exactly what the present situation required. There was no way to do a neat job of flying a six-place aircar with fourteen spacers aboard. Unlike a better driver, Barnes wasn't disconcerted by the number of skidding collisions they'd had on the way to the Anyo Nuevo.

Barnes was a big man, handy with a club or his fists. That was good too, as was the fact Woetjans brought twelve in the car instead of ten like Daniel ordered. He hadn't put them out on the street when he and Hogg squeezed aboard, and now that they'd arrived at their destination he was glad for the bosun's better judgment.

It'd been a near thing, though. *Bloody* near, he'd thought when he saw the van nosing straight across their path.

"Turn right at the next intersection and stop!" Daniel said, his left hand on Barnes' shoulder to get his attention. He was watching the road through a street map projected as a thirty percent mask on his faceshield. A moving red bead indicated the aircar, a gold one their intended destination.

Barnes tried to corner and tried to stop, each with partial success. The streets joined at more than a right angle, and they had the speed up to keep the overweight car from dropping like an anchor. At the last instant Barnes did the best thing possible, jerking the steering yoke hard right so that they were banked at 45 degrees when they slammed into the front of a food stall, then caromed off before bouncing to a halt.

Locals who'd a moment ago been gaping at the vehicle coming toward them on screaming fans scattered like a covey of birds. Daniel was pretty sure the aircar hadn't hit anybody—all the people he could see were running and cursing at the top of their lungs— but the good Lord knew there'd be damage claims from at least the stall-holder whose soup tureens were sprayed across her back wall. That was a matter for later, and for Count Klimov—if they got him out alive.

"This way!" Daniel shouted, forcing his way up against the weight of several spacers using his body to launch themselves out of the moaning vehicle. "And keep out of sight till I'm through the door!"

Daniel handed Hogg the commo helmet Woetjans had brought for him, donned his gleaming white saucer cap—slightly squished in the controlled crash of their landing—and straightened his rows of medal ribbons. When Daniel was as presentable as possible under the circumstances, he strode into an alley whose sides he could've brushed with both elbows. Twenty feet down he knocked at the metal back door of the Anyo Nuevo.

The door didn't have a peephole, but the diode on a thumb-sized camera clipped to the transom went red. "Name?" squeaked a sexless voice from the camera's speaker.

"Daniel Leary of Bantry," Daniel said, brushing the name tape on his left breast: LEARY in gold letters against the white cloth. "The password is 'Lusiads,' whatever that means."

And your name is Ramon Echevaria, he thought. *My signals officer has told me absolutely everything on record about this house.*

"You're not on the list," the voice said in puzzlement. "Who recommended you?"

"Commander Adrian Purvis," Daniel lied nonchalantly. "My cousin."

"All right, get out of the way," said the voice. "The door opens out."

Daniel moved sideways as he heard the bolts withdraw. The door—goodness, it was two inches thick and solid metal!—whined open on hydraulic rams. Echevaria, a small man with a goatee, sat on a cushioned chair, watching a hologram involving two women and a wombat.

Daniel grabbed him by the throat, not hard until Echevaria tried to reach the holstered pistol hanging from his chair. Hogg thrust a wedge of tool steel—an antenna lock—into the door hinge and waved forward the spacers waiting at the head of the alley.

"I got him, master," said Hogg as he wired Echevaria's wrists together. "Now listen—if you're a good little wog and don't make a peep, I'll cut you free when I come back by. If you start screaming, I'll pull your tongue out instead. Understand?"

Daniel started up the stairs to the private room on the third floor, above the saloon at ground level and the women's apartments on the floor above. He wasn't sure Hogg would bother to free the doorman if he stayed quiet, but he'd bet his hopes for a captaincy that the rest of Hogg's promise was real.

Amber-colored rods inset into the wainscoting lighted the stairs. Figures of a darker golden color danced in their depths. There wasn't a door at the top, only a plush drapery. Daniel pushed it aside and stepped through, leaving Hogg behind in the archway.

Daniel expected to arouse attention when he entered, but the twenty or so people already present were focused on the table at the edge of the lush room.

A house man sat on the side, dealing five-card stud to Count Klimov at one end across from a short, trim man with brush-cut hair—Captain Bertram. The Alliance officer wore a suit of lace ruffles over puce that made him look like a clown. Daniel knew that the civilian outfit was the height of fashion on Pleasaunce, so far on the cutting edge that it'd been only just beginning to be copied on Xenos when the *Sissie* lifted.

Chandeliers of rainbow-colored pinpoints twinkled to light the room. Hangings of monochrome plush covered the walls in thick folds to deaden noise. The roulette table in the center was untenanted; the croupier, a sultry woman in a fishnet top, held her rake as she watched the poker game. Half those present were staff, but like the patrons they were now merely spectators around the poker table.

The top cards were face down. Klimov looked at his and said, "Up twenty."

He deliberately added stacks of gold markers, five and five and five and five, to the considerable amount already on the table before him. He had three queens showing. Bertram had the nine and ten of hearts and the seven of clubs.

Daniel scanned the room quickly, making a keep-back gesture to Hogg with his left hand. Only high rollers and the house staff had access to this sanctum. None of the spacers escorting Klimov and Bertram were present, nor did the other gamblers have servants with them. Two heavies stood at the stairs to the lower floors. Although they were well-groomed, they weren't there to serve drinks.

The Alliance officer glowered and took a fierce drag on his cigar, making the tip glow like a demon's eye. He glanced at the palm of his left hand, seemingly empty, and said, "Yes, all right. I call."

Bertram shoved out chips with an angry, nervous

motion. Some of his bet was in gold, some in violet, and the rest in a scatter of lesser colors. Daniel didn't know what the denominations were, but judging from the way everybody watched the poker table he could venture a guess.

The dealer's hands fluttered over the final bet, taking the house percentage. The motion was as swift as sunlight glancing on the ripples of a pond.

"So," said Klimov equably. He turned over his top card, a five of clubs.

"So!" said Bertram. He snapped up the jack of spades and the eight of diamonds, then leaned back and took a long drag on his cigar. "My straight beats your three queens!"

Klimov turned up his hole card, the fourth queen.

The Alliance captain gave a disbelieving gasp. He stared into his left palm again, then jumped to his feet. "That's not a queen, it's the ace of spades!" he shouted. "You think you'll cheat me, you hog-fucking hayseed?"

Bertram reached under the blouse of his tunic and started to come out with a gun. Spectators scrambled back like roaches startled by a light. Daniel went through them like a ball scattering ten-pins.

"Sissies to me!" he shouted, catching Bertram's gunhand and elbow. He bent the wrist backward till the gun came loose and Bertram's call, "Alliance! Alliance!" turned to a scream.

The toughs at the door had either missed Bertram's gun or been paid to miss it. Now they jumped out of the way instead of trying to stop the solid mass of Alliance spacers coming up the stairs. There were more than twenty, that Daniel could see in the brief glance he got as he lifted Bertram over his head and hurled him down the stairwell.

"Get your fucking ass outa the way, master!" Hogg shouted. Daniel threw himself to the side. Woetjans

and half a dozen more Sissies went by and with an
explosive grunt—

*Good God almighty, they had the roulette table on
its side! A thousand pounds of baize and dark, lustrous
wood if it weren't twice that heavy!*

—sent their huge missile into the faces of the
Alliance spacers trapped in the stairwell.

Lights hidden in the curtain valences came on, flood-
ing the room brilliantly. The last of the dozen Sissies
were coming through the back door, holding clubs and
looking for somebody to fight. There weren't any
hostiles left at the moment. A doorman who'd stumbled
into Dasi while trying to dodge the roulette table
might need surgery to remove his balls from his chest
cavity, though.

"Hogg, where's my—" Daniel began, but before he
got the rest of the question out of his mouth Hogg
tossed him the commo helmet he'd stuffed into a cargo
pocket. Hogg's trousers and loose tunics could hold—
and often had held, to Daniel's certain knowledge from
when he was a boy on Bantry—whole coveys of game
birds without a soul realizing the fact by glancing at
the hick with the slack-jawed grin.

He settled the helmet in place as he turned. Woetjans had the Count with one arm around his waist and
the other gripping the opposite shoulder. Neither of
Klimov's feet touched the ground in the normal fashion but his right boot tapped down occasionally as
Woetjans headed for the back stairs as planned.

Klimov must figure to cash out some time, though
it wouldn't be tonight; he'd swept up the chips before
the bosun grabbed him. That was fair, he'd won the
hand, but there was *something* screwy about the
game. . . .

Which could wait for more leisure than Daniel had
right at this moment. "Six-three—that's you, Adele—

get the men from the bar clear," he said. "We're coming out the back way with the Count. He'll fly back—"

If the car was still flyable; which it likely was, carrying just Klimov's weight and that of a couple spacers as driver and escort.

"—while the rest of us return overland. Out."

Four Sissies watched the stairs down which they'd thrown the roulette table. Daniel glanced past them. Save for sprawled bodies, none of the Alliance spacers were closer than the first landing. They had their captain, Daniel'd seen to that, so there wasn't any reason to continue the fight except for honor—but that was a good enough reason, maybe the only good reason there was. With luck the roulette table would dampen their ardor enough to give the Sissies enough of a head start, though.

"Stand clear!" Daniel said to the self-appointed rear guard. They stepped sideways and he hurled a chair at the faces peering up from the landing. It struck the wall and shattered, flinging splinters and bits of delicate inlays in all directions.

"When I give the word," he continued in a low voice to his spacers, "we'll cross the room and head down the back stairs after the others. Ready?"

Shouts and the deadened crunch of battle burped up the back stairs. Daniel turned, his face blank.

"Bloody hell, captain!" shouted Lamsoe who'd just reached the curtained doorway on his way down. "They got around us, sir! Bloody hell, there's a whole army of 'em!"

"Sissies defend the doorways!" Daniel bellowed. Some of the spacers had commo helmets on, but most did not. "Woetjans, back to the doorway and we'll hold them here!"

For a while, but there'd better be another way out than the two I know about, Daniel thought, absently picking up another of the chairs. They were too flimsy to make good clubs or missiles, but four chairlegs in the face would give pause to a man willing to charge a brandished axe.

The staff and the room's other patrons squeezed themselves against the walls. An elderly man in striped robes was dabbing the pressure cut on his left cheekbone, and a mannishly handsome woman was counting chips from the palm of her left hand into her reticule with an eye on the croupier shivering beside her clutching her own shoulders. In the bright overhead lighting, the female staff in their net tops looked like fish being landed rather than exotically sexual figures.

The wall hangings were disarrayed. Close to the back entrance, Daniel saw the jamb of a closed door. He stepped to it, tried the knob and found it locked.

"Careful, sir!" Dasi shouted. Daniel jumped back. Dasi and Barnes—mates from long before Daniel had known them—lunged forward with the porphyry shelf they'd wrenched from the wall. They smashed it into the latch.

The whole doorpanel disintegrated. Daniel jerked the remains out of his way and stepped into a service area. The floor manager was talking in violent agitation to someone over a flat-plate communicator. He saw Daniel, screamed, and reached into the half-open drawer under the communicator.

Daniel caught the fellow's arm and twisted it up, taking the pistol out of the drawer with his free hand. He didn't want a gun, but in a situation like this he didn't intend to leave it in the hands of somebody who certainly wasn't a friend.

"How do we get out?" he said, still holding the manager's wrist but no more firmly than necessary to keep the pudgy little man from wriggling away. "Quick, if you please, so that we can take our troubles away from here."

"The back stairs!" the manager gasped. "The way you came in, for God's sake!"

"That's blocked now," Daniel said, speaking calmly. "Is there a way to the roof?"

Behind Daniel sounds from the card room suggested a demolition team was at work. That was more or less the truth. His people had brought clubs, but weight of numbers was going to tell very quickly if it came to hand-to-hand slugging against the *Goldenfels'* crew. The Sissies were converting the furnishings into missiles, and they'd very shortly be using the studs for spears if they managed to tear them out of the walls.

"In there!" the manager said, pointing to the toilet half-screened in the corner. "In the ceiling, there's a ladder pulls down. But it won't help you!"

Daniel turned to give an order but Hogg and Portus, a technician with blood now matting her blond hair, had gotten to the alcove before the words were out of the manager's mouth. Daniel stepped to the card room door, still holding the manager. The fellow was probably harmless, but there wasn't enough margin for survival in this affair to learn that there was another pistol stashed somewhere in the service area.

His Sissies were holding the tops of both staircases, but Lamsoe was sprawled unconscious in the middle of the room and most of the others Daniel could see had injuries. If there was only a trap door to block they'd survive that much longer, but retreating up a ladder would mean sacrificing the rear guard; which Daniel wasn't willing to do, not yet.

"Got it open!" Hogg shouted. "I'll check the—"

"Negative!" Daniel said. "Portus, check the roof for a way out. Hogg, come here and—"

"There's no way off the roof!" the manager said in a piping voice. "You'd have to jump!"

"—rig a snare across this doorway for after we're clear. Sissies, start withdrawing to the roof. Horn and Kolbek—"

Two techs who weren't involved in the immediate fighting, waiting for a chance to replace somebody in the groups fighting at each stairhead.

"—carry Lamsoe *now*! Move it, Sissies!"

Jumping from a third-floor roof would mean broken legs and maybe broken necks—which wasn't any worse than what the Alliance spacers would do to them if Daniel didn't get his people clear in some fashion. Aircars, maybe? But where to steal enough of them quickly, and few spacers could drive one anyway.

Of course if the fight went on long enough the local authorities might intervene. At this point that was looking like a less bad option than it'd seemed at the beginning.

Three spacers trundled past. Lamsoe was on his feet, but his face was slack and he was moving only because Horn directed him.

"Woetjans, start sending them back!" Daniel said. "We're moving out!"

Hogg knelt nearby, wearing gloves and paying out the length of deep-sea fishline he always carried. The line was boron monocrystal, strong enough to hold a whale but so thin it cut like a knife if you weren't careful handling it. He'd looped it around the lower hinge of the shattered door and was running it back to the legs of a couch on the other side.

There was a burst of particular violence at the main stairs. Barnes and Dasi charged some ways down the steps after the retreating Alliance spacers; when they came back up, Barnes had lost his left sleeve and his mouth was bloody. The blood wasn't necessarily his own, of course.

"Now!" Daniel said. "We'll hold at *this* door. *Now* by God or you'll none of you ship under me again, damn your bloody souls!"

"Captain . . . ?" said Count Klimov, looking aristocratically puzzled and holding a baize bag bulging with chips.

Bloody Hell, I'd forgotten him! Daniel grabbed his employer by the lapel and dragged him into the service room to relative safety. "Somebody get the Count up the ladder!" he shouted over his shoulder. "Soonest! Move! Move! Move!"

All but four Sissies broke back immediately, not in panic but out of the ingrained habit of obeying orders instantly. Horn was feeding them up the ladder; there was a brief delay as spacers helped/tossed the Count up to hands waiting on the roof, but the spacers themselves climbed as they would the companionways of a starship. Not even the largest battleships had elevators. A cage would catch and become a fatal trap if the vessel's fabric worked enough to kink the shaft. That could happen while transiting from one bubble universe to another, let alone as a result of enemy action.

"Come on back, the rest of you!" Daniel ordered. "Hold this doorway!"

He tossed the manager into the corner diagonally away from the toilet alcove. If the fellow had good sense he'd stay there, squeezed into as tight a ball as his waistline would allow. If he didn't, well, that was his lookout.

Barnes and Dasi, Woetjans and Szurovsky, jerked themselves away from the struggle at the two stairheads. Alliance spacers followed, but not instantly. The newcomers pouring up the stairs turned their first

attention to the civilians in the card room who'd
begun to move when they saw the Sissies leaving.

"I'm ready!" Hogg said. "Master, get up the ladder!"

"I'll wait till—" Daniel said.

"Woetjans, haul his ass out of here!" Hogg said.
"Quick!"

The bosun turned and reached for Daniel's arm. He
was ahead of her, springing for the ladder. Knowing
when to decline battle against overwhelming force was
a necessary skill for an RCN officer. The ladder built
into the wall was iron, red with rust inhibitor and
rust—mostly the latter, but the metal remained sturdy
enough for the job.

Woetjans was directly behind him. As Daniel went
through the trap door he shouted over his shoulder,
"Szurovsky next, Barnes and Dasi follow as soon as he's
on the ladder. Move it—"

Hands, at least three sets of them, jerked Daniel
onto the roof.

"—Sissies!"

"There's no way down!" Portus said. "There's Alliance spacers all around the building, sir, it's like the
tide coming in down there!"

Daniel rolled to his belly and glanced back through
the trap door. Woetjans was out and Szurovsky, a lanky
man of nearly six feet six, slithered up behind her. Dasi
and Barnes ran back from the doorway. As they did
Hogg rose to his feet, lifting with him the chairleg on
which he'd wrapped the other end of the fishline
crisscrossing the doorway as an invisible shimmer.

Three Alliance spacers charged into the doorway,
then tripped screaming onto the service room's floor.
One had a cut deep into his shin bone. There was
blood on the threshold and blood in the air, clinging
to the boron fiber and giving it visible presence.

Hogg dropped the chairleg with which he'd tensioned

the snare and ran for the ladder just as Barnes cleared it. Nobody else rushed into the service room for a moment. An Alliance spacer threw a statuette into Hogg's back as he mounted the ladder; Hogg climbed the rest of the way with only a grunt and a curse to show he'd been hit.

Sissies jerked Hogg onto the roof; Portus and Lamsoe, bright-eyed again, slammed the door down on its jamb. There wasn't a lock on this side, but the two spacers stood on the panel while four others staggered over with a section of stone cornice they'd torn from the facade.

Daniel stuck the pistol he'd taken from the floor manager back into his sash. He hadn't been going to let Hogg be kicked to death in front of him, even if that meant shooting somebody.

Only now did Daniel step to the edge and look down. He'd hoped they'd be able to jump to the roof of the building on the other side of the narrow alley, but it was two stories taller and the brick wall facing the Anyo Nuevo was blank.

The alley itself was full of green Alliance utility uniforms. Some of the more enterprising of the *Goldenfels'* crew were climbing the gap, bracing themselves between the walls as they would in a narrow crevasse. They weren't a serious threat, but in all likelihood their fellows would be on top of the adjacent building shortly and using twenty-foot height advantage to hurl bricks—if they didn't use guns.

"Bloody hell, sir, come look at this!" Woetjans shouted as she gazed over the front of the building. Daniel stepped to her side, grimacing at the damage to his dress uniform. Still, it'd gotten him into the card room without alerting the mob of Alliance spacers below.

He followed Woetjans' gesture. Up Straight Street—

it wasn't particularly straight, except by comparison with most streets in San Juan—from the direction of the harbor came a line of vehicles. Most were armored after a fashion, and all were armed. They flew streamers and flags of many varieties—house colors, Daniel assumed—but every single one of them wore the red-on-gold—

"Great God, our help!" shouted Portus. "That's the Cinnabar sandal! They're not the cops, they're Cinnabars come to save us!"

A pair of large aircars, laboring to stay airborne, roared around the side of the tall building behind the Anyo Nuevo. They flared to land, their skids sparkling on the roof's covering of asphaltic concrete. One had a cloth-of-gold canopy, the other red silk which had torn to tatters on the flight just ended.

Most of those aboard the two vehicles were heavily-armed locals, but the men in the middle, the seat of honor, were Cinnabar natives dressed in local pomp. Daniel recognized both of them.

He stepped to the gold-covered car and saluted. His right arm caught him in mid-motion—he'd strained his triceps somehow—but he carried through anyway.

"Sir!" he said to Admiral O'Quinn. "Lieutenant Daniel Leary, RCN, reporting!"

He coughed. "Ah," he added. "That is, RCN Reserve, sir. And we're *very* glad to see you!"

O'Quinn got out of his vehicle with the hesitation of a man more hindered by ill health than old age, but who was old as well. "If you're on half pay, Leary," he said, "then you're more RCN than I am by a long ways."

He peered over the front of the building. "I think the boys are sorting out the Alliance well enough," he went on. "It's our household guards mostly doing the heavy work, but I see some of the old crew are showing they're not too old to swing a wrench."

"Sir," said Daniel, nodding to Commander Purvis as he joined them from the other aircar. The mob flying the Cinnabar flag was weighing into the *Goldenfels'* crew all right. There were hundreds of the newcomers, and more were arriving from several directions in addition to the initial batch from the harbor. "Ah, I'm very grateful, as I said; but how is it that you came here like this?"

O'Quinn looked at him in surprise. "Came here?" he repeated. "Why, Mistress Mundy sent a warning through the alert network we Cinnabars set up in case, well, things changed in our relationship with the Governor. Our private network."

"I don't see how she got the codes to do that," Commander Purvis said with a sudden frown. "I certainly didn't give them to her. I don't know how she even realized the network existed!"

"We'd have done the same if it was your father, Leary," said Admiral O'Quinn. "Of course I might've hanged him afterwards, but I wouldn't have left him to the Alliance."

Daniel nodded crisply. "Yes sir," he said. "I appreciate the distinction. So would he."

Count Klimov, looking very little the worse for wear, strolled over to them. "So, Captain Leary," he said. "These men are friends of yours?"

Daniel quirked a smile at his employer. "Yes, your excellency," he said, "they're my colleagues and most certainly my friends."

He took a deep breath and went on, "And if you don't mind my appearing to give an order, your excellency, I strongly recommend that the *Princess Cecile* lift from here as soon as we and the rest of the crew are back aboard!"

you were without it.

"We're carrying no cargo whatever, Commander Mendez," Daniel said to the pasty-looking official who'd

CHAPTER 14

It'd been a wryly pleasant surprise to Adele when she learned that most spacers didn't like weightlessness any better than she did. A properly-functioning starship was almost always accelerating at 1 g, providing the illusion of weight.

The exception was during the time a ship was in orbit, preparing to land. Tegeli now rotated below the *Princess Cecile*, a haze of greenish seas and the varicolored smears of low-lying islands and the life-encrusted shallows around them. It wasn't particularly inviting, but at least when the officials from the picket boat cleared the *Sissie* to land, there'd be gravity again.

Adele smiled at her display. The secret to contentment appeared to involve finding pleasure in small things. Though gravity didn't seem a small thing when you were without it.

"We're carrying no cargo whatever, Commander Mendez," Daniel said to the pasty-looking official who'd come aboard on a line from the picket boat. For all the fellow's impressive rank, his vessel was a bucket with neither antennas nor High Drive; the crew establishment

was five, but according to her log she'd been operating with four these past two months. "Only stores for
our own use, and those are rather sparse at the moment.
Because of riots in San Juan, we left Todos Santos
before we'd completed loading."

Adele, examining Tegeli's starship landing records,
pursed her lips. Although technically Daniel wasn't
lying . . . and under the circumstances a flat lie would
probably have been a better choice than telling the
Commander that the *Princess Cecile* had fled San Juan
after her crew fought a street battle with Alliance
spacers, eventually drawing in large numbers of the
local military.

Not that it had been the Sissies' fault, of course, but
that was the sort of detail that local officials might find
less than reassuring.

Mendez sniffed. "Politics!" he said. "We don't go in
for that sort of nonsense on Tegeli. People mind their
own affairs."

Such as they are, Adele thought as she reviewed the
records she'd just copied from the planetary database.
Tegeli had logged only thirty-eight landings in the past
quarter; Todos Santos saw that many in a day or two.
Fishing and marine products were the planet's main
exports; imports were a limited quantity of luxury
goods, supporting the *Sailing Directions*' description
of Tegeli as having a highly-stratified society.

Stratified but languid, which is another way of
putting Commander Mendez' comment about people
minding their own affairs. The planet had almost no
volcanic activity. There was no moon, and because
Tegeli was 108 million miles from its sun the solar tides
were mild. The human inhabitants appeared to live in
a pattern that mimicked the placid nature of their
environment.

"Now, I see that you're not the owner of this vessel,"

said Mendez, consulting the uppermost of the sheaf of flimsies in his gloved right hand. He wore a skin-tight vacuum suit whose patches made Adele's lips wrinkle sourly just to look at, though she supposed the holes weren't life-threatening. A split in the fabric would just mean minor hemorrhaging, a few more spider veins in the Commander's skin. Prolonged weightlessness— because the picket boat didn't carry sufficient reaction mass to keep a weigh on—had done more serious damage to his body. "The owner is Count Klimov?"

"We are the owners, Georgi and I," said Valentina, standing with her husband at the front of their annex. "Is there a problem?"

The Klimovs hadn't mastered weightlessness, but they were able to hold themselves vertical in one place instead of drifting about the way Adele would've done if she hadn't been strapped in. She *was*, of course, strapped in.

"Not at all," said Mendez, turning to face the Klimovs. "Not at all! But I note that you haven't listed guest-friendships with anyone on Tegeli. Is that the case?"

"No," the Count said. "I regret to admit that we'd never heard of your planet until just before we took off from Todos Santos. Our arrival here was whim."

The truth was a little more complex than that, though Count Klimov might not understand clearly the reason Daniel had shaped their course to this backwater. Tegeli was an unlikely landfall for any vessel but one deliberately setting out for it. While the *Princess Cecile* wasn't short of food, air, or reaction mass, she couldn't afford to spend an indefinite additional period in space without replenishing those stores. Tegeli could supply their needs without a likelihood of the *Goldenfels* arriving before the corvette had finished loading.

"Well, a fortunate whim for us, then," said Mendez. "Particularly for the Pansuelas of Lusa City."

He consulted a second sheet of the flimsies he held. "Yes, that's right," he said. "Since they were the next on the rota, they were alerted as soon as your vessel announced its arrival. They'll be very pleased."

Mendez glanced around the bridge, then focused his attention on Daniel. "I wonder, Count Klimov," he said. "Are any of your ship's company of the landowning class as well?"

Instead of waiting for the Count to speak, Adele said from her console, "Lieutenant Leary, our captain, is the son of Speaker Leary. I myself am a Mundy of Chatsworth."

She waited for Mendez to turn before giving him a cold smile. "I'm *the* Mundy of Chatsworth, as a matter of fact. If it matters to you, we're members of what're called the Best Families of the Republic of Cinnabar."

Daniel looked surprised at Adele's forwardness; she hadn't had a way to warn him before she spoke. According to the information she was pulling together, there wasn't a private inn anywhere on the planet that was better than a hog wallow.

It wasn't of great concern to Adele if she lived aboard the *Princess Cecile* while they were on Tegeli. She wanted to use what written archives were available, though, and she knew Daniel liked the opportunity to socialize whenever they touched ground. That required they be received by the Patrons, the landowners of the planet.

"Oh, but that's wonderful!" Mendez said. He glanced at his first flimsy again. "I'll be able to accommodate two more of the Patrons! That will be—"

"No," said Daniel, drawing eyes back to him. "Commander Mendez, it won't be practical to divide our group while on Tegeli. If the Pansuelas can't receive so many as four of us, then I'm afraid Mistress Mundy and I will have to remain aboard our vessel."

"That isn't the difficulty," said Mendez. "You see, we have so few visitors of proper quality that the regulations allotting them among our Patrons are very strict. Still, if you insist . . . ?"

Shuffling the printouts he'd boarded with had caused him to rise slightly. He raised an arm absently, tapped the ceiling with his finger, and reversed his slow progress. While not a prepossessing man, the time the official spent on picket duty had obviously made him a past master of maneuvering in weightlessness without overcorrecting.

"I do," said Daniel formally. "I must."

"Then I must perforce agree," Mendez said with equal formality. "I will inform the Pansuelas that they have the honor to receive four visitors of the very highest rank."

He shook his head in wonderment. "They'll be the talk of all Tegeli, they will," he added. "They always had a reputation for being a lucky house, but now, goodness!"

Mendez turned, angling his body so he could push off for the airlock by which he'd boarded.

"Excuse me, Commander?" Daniel called to the official's back. "Are we cleared to land, then?"

Mendez continued his rotation, bringing himself fully around. "What?" he said. "Why yes, of course—at Lusa City, as I told you. Welcome to Tegeli, patrons!"

"Welcome indeed," Daniel agreed, giving Adele a broad smile of anticipation.

"We'll let you lead," Count Klimov said. In response to his gesture, Daniel strode whistling across the boarding bridge ahead of his employers. The vehicle waiting on the wooden quay beyond looked like a boat with fat tires.

The *Sissie*'d cooked the basin's mud bottom while setting down. Though warm brackish water had immediately flowed back around the vessel, the stench of burned organic material formed a haze in the muggy air. It was nothing to spacers used to working high in the yards of a starship in the Matrix, but landsmen like the Klimovs might reasonably find it daunting.

Insectoids flew about the harbor, visible mostly as glitters in the air or dimples on the surface of the black water. One hovered momentarily before Daniel's eyes, a body as small and round as a pea supported on transparent shimmers; before he could decide whether to brush it away or just duck, it zipped off on business of its own.

Daniel's duties as captain of a ship which'd taken off hastily had kept him too busy to give more than cursory attention to Tegeli's natural history. The planet's seas included impressive specimens of marine life, but he should have studied the fauna of the tidal basins with greater care. That was what he'd be in contact with.

Daniel grinned. It was no different in the RCN: people ooh-ed and ah-ed over the battleships, but fleet actions were rare even during periods of full-scale warfare. The commanding officer of the corvette *Princess Cecile* had seen more action than some full admirals. . . .

The tangled forest surrounding the Lusa City harbor might have been a single plant. Individual stems/trunks/branches were rarely more than four inches in diameter, and the treetops were only sixty or so feet high. From above as the *Sissie* descended, the forest looked like a dark green pillow; viewed from sea level, the woody substructure was rigidly black against softer shadows, with air plants and parasites scattering a myriad of bright splashes.

Daniel stepped aside to allow the other three to reach firm—well, slightly muddy—ground. The Klimovs strode on toward the vehicle, but Daniel gestured Adele close and murmured, "Is there a customs official or the like on his way? I don't want to miss some necessary formality because we left before the Port Commandant finished his siesta."

"They appear to take a relaxed attitude toward that sort of thing," Adele said. She too spoke quietly, though there probably wasn't any need for it. Across the tree-fringed harbor a barge was unloading containers into a warehouse; that and the waiting vehicle were the only signs of life. "I couldn't find any customs records. Ships pay a landing fee irrespective of their cargo or even their size—though that may be because none of the ships landing on Tegeli are very big."

"Daniel, come!" Valentina said, waving. "The boy is waiting to take us to Pansuela House."

Daniel nodded assent and walked the rest of the way up the path to the car. At his side Adele murmured tartly, "The 'boy' is forty if he's a day. Based on what I've found regarding Tegelan society, the Klimovs should find themselves right at home here."

The driver—who was indeed forty or more, a swarthy, muscular man with flaring mustachios, held the rear door open for them. Daniel suspected the car's thick sides were floatation chambers. The wheels and their balloon tires were wider than they were high; instead of normal treads they were scooped into a series of curved paddles. Though the vehicle had very low clearance, its muddy underside was obviously intended to skid through muck as the wheels splashed forward.

For all the vehicle's external size, space within was at a premium. The Klimovs had taken the central pair of bucket seats. There were two more seats in back and an uncushioned bench in front.

As the driver handed Adele into a back seat, Hogg and Tovera conferred under their breath. Tovera stepped in after Adele, seating herself on the rear deck with her legs between the bucket seats; the attaché case was in her lap. Hogg got into the front while the driver stared in puzzlement at Tovera.

"That's quite all right," said Daniel as he got in. "We prefer having a servant with us in the back."

It wasn't worth arguing about. If Hogg and Tovera had decided it between them, that was most likely the way it was going to be.

"Just drive us to the Pansuelas," he continued aloud as he pulled the low door out of the driver's hand and closed it. "How far is it, anyway?"

"Not far, patron," the driver said, bowing again. He walked around to his door.

"It's one point seven miles," said Adele quietly. She started to get out her data unit. "I can show you—"

"No need for that," Daniel said, smiling. "Though when we have some leisure, if you have a natural history database—"

"Of course," said Adele, in much the same tone as if he'd asked if she'd remembered to bring a change of clothes. Come to think, it was much more likely that she'd have failed to pack clothes than that she'd neglect information she knew was of interest to Daniel.

"Excellent," Daniel said as the driver clutched in the diesel engine and turned the car tightly. "This appears to be one of those worlds where nature comes to us." They moved off at gathering speed. The road was a dirt causeway, built a few feet up from sea level by mats of plastic sheet-stock anchored by pilings cut from the interlacing trunks of the forest itself. So far as Daniel could tell the region was a tidal flat with no features except for the homogenous forest, but for some reason the road curved back and forth like a snake's track.

The tires rolled smoothly over the soggy ground, though their thrum was loud enough to prevent normal speech. Sheets of mud and muddy water sprayed out to either side as the car negotiated particularly soft places, but the splashes didn't soak the passengers as Daniel had expected they would.

He leaned close to Adele's ear and said, "I see why they were bringing processed fish to the warehouse by barge. Ground transport of bulky goods would be next to impossible, even between points on the same island."

Adele looked at him and nodded, indicating she'd heard him and understood. Then she went back to whatever she was doing on her data unit, regardless of the car's motion—indicating that she didn't *care* about the difficulties of bulk transport on Tegeli.

Daniel grinned. Unless she'd found the information during one of her data searches, of course; as she probably had. He supposed this was another case where his interests and Adele's complemented one another.

Given the amount of noise the wheels made, Daniel didn't expect to see much in the way of wildlife. As they came out of the forest onto a road with high curbs and houses to either side, however, a blister swelled suddenly from the trunk of a tree and launched itself outward with an undulating motion. While flying the creature had a glistening translucence, but it vanished completely as soon as it landed on the weathered slats of a house a hundred yards away.

The wooden buildings on the road from the harbor had been raised four or five feet above the ground on pilings. Chickens scavenged around the houses and in the street, sometimes scattering noisily as children playing ball rushed too close. Women sat on the steps, sewing and cutting vegetables against their thumbs as they chatted in high, musical voices.

In actual money there probably wasn't the equivalent

of ten Cinnabar florins as far as Daniel could see up and down this street, but the impression he got of the district was simplicity rather than poverty. The women's clothing was a mix of colors tending toward reds and yellows, and the houses were painted bright pastels even though much of the paint had flaked away.

The street was wide, but pedestrians were the only other traffic. Once the car passed a pair of men trudging along with the carcase of a pig slung between them, but for the most part Daniel saw women with bundles or wicker baskets on their heads. Occasionally they stopped and looked at the vehicle in blank-faced wonder.

Adele leaned close and said, "There's canals at the back of the houses. They carry the commercial traffic; and act as sewers, I gather."

Daniel nodded in understanding.

They were coming to the dwellings of the wealthy, though as they approached Daniel thought what he saw ahead was the industrial district. The three- and four-story houses were built of concrete, but their window gratings were iron worked into patterns of remarkable art and delicacy despite the smears of rust on the walls beneath them. Here drainage ditches bordered the road on both sides. Some of the houses had culverts to their substantial front gates, but many used instead draw-bridges—which they kept raised.

Bunting draped the facade of a building a quarter mile in the distance. The gates were open and servants stood in the street waving flags. Daniel increased the magnification of the goggles he wore with his 2nd Class uniform. "Good God, that's a Cinnabar sandal!" he said.

"The Novy Sverdlovsk flag is a red eagle on a black and white ground!" Adele said into his ear. "Is that . . . ?"

"Yes, by God, it bloody well is!" Daniel said, focusing on one of the flags alternating with those of

Cinnabar. "Good heavens, they didn't have long to run them up, did they?"

The tires slowed from a *thrum* back to a *flop-flop-flop*. The driver turned hard—the horizontally-mounted steering wheel didn't have power assist, Daniel noticed—and drove through the arched gateway into a courtyard almost filled by the dozen or more similar vehicles which were already parked there.

A priest in black robes and a score of other people in glittering finery—the headdress of some of the women was remarkable—looked down from second-story balconies. In contrast to the animated servants, these folk were working very hard to impersonate statues.

The car stopped and the diesel rang silent. Adele leaned close to Daniel as they got out, murmuring, "The Pansuelas invited all the other landowners in Lusa City when they learned we were arriving. There'll be additional guests from neighboring islands later in the evening."

A couple accompanied by footmen walked down the spreading stone staircase from the wing opposite the entrance. The man was a tall, distinguished sixty-year-old; the woman was somewhat younger and her bosom could almost be described as overdone. She embraced Count Klimov while the man took Valentina's hand and held it as he said, "I am Enrique Pansuela; this is my wife Flora. We are honored, deeply honored, to have guests of your obvious nobility!"

The locals on the balconies broke their stasis and waved: the men handkerchiefs, the women ribbons or lengths of lace. Though they didn't raise their own voices, the servants standing behind them cheered loudly.

Flora released the Count and threw herself into Daniel's arms. "Master Leary of Bantry?" she said, raising her lips for what was certainly not intended to be a peck on the cheek.

"Madame Pansuela," Daniel said, keeping his own face lifted toward the women waiting on the balcony— some very nice ones there, yes. He patted the lady's shoulder-blade with a masculine firmness. "Honored to meet you, Madame, and your esteemed husband."

By making a quarter turn to the right, then quickly reversing his motion, Daniel detached himself. He extended his right hand to Enrique, effectively preventing Flora from gripping him again. From the corner of his eye he saw her return her attention to Count Klimov with a moue of frustration.

A striped creature the size of a cat humped half-way across the courtyard, then stopped to raise and lower its front half repeatedly in quick succession. It had either no legs or very short ones; a pair of tiny, bright eyes framed its prehensile nose.

"Very good of you to grant us your hospitality," Daniel said as he pumped his host's hand with verve, trying to mask the fact of Madame Pansuela's obvious play for him. Though he didn't imagine it was a new experience to her husband.

Bloody Hell, perfumed powder from the lady's bosom was smudged across the front of his Dress Grays. He'd be lucky if he didn't sneeze!

"Ours is the honor, Captain," Pansuela said. His speech had a slight glaze and he moved with the stiff formality of a drunk. Daniel couldn't smell alcohol on his breath, but the old man was either ill or on some drug. "Will you and your fellow Patrons accompany me? I wish to introduce you to our friends before dinner and to show you Pansuela House."

"Yes, I'd like to meet your friends," said Valentina, eyeing her husband with mild distaste. "Some of them, anyway."

She offered Pansuela her arm imperiously. He took it, bowed, and started up the broad stairs with her at his side.

Adele set her hand firmly on Daniel's biceps, providing both of them with cover. That probably wasn't necessary, because Flora had welded herself to Klimov; the Count seemed pleased with the attention. The priest watched them from the landing with eyes like chips of obsidian.

As Daniel and Adele followed the other couples to the second floor, he caught a glimpse of the striped animal. It resumed hopping toward the far wall. Following it now were a half dozen similar creatures of half the size, making cheerful little squeals.

A good omen, Daniel decided; but from the hard line of Adele's lips as she watched Flora Pansuela, he decided not to whisper the thought to her.

CHAPTER 15

"Do have a bite of this breast, Captain Leary," said Estrella, the strawberry blonde on Daniel's left, offering him a tidbit of chicken between her thumb and index finger. She giggled and with her other hand plucked the deep-scooped neck of her blouse momentarily below her nipples. "Wouldn't you like that?"

"I think Dannie prefers dark meat," said Margolla, the brunette on his other side as she leaned against his arm. Her top covered her from chin to wrists, but the fabric was translucent even in dim light and so thin he felt not only her warmth but her heartbeat. "Do you like dark meat, Dannie?"

"At the moment . . . ," said Daniel with a catch in his throat. "I think I'll have some more of this excellent wine."

He emptied his glass and looked around for a waiter. Two servants converged on him, each carrying a ewer. They jostled for a moment, then one poked the other in the ribs with his free hand.

"Boys!" Daniel snapped. He pointed his finger at the servant who'd jabbed the other and said, "Stand back!"

When the servant obeyed, bowing and scraping with his free hand, Daniel offered his glass to the other fellow to fill.

Daniel saw Adele reach into her jacket pocket when he raised his voice. She alone of the forty-odd diners appeared to have noticed anything. She sat at the end of the table on Enrique Pansuela's right; he'd been lecturing her about the curio cabinets covering the walls to the mezzanine walkway.

"Oh, you're so masterful," Estrella murmured, absently swallowing the bit of chicken she'd been holding. "I wish we had men like you in Lusa City, don't you, Margolla?"

The women were young, pretty, and obviously willing—all the traits Daniel looked for in his off-duty socializing; but they were also forward enough to make him a trifle uncomfortable in a setting whose rules weren't necessarily as clear as they seemed. He'd done enough snaring in his youth on Bantry to worry that the open path before him might end in a demand for marriage or huge damages to a suddenly-aggrieved father.

Come to think, he wasn't even sure the girls were daughters rather than wives with God *knew* what sort of complications. The way Flora was crawling over Count Klimov at the far end of the table showed that was a possibility.

The hall filled the second and third stories of a whole wing; even with scores of guests and seemingly twice that number of servants, it was a hollow cavern. Now that night had fallen, chandeliers hanging from coffers between the darkened skylights were the only illumination.

The curio cabinets along the walls weren't separately lighted, but as a result the few items that reflected the glow from above stood out like stars on a moonless night. Daniel was in a reverie that was part wine, part the warm pressure of the girls to either side, and part concern about that pressure. It took him almost a minute to understand the image he'd seen gleaming on a shelf behind him when he separated the squabbling waiters.

He set his refilled glass down untasted. "Excuse me, my dears," he said, sliding his chair back so quickly that the girls might well have toppled sideways together had he not kept a guiding hand on the nearer shoulder of each.

Daniel stepped to the cabinet; as before only Adele paid any attention to him, though in this case there was the excuse that the others probably thought he'd risen to go to the jakes. He took the object out of its niche beside a goblet of tarred earthenware, seemingly ancient, and a sheet of native copper covered mostly with black sulfate corrosion. It was a military belt buckle. That was common enough, but judging from its weight and lack of tarnish this one was made of platinum.

A golden eagle stood out in high relief from an incised shield whose lower portion was crosshatched to indicate a separate color. Daniel turned and found that Adele and their host were already coming around the long table toward them. He was surprised, but he knew Adele well enough that he shouldn't have been.

Pansuela getting up *did* create some interest; half the diners began craning their necks to see what was happening. Count Klimov was too far into his wine to care, but the Klimovna was looking. Daniel caught her eye and hooked a finger toward her. She shook off the hand of the local gallant—from his features very possibly Margolla's brother—and got up to join Enrique and Adele before they reached Daniel.

"Master Pansuela," Daniel said, holding out the belt

buckle, "this appears to me to be a representation in metal of the Novy Sverdlovsk flag. I was wondering how it came to be here?"

"May I?" said Valentina; the form of her words was polite, but she snatched the buckle from Daniel with the ravenous enthusiasm of a predatory fish taking chum. "Yes!"

She turned, folding the buckle in her palm. "Georgi! Come here! The Captain has found the buckle from John Tsetzes' regalia!"

"What?" said Pansuela. He reached for the buckle, but Valentina obviously wasn't in a mood for anybody else to touch it at the moment. He shrugged. "I'm afraid I don't have any idea, Leary. One of my uncles catalogued this, but that was . . ."

He waved a hand, indicating a past lost in the mists of time.

"And anyway," he added, "we all thought he was likely to start chirping with the birds, you see. Not quite right in the head."

"John Tsetzes left Novy Sverdlovsk sixty-one standard years ago," Adele said. Her voice was calm but she wore a tense expression—possibly because she couldn't use her personal data unit unless she sat down and set it on her lap. At the moment sitting on the floor meant she'd be stepped on. "The chances are that were he to have arrived here, it would've been within six months of that time. Is that helpful?"

"Who knows?" Pansuela said. "I suppose you could check the guest book. You noble patrons haven't signed the book yourselves yet, have you? Or did you? I forget things sometimes."

"Where would the guest book be, if you please?" said Adele more sharply than perhaps she intended. One didn't want to get between Adele and information, though. "I'd like to look at it now."

The Count and Flora Pansuela struggled through what was by now a gathering crowd. Given the limited amount of light, it was rather like being in a forest after sunset. Hogg stood nearby—he'd been against the wall behind Daniel's chair during dinner. Daniel didn't see Tovera, but then one *generally* didn't see Tovera. He had no doubt Adele's pale reptile was wherever she felt she could best safeguard her mistress.

"Georgi, you see?" Valentina said, holding the buckle toward her husband in her cupped hands. She turned to Daniel and said, "Tsetzes always appeared in public in a white uniform with appointments of platinum picked out with gold: the braid, the buttons, and this buckle of course. He even had a pistol of platinum, they say."

"And the Earth Diamond," the Count said. He caressed the buckle with his fingertips but didn't try to take it from his wife's hands. To his host he went on, "Master Pansuela, have you perhaps in this potpourri—"

A sweep of his left arm indicated the egg-crate shelving which held the curio collection on this side of the room.

"—a diamond the size of a child's head, etched with the continents of Old Earth? Because if you do, my wife and I can offer you. . . ."

Pansuela shrugged. "I really don't know," he said. "I've never seen such a thing. But the last person to take an interest in the cabinet was Uncle Manuel, as I said."

"Did your uncle leave a written catalogue?" Adele said. She and the Klimovna sounded like a pair of hounds on a very fresh scent. "Or perhaps electronic files? Either would do."

"I suppose he must have," Pansuela agreed, wrinkling his brow. "He had a study off the mezzanine." He nodded toward the railed walk midway to the hall's coffered ceiling. "I'll show it to you, but you'd know better than I what sort of thing you're looking for."

He turned to the Klimovs. "And you're welcome to search the collection itself if you like," he went on. "But a diamond so large, I'd expect to have heard about it. Though perhaps not."

"You will not be looking at dusty shelves tonight, Georgi," said Flora Pansuela, pressing her ample form so firmly into the Count that he shuffled sideways to avoid being knocked over. "We have other business."

"Not tonight, Lady Pansuela," said the priest who'd been glowering from the moment Daniel first saw him. "You and I will spend tonight in our devotions."

"No, Rosario, not tonight," said Flora with an unmistakable edge in her voice. "Perhaps next week—"

"No!" said the priest. He tried to force his way between Klimov and Lady Pansuela, but he was so short that the wide brim of the hat he wore even at dinner brushed the Count's chin. "I will not permit you to risk your immortal soul by putting off your devotions!"

"Rosario!" said Flora. "You are my chaplain, not my jailer. If you forget that once more, I'll have the boys put you out the door—and if I do, you'll not be allowed back, I warn you!"

"Father Rosario," Enrique Pansuela said, putting a hand on the priest's shoulder. "Come upstairs with me and Lady Mundy to find Uncle Manuel's papers. Afterwards you and I can have a nightcap and get some sleep. It won't seem so important in the morning, I'm sure."

"Faugh, you complaisant *lump!*" the priest shouted. He glared at the Klimovna, adding, "And you're no better!"

"Rosario, these are our guests!" Pansuela said. The priest shoved his way out of the assemblage and tramped toward the doorway at the end of the hall.

Daniel let his breath out slowly. He'd been in enough situations of the sort himself to realize that you couldn't be sure just where they were going to go in the next few seconds.

Enrique Pansuela turned to Adele with a sad smile. "Lady Mundy," he said, "have you had your fill of dinner? Because I can show you Uncle Manuel's study whenever you like."

"I've eaten all I need to, Master Pansuela," she said. "I'd like to see the records as soon as is convenient."

Daniel felt friendly warmth against his left arm. "And you, Dannie?" a voice murmured. "Would you like to go somewhere too?"

"I would indeed," Daniel agreed. As he settled his arm around Margolla's waist, it struck him that he and Adele both in their different ways were finding Tegeli an unexpectedly pleasant landfall.

The guest book lay open on the folding table servants had brought into the room at Adele's direction. Uncle Manuel's desk of boldly-carved wood was here also, but his study—and for how many generations would it be known by that name?—had become a place to dump whatever the Pansuelas decided they didn't need but weren't ready to discard.

Boxes and odd lots—a set of curtains, rotted halfway to the rod on which they were rolled; a holographic entertainment deck, certainly ancient and probably nonfunctional—stood along one side of the hallway, the overburden removed to get down to the layers of Uncle Manuel's occupancy. Stolid servants waited just outside the door to execute Adele's next direction.

She smiled faintly as she twisted off the top of a canister which rattled hopefully. *This is really more a task for an archeologist than a librarian*, she thought, but she wasn't about to complain. Not only was this a job well within her capacity, it gave her a familiar warm feeling to unearth information that almost no one else could have dragged from the tangles where it hid.

The canister contained commercially-loaded holo-chips. According to the legends printed on their sides they were cookbooks. The chips were of a non-standard variety. Adele could probably manage to read them with her data unit, but she didn't bother. Even if they were something other than they claimed to be—a collection of pornography, for example—they weren't going to bring her closer to John Tsetzes.

She closed the can and set it in the box of discards beside her. It was full enough, so she called, "Boy!" and went on to the next item.

This was a diary, handwritten by a woman with a penchant for purple ink, though she'd used a number of other colors. Adele skimmed the contents: an empty chronicle of an empty life, very like most other lives. It was from twenty or so years ago, far too recent for the period she was researching, so she set it into the empty box with which a servant had replaced the one he'd carried into the hall.

Adele caught movement from the corner of her eye. These servants didn't need to be geniuses to understand "Stay out of the room until I call you," which she'd already had to repeat twice since her initial briefing. "I told you—" she said, looking up in irritation.

Enrique Pansuela had come back. He'd watched her for half an hour initially, then given the servants directions to do whatever Lady Mundy said and to her relief gone off to his own occupations. "Oh," Adele said. "I'm sorry, Pansuela, I thought . . ."

She let her voice trail off. "I thought you were a servant," was the honest truth, but it probably wouldn't be politic to say. She sneezed instead, a natural consequence of the work she'd been doing, and well timed for a change.

"Don't bother getting up," her host said with a little gesture. Adele blinked, amazed that he'd thought she was going to. She'd been sitting cross-legged on the floor for hours, so it wouldn't be a quick process. "I just came over to see how you've been getting on."

He cleared his throat. "I haven't been able to get to sleep, you see."

Adele nodded, understanding more than she'd been told. Pansuela had been under the influence of something when he greeted them this afternoon—yesterday afternoon, by now—but he apparently hadn't taken any more of his drug of choice since the *Princess Cecile's* arrival. She supposed she should praise her host for fighting his addiction instead of sneering within herself at somebody weak enough to become addicted in the first place . . . but so long as she kept it within her, not even Pansuela himself had a right to complain about her attitude.

"Yes, well," she said aloud. She decided to get up after all; now that she was back in the world outside her own head, she realized that she really ought to move. "I've found John Tsetzes in the guest book, that was easy enough."

She gestured to the leather-bound volume on the table she'd had brought in. Finding the page hadn't been as easy as she implied—well, it wouldn't have been easy for somebody else. The ink and the pages—which were some sort of leather, perhaps fish bladder—had turned an identical sepia tone in the sixty-one standard years since they'd been created. She'd scanned the sheets into her data unit, sharpened the contrast, and then let the processor do the sorting, managing the job in a reasonable hour or so.

In place of the original muted lighting, a battery-powered lantern which Hogg had found for her flooded the room with hard illumination. He said it came off the bow of a fishing vessel where it'd been used as a night lure. Pansuela winced, though whether from the glare or the disorder it threw into high relief Adele couldn't judge.

"He signed using the name Ion Porphyrogenitus, commanding the yacht *Nicator*," she explained, "but the timing was right and he gave his homeworld as Novy Sverdlovsk. Since then I've been looking for your uncle's catalogue of the collection, hoping that there'll be some reference to provenance as well—at least for the accessions within his own lifetime. Your Uncle Manuel would've been an adult sixty-one years ago, wouldn't he?"

Pansuela rubbed his forehead with his fingertips. "What?" he said. "Yes, I suppose so. In his thirties, I believe."

He scanned the room; it was emptier than it'd probably been in a generation but it was a jumble by any reasonable standards. Pansuela swivelled—he still stood in the doorway—and looked down the hall in both directions and returned his attention to Adele.

"I wonder," he said unexpectedly, "what might have happened if I'd grown up differently. If I'd gone off-planet, I mean. I almost did, when I was eighteen. A Kostroman merchantman landed. They'd been damaged in a fight with pirates and needed repair. They'd lost some crew as well. The captain stayed with us while they were fitting new antennas. He offered to take me as a trainee officer."

Adele looked at Pansuela and tried to imagine him as a spacer, as a starship officer. She shook her head unconsciously. He had the intelligence and probably the education, but with the best will in the world she couldn't pretend he had a backbone. Though perhaps the drugs had leached it out of him. . . .

Pansuela gave her a bitter smile. "Do you ever wonder how things might have been different in your life, mistress?" he said.

How much did he know about her? And of course the answer was, "Nothing whatever."

"No, I do not," Adele said, bending backwards to loosen muscles that'd tightened during the past several hours of her hunching forward. "There was one major . . . crux point, I suppose you could call it, in my life. Occasionally I wonder what it would've been like had that developed otherwise—"

Had the Mundys and all their close associates not been slaughtered in the Proscriptions which she'd escaped by being off Cinnabar at the time.

"—but I find it's like trying to look through a brick wall. It's a completely pointless exercise, so I don't do it."

Adele cleared her throat and glanced down at the pile she'd been working through. She said, "Well, I'd better get back—"

Somebody shouted in mad fury, his voice echoing down the hallway like the roar of a balked predator. Metal hammered on wood.

"What on—" Pansuela said.

A heavy electromotive pistol *crack*ed. The slug hit metal with a bell note and the splintering of wood.

"That's from the guest wing!" Pansuela said. His mouth dropped open. The servants in the hallway had exchanged brief glances and vanished in the opposite direction from the shooting.

Adele stepped to the doorway. Her left hand was in her pocket.

❖   ❖   ❖

Daniel had eaten well, drunk very well, and thereafter exercised with an enthusiasm appropriate to a fit
young man who took pride in good workmanship. Even
so the first shouting brought him to his feet out of a
dreamless sleep. He didn't know what was going on
or even where he was, but he knew something was
wrong and that made it the business of Lieutenant
Daniel Leary.

God in heaven, it was dark! They'd had a candle
lantern that burned with a pinkish flame. The girl,
whatever her name was—Margolla?—thought it was
romantic and Daniel was happy with whatever a girl
thought was romantic. It'd burned out, though, and
the course of the evening he'd kicked heaven knew
where the trousers he'd laid neatly over the bunk's
footboard when he took them off.

He groped on the floor, still disoriented—it was dark
as six feet up a hog's bum!—and grabbed a handful
of the silky synthetic fabric as the girl said, "Dannie,
what's happening?" and somebody started banging on
a door just down the hallway.

The girl—her name *was* Margolla—switched on a
bedlamp. She was leaning toward him. Her breasts
were firm, full, and shapely—enticing under most
circumstances but right now of less interest to Daniel
than the fact that *Bloody hell, I've got my trousers on
backwards*!

"Daniel, where are you going?" Margolla said on a
rising note. Daniel jerked the door open.

Electric sconces at either corner illuminated the
hall with wan sufficiency. Father Rosario stood at the
door of the next suite down. His wide hat had fallen
off and lay like a soup dish on the floor beside him.
As Daniel stepped into the hallway, the priest put the
muzzle of his gleaming pistol against the lock-plate
and fired.

The brilliant white flash of oxidizing aluminum lit the hallway. The pellet hit the lock a clanging hammerblow that blew it out of the panel. The door-panel swung inward.

"Hey!" Daniel shouted, waving his arms as he started forward. He didn't have strong feelings about Count Klimov as a person, but the Count was a Sissie, a member with Daniel of a family bound tighter than mere genetics could do. "Drop it!"

Father Rosario turned, bringing up the pistol. Daniel, ten feet away, saw the tiny black hole of the muzzle and threw himself sideways.

The first slug missed, blasting a divot from the wainscoting before it ricocheted off the concrete core with a spiteful howl. Recoil lifted the barrel so the priest's next two shots smacked into the ceiling.

Daniel'd squinted as he rolled, but the flashes still left vivid afterimages quivering across his retinas. He saw Count Klimov, a gangling ghost of a man, lunge out of his room and sprint down the hall in the other direction.

Father Rosario turned, aiming through the doorway again. He was blinking, blinded by his own shots, but he caught motion from the corner of his eye and blasted twice more down the corridor just as the Count disappeared around the corner. The priest started after him, waving the pistol and screaming.

Bloody hell, it sounded like a whole stadium of people screaming, including Margolla bawling, "Dannie, don't do it!" Daniel launched himself in a flying tackle that would've smashed the priest to the floor hard enough to jar his teeth loose, let alone his gun— except that Flora Pansuela, darker and more rounded than the Count but just as naked, ran into the hall-way just at the wrong moment. Daniel crashed into her, knocking Flora into the doorjamb and slewing himself into the opposite wall. For all her softness, the lady was a solid weight.

Daniel rose to his feet again like a sprinter launching himself from the blocks. He'd never lost forward motion, just channeled it at the cost of some bruises. He'd feel them in the morning but they didn't slow him tonight.

Rosario stumbled on the hem of his long robe, triggering another shot into the floor. It caromed into the ceiling, then back to punch a hole in the door of the thankfully unoccupied room at the end of the hallway.

The priest stopped at the corner and pointed his weapon down the intersecting hall. Daniel caught him around the shoulders and crushed him against the opposite wall. He thought he heard bones crack, and he bloody well *hoped* he heard bones crack. The pistol bounced away harmlessly.

Father Rosario crumpled to the floor. Daniel fell on top of him, breathing through his mouth and suddenly queasy from the adrenaline he hadn't burned out of his system. He glanced down the hall through blobs of purple and orange flickering across his retinas. Count Klimov had tripped on a pile of boxes and was crawling on all fours toward the lighted doorway where Enrique Pansuela stood with a shocked expression.

Adele, her face still as marble, lifted the muzzle of the pistol on which she'd been taking up trigger-pressure. She breathed out, then slipped the weapon away in her pocket.

Daniel managed to rise to his hands and knees. He patted the priest on the back. "You may not be ready to thank me now, Rosario old boy," he said through dry lips. "But I just saved your worthless life!"

CHAPTER 16

Adele looked at the sky as Daniel and the Chief Engineer made a final inspection of the thrusters. She wasn't a weather expert, but . . .

She glanced at Hogg, standing beside her on the quay alongside the *Princess Cecile*. He nodded gloomily. "Aye, be coming down like a cow pissing on a flat rock before long," he said, answering the unspoken question. "God knows what it'll be like to take off in."

Adele frowned, thinking back. She had to restrain herself from getting out the data unit. "We've taken off in the rain before," she said, frowning deeper. "I don't recall it making any difference, did it?"

"Yeah, well," Hogg said. "We'll see."

The Pansuelas' open car splashed toward the harbor, flanked by the rainbows its tires cast up. The Klimovs, warned by Vesey on the bridge, appeared in the main hatch to await their visitors. The Count had been adamant about getting out of Pansuela House immediately after the shooting. Valentina had come back to the ship with him, though she'd exhibited more amusement than concern.

"He could've got his head shot clean *off*," Hogg said, glowering at the Count but obviously referring to Daniel. "And for what? For some wog who thinks he's something!"

He glared at Adele in outrage. "What *I* know, mistress, is when two guys have a problem about a girl, then the job of *every*bloodybody else is to keep outa the way and let 'em settle it! Right?"

"You'd have done the same thing if Daniel instead of the Count had been at risk, Hogg," Adele said in a neutral tone. She wasn't willing to have her silence read as assent, but neither did she want to argue with Hogg in his present mood. At least now she knew why he was so angry.

Hogg flashed her a slight, hard smile. "Aye, I would, mistress," he said, his tone minutely lighter. "But you and I will be a lot older before we see Daniel Leary crawling on his belly to get out of a fight, eh?"

The idea was so incongruous that Adele chuckled. "Yes, there's that," she said.

The Pansuelas were coming down the path, followed by a servant carrying a small box under a piece of damask. The Klimovs started across the boarding bridge to meet them on the quay. Somebody representing the ship ought to be present also. . . .

"Besides *which*," Hogg said venomously, "nothing more was going to happen to the Count if the young master'd just let things take their course. That so-called priest was going to be sporting a third eyehole before he got another shot off, right?"

"Yes," said Adele, "he was. But that didn't happen."

She cleared her throat. "Daniel is busy under the ship and it doesn't look like Mr. Chewning is going to appear," she said. Though it wasn't the duty of a junior warrant officer, she knew the crew expected Signals Officer Mundy to deputize for the captain when necessary in any sort of social setting. "I suppose I'll join our employers."

Adele thought about the night before as she walked to the foot of the boarding bridge where the two parties would meet. She'd killed in the past, and due to the life she now lived—by her own choice—she would very likely kill again. That was part of what she was.

But at the point she stopped caring that she killed, she'd be another creature like Tovera. There'd be an Adele Mundy who was intelligent and cultured, but who was no longer human and who'd never regain her soul.

She wasn't sure that those close to her, even Daniel, would recognize the difference; but she herself would know . . . and Tovera would know, looking into Adele's eyes and seeing a mirror.

"Lady Mundy," Enrique Pansuela said when he at last noticed Adele. He was drugged again, walking stiffly and talking with a complete lack of affect. His addiction allowed him to function with his normal intelligence, but he showed no more emotion than the concrete quay.

"Patron," Adele said, nodding crisply. *It's by his choice, just as I carry a gun by my choice.* The sight gave her a twinge of sadness nonetheless. "Lady Pansuela."

Flora acknowledged with a toss of her head; makeup couldn't hide the bruise on her right cheekbone. Her hair was teased high onto a series of combs, hand-carved from some opalescent material. Fish scales? Or perhaps bones? Something to look up as soon as Adele could with propriety bring out her data unit.

The Klimovs reached the quay, Valentina leading the Count. She offered Enrique her hand while eyeing his wife with cool amusement. Enrique touched the Klimovna's fingertips and dipped his head in a scant bow, seemingly oblivious of any emotional currents.

Count Klimov cleared his throat. He kept his eyes on the concrete except for quick glances at the others around him, the way a mouse might look from its hole to a roomful of people.

"You'll be returning to Todos Santos?" Enrique asked with bland friendliness. He glanced at the sky without any sign of concern that he'd be riding back to his house in an open car.

"No, Captain Leary has suggested a planet called Morzanga," Klimov said to his boots of tooled leather. "It's not on the way to anything, but time isn't of concern to us. His uncle found the wreckage of a starship there which the Captain now thinks might be John Tsetzes' yacht. Since we know Tsetzes passed this way, from the buckle."

"Yes, you'd explained your interest in this John Tsetzes," Enrique said. "We'd like to give you a present. Flora dear, will you make the presentation?"

His wife colored under her dark skin. "No, you do it," she said, looking away from everyone.

"As you please, dear one," Enrique said. "Ector, bring the gift forward."

The servant stepped between the Pansuelas. Enrique flicked off the damask and opened the box, still in the servant's hands.

Count Klimov began to tremble; Valentina laughed. Adele leaned forward, expecting to see John Tsetzes' belt buckle. Instead the box held the pistol Father Rosario had been using. Now that she had time to examine it, she realized it was of platinum with the Novy Sverdlovsk flag picked out in gold on the receiver.

"I hope this will make amends for the difficulties of last night," Enrique said. "It seemed a suitable gift, all things considered."

"No," said the Count in a choked voice. "No, no, you keep it."

"On the contrary, Georgi, dear one," said the Klimovna. She took the pistol from the box, pursing her lips at its unexpected weight. "I think this is a wonderful gift. And think of the story we'll have to tell when we return home."

She looked at Enrique and bowed. "I wish there were something we could give you in exchange," she said. Her eyes turned minusculely to lock on Flora. "But perhaps my husband already has, darling . . . ?"

Thunder rolled. Daniel called something cheerful. The spacers holding the lines pulled his inflatable raft toward the quay.

Adele looked at the two couples. She said nothing and showed nothing. But she was glad the *Princess Cecile* would be lifting from Tegeli very soon.

CHAPTER 17

While the *Princess Cecile* continued to orbit eighty miles above Morzanga, Daniel locked the frozen image of the village adjacent to their intended landing place on his display, then increased the magnification to where he could see the poles supporting the individual houses. A central circle contained about half the fifty-eight dwellings, and the remainder straggled away into the jungle in several directions.

Natives walked among the houses and tended fish weirs in the broad, mud-brown river nearby. A border of jungle concealed the village from anyone in the channel, but the weirs were a dead giveaway to its presence.

"According to Commander Bergen's logs, he landed the RCS *Granite* in the slough just east of this village," Daniel said. Ships, even exploration vessels like the *Granite*, didn't land in moving water if they could avoid it. Besides, landing directly in the river would destroy the weirs and very possibly incinerate some fishermen as well, not a good way to make friends of the locals. "It doesn't appear to have changed in the twenty-seven years since the *Granite* landed. Now, you'll notice here—"

He was speaking to the Klimovs, but he suspected half the crew was listening to his exposition. The riggers had come aboard after they retracted the antennas and stowed the sails, and so long as the *Sissie* was orbiting the Power Room technicians had nothing to do but watch gauges which didn't flicker more than an eyelash from a flat response.

"—the jungle is unbroken," Daniel continued, sliding to another portion of the main image. "When we scan for magnetic anomalies, however, we get this."

He cut in a cylindrical overlay with a ragged shadow spraying out to one long side where a crash had thrown debris. As with the optical image, the software had sharpened this considerably, though in a fashion that only an expert would recognize.

"Uncle Stacey—Commander Bergen, that is," Daniel continued, "noted this wreckage in his log, but he didn't bother to explore it. His orders were to chart a course through the cul-de-sac in which Morzanga lies, and from the anomaly's dimensions he assumed that the ship had been a Commonwealth vessel. They're known to trade in the region occasionally, and no doubt to raid as well."

Daniel cleared his throat. "Now, the chances are that the wreck *is* a Commonwealth ship," he said. "But it might just possibly be the yacht on which your John Tsetzes escaped. There's no way to tell without examining it on the ground, but that should be easy enough to accomplish."

"What do you mean by 'cul-de-sac'?" Valentina asked. *"Space is space, not so?"*

From the first the Klimovna had been the one to take an interest in the working of the ship. Her husband was good enough company, but he spent his time either drinking alone or playing cards for rice grains with Hogg. To Daniel's amazement, Hogg barely held his own. According to him, the Count's real edge came from equipment that allowed him to deceive sharpers who cheated with electronic aids. By spoofing their hardware, Klimov's natural skill allowed him to clean them out when they bet on what they thought was a sure thing.

"No, madam," Daniel said. The miniature of the Klimovna's face at the top of his display frowned at the formality, but her question had put him unconsciously into lecture mode. "If it were, we wouldn't be able to travel between stars. Each bubble universe within the Matrix has different physical constants; the only universal constant is the pressure of Casimir radiation which we use to drive our vessel. By entering bubbles where time and space vary in known fashions, we're able to adjust our position relative to objects in the sidereal universe when we return to it."

"Yes, Dannie," Valentina said with a hint of fraying patience. *"But what has that to do with culs-de-sac or whatever? Does your Matrix have walls in it?"*

A ghost image of Adele frowning flashed onto Daniel's display. She didn't speak, but her stern visage warned him to remember who he was speaking to. Not even his signals officer should've been able to crash the barriers onto the command console. In all likelihood, no other signals officer could have.

Daniel grinned, a conscious expression but an honest one as well. Imagine *her* warning *him* to show proper deference. And being right, of course, a fine example of "Do as I say, not as I do."

Aloud Daniel continued, "There's no brick wall, no, but there are locations in the sidereal universe where the energy levels of the interpenetrating bubbles are so high that the gradients would damage or destroy a ship which tried to enter them. This arm of the galaxy is such a location, a cul-de-sac."

He grinned more broadly, glad as he always was to be able to brag about Uncle Stacey's skill. "Now in fact Commander Bergen *did* find a way through the bottom of the sack, so to speak, but it was a wormhole that very few astrogators could conn even with the benefit of his logs. As a practical matter, traffic to Morzanga would have to come by way of Tegeli at the mouth of the sack. I doubt there's more than a ship or two in a generation."

"John Tsetzes was a space captain himself before he and his mercenaries hired themselves to our planet, then seized the government," Count Klimov said. *"A tyrant and a thief, but a great captain. Perhaps he found the passage out the other way before your Commander Bergen did, eh?"*

"Perhaps he did, your excellency," Daniel said. "All we know at this point is that Tsetzes didn't return by way of Tegeli, because there'd be record of his reappearance there if he had."

Daniel had been hot-tempered when he was a boy. Indeed, he still was when it was a matter of himself as a private person. But a junior officer in the RCN gets a great deal of experience in biting his tongue when those higher on the chain of command make stupid or even insulting statements, and the experience stood him in good stead now.

Adele inserted her image at the top of Daniel's display, joining the conversation formally. She kept the image slightly smaller than the Klimovs' and washed it out so that it was almost monochrome.

"Captain Leary?" she said obsequiously. *"Might Tsetzes have tried to reach the Commonwealth by the route Commander Bergen later found, but miscalculated and destroyed his ship in the process? If he'd gotten*

*through, I think there'd have been some mention of him
in the files I was able to copy in San Juan. As it is,
there's no record of John Tsetzes after he landed on
Tegeli . . . and nobody knew about that landing until you
uncovered the artifacts at Pansuela House."*

"I agree that's a possibility, Mundy," Daniel said, feeling himself relax as Adele spoke. "I'll continue to hope
that the *Nicator* crashed on Morzanga, though. If it
disintegrated in the Matrix, I'm afraid there's no hope
of ever recovering the Earth Diamond."

"Then set us down, Captain," the Count said with a
wave of his hand. *"By all means, set us down and we
will search the wreck in all hope. But for myself . . .
diamonds are sturdy things, that is so; but I fear that
a crashing starship would break even a diamond into
little bits."*

"Adele?" Daniel called over her helmet intercom.
*"We're about to receive a deputation from the village.
Unless you're doing something particularly important,
why don't you join us on shore."*

"I'm on my way," Adele said, closing up her data unit
and slipping the control wands into their sockets.
"There's nothing on this planet's RF band except
thunderstorms."

She walked to the companionway as she stowed the
data unit, wobbling for the first few steps. She'd been
sitting for a long time. In a way Adele's determined
search for radio transmissions was a failure, because
she hadn't turned anything up. On the other hand, it
was important to know the crew of the *Princess Cecile*
were the only civilized people on Morzanga.

Adele smiled faintly. Her mother would've objected
to the term "civilized people" because it implied that
the natives of Morzanga were something else. They
were something else. "Uncivilized" was a description,

not an insult. The natives of Morzanga didn't live in a technologically advanced civilization like the one whose officials had shot her mother dead and staked her head onto Speaker's Rock in Xenos.

Though the Morzangans probably had their equivalent. They were human, after all.

The corvette was open to vent the recycled wastes of ten days in space. Crewmen had locked automatic impellers capable of throwing streams of half-ounce slugs into the access ports on both sides of A Deck and at the cargo hatches on C Deck. The forward turret was raised; its twin plasma cannon were trained toward the village just out of sight to the west.

The gun crews looked tense. Not frightened, nothing like frightened; but very grimly prepared to turn everything within a mile of the ship into a shattered wasteland.

The squad on watch in the access hatch had similar expressions, holding their weapons instead of carrying them slung or leaning them against the bulkheads. They nodded as Adele stepped past.

Tovera carried her miniature sub-machine gun openly instead of concealed in her attaché case. She followed Adele onto the boarding bridge over the slough whose waters had absorbed the blast of the starship's landing.

"I feel underdressed," she murmured, nodding to the spacers holding stocked impellers and full-sized sub-machine guns. Occasionally she chose to demonstrate that she had a sense of humor.

"I doubt it'll be that sort of party," said Adele, resisting the impulse to hold her arms out for balance. The bridge was a full meter wide, and though footsteps made it quiver, Adele knew it was stressed for three-ton loads. "If it is, I'm sure they'll make allowances for us."

Some of the Sissies were good shots, and a few were excellent. The picked detachment of twenty waiting on the shore with Daniel and the Klimovs could withstand the attack of hundreds of Morzangans armed with bows and spears.

But nobody on the *Princess Cecile* was Tovera's equal with a pistol . . . unless it was Adele herself. As she'd said, that shouldn't matter today.

Crewmen had unloaded the aircar while Adele sat at her console. She hadn't seen it since Barnes flew staggeringly back to the *Sissie* in San Juan, barely able to stay airborne carrying the Count and three of the worst-injured spacers. Nobody'd mistake the vehicle for new, but the dents were hammered out and the twisted fan blades replaced.

Barnes stood beside the driver's seat again; his friend Dasi was across the vehicle from him. Both cradled stocked impellers and were eyeing the vegetation fifty yards inland where the ground was dry enough to support sizeable trees. Most of the other spacers were looking that way too.

"There's six men with spears at the edge of the jungle," Tovera said in a low voice. "They're watching us."

"I'll take your word for it," Adele said as she joined Daniel.

"With your permission, your excellency," Daniel said to Klimov, "I'll walk toward them alone. They're probably afraid to come out in the face of our weapons. Hogg, hold this if you will."

The Count didn't even bother to shrug assent to what was obviously a *pro forma* request. Daniel offered Hogg his stocked impeller.

"Like hell you're going without me!" Hogg snapped. He held out his own weapon to the nearest spacer. "Here, Castro," he said. "Hold this for a bit while me and the master prove we're bloody heroes."

"I'll go with the Lieutenant, Hogg," Adele said quietly. "You can cover us from here."

Hogg opened his mouth to protest, then closed it into a grin. "Yeah," he said, "I guess there's nothing I can do with a knife that you can't handle your own way. Eh, Tovera?"

Tovera shrugged. Her smile could've cut glass.

"I'm glad to have your company, Mundy," Daniel said with a grin that melted the public formality of the words. "It's always reassuring to know that whatever information I need will be immediately available."

They stepped forward, side by side. Near the ship, plasma had seared the ground cover into a twisted mat over mud which had dried to a crust. It bore Adele's weight, but Daniel repeatedly broke through and splashed his boots and trouser legs.

"This is awkward going . . . ," he murmured, grinning. "But by landing in the slough, I didn't risk the reflected exhaust flipping us over on our back as I would on dry land. I think of the mud as one of life's minor trade-offs."

"I don't mind the mud," Adele said. "But nobody else aboard is afraid you'd botch a landing, so I don't see why you should be."

"Ah, perhaps so that nobody else has *reason* to be afraid," Daniel said. He raised his left arm, palm forward, and waved to the brush twenty yards away. Trees more than a hundred feet tall rose in a green/black backdrop slightly farther inland.

"Good day, gentlemen!" he called. "We're visitors from Cinnabar, and we hope you'll accept gifts from us in return for our intrusion."

"Do they have atlatls?" Adele asked in an undertone. "Spear-throwers, that is?"

"Uncle Stacey didn't say anything about that," Daniel said, "but of course it wasn't the sort of thing that

interested him. Mind, we're far too close ourselves for
that to matter."

A lanky man nearly seven feet tall rose from the
brush. He wore only a feather breechclout, but for a
moment Adele mistook his tattoos for a woven garment
covering his torso from neck to elbows. His spear was
made from a thin jointed reed. Adele noted with a flush
of pleasure that it was fitted into a knobbed stick whose
leverage would more than double the cast possible with
an unaided arm.

"What gifts?" the man demanded. He spoke Universal, the pre-Hiatus trade language, with a thick but
intelligible accent. Where he wasn't tattooed, his skin
was startlingly white, and his red hair didn't seem to
be dyed. "Do you have slash?"

"Indeed, we'll give you enough slash that your
whole village can drink yourselves into a stupor,"
Daniel said, continuing to walk forward till he and
Adele were only six feet from the brush. "But we'll
do that as we're leaving, sir, so there won't be any
awkwardness. Though—if you're the chief of your
village, we'd be more than happy to offer you a taste
of something now."

Even this close, Adele couldn't see the five other
natives Tovera had mentioned. Well, Tovera would be
at a loss to find a snatch of pre-Hiatus poetry.

Adele consciously avoided a grimace. Slash, home-
made liquor, was as much a part of star travel as
Casimir radiation; and equally necessary, many spacers would've claimed. Anything organic can be fermented; anything fermented can be distilled into liquor
strong enough that you might be able to get drunk
before nausea emptied your gorge.

Adele had never found an attraction in numbing her
mind, and if she had she'd still have been unwilling
to use slash for the purpose. In this, however, she

realized she was in the minority of those aboard the *Princess Cecile*.

The native hesitated, his eyes flickering to his left. Another man, of similar build but much older, rose from a twisted bush close enough for Adele to have touched him. Four more men of intermediate age stood up also; it was as if they'd coalesced out of thin air.

"I am the Captain!" said the oldest native emphatically. The flint point of his spear was bound to the shaft with copper wire, the only metal Adele saw among the six of them. "He's only the Purser, and that because the Lieutenant died yesterday and the Purser was promoted to Engineer. You must give *me* the slash."

A burly man, stocky only in comparison with his fellows, nodded enthusiastically. In addition to his spear, he carried a stone axe whose head with a little imagination resembled an adjustable wrench.

"Indeed we will, Captain," said Daniel, his voice formally portentous. "For you, and some for your officers too. Then—"

He paused, smiling broadly.

"—we'd be pleased to have you accompany us on a visit to the wrecked ship nearby."

He gestured toward the *Princess Cecile*, bowed to the Captain, and turned. As he started back with Adele beside him, Daniel whispered, "Because if he's with us, I'll worry less about his friends suddenly deciding that they might get their slash quicker if they grabbed some of us for ransom."

CHAPTER 18

"Captain Leary?" said the Count, shuffling down the boarding bridge between a pair of riggers. He'd changed clothes after he'd slipped off the bridge earlier. The shock seemed to have sobered him as well—he'd been sampling the slash with the village officers—but it hadn't done anything positive for his state of mind. "When we come back I order you, I *order* you, to move the ship to dry ground. Do you understand?"

"Certainly, your excellency," Daniel said, bowing from the waist. He turned to his lieutenant and continued, "Mr. Chewning, while I'm gone I want you to move the locals out of the way so that on my return I can shift the vessel to the clearing three hundred yards west of here. Don't use any more force than you need to, but I don't want to burn up half the village."

Moving a starship overland on its plasma thrusters was a simple piece of shiphandling by comparison with coming down on full braking thrust and suddenly having to deal with reflections from a solid surface. The only real difficulty was that all the villagers were now clustered on shore beside the *Princess Cecile*. The corvette would incinerate everything it overflew at low altitude. Daniel figured forest fires were enough of a problem without having a couple hundred dead natives on his conscience as well.

"Can I give 'em a tot when I get 'em out of the way?" Chewning asked.

Daniel considered. The officers had had their treat, but he'd remained adamant than the ordinary villagers weren't to have liquor until the *Sissie* was ready to lift off-planet again.

"Yes, of course," he said. "But two ounces only and make sure they all drink their own share, Chewning. The locals don't seem to have much of a head for liquor, and I'm afraid of what'll happen if they get too much in them."

The native officers—Captain, Lieutenant, Bosun, Engineer, Gunner and Purser—had been given four ounces, a quantity all the spacers thought was safe. Either the batch had been spiked with a little too much hydraulic alcohol, or the local tipple was pretty mild. All six were drunk: two sleeping, two arguing violently about something Daniel couldn't understand, and the Captain was singing loudly with his eyes closed.

The Lieutenant had gotten extremely affectionate with Barnes. Under other circumstances Barnes might have been interested, but as things were he'd held the native's arms until Dasi laid the fellow out with a judicious punch to the jaw.

Having delivered his ultimatum, Klimov stalked to the waiting aircar. Valentina walked behind him, throwing Daniel a bemused glance over her shoulder. It was going to be crowded with eight aboard, but it wasn't a long flight.

Daniel glanced at Adele, standing beside him. She'd been reading something projected on her visor—her handheld data unit was stowed—but she looked up when she caught his movement. "I'm ready," she said simply, answering the question he hadn't needed to ask.

Daniel nodded and they walked together to the aircar. Hogg and Barnes, who'd be driving, had walked the Captain into the front seat between them. The bench wasn't made for three, but planting the native between two strong men was the best way to be sure he wouldn't decide to get out at a hundred feet in the air.

"Your excellency," Daniel said. "Valentina. If you'd be so good as to take the rear pair of seats. That'll allow me to sit directly behind our guest in case he needs steadying in the air."

In case he needs to be cold-cocked, of course; but if Daniel said that, the Count in his present mood might insist he was able to take care of that if it became necessary. Daniel didn't trust Klimov to act as quickly as might be required.

"Come, Georgi," the Klimovna said, leading her husband into the back before he could decide to protest. The Count was a generally pleasant companion, but his tipsy fall into the muck had made him ridiculous in his own eyes . . . and, he correctly suspected, in the eyes of his wife and the spacers as well. He was in a foul mood.

Tovera smiled her cobra smile as she and Adele got in, squeezing themselves to opposite sides of the middle bench so that Daniel could sit between them. Tovera, like Hogg and Daniel himself, carried a sub-machine gun from the corvette's arms locker. It was a good weapon for dense forest. In addition she had her own smaller weapon in a holster under her left shoulder.

The Captain was still singing, but the words were so slurred that Daniel wasn't sure whether they were meant to be Universal. Barnes brought the drive fans up to 90% power, angling them against one another so that the aircar hopped and quivered like a hound straining at its leash.

"If you're ready, Barnes," Daniel said, "then take us along the plotted course at just above the treetops—and no faster than you have to, either."

Barnes synched the fans and poured on the coal. He'd chosen too steep an angle for the present load: the car leaped upward at 30 degrees for a few seconds, then mushed and would've crashed into the slough if Barnes hadn't slammed his yoke forward to drop the nose. They picked up speed in a swoop that he converted into a climbing turn just before they plunged into the forest. The car zoomed over the trees and kept rising till Barnes tilted the yoke at five hundred feet—overcorrecting again but this time with enough height that the maneuver wasn't immediately dangerous.

The Count and Countess were shouting in terror. Daniel wasn't especially worried, though now that he thought about it he understood why the Klimovs would be. He supposed he'd gotten so used to Barnes' driving that it didn't bother him any more than walking along a spar in the Matrix did.

The native in the front seat sat upright and stared in all directions, his eyes seeming twice the size they'd been when he closed them on the ground. "I'm dead!" he screamed. Daniel put a hand on the fellow's shoulders, but he stayed firm in his seat. "I'm dead! I'm in Hell!"

The aircar pulled out of its dive twenty feet above the treetops, then started to climb again. "Barnes, slow down!" Daniel said. "We're there, just bring us down by the tree with the orange foliage over there to the right!"

He wasn't actually sure that was the right place, but he knew he'd better give Barnes a specific target or the good lord knew where they'd end up. The car banked and came around in a tight starboard turn, losing altitude more rapidly than it slowed. At what seemed to Daniel to be the last possible instant, they slid between the tops of two emergent trees and dropped to the height of the undergrowth where they hovered, barely crawling forward. Ahead of them was a battered metal cylinder covered with vines, tree roots, and generations of composted leaf litter.

Barnes landed softly. *He's a better driver than I realized*, Daniel thought.

Barnes turned and beamed at him. "How about that, sir?" he said cheerfully. "I thought we were going to auger right in, but what d'ye know, she leveled out after all!"

And then again, maybe Hogg should drive the car back. . . .

They got out of the aircar gratefully, stepping onto black leaf-mold from which fungus sprouted in a score of different shapes and colors. Daniel found a prism of rock just beneath the surface and slid his boot to the side before putting weight on it. Valentina, not a woodsman, wasn't so careful. She shouted as her ankle twisted. She'd have tumbled forward if her husband hadn't caught her.

"Careful, dear one," the Count said as he set her upright. He was smiling for the first time since he plunged into the slough. "The footing here is tricky."

The wrecked starship was belly-up or nearly so. Thinking aloud for his companions' sake, Daniel said, "It wasn't moving very fast when it went over, so they probably didn't crash while landing. Now, I wonder if . . ."

He strode purposefully toward the vessel, oblivious of the others and confident he was safe in ignoring everything but his personal question. Hogg was watching the forward arc about them while Tovera took the rear, a division of concern they'd made without discussion so far as Daniel could tell. The two worked well together.

He extended the wire butt of his sub-machine gun and used it to scrape litter away from the ship's steel hull. "Yes!" he cried, pleased to have support for his surmise.

"You've found Tsetzes' yacht?" Valentina called eagerly.

Her husband in almost the same breath said, "How do we get in? Good God, if the regalia's still aboard her, think of it!"

"Excuse me, your excellencies!" Daniel said hastily as he straightened. "I was unclear, I'm afraid. This isn't the *Nicator*. It's a typical country craft, the sort of trader-*cum*-raider we saw in San Juan and all over the Commonwealth. But judging from the height of the trees that've grown around it—"

Which could only be an estimate, based on what Daniel knew of similar trees on similar planets.

"—I'd say that the wreck is of roughly the same period as when John Tsetzes might have arrived on Morzanga. And the wreck was destroyed—"

He tapped the hull's smeared bands of rainbow discoloration.

"—by plasma bolts at short range. It's possible that two pirates fell out with one another, of course; but it's also possible that John Tsetzes forestalled what he suspected was an attempt at piracy by destroying a strange vessel as soon as it arrived. He was, I gather from his history, a man who might have made that sort of decision?"

"He was a butcher," said the Count. His tone was more approving than not. "A bloody-handed butcher."

The native stepped forward purposefully and stabbed

his long spear into the leaf litter. He brought it up with something the length of his finger wriggling on the point. Before Daniel got a good look—it was multi-legged but seemed to have a soft body—the fellow lifted his head and dropped the creature down his throat without chewing. If you *were* going to eat the thing, swallowing it whole in that fashion was probably the better course. . . .

"Captain?" Valentina said to him. As she spoke, she walked toward where a vine bearing hard-shelled fruit crawled along hull-plates whose seams had ruptured. "How long has the ship been here? Do your people have year records?"

"Missy, not there!" the native warned in sudden alarm. He thrust his spear before her in bar. "The firebugs will gnaw your bones!"

"What?" Valentina said. She stopped and turned to the native, but she was still within a foot of the dangling fruit.

Daniel, guessing the problem without knowing the specifics of it, touched Valentina's forearm and moved her back more by guidance than force. "See the little holes in the rind of those orange gourds?" he said. "I think the chief means that there are insects, insectoids, living there that defend the fruit."

The Captain nodded approvingly at Daniel. He tapped the vine with his spear-point, then stepped back quickly. From three holes in the nearest gourd spilled insects so tiny they looked like a seepage of liquid. Individually they had black shells with a line of red.

"Firebugs!" the fellow said. "They guard the money plants. Maybe tomorrow I smoke them out to get the money seeds, but today we must bury the old Lieutenant."

He looked shrewdly at Daniel and added, "Perhaps you fly me here again quick-quick in your flying boat?"

"Perhaps," Daniel temporized. "But answer the Countess' question: how long ago did this ship crash?"

The Captain shrugged. "Long long time," he said. "My mother's father's father came on this."

"So the crew survived?" said the Klimovna. "Do you have artifacts from the ship?"

"Some live, some die," said the Captain with another shrug. "Now all dead."

He looked at the wreck with a spark of interest which quickly faded. "Once our village was rich from this," he said, "but that was long long past. There's nothing left to take, not for long long time."

Klimov frowned. "Perhaps there's a locked compartment these natives couldn't get into? he said to Daniel. "One that might hold the Earth Diamond?"

"If a number of the crew survived, they'd have been able to open any compartments—by force with tools from the vessel if no other way," Daniel said. "And this *wasn't* John Tsetzes' ship, your excellency."

"Yes, yes, of course," Klimov said, sinking into himself again. "Damn it, so close and nothing!"

Perhaps close, thought Daniel. But in his heart he was just as disappointed as the Count.

"You take me back," the Captain said. "We bury the old Lieutenant today. There be much food, much drink."

He smacked his lips; for further emphasis he slapped his belly with his free hand. His palm and spread fingers cracked like pistol shots.

"Yes, we'll take you back," said the Klimovna with a look of calculation. "And we'll supply you with a tub of slash if you let us—let me, at least—record the funeral celebration."

Daniel's protest didn't make it to his tongue. He thought it was a *bloody* poor idea to get the villagers drunk and sit in the middle of them, but Valentina already knew what her employee thought. She was going to do as she pleased anyway.

Well, Daniel had obeyed orders before that he disagreed with. That was how a chain of command worked.

"Yes, missy!" the Captain said. He laughed heartily, then added, "Poor bastard Lieutenant, he miss all this slash by one day only! He chew rocks when we put him in the ground!"

"Right!" Daniel said. "We'll get back then, shall we?"

Speaking from his side, Adele said, "I've radioed ahead, in case Mr. Pasternak needs to run more liquor. Fortunately, slash doesn't seem to require aging."

"And I," said the Klimovna, "will fly us back. You will not argue."

Daniel bowed to her. "I wouldn't think of arguing, your excellency," he said. "It's a fine idea."

"Yes," said Adele. "A lifesaver, I would put it."

Adele, walking alongside the aircar with Daniel, hadn't thought much about what the funeral feast would entail. She was shocked to see the dead man tied to the base of a tree in a seated position, his legs splayed out in front of him. His scrawny body was stark naked, but he'd been painted orange, blue, and yellow. If there was a pattern, it was too subtle for Adele to recognize it.

His arms were curled around the bushel-sized pile of strung beads resting on his lap. Beside the corpse, one hand toying with the beads, stood a younger man with similar facial features. His chest was splotched orange, blue and yellow also, but he wore a feather breechclout like other adult natives; children under the age of ten went naked.

The whole village was assembled, close to two hundred people above the age of nursing infants. They had neither plates nor utensils, but each held a polished wooden drinking bowl.

On reed mats stretching from where the dead man sat were baskets of fruit, trays of broiled fish, and wooden tubs cut from sections of large tree-trunks. Some of the tubs held porridge, but most of them were filled with pale yellow fluid on which floated chewed bits of vegetable matter. Adele assumed it was alcoholic, but she couldn't imagine circumstances in which she would taste it herself.

Valentina drove the aircar slowly into the clearing with twenty heavily-armed spacers walking alongside. The Count sat beside his wife; Woetjans and the native Captain had the rearmost pair of seats. Mr. Pasternak's technicians had removed the middle bench and put in its place a 50-gallon tank, previously part of the water purification system.

The Sissies pushed back the crowding natives until the car could halt beside the corpse as the Captain had directed. As soon as the vehicle stopped, eight crewmen began filling gallon buckets from the tap in the big tank while the others remained on guard.

Adele felt prickly, prepared for serious trouble but not seeing any way to prevent it. She clasped her hands in front of her. She'd have been less nervous if she could've taken out her data unit, but that would've been silly.

Daniel, walking beside her, looked cheerfully at ease. He wore a pistol in a full-flap holster, but Adele didn't recall ever having seen her friend use a gun. He had a baton of structural plastic as long as his forearm, however. Given the strength of Daniel's wrists and shoulders, it would lay out anyone as quickly as a shot from his service pistol.

Daniel eyed the beads in the dead man's lap. "Look, Adele!" he whispered. "They're seeds, little hard seeds.

They must come from gourds like those near the wreck. Of course! The seeds are valuable because the insects, the firebugs, make them difficult to gather!"

Adele looked carefully at the strings because they were of interest to her friend, though she didn't share Daniel's enthusiasm for natural history. The individual seeds were about the size of her little fingernail and flat, running ten or a dozen to the inch the way they were strung. She frowned: there must be many thousands of seeds in the pile. Cleaning and drilling each one would've taken time, quite apart from the risk of being attacked by the insects.

The Captain rose to his feet in the back of the aircar. "My people!" he shouted. "My great friends from the sky have brought me slash! I will share it with you out of the goodness of my heart!"

When the aircar stopped, the villagers had been seated to either side of the long mat; the elders—the officers—and their families were on the end close to the dead man. The crowd gave a great bawl of sound and surged upright, about to rush the aircar like a tidal wave pouring over the shore.

"Hogg!" Daniel said.

Hogg fired his stocked impeller into the treetop, blowing a thigh-thick limb off in a shower of matchstick-sized fragments. The gun's buzzing whiplash was lost in the *whack*! of the slug disintegrating thick wood a heartbeat later. The limb sagged with a series of pops as it tore the few remaining fibers holding it to the trunk; then it plunged twisting to the ground.

Natives nearby wailed as they scrambled back. Hogg watched with a disdainful expression as heat waves shimmered above the barrel of his weapon. The powerful slug had kicked the limb enough to the side that no one in the crowd was in any danger.

"If you, our honored hosts, will remain seated with

your bowls waiting . . . ," Daniel said in a voice easily
heard even by ears stunned by the sudden gunshot.
"Then members of my crew will pour out the amount
of our gift to you. Anyone who gets to his feet instead
of waiting will show himself to be unworthy of the gift.
Do you understand?"

The natives made a variety of noises. Collectively
it sounded like a growl, but those who were still standing scrambled to places at the mat; none of those
seated got to their feet.

The Captain nodded to the painted man standing—
now squatting—beside the corpse. He hopped to his
feet and squeaked, "My father bids the feast begin!"

The natives set in with a will. The preferred technique seemed to be to stick the left hand into the porridge tubs and use two fingers of the right to guide any
overflow back into the corners of the mouth. Fish up
to the size of the diner's palm were swallowed whole;
larger chunks were devoured in mouth-sized increments.

Layton dipped a standard ten-ounce mess mug into
his bucket of slash and handed it to the gleeful Captain,
while the dead man's son got a similar amount in a bowl
fashioned from a seed pod. Adele didn't see any pottery,
even low-fired earthenware; the tubs were waterproofed
with pitch on the inside and painted on the outer surfaces with geometric designs in several colors.

Hogg edged close to Daniel and Adele. "Reminds
me of my old man's wake," he said, chuckling. He
grinned at Adele and added, "Of course, these folk're
neater about the way they chow down than we was
back at Bantry, eh, young master?"

"Perhaps a trifle," Daniel said judiciously, watching
food flying in all directions. "Of course, they haven't
been drinking all afternoon the way everybody was at
Old Guzzler's wake."

The native Bosun, a grizzled man with feathers stuck

through holes in both earlobes, tossed off his slash with thoughtless haste. He choked, spewed the clear liquid out his nose, and fell over on his back retching. After a moment he rolled upright again and dipped a bowl of the local brew.

The Klimovna squeezed down between the dead man's son and the Captain, seated to his right. The natives made room cheerfully, talking to her and to one another as they ate.

The Count stood behind his wife, looking awkward and out of place. When he happened to catch Adele looking at him, he flashed her an embarrassed smile; they both quickly looked away.

Adele thought about the Klimovs' relationship. Obviously it worked for them. . . . She realized, not for the first time, that one of the reasons she liked dealing with information that had already been compiled was that it was much simpler than understanding people in the raw.

Spacers carrying buckets of slash bustled about behind the facing rows of natives. They were working from several points around the mat, taking the bowls and dipping them full before handing them back.

Adele looked at Daniel with pursed lips. He shrugged and said, "Since I wasn't able to carry out my original plan, I'm proceeding on the second option: getting them all falling-down drunk before they have time to go berserk."

"Ah," Adele said, nodding. She pursed her lips again. "But the children?" she said.

"All the boys old enough to wear a nappy," said Tovera, standing behind her, "have flint knives as well. For myself, I don't assume the girls of similar age are harmless either. I wasn't."

Adele cleared her throat. "Yes," she said. "There's that."

Better that she watch the children drink themselves comatose than that she see what happened when one of them did something Tovera thought was threatening. Having a servant like Tovera was in some ways like walking around with a live grenade.

Sometimes, of course, you *need* a live grenade. Signals Officer Adele Mundy did, at any rate.

A native turned and vomited over the ground behind her. She wiped her mouth with the back of her hand and resumed eating. Halfway through another bowl of porridge, her eyes rolled up and she toppled onto her face in the tub. The man sitting next to her lifted her out, apparently because she was in the way of him getting porridge.

Daniel was no more an ethnologist than Count Klimov was, so instead he kept up a breezy discussion of the animals that were coming to light. Most of them appeared by crawling over or into the food. Adele noted with wry amusement that bugs which looked like black rice-grains had a particular affinity for the native beer in which they spun like tiny boats; those which landed in cups of slash quickly sank.

After a few minutes, Adele seated herself cross-legged and got out her handheld unit. There were enough people to keep an eye on the natives—who appeared to be happy drunks after all, so long as spacers continued to pour refills—while Daniel and Tovera between them would prevent anybody from accidentally stepping on the librarian sitting in the dirt. When Daniel pointed out the feathered creatures flitting about the stump from which Hogg shot the limb, Adele could plunge straight into the database to see what was known about them.

Apparently nothing was known. Commander Bergen's was the only formal account of Morzanga in the Cinnabar archives, and Uncle Stacey hadn't shared his nephew's interest in natural history. Perhaps a paper: *Notes on Aviform Species of Morzanga*, by Daniel Leary, Lieutenant RCN. . . .

"Friends!" called the son of the dead man who now stood, a trifle wobbly, beside the corpse; he held a flint knife. He must've gotten to his feet while Adele was lost in her unsuccessful data search.

The whole assembly rose; those who were able to, at any rate. Daniel kept his eyes on what was happening around him, but he held his left arm out as a bar on which Adele could lift herself. She gripped it and pulled herself upright with one hand as she put away the data unit with the other.

"My father bids you greet him so that he can give you his final gifts!" the son said. "Praise him as you go about your business in this world, so that he may have honor in the afterlife!"

The Captain walked forward, tugging the uncertain Klimovna along with him. The son raised a string of money and snipped it with his knife. He tossed the section to the Captain, cut another and gave it to Valentina, and—as the Captain pulled Valentina out of the way—gave a third piece to the new Lieutenant.

The whole village began filing past the corpse, getting gifts of money. The length of the string didn't seem to matter; the sections ranged from a foot or so long to about a yard. The son flicked a loop up with one hand and clipped it with the other, thus stretching a greater or lesser amount depending where the other end lay in the pile.

The Klimovna showed her string to the rest of them. Daniel and the Count learned forward; after a moment, and with a vague sense of irritation, Adele bent closer also. Deep in her soul she believed that information was something you looked up instead of collecting yourself, but the *Sailing Directions'* cursory description of Morzanga didn't cover seed money any more than it did feathered creatures.

The seeds were symmetrical ovals, flat, and of a pale ivory color. The string was some sort of vegetable fiber, knotted on either side of each seed. The money seemed to smell faintly of camphor, but the odor might've come from the paint covering the dead man's body.

A good half the village had filed past to get their gift. The son jerked a fresh string loose. Now that so much had been dispensed, Adele could see that the money was heaped around a glittering ball resting in the lap of the corpse. She nudged Daniel and pointed; he adjusted his visor magnification with a quick ease that she could never manage. The Klimovna turned to see what they were looking at.

Husband and wife reacted simultaneously—she by screaming, him with a choked cry, "The Earth Diamond!"

Valentina lunged for the gleaming object, the string of money dangling forgotten from her right hand. Daniel grabbed her from behind by the collar and jerked her back, so quickly and hard that her feet both kicked off the ground for an instant.

"What?" said the Count, an outraged expression forming. He started toward Daniel; Hogg body-checked him dead in his tracks.

"Valentina," Daniel said, releasing the woman but keeping himself between her and the adorned corpse. "Please. We'll get it, I promise you; but not in a fashion that we're all butchered on a pile of wog corpses, *please*."

The Klimovna shook herself. Her icy fury melted with the suddenness of snow slumping off a roof. "Yes, Captain," she said. "You will fetch us the diamond when you can; but if you please, don't be too long about it."

The Captain stood sipping his liquor in the midst of the party from the *Princess Cecile*, ignoring—apparently unaware—of the by-play among them. Daniel turned to him and, gesturing a rigger named Nussbaum closer with his just-refilled bucket of slash, said, "Captain, is that jewel on the old Lieutenant's lap going to be given away also? And say, why don't you have another glass of slash?"

The Captain gulped down the last of what was in his mug, then doubled up coughing. Daniel worked the mug out of his grip and gave it to Nussbaum to dip full. The native straightened and drank again, but with proper care.

The dead man's son whipped more money from the pile; Adele took her left hand out of her pocket and relaxed. Whatever the object was, it wasn't a diamond.

Now that she could see almost the whole thing, an engraved sphere a foot in diameter, she wasn't even sure it was mineral. It had the opalescence of a soap bubble rather than a diamond's sharp refractions. Besides, the Earth Diamond was supposed to be flawless. Granted that historians might gild reality, even a politician would've choked before claiming purity for an object so translucently milky.

"Ah, the Sky Ball," the Captain said. He leaned down and wriggled his free hand under the sphere to lift it from the strings of money. The other natives continued with their business, unconcerned by what was happening. "It stays in Captain's House, except when officer dies."

He handed it to Daniel. Before Daniel could pass it to the Klimovna, she snatched it greedily away from him.

"It's light!" she said. "But—Georgi, look at this! It's not a diamond, but it's carved with the continents of Earth as they were before the Hiatus. Is it not?"

"Daniel, hold this for me," Adele said curtly as she handed him her data unit. She couldn't hold it and operate it at the same time, so in lieu of a table in this present need her friend's hands would have to do. Her wands flickered, retrieving the image of the Earth Diamond, the real one, where she'd cached it. She projected it as an omnidirectional hologram in the air beside the clumsy fake that the Klimovna held.

"Waugh!" said the Captain, jerking backward. His feet didn't move as they might have done ten ounces of slash ago; he'd have fallen if Hogg hadn't caught him around the shoulders with the reflex of long experience in dealing with drunks.

"In addition to the obvious differences in outline . . . ," Adele said. The "continents" on the Sky Ball could've been outlined by a child drawing in mud with his fingers. "You'll note that the Earth Diamond is etched on the interior of the sphere by an artist working through a pinhole at the North Pole."

She expanded the northernmost ten degrees of the image, then rotated it to bring the concave interior into view. The Captain stared at the transformations with the complete amazement of a man seeing a pig walk down the street on its hind legs.

"Whereas this object, the Sky Ball . . . ," Adele continued. She needed to record imagery of the object, she realized as she spoke. "Is carved on the outer surface in the normal fashion."

"It appears to be of vegetable origin," Daniel said, frowning. He straightened, looking across the faces turned to his. "Though the important fact is that whatever its origin—and I assume it's local—it could only have been made by somebody who'd seen the Earth Diamond. John Tsetzes or at least the loot he escaped from Novy Sverdlovsk with *has* been here on Morzanga."

"Can we buy it?" the Count said, looking troubled.

"It's trash!" Valentina said angrily. "Why would we want to make fools of ourselves?"

She shoved the ball back at the Captain. Startled and unprepared, he'd have let it hit the ground had not Daniel snatched it as it fell.

Valentina's fierce eyes locked on the Captain's. "Where did this come from?" she demanded. "Do you have the original it was carved from?"

"It's from seaweed that floats up on the beach of the big water three days journey toward sunset," the native said. He blinked and rubbed his eyes with the back of the hand that didn't hold the mug of liquor. "This is *very* big bubble, though. Nobody ever has seen so big a one again."

Daniel nodded approvingly. "Yes, of course," he said. "A flotation bladder from a deep sea plant. Storms would occasionally break pieces loose to where the currents could carry them to shore."

"I don't care where the plant came from!" Valentina snapped. She jabbed the Captain with the tips of her index and middle fingers. "It's the design that matters. Where did you get the design, you?"

He looked even more puzzled. "We've always had the Sky Ball," he said. "My father's father had it."

The second part of the statement was probably true, Adele realized, since he'd said his *mother's* father's father had been from the crew of the ship destroyed by gunfire. Daniel's suggestion, that John Tsetzes had destroyed the other vessel when it first appeared, looked increasingly probable.

The alert from the *Princess Cecile* winked simultaneously in her helmet and Daniel's. They straightened together.

"What ship? What ship? What ship?" queried a vessel in orbit above Morzanga. Its transponder declared it was the *Belle Ideal* of Condon's Planet, one of the independent worlds loosely allied with Cinnabar; Adele recognized the signal as coming from the *Goldenfels* even before the analysis program—which was part of Mistress Sand's equipment—confirmed her assumption. No two radio transmitters are perfectly identical, any more than any two human voices are.

Because Adele had set her handheld unit to echo emergency signals automatically, she didn't have to bring up the commo display. Her wands twitched, locking the bridge and Battle Center transmitters so that the duty officer—Chewning—couldn't respond. The wrong response—the truth—would be suicide.

Her eyes met Daniel's. The rest of the group from the *Princess Cecile* continued to talk among themselves, scarcely aware that the two officers were only physically present at the moment. "Daniel, it's the *Goldenfels*," she said. "Will you trust me to handle this my way?"

"Yes," he said. The data unit was rock steady in his hands, though he couldn't see its display or guess what she had in mind. "Woetjans, move other people away from us, please. There's a problem and Mistress Mundy mustn't be bothered while she's dealing with it."

"*Goldenfels*, this is Adele Mundy of Bryce," Adele said. There was a bustle among those nearby, but her world had shrunk down to her screen and her mind as she used the only weapon that could possibly save them: information. "I'm secretary to a pair of rich boobs from Novy Sverdlovsk. Listen, they've found the Earth Diamond! I repeat, they've found the Earth Diamond! If you'll help me, we can save it for Guarantor Porra instead of having it go decorate some hog farm in the back of the beyond! Over."

She was taking a series of risks, the first and greatest being that she'd replied using the *Goldenfels'* real name instead of the false identity coming from the ship's transponder. Adele's offer was only believable if it was made by an Alliance citizen to an Alliance ship. With luck they'd overlook the question of how she'd recognized them or at least give her a chance to explain.

The fact the *Goldenfels* had tracked the *Princess Cecile* from Todos Santos and was giving a false name indicated that Captain Bertram hadn't come to talk. Because of their relative locations, the *Sissie* was a sitting duck.

High Drive motors didn't do a perfect job of combining antimatter and normal matter to create thrust; unconverted antimatter in the exhaust reacted violently with any normal matter outside the nozzle. A ship in vacuum could fire missiles to the surface with reasonable accuracy, but missiles fired from the bottom of an atmosphere would destroy themselves before they climbed to a target in orbit.

"*What ship? What ship?*" continued for two beats before the transponder shut off. After a brief pause, a male voice said, "*Unknown caller, identify yourself. Over.*"

"This is Alliance citizen Adele Mundy aboard the yacht *Princess Cecile!*" Adele said. She'd lived on Bryce long enough, working in the Academic Collections, that she could easily counterfeit an upper-class accent. "I'm alone in the control room because the officers are all getting drunk with the local savages, but somebody may come in at any moment. Listen, the Klimovs have bought the Earth Diamond from the savages! Look it up, I don't have time to explain, but it's valuable beyond belief! Land your ship nearby, pretend to be friendly, and I'll see to it that we get the diamond without any fighting. The Guarantor will reward us all. Do you understand, over?"

There was another pause. The *Goldenfels'* signals

compartment was separate from the bridge. The hatch had remained closed while the inspectors boarded above Todos Santos, so Adele had only her imagination and the speaker's tone from which to picture her opposite number: a little angry, a little worried; frowning because now he must relay uncertainty to a superior officer who expects merely assurance that they have the correct target for their missiles.

"Citizen Mundy, hold one," the voice said. *"Do not break contact or it'll be the worse for you! Over."*

There was a longer pause. Adele took a deep breath and became aware that she was the center of attention. Concerned spacers had enforced a ten-foot circle about her by shoving people back with their weapons; they glanced at her. The nervously angry Klimovs glared at her from the other side of the spacers. Puzzled natives watched her and the Sissies do unintelligible things. And Daniel Leary, holding the data unit more steadily than any terrified slave could've managed, smiled engagingly through the hologram at her.

"I think they're trying to learn what the Earth Diamond is," Adele said. Her first syllables were croaks, because her throat was very dry. "It'll take them longer than it did me, but a vessel like that—"

A spy ship.

"—will have a data bank with enough of a description to make them believe me. Then—"

"Citizen Mundy," a different voice said through Adele's commo helmet. *"We will be setting down after the next orbit. We'll invite the owners and officers of your ship aboard ours for a banquet. See to it that you come with them. Goldenfels out."*

Adele cleared her throat. She smiled at Daniel, knowing that her expression was wan compared to his.

"Then," she concluded, "we'll figure something else out."

"I think I already have," said Daniel, who'd smiled even more broadly when he heard the final orders from the *Goldenfels*.

CHAPTER 19

There was seating for twenty at the *Goldenfels'* banquet table. The compartment was austere—it was ordinarily the petty officers' mess, the lieutenant to Adele's left had informed her—but the attendants were uniformed and she didn't recall ever seeing a better wine list, even in the old days when her parents were entertaining the rich and powerful of Cinnabar.

"How did you come to your present position, Mistress?" the lieutenant asked politely. His fingers played with his wine glass but his eyes were on her with the intensity of a bird of prey. His name was Greiner, the *Goldenfels'* Signals Officer. His was the voice she'd talked to four hours earlier.

Adele snorted. "Necessity," she said. "My father was in shipping and lost everything to Cinnabar privateers. What do you think? Did you suppose I like working for unlettered boobs from Novy Sverdlovsk? Though the woman isn't so bad, for a farmer."

She glanced past Greiner toward the head of the table, pretending to be concerned that she might be overheard but too resentful to keep a close bridle on her tongue after the second glass of wine. Adele was playing a part, but it was an easy one: any one of a score of the pupils she'd studied with at the Academic Collections would do for a model. Given the way the recent war had gone—the reference to Cinnabar privateers was perfectly believable—she suspected that several of them were trading on their education to stave off poverty instead of living as cultured dilettantes as they'd expected.

The same thing had happened to Adele, of course; but a little earlier, and the result of the Three Circles Conspiracy rather than war. The worst trouble she'd had in being the librarian to the Elector of Kostroma wasn't the pay or even the conditions; it was quite simply that nobody really cared about the things an educated person knew and did. Her presence had been only a bauble for the Elector to dangle in front of other vulgarians.

Oh, yes; Adele Mundy understood the feelings of a resentful savant working for wealthy Philistines. . . .

"And yet it appears most of your yacht's crew come from Cinnabar," Greiner said. "Don't you find that very difficult, given your background?"

"If it were my yacht," Adele said with a trace of asperity that wasn't feigned, "then you'd have a right to be puzzled. As it is, I find the situation less difficult than starvation—which was the only choice on offer."

She looked around morosely. The *Goldenfels'* purser sat to her right and Vesey to the purser's right at the far end of the table. Betts was directly across from Adele, but even if he'd tried he couldn't have heard what she was saying. In addition to the general noise of dinner, the music of a live pipe band was being transmitted through the ventilating ducts.

The Klimovs sat beside Captain Bertram and his first officer at the head of the table. They were talking loudly and with animation; from snatches Adele heard, John Tsetzes was the primary subject. Daniel was across the table between the *Goldenfels'* Second Lieutenant and her Engineering Officer.

"And yes," Adele continued. "They're not only from Cinnabar, most of them, they were the ship's crew while she was in the Cinnabar navy—"

She carefully avoided saying "RCN," because the acronym was RCN jargon. She'd known as a scholar, long before she became a spy, that sometimes the form of a statement was as important as its content.

"—until a few months ago. The Klimovs bought the ship and hired the crew at the same time."

"Remarkable," Greiner said, though he must have been aware of that ever since the two vessels had rubbed against one another on Todos Santos.

"That's why I didn't suggest you capture the officers tonight and rush the ship," Adele said, taking a spoonful of the excellent pork fricassee a steward had just served in response to her nod. "I heard them discussing it before they accepted the invitation. The watch officer, he's a clod named Chewning, will vent the fusion bottle into the hull if that happens. That'll destroy the Earth Diamond, and I shouldn't wonder if it'd damage your ship as well since it's so close."

"You're sure they'd do that?" Greiner said, his eyes narrowing. "That would be suicide—literal suicide."

Adele shrugged. "I know the captain believes Chewning'll do it," she said through a mouthful. "They're hardcore navy, as I said. Apparently they've got quite a reputation, or anyway they think they do. Death before dishonor and that sort of nonsense."

She grimaced at the Alliance officer. "They're dolts like the farmers I work for," she said. "But I will say that they seem to know their business."

"Yes," said Greiner without expression. "The *Princess*

Cecile did indeed have a reputation when she was in naval service. And I'm inclined to agree that her crew know their business."

He looked hard at Adele, holding his part-full wine-glass but wholly concentrated on her reaction to what he was about to say. "So, Mistress. . . . The object you mentioned does appear to be a remarkable one. If not by force, then how *do* you plan to bring it into hands where it will be properly appreciated?"

A steward offered a bowl of something starchy whipped with bits of onion. Adele nodded, then nodded again for a second spoonful.

When the servant left, she said quietly with her eyes on her plate, "I told you my father was in shipping— he had seventeen vessels until the bloody war. He saw to it that I learned their systems back to front. If you'll give me fifteen minutes with your own transmitter, I'll set up a program that'll shut off all the yacht's power when you send the signal. If you do that at three in the morning, the worst there'll be is a shot or two from the sentries—if they don't throw their guns down when the lights go out."

"I don't understand," said Greiner. He didn't raise his voice, but when a steward came by with a carafe of wine he waved the fellow away curtly.

Adele grimaced. "Perhaps we can get out of here for a few minutes?" she said under her breath.

Greiner glanced at the head of the table; Captain Bertram was entertaining the Klimovs with a story that required a great deal of hand-flourishing. A less arrogant fellow might wonder why a man whom he'd first cheated, then humiliated, was working so hard to be engaging, but not the Count. Arrogance wasn't the same thing as stupidity, but it tended to have similar results.

"Yes," Greiner said, shoving his chair away from the

table. It was bolted to deck rails that allowed it to slide six inches forward or back. "Follow me in a minute and I'll take you to the Signals Room. We won't be disturbed there."

Adele ate her starch—which hadn't begun as potatoes, though she didn't know what the source was—in precise forkfuls, using it to sop sauce from the pork. She was nervous, but she'd spent many years poor to the point of starvation. Emotion might rob her of her appetite, but nothing took away her ability to eat.

After a minute, neither more nor less, Adele rose, folded her napkin beside her plate, and walked out the hatch at her end of the compartment. Mr. Pasternak was coming the other way, guided by a discreet steward. The engineer's eyes brushed over Adele without focusing: whether or not Pasternak recognized the vintages, he'd certainly shown his appreciation of the *Goldenfels'* wine.

The nearest rest room—the head, as she'd learned to call it in the RCN—was just outside the banquet hall, but Lieutenant Greiner gestured to her from the hatch of the companionway down the corridor instead. She followed him upward. The whisper of their boot-soles on the steel treads set up pulses in the armored tube that rushed back and forth like heavy surf.

Greiner motioned her up alongside him; the *Goldenfels* was a much bigger ship than the *Princess Cecile*, and even her companionways were on a larger scale. "I was surprised when you signaled us as soon as we fell into orbit here, mistress," Greiner said under the cover of the echoes. "Not every rich man's secretary would know how to use a starship's communications gear even if it were left unattended."

"I told you," Adele said. "The Klimovs pay me as their secretary, but my father trained me as an assistant engineer—*his* assistant. He shipped as engineer on a privateer before his share of a convoy of fullerenes let him buy his first vessel."

Greiner looked at her in the green light of the glowstrips forming long circles up the companionway, but he said nothing till he opened the hatch marked A LEVEL and led her out. At the end of the corridor to the left—directly above the banquet room—was the bridge. Its hatch was open, but a spacer with a submachine gun stood guard there.

Greiner stopped instead at an unmarked compartment on the left of the corridor, opening the hatch with an electronic key. "Go in, mistress," he said.

There were three consoles, one of them occupied. The man on duty looked up as Adele entered.

"I have some questions to ask the lady, Bandeng," Greiner said as he closed the hatch. "I'm not sure how she's going to react, so I'd like you to be prepared."

The duty man gave Greiner a flat stare, then looked at Adele. He ostentatiously reached into a drawer of his console and withdrew a service pistol which he pointed toward the corner past her head. If Adele *had* been armed—she wasn't; the contingent from the *Princess Cecile* knew they'd be searched before they were allowed to board the Alliance vessel—she could've shot Bandeng through the eye before he realized a gun isn't a magic wand that you wave to make people do what you want.

"So, Mistress Mundy . . . ," Greiner said. "How is it that you knew you were speaking to the *Goldenfels*? We identified ourselves as the *Belle Ideal*."

"You did after you reached orbit," Adele said with a justified sneer. "When I pinged you half an astronomical unit out, a few minutes after you returned to sidereal space, your transponder was still saying you were the *Goldenfels*. When you changed the identification, I knew you'd be willing to help me get the Earth Diamond."

Greiner's expression was becoming locked into frustrated surprise. "You queried our IFF when we were that far out?" he said. "How did you locate us so quickly?"

Adele shrugged, a gesture that was becoming as habitual in this conversation as the Alliance officer's amazement. "The yacht still has its naval sensors," she said. "I suppose they wouldn't always have picked up your arrival while we were on the ground, but they did this time."

That was a lie: the *Sissie* hadn't been aware of the new arrival until the *Goldenfels* announced herself— falsely. But it was a perfectly believable lie, one which fit all the facts at Greiner's disposal.

"Wait in the corridor, Bandeng," he ordered without taking his eyes off Adele. Part of his mind was probably considering the fact that he hadn't bothered to reprogram the automated system while the *Goldenfels* was still in the Matrix. "Go on, *now*."

Bandeng glared at him and ostentatiously stuck the pistol in the waistband of his fatigues before he obeyed; but he did obey. Greiner hand-locked the hatch behind him.

The Alliance officer forced a smile. When the interview began, he'd believed the power was in his hands. Now that Adele had demonstrated Greiner's lapse in security—and had done so in front of a subordinate present because of Greiner's own decision— he was extremely vulnerable.

She returned the smile coldly. Based on what she knew of the Alliance intelligence services, Mr. Bandeng would have to be careful if he were to avoid dying in a freak accident before the *Goldenfels* reached her home port.

"You're obviously a resourceful person, Mistress Mundy," Greiner said. "If matters work out as you say they will, I'll arrange a career path for you more suitable than nursemaiding farmers. But just how *is* it you propose to hand the *Princess Cecile* and her cargo over to us?"

Adele brought out her handheld unit. "I've built a program to modify all the yacht's control codes," she said nonchalantly. "I'll download them into your system."

She gestured to the nearest console, the one where Bandeng had been sitting. In fact Adele hadn't had anything to do with creating the program: that was primarily Daniel, with input from Pasternak, Vesey, and even Chewning. The actual work was done by the ship's navigational computer, but devising the pathways by which to achieve the plan was the job of human minds. Very resourceful human minds.

"When you send the program via a signal to the yacht over the normal watch frequency," she continued, "everything including the fusion bottle will shut down. They won't be able to fire the plasma cannons, close their hatches, or do anything at all else. They have backup controls, of course, but it'll take minutes if not hours before the ship will be operable again. By that time it'll be in your hands—and the Earth Diamond with it."

"It strikes me that if this doesn't work . . . ," Greiner said. His voice was completely expressionless, but his tongue clipped the syllables out like individual projectiles. "That the *Goldenfels* herself will be in a very dangerous position. Half her crew would be between the vessels, in what would turn into a killing zone if the *Princess Cecile*'s cannon were *not* disabled."

"Yes, of course," Adele said, as if unaware that Greiner was suggesting the possibility of her treachery rather than merely simple failure. She seated herself at Bandeng's console and brought it live. "We'll test it before we leave here. You can display the yacht in realtime, can't you?"

As if the matter were already decided, Adele synched her handheld unit with the console's input port. Greiner opened his mouth to protest, then reverted to the vaguely superior sneer which he'd affected at the start of the conversation. "Yes, of course," he said, switching the standby milkiness of a second console's display to a three-dimensional hologram of the *Princess Cecile*, a hundred and fifty yards from the *Goldenfels*.

Adele kept her expression blank as she worked, but her heart was singing in triumph. Like most of a librarian's triumphs, of course, it was completely invisible to everybody else.

The results, however, would be quite evident. Of that she was sure.

The sun had been setting when the *Sissie*'s officers trekked across the smoldering meadow to dinner, a performance commanded by the Alliance vessel's vastly greater power. The *Goldenfels* had landed more than a mile upstream where she wasn't vulnerable to the corvette's plasma bolts while she was setting down. The Alliance captain hadn't been concerned about damaging the natives' weirs while his ship thundered a few feet off the ground toward a spot beside the *Princess Cecile*.

At this hour the *Princess Cecile* lay in a darkness which the gleam of her many open hatches picked out. Four guards sat on upturned buckets under a tarpaulin stretched into a marquee from bitts above the main access port. One man—the image was crystal clear but too small to show facial features—was playing a harmonica or ocarina.

"All right," Adele said, turning to Greiner; she held

her control wands ready. "Tell me what signal you want for the trigger. I suggest something simple, but it's entirely up to you."

Greiner frowned like thunder. "All right," he said abruptly. "RCN. Use that—the three letters, RCN."

Adele's wands flickered. She looked up again.

"All right," she said again. "I've entered that. Simply transmit the program at . . . fifteen point oh-five-oh kilohertz with enough power that the *Princess Cecile* can pick up the signal. As close as we are, that's less power than it takes to light a match."

Greiner hesitated. "Go ahead," Adele said impatiently. "For the test it'll only shut them down for two seconds. When you've seen the demonstration, I'll set it to make the shutdown permanent the next time . . . which is for you to choose, but three or four in the morning seems to me to be suitable."

"First show me," Greiner said. "Now."

Adele set down her wands and crossed her hands in her lap. "No," she said. "Send the signal yourself, Lieutenant. RCN, you said. Send it."

Greiner dropped heavily into the seat of the console he'd used before; with the virtual keyboard he brought up a communications display as a sidebar. The realtime visuals of the *Princess Cecile* remained the main image. He checked his setup, then locked eyes with Adele momentarily before stabbing the Execute button.

The *Princess Cecile*'s lights went out. Her hull gleamed faintly in the starlight. Battery-powered lights appeared, beads of illumination which emphasized the greater darkness. If there'd been an audio pickup, Adele and Greiner would've heard angry shouting.

The corvette's lights came on again, generally with a rush; a few quivered for a time as overage exciters struggled to build the charge. Adele, smiling with satisfaction, made a further adjustment with her wands. She put her handheld unit back in its pocket and rose.

"They'll be wondering where we are," she said. "And I'm sure Captain Leary is getting a panicked call from the duty officer, saying that a fault shut off the ship's power momentarily. He'll leave and probably recommend the rest of us leave with him. If I don't accompany them, there may be awkward questions."

"Yes, we'll go back to the banquet compartment," Greiner said, unlocking the hatch. "There've been enough odd things happening already tonight!"

"Ah, Adele?" Daniel asked. "I know you have, ah, ways of listening. Have you learned anything about what's happening in the *Goldenfels*?"

He spoke in a low voice, pitching his words to carry across the hum of the bridge consoles operating on standby. The *Princess Cecile* waited under a complete lockout of radio communication, ordered by Daniel and enforced by Adele through the Signals Console.

Adele turned to look at him, past Sun and Betts at the gunnery and missile boards respectively. The holographic displays, though blank, shed a pearly luminescence over the compartment. There was plenty of light to see by.

"I haven't tried," she said. "I won't try. Too many things could go wrong."

"Yes, of course," Daniel said. "Forgive me. Part of me keeps thinking of the *Goldenfels* as a freighter, and of course it's not."

The Alliance vessel could be, must be, presumed to have electronic defenses and countermeasures equal to the material armament which Daniel could deduce from structural hints. The only visible plasma weapons were the twin 10-cm guns in the forward turret, comparable to the *Sissie's* own guns. No freighter would voyage the North with less.

Two double-opening hatch covers on the *Goldenfels'* port side, toward the corvette, and similar ones to starboard, were of the correct size to cover twin 15-cm guns, however; or, less probably, individual 20-cm plasma cannon, weapons whose single bolt would at this range vaporize half the *Princess Cecile*.

Daniel assumed that the Alliance vessel had a missile armament as well, though that wasn't a matter of immediate concern. If things went as wrong as they might soon do, the *Goldenfels* wouldn't need missiles to destroy the *Sissie* utterly.

Daniel chuckled. Sun looked over at him. "Sir?" he said.

A sub-machine gun hung from the back of the gunner's seat, though his primary task was to operate the plasma cannon if necessary. If things went as everyone hoped and expected, there wouldn't be shooting of any kind tonight.

"If we think of this as a children's game, Sun," Daniel said, "us hiding in the shadows waiting to jump out and surprise our friends, then it doesn't seem so frightening, does it?"

"Sir, I was raised in a tenement that looked out at Harbor Three," Sun said. "It was a tough place, I grant. But I don't recall having any friends with six-inch guns."

After a moment he chuckled at the thought; a moment later, Betts guffawed. Daniel smiled with appreciation. They were a good lot, a good crew for hard times.

And this was a very hard time.

A bell chimed through the ship. Machinery purred or hissed according to its needs, but the vessel's human environment remained the same. The watches would change at the next bell, but not now; this was the last hour of sleep, the last hour of watching silent gauges or the alien night before giving the boring duty over to your relief.

If it was going to happen, it wouldn't be long; and it was certainly going to happen.

Daniel had issued small-arms to half the crew. He'd chosen from among the solidest personnel, but he'd also picked men and women who'd used guns in the past and were comfortable using them again—on human beings.

That eliminated many otherwise suitable members of the crew. A man wasn't necessarily a coward because he wasn't willing to kill another person; a woman wasn't necessarily a monster because she *was* willing.

He glanced at Adele, who was doing something at her console—the only unit on the bridge which was active. He, Betts, and Sun sat quietly at their posts, ready to act when the balloon went up but electronically silent till then.

Normally at this hour only the duty officer would have a live console; they had to assume that the *Goldenfels* could tell whether or not that was so tonight. Adele said hers needed to be operating, and Daniel assumed she had a reason. She always had in the past.

The Klimovs were in shock cradles in their own quarters, not in the bridge annex. "For your safety," Daniel had told them; but in all truth, to keep them out of the way when he and his Sissies had to react instantly and possibly in unplanned fashions. The Klimovs weren't fools, but they were sometimes willful. Survival tonight required discipline.

And skill. And not a little luck. . . .

Daniel's eyes fell on Tovera, sitting on the deck with a sub-machine gun where she couldn't be seen through the open access hatch. She was smiling faintly.

Sometimes, of course, people willing to kill other people *are* monsters.

Though Hogg, prepared to fire his stocked impeller from the hatch beside her, wasn't inhuman: he was just a countryman who killed as a normal part of life and in the full knowledge that he too would die in his time. It didn't seem to make much practical difference; but it made a difference in Daniel's mind.

"They're about to move," Adele said. She didn't sound tense, but she spoke very precisely. "They're passing orders—by voice only. They're being careful."

"For what we are about to receive," Betts said, voicing the warriors' ancient joke, "the Lord make us thankful."

All the lights aboard the *Princess Cecile* went out. Metal shrieked on the *Goldenfels*, the shutters sliding open to unmask the hidden turrets.

"Wait for it!" Woetjans bawled from B Deck, audible up the forward companionways. "Don't nobody fucking move!"

Daniel poised with his mouth and eyes both open. He heard the four guards outside the *Sissie*'s main hatch run aboard, their boots clanging. Nothing more happened for a beat, a second beat—Captain Bertram wasn't acting rashly. Then, from hundreds of throats on the other side of the burned-over clearing, came the cry, *"Urra!"*

Adele's wands flicked. All the lights and displays aboard the *Princess Cecile* returned to full brightness.

"Initiating ignition sequence . . . ," Daniel said. His finger stabbed EXECUTE on his virtual keypad, sending reaction mass to the thrusters to be stripped of electrons and expelled. "Now!"

The *Princess Cecile* jolted as if eight trip-hammers had struck her hull in close sequence. Normally he'd have brought the thrusters up gently, equalizing the impulse into perfect unison before jumping them to real power. This wasn't a time for delicacy.

Their gushing ions rebounded from the soil, some of it curling back in through the corvette's open hatches. Daniel's faceshield protected his eyes, but the skin of his throat and the backs of his hands tingled. It'd be worse on the lower decks, but he very much doubted that the spacers there cared any more than he did.

Hydraulic jacks rammed the *Sissie's* hatches closed as quickly as possible, but that still took time. An Alliance spacer fired his handheld weapon, without orders or possibly against them. Slugs rang *kling/kling/kling* against the forward hull before a single ricochet moaned through an opening and across a compartment. Somebody cried out, but perhaps that was surprise rather than pain.

The *Princess Cecile* shivered in balance: her bow a yard above the ground, her stern six inches lower. Daniel slid the vessel toward the river, using his manual controls because he didn't trust the software on a task with so many variables.

The lower two-thirds of Daniel's display mapped the terrain in the corvette's direction of travel with sidebars for his gauges, but the top portion showed the *Goldenfels* in realtime. She'd unmasked both starboard lateral turrets, each mounting twin 15-cm guns as Daniel had surmised. They and the dorsal 10-cm cannon were aimed straight at the *Princess Cecile's* midpoint. A salvo would turn the corvette into a fireball visible from Morzanga's distant moon.

The guns didn't fire. Half the *Goldenfels'* crew had rushed from her hatches in the fifteen seconds before Daniel lit his plasma thrusters. To avoid the *Sissie's* rainbow exhaust, members of the would-be assault party had thrown themselves down on the burned-over sward or turned hesitantly back toward their own vessel.

Side-scatter from plasma cannon fired so close-by in an atmosphere would incinerate scores, perhaps hundreds, of unprotected Alliance spacers. Captain Bertram wouldn't sacrifice so many personnel just to stop a fleeing foe, if only because he knew the survivors would lynch him if he did.

The assault force had left the *Goldenfels* by sliding down chutes of sheet plastic from access ports on the upper decks as well as from the main hatch, but they could return only by the regular boarding ramp. All the curses and threats from their officers couldn't get hundreds of weapon-burdened spacers up a single two-meter ramp quickly.

The *Princess Cecile* slid into the slough where she'd first landed. The terrain between here and the clearing was regular, but there was enough variation that the *Goldenfels* was no longer in direct sight: the *Sissie* would be safe from plasma bolts so long as the two ships remained in the same relation to one another. Dorst had tacked a surveillance camera to a tree at the edge of the clearing before the *Goldenfels* landed; it continued to provide visuals for the top of Daniel's display.

Daniel kept the *Sissie* just above the surface, her forward speed no more than a fast walk. She roared in a blanket of steam over the mouth of the slough to the river proper, which was nearly a mile wide at the confluence. The last of the assault party was boarding the *Goldenfels*; the Alliance vessel was closed up save for her main hatch.

"Signals Officer," Daniel ordered, his hands busy with controlling his own ship. "Let the whole ship watch the visuals from the *Goldenfels*, out."

An icon flickered, indicating that Adele had obeyed; she hadn't remembered to verbally acknowledge the command. RCN Signals School would have made Adele more conversant with military proprieties, but it wouldn't have taught her to do what she'd learned as a librarian—and those were the things on which the *Princess Cecile* and her crew depended.

"Captain Bertram has just announced he's lighting his thrusters," Adele said over the ship's general channel.

There was a rippling flash like chain lightning beneath the *Goldenfels*. The Alliance freighter lurched over on its side. Steam rose; for a few moments a stutter of matter/antimatter winked like a devil's eye. All twelve High Drive motors had devoured themselves, taking with them divots from the vessel's belly plates.

Daniel brought the *Princess Cecile* to a standstill, hovering over the broad river in a ball of steam. Normally he wouldn't lift into orbit until he'd lowered his vessel to the surface, but that itself would be tricky under the present conditions.

The *Goldenfels* was almost certainly out of action for the future indefinite, but "almost" wasn't the same as "certainly." Daniel didn't want to learn the hard way that Captain Bertram was an unusually lucky or resourceful officer.

"Ship," Daniel ordered over the PA system and general push. "Prepare for liftoff. Over."

He reviewed the pre-lift checklist, knowing that Chewning, Pasternak and the two midshipmen had already done the same thing. Three open hatches showed red when the display came up, but two winked out as he watched and the third—a C Deck bulk port—had shown a false positive once before.

"Six, this is Four," said Pasternak from the Power Room. *"I've got a team checking PC-17 but it may be five minutes. Over."*

"Roger, Four," Daniel said. "We're not in so much of a hurry that we need to chance dumping our whole atmosphere. Six out."

Because of the necessary delay, Daniel leaned back and took a deep breath for the first time since he'd returned from the *Goldenfels'* banquet a lifetime ago. Grinning with a sudden thought, he resumed, "Ship, this is Six. Those of you who watched the *Goldenfels* a few minutes ago have seen what happens when a ship engages its High Drive motors at the bottom of an atmosphere."

He glanced toward Adele. Before he could ask her to do so, she began to rerun the explosions as an imagery loop available to all crewmen on their helmets if they didn't have access to better displays.

"I'm sure you'll all join with me in thanking our Signals Officer, Mistress Mundy," he continued, "who entered the *Goldenfels'* operating system and cross-connected it so that a signal to light the plasma thrusters would engage the High Drive instead."

Daniel grinned broadly at the Signals Console, but Adele kept her head resolutely turned toward her display.

"Hip-hip!" Daniel said.

And the whole ship's company echoed, *"Hurrah!"*

CHAPTER 20

Adele came back to the bridge after showering and putting on a clean utility uniform. The attack console was empty; like Adele, Betts had gone off-duty when the *Princess Cecile* entered the Matrix. Neither a missileer nor a signals officer was of any use until the vessel returned to sidereal space. There was no need of a gunner, either, but Sun had remained at his board; he shot Adele a worried look.

Daniel must've released the Klimovs from their quarters when the *Sissie* left sidereal space, because now they stood to either side of his console. Adele heard their raised voices while she was down the corridor, the Count saying, "... didn't intend when we engaged you that you'd use the opportunity to wage war on your national enemies!"

"Captain Leary," Adele said sharply as she stepped to her console. "Pray help me adjust this knob on my couch, if you'd be so kind."

Sun started to rise, his mouth open with an offer to help. Adele pointed her left index finger at the gunner's face and gave him a look that would've melted rock. He subsided with realization dawning in his eyes as thought replaced reflex.

"One moment, your excellency," Daniel said, rising from his couch and by doing so forcing the Count to back away. Daniel stepped to Adele's console, his lips pursed.

"I see . . . ," he said. He deliberately kicked the knuckle of the hydraulic support with the heel of his boot. "I think you'll find it satisfactory now, Mundy."

The Klimovs had trapped Daniel, perhaps by conscious plan, by standing in their anger so close to his couch that he'd have had to touch one or the other of them to get up. His unwillingness to escalate the encounter in that fashion meant he stayed pinned on his back for them to hector from above. By implicitly ignoring the Klimovs as she intruded on the equation, Adele had freed her friend.

"Thank you, Captain," she said politely. Turning to Klimov before he could resume his harangue, she continued, "Count Klimov, while I was in the *Goldenfels'* data bank for other purposes, I downloaded all files dealing with the *Princess Cecile* or her personnel. Among other things, they indicated that Captain Bertram was able to track you because you discussed your plans with locals on Todos Santos and Tegeli. This of course is your right as owner of the *Princess Cecile*; but given Bertram's animus against you, I thought you should be made aware of the risks your talk created."

"Animus against *me*?" Klimov shrieked. "Animus against Cinnabar, you mean!"

"Not at all," Adele said calmly, setting her data unit on the edge of her console and bringing out the wands. "Bertram was furious that you'd cheated him— *out*cheated him, I gather—at cards. Reading between the lines, I suspect that he was gambling with government funds and that he expects very serious personal consequences on his return to Pleasaunce unless he gets the money back."

"That's a lie!" Klimov said.

"Georgi!" shouted his wife, her voice rising. She stepped in front of the Count, her hands pushing him back. She shot Adele a glance over her shoulder; there was real fear in her eyes. "He didn't mean that!"

It struck Adele, standing as still as a deck stanchion, that Valentina knew more than Adele had ever told her. There were plenty of people aboard who might've talked, of course. The Sissies were proud of their Signals Officer: the lady who'd as soon shoot you as look at you, who knew everything, and who never missed. . . .

"Count Klimov," Adele said in a general silence of fear, "I'd sent a prepared search signal into the *Goldenfels'* computer during the banquet. Yesterday evening and night I had time to analyze the results while we were waiting for Captain Bertram to attack. I'd be pleased to show you the information in both raw and processed form."

She cleared her throat. "Now," she went on. "I believe you started to say something which I was too abstracted to hear. If you'd care to repeat your statement, we can proceed as the situation dictates."

Valentina pinched her husband's lips closed and whispered viciously into his left ear, watching Adele sidelong. Klimov stared at Adele, nodded, and then moved his wife's hand away from his mouth.

"Your pardon, Lady Mundy," he said, bowing. "I've completely forgotten what I started to say. Knowing me, it was probably something very foolish anyway."

"Yes," said Valentina, glaring at her husband. "It was."

Daniel cleared his throat, his eyes on a bulkhead, then turned to the Klimovs with a smile as though seeing them for the first time today. "That's all in the past, of course," he said, "but it does bring up an associated point. I don't believe the *Goldenfels* will be pursuing us any longer—"

Adele glanced at the Klimovs. While in their stateroom they could've accessed the visuals of the Alliance vessel rolling over on its side, but she wasn't sure they'd done so.

"—but other Alliance vessels may be searching for them. Any such ship that arrives on Morzanga and learns what happened will become a new problem for us. I suggest that we not leave via the ports from which we arrived."

"What choice is there?" the Klimovna asked. "A cul-de-sac, you called this."

"Yes, with the exception of the passage Commander Bergen traversed," Daniel said, nodding. "For part of the way, that route requires travelling between rather than through bubble universes. I don't honestly believe anyone but Uncle Stacey could have opened the route. I hope—I believe—that using his log books, I can retrace it, but I won't pretend there isn't serious risk."

"You think John Tsetzes tried this passage and was destroyed, not so?" Valentina said.

Daniel nodded. "I think that's possible," he said. "After finding the copy of the Earth Diamond on Morzanga and no evidence that Tsetzes ever left this cul-de-sac, I think in fact that it's very probable. We have the advantage of Uncle Stacey's logs over him, of course."

The Count looked at his wife, then back to Daniel. "If it's so risky," he said querulously, "why would we do it?"

"Because the risk is less than that of being shot by the people you and your card tricks put about our heads,

Georgi!" Valentina said; summing up the situation in much the way Adele would've done herself, and in an equally peevish tone. "That's what you mean, Daniel, isn't it?"

"Yes, that's what I mean," Daniel agreed. "I'm not seriously concerned about meeting Alliance ships here in the North, but . . . this is a lawless region at the best of times. An Alliance vessel which found the *Goldenfels* and offered a reward on Todos Santos would get many takers. Whereas if we first make landfall at New Delphi, the planet with the tree oracle you know, I think we'll have outdistanced potential trouble."

"Faugh, do what you please," the Count said abruptly. He turned on his heel. "I'm going to play cards in the wardroom."

Valentina watched her husband stalk off the bridge. "Cards and women," she said in a tone of disgust. "Other men manage to amuse themselves without risking the lives of everybody around them!"

She shrugged. "I have notes from Morzanga to organize," she said as she walked toward the companionway. "Men are all fools!"

Daniel smiled faintly. Adele raised an eyebrow. "I hope you don't expect me to argue the point," she said. "Of course, I don't have a high opinion of women either."

"Mr. Chewning," Daniel said, cueing his helmet. "You have the watch. I'll return to the bridge in three hours, when we're ready to drop back into sidereal space for a final star sight. Six out."

He grinned broadly at Adele. "I anticipated the owners' agreement, you see," he explained. "We'll be attempting the passage shortly. Until then, I'm going to take a nap."

"But it's only three hours, you said?" Adele said. She pursed her lips but took care not to frown.

"Yes, well, it's not long," Daniel said, his grin becoming rueful. "But you see, I'll be on the truck of Antenna Dorsal A the whole time we're in the passage. Which will be thirty-four hours, if all goes well."

Daniel stood at the top of the leading mast of the dorsal row, the point farthest from the *Princess Cecile*'s hull. There wasn't—there couldn't be—a more gorgeous and awesome display than the blaze of the hundred universes now beating down on him. He didn't feel like a starship captain or a Cinnabar nobleman, he felt like the Lord God Almighty. It was all he could do to fight down the urge to raise his arm and shout, "Let there be light!"

The *Princess Cecile* was a universe of her own, a fragment of sidereal space-time thrust through universes by the pressure of Casimir radiation, the one true constant which permeated every bubble of the Matrix and the immaterial spaces separating those bubbles. Her antennas and yards stretched molecule-thin sails of conductive fabric. Their area, angle and electric charge determined the vessel's course within the Matrix and therefore her location when she returned to the sidereal universe. The navigational computers which plotted those relationships were the most powerful available to humanity, but even so a course computation was likely to require an hour or more.

Daniel eyed the heavens' pattern of color and intensity. He knew the next programmed correction: adjustment by ten percent of the maincourses of all twelve lateral masts while the dorsal and ventral sails remained the same.

That was what the computer said, based on observed gradients . . . and if they followed that program, the *Princess Cecile* would drive herself into a bubble where a photon had three orders of magnitude greater energy than that of the universe where men had built her. She might survive those pressures long enough for her automatic systems to dump her back into the sidereal universe . . . but the chances were that she wouldn't survive, and there was no chance at all that she'd be able to proceed with the course the computer had planned.

Daniel raised his right arm as an attention signal; the quartermaster, waiting at the semaphore control panel at the base of Dorsal Two, gestured back. Daniel's arms made a quick series of signs as precise as the movements of a trapeze artist and as certain to bring disaster if bungled.

The quartermaster dialed the new orders into his mechanical computer, then pulled the long lever on the side. The arms of semaphores at twelve locations across the *Sissie's* hull sprang to life. A person anywhere on the outer surface of the vessel could see at least one of the stations.

Only mechanical and hydraulic equipment was used to control operations on the deck of a ship in the Matrix. A radio signal or even the field generated by an electrical conductor within the bubble of sidereal space was enough to throw a vessel off-course to a literally incalculable degree. A fiber-optic cable didn't set up a field—but neither could it do any work at the far end: that would require an electrical booster with the same attendant problems.

Cables and hydraulic lines worked. Oh, they stretched and broke and leaked and sometimes froze, but for the most part they worked. And the riggers worked, the human beings who used their eyes to spot trouble and their muscles to correct it; knowing that if they misjudged they might drift into a bubble universe whose very matter was hostile to them.

The sails of the lateral antennas began to skew

counterclockwise, coming slightly closer to alignment with the axis of the ship. In response to Daniel's order, riggers moved across the *Sissie's* hull to the capstan at the base of each dorsal mast. Daniel felt through his boots the vibration of pulleys turning, shifting the set of Dorsal One's lower course as other riggers were adjusting the sails of the antennas behind his in the file.

The effect of Daniel's order would be to rotate the corvette on her axis instead of skewing her in plane. The *Princess Cecile* would squeeze between unacceptable gradients instead of smashing directly into one.

Daniel eyed the heavens pressing against the very existence of the *Princess Cecile*. The Matrix wasn't hostile, but it was pitiless and vastly beyond the ability of Mankind to conceive, even to the degree that Man understood the universe which had created him.

The *Princess Cecile's* transition would come shortly. The astrogation computer had used Uncle Stacey's logs to determine the course—but the Matrix changed, and a computer could predict but could not feel. Daniel, here on the leading mast-truck of a ship not very different from Commander Bergen's, was doing what his uncle would have done. If he misjudged, they'd go off course or very possibly disintegrate.

He wasn't as skilled as Uncle Stacey, of that he was sure. But in his heart Daniel believed his judgment was good enough.

Someone moved on the hull below him. Daniel looked down, gripping the mast with his left hand because the helmet of his heavy rigging suit distorted his peripheral vision. Yes, somebody had just emerged from the forward hatch and was handing his way along by the lubber lines which acted as guides and support for the non-riggers who were forced by circumstances to work on the hull.

Daniel smiled. The only person so clumsy who'd have come out now was Adele. She knew better than to try to climb to him; even if she'd been able to do so without drifting away, there was no room for her here at the peak which he already occupied.

She stopped at the base of the antenna and attached her safety line to an eyebolt, then bent backward to look up. She didn't signal and he couldn't see her features through his faceshield and hers; but she was there. She had nothing to offer but her presence nearby, so she was offering that.

Daniel looked at the heavens again. The lights surrounding him, surrounding them all, shivered and changed like the cascading images of a kaleidoscope, each linked to the one before it but utterly different.

The *Princess Cecile* slid between universes. Her sails blazed. Though the rippling heavens gave the impression of movement, the reality of her change in relation to the sidereal universe was beyond human understanding.

Daniel felt transitions ripple swiftly, each within safe parameters. Once a violet glare shoved against the bubble in which the corvette sailed, but only for a heartbeat; then the *Princess Cecile* was through the throat, the danger point, and proceeding on a course that an intrasystem scow could've navigated safely.

We'll make it, Daniel thought. *Of course. Together we'll make it again.*

He even had mental leisure to wonder what the oracle of New Delphi would be like. . . .

CHAPTER 21

Adele's only warning that the *Princess Cecile* had reached the surface of New Delphi came when the plasma thrusters shut off. There was no jolt, no violent buffeting—just silence and an end to the juddering vibration of ions expelled at high velocity to counteract the pull of gravity.

"Ship, this is the captain," Daniel announced over the common channel. *"We've landed, but the surface here is sand, not water. We'll wait ten minutes for the site to cool before opening any hatches. I repeat, ten minutes—and I mean it, Sissies, I'm not having a bubble of molten glass pop and spit through a port. Captain out."*

"We're on the ground already?" the Klimovna said, her tone mixing surprise with at least a hint of irritation. With the thrusters shut down, probably everyone on the bridge could hear her; certainly Adele could. "I thought this landing was supposed to be very dangerous!"

Adele unstrapped herself from her couch and sat up. Forcing a smile, she looked at her employers in the

317

annex and said, "I'm sure many captains could have
given you all the danger you could imagine on such
a landing, mistress. Fortunately you were wise enough
to hire a man with a talent for making the difficult look
easy."

Daniel rose to his feet with a satisfied smile. "Loose
sand is a better surface than I'd feared it might be,"
he said. "Though of course walking to the monastery
is going to be a chore."

He cleared his throat. "Mistress Mundy?" he went
on. "While we're forced to wait, would you please run
through a description of New Delphi for me and the
crew?" He bowed toward the annex. "And for our
employers, of course, if they're interested."

"Yes, of course," Adele said. She settled back on her
couch, thumbing electronically through images to pick
the best sequence for the purpose. She didn't know
whether Daniel was really interested in a presentation
or if he simply wanted her to fill time that might
otherwise permit awkward questions.

It didn't matter, of course. She'd been asked to
provide information, so she'd do just that.

"There's no certainty of when New Delphi was discovered," she said, transmitting over an alert channel.
The signal went to everyone aboard the *Princess Cecile*,
but nobody else could respond by it. "It was settled
and named three hundred years before the Hiatus by
what appears in the beginning to have been a scientific expedition. They're now a religious order calling
themselves the Service of the Tree. There've never
been more than a hundred acolytes under a prior on
New Delphi. They're volunteers from all over the
human galaxy. The Service has extensive charitable
works on many scores of planets, staffed by Lay Servants and funded from the fees charged for incubation within the monastery."

Sun looked at her with a worried expression. "Pardon, mistress?" he said. "But 'incubation'? There's disease here?"

There aren't even any brothels here, so you needn't worry about disease, Adele thought in irritation at being interrupted. But because Sun probably spoke for scores of spacers throughout the ship, she continued aloud, "Incubation means sleeping; in this particular instance it means sleeping in the Chamber of the Tree to receive dreams which are said to be prophetic."

She cleared her throat and added, "Some of those making the claims of prophecy are in fact scientific bodies of the highest repute. A delegation from the Academic Collections on Bryce made a detailed study thirty-three years ago. It concluded that the so-called Tree Oracle did in fact foretell the future in statistically-verifiable fashions."

It embarrassed Adele to repeat superstitious non-sense, but she was unwilling to suppress evidence simply because she was sure those listening would misinterpret it. There was some explanation other than godlike wisdom housed in a tree; it was just that no one had discovered it yet.

There was a general buzz of voices which Adele ignored as she selected visuals, of the planet generally and of the monastery a quarter mile away. In a commanding tone, Count Klimov said, "What is the amount of the fee the monastery charges, if you please?"

Adele looked expressionlessly into the annex. Over the alert channel she answered, "The fees are variable, according either to whim or to rules which have never been stated to outsiders. The only certainty is that they're very high."

Before somebody could interrupt with another question, Adele projected the images she'd picked from her files. She supplemented them with one which the

Princess Cecile took from orbit and with a realtime display from the corvette's dorsal sensor pack.

"New Delphi is arid," she said, "with no surface water at present. There are significant stocks of water in deep aquifers, however, and in some locations plants which rooted before the onset of the final drought have been able to survive by tapping that water. One of these . . . oases is the wrong word, no seedlings have rooted for millennia. One of these existing plants is the so-called Oracle Tree, which has been growing out from its center to a present diameter of nearly six miles. We've landed beside it."

She highlighted the realtime display. A tangled mass of trunks and branches reached a hundred and twenty feet high. It didn't look like a single tree to her, but she accepted the opinion of the experts.

The mass didn't even seem to be alive, but again Adele supposed the experts must know. The gray leaves were sparse and individually tiny, but presumably they proved sufficient to the tree's limited requirements.

"The monastery's built within the tree," she continued. "It's only the outer ring that's alive; the wood of the interior is dead and in the center has rotted away. There are extensive passages through the dead portion of the trunk and in the soil beneath, though five years ago—that's the latest report I could find—there were only forty-one acolytes on New Delphi."

"What kind of defenses does the monastery have, Mundy?" Daniel asked. "The wealth of the Delphi Foundation would be a tempting prize even in a more settled part of the galaxy. Here in the North I'd judge it'd be a race between pirates and the Commonwealth government itself as to who'd be the first to loot the planet."

"The Tree Oracle funds the operations of the Delphi Foundation all over the human galaxy," Adele said, remembering that she was speaking to members of the crew who couldn't hear Daniel's question. "Orphanages, hospitals, development schemes—nearly a thousand projects on several hundred worlds, and I doubt that's an exhaustive list. But none of the wealth is *here*."

Her wands sequenced through a dozen images of the monastery's interior: the bare walls were either rock or wood textured by its grain; individual rooms—cells—with a table, a stool, and a sleeping mat unrolled on the floor; and a dining hall in which acolytes wearing identical robes of coarse gray fabric filled their bowls from a common urn.

The only exception to the general starkness was the library containing tens of thousands of volumes and data consoles of advanced design. Adele smiled wryly as she flicked that image up, then replaced it with one of the Chamber of the Tree; its only furnishing was a couch carved into the trunk of the Tree itself.

Adele was probably the only person aboard the *Princess Cecile* to whom a library like that one suggested extreme wealth. Pirates would react much the way Sun did, with blank incomprehension.

"The acolytes live an ascetic existence, even by the standards of the RCN on active service," Adele said, allowing herself a straight-faced joke. "The oracle is open to all who pay the fee; the Foundation is wholly apolitical, acting for the betterment of Mankind without regard to government, religion, or any other factor save the perceived need of the recipients of the proffered aid. The combination of neutrality and poverty has preserved the monastery as no conceivable armament could have done."

She smiled coldly. "A cynic might believe that the poverty alone was sufficient protection."

"Six?" said Betts on the command channel. "*There's people coming toward us. A little door opened in the*

*side of the tree. Do you want we should let 'em
aboard, over?"*

Adele increased the magnification of the realtime
display at the top of her screen. A young woman and
an older man with white-trimmed hem and cuffs had
walked from the tree and to within a stone's throw of
the *Princess Cecile*. They were barefoot and bare-
headed, squinting slightly against dust blown by the
steady wind. Occasionally the man would wobble; each
time the woman took his arm to steady him.

"I think," said Daniel, rising from his console, "that
instead we'll go meet them. Ship, this is Six; all personnel may open the hatches in their area. Woetjans,
meet me in the main lock with a twenty-strong escort;
we're going to view the monastery of New Delphi. Mr.
Chewning, you're in charge in my absence."

He looked at the Klimovs. "Your excellencies?" he
said. "Would you care . . . ?"

"Yes," Valentina said as she and her husband rose
stiffly. "Of course we'll come!"

Adele got up from her couch and twisted her
upper body one way, then the other, to loosen her
muscles. "Ah . . . ?" she said, catching the "Daniel"
before it left her tongue. "Captain? I'd like to accompany you. To see the library."

"Yes, of course, Mundy," Daniel said with his usual
bright smile. He buckled his equipment belt with the
holstered pistol on over his utility uniform. "You'll be
able to tell us what to look for."

The group from the bridge trooped down the echoing companionway. Adele frowned when she saw that
the escort waiting in the entryway within the open
main hatch was armed to the teeth. "Daniel?" she
murmured in her friend's ear. "Do you think the guns
are necessary?"

"No, I don't," he said, pursing his lips in thought.

"But your most recent information is five years old, and there's no foreign ship on the planet so far as we could tell from orbit. The personnel Woetjans chose for our escort are well-disciplined, so we needn't fear accidents on our side . . . and I'd just as soon view the situation on the ground myself before I assume it's perfectly safe."

The air blowing in through the hatchway was cool and dry with the hint of a vegetable odor. Adele would've described the smell as cinnamon if she'd been forced to pick, but of course she wasn't.

"I'll lead," Daniel said nonchalantly and strode down the boarding bridge. Hogg was directly behind him, and Woetjans with her armed band followed ahead of the Klimovs, Adele, and last of all Tovera. Because the *Princess Cecile* stood on solid ground, the entry port was some distance in the air. High enough to break a leg or your neck, Adele suspected; and there was enough wind to make a fall possible even for someone sober.

The ship's exhaust had fused the ground into coarse glass. There were similar patches at many places along the south side of the tree's vast circle. Archeologists could probably identify thousands of earlier landing sites, covered or broken up by ages of blowing wind.

The Service of the Tree had pointedly chosen not to encourage visitors by improving the facilities. Even the small vessel the Service kept for its own purposes stood in the open. Its only protection was a fence upwind which formed a berm of sand dumped on the other side of the slats.

Daniel had waited with his hands crossed behind his back until the Klimovs arrived. "Count and Lady Klimov," he said, "allow me to present the Prior of the Service of the Tree and Sister Margarida, a novice of the order."

Adele noted with amusement she was careful to hide that the Count didn't know whether to react to Margarida as an attractive young woman—which she certainly was, at least in the slightly plush fashion that Daniel favored—or as the religious figure which her title and gray habit suggested. In the end he bowed to both man and girl, without offering to kiss the latter's hand.

"Please come in with us," the Prior said, turning with the careful determination of age. "You'll find it more comfortable out of the wind, I'm sure."

He chuckled, adding, "And so will we, to tell the truth, though I don't remember it bothering me so much when I was as young as Margarida, here. That was a very long time ago, of course."

The door set into the rock was wooden, but it had weathered to such a degree that valve and jamb blurred visually from any distance. At ground level the Tree was a mass of trunks, surface roots, and low-hanging branches. The different portions were indistinguishable to Adele and probably confusing even to Daniel, whose knowledge of natural history was more than a dilettante's. Everything—bark, wood, and the underlying stone—was the same color: gray with tawny undertones.

Margarida opened the door. Before she could help the Prior through, Woetjans pushed inside with her stocked impeller pointed forward at waist level.

"Most of the Acolytes are at their duties in other parts of the monastery now," the Prior said with a faint smile. "I don't believe you'll find anyone in this section of corridor, but if you do I assure you that they'll be friendly."

Daniel bowed to the old man. "May I help you, sir?" he said. "I appreciate you inconveniencing yourself in order to greet us."

The tunnel within was eight feet wide and not quite that high. The ceiling was a mass of wood with a ropy pattern. Daniel, the Prior leaning on his right arm, looked up and said, "Is that a root, sir? It certainly appears to be."

Margarida closed the door behind Tovera. Glow strips on the walls cast a yellow-green illumination to which Adele's eyes quickly adapted, though she noticed that as soon as the spacers stepped inside they slid down their light-enhancing goggles.

"Yes, the tree's still alive in this section," the girl called in answer to Daniel's question. "You'll notice that the roots have grown over some of the lights a little way up the corridor."

She smiled pleasantly to Adele as she passed, moving up to the front with the Prior, Daniel, and the Klimovs. Adele thought there was something appraising in the glance Margarida gave each of the Sissies in turn, but she supposed that was natural enough for a member of a small community suddenly visited by strangers three times its number.

"This is the refectory," the Prior was saying as Adele entered a long room that grew from the tunnel rather than being served by it. "We eat twice a day here, though I should mention that our days are only nineteen standard hours. You're welcome to dine with us while you're on New Delphi, though please give us at least a few hours warning."

He smiled; he still had his hair, but it was so fine and white that his scalp shone through. Since the only light was that of the glowstrips, what would normally be pink had a disconcerting purplish tone.

"Normally two acolytes prepare each meal, a senior and a novice," the Prior explained. "I would wish to considerably increase the numbers in the kitchen if we're to feed all of you."

According to all Adele's sources, the acolytes ate cheese, gruel and dried fruit, all of them imported but nonetheless of the simplest sort. They washed their identical meals down with water drawn up from the same aquifers which fed the Tree; reportedly it had enough iron to stain cups after a week or two of use.

"I believe we'll eat aboard the *Sissie* rather than strain your resources, sir," Daniel said. Count Klimov looked vaguely irritated, probably by the fact his employee had spoken rather than the decision itself, but he didn't intervene. "His excellency the Count remarked that he'd like to see the incubation chamber. Is that permissible?"

"Why yes, of course," the Prior said. "Those of us in the Service of the Tree have no secrets. There *are* no secrets from the Tree, you see."

He led them between the long tables to one of the several doors opening off the left sidewall. An older woman in the robes of an acolyte entered the refectory, bowed to the party, and went out through the opposite side on an errand of her own. The large room could seat hundreds, but only two tables at the far end appeared to be in use.

"In fact, I'd like to hire a dream myself," the Count said, his voice needlessly loud with nervousness. "How much will it cost me?"

The Prior, leaning against Daniel while Margarida hovered close to his other side, glanced at Klimov but continued his careful shuffle to the door. "We can discuss that at a later time, if you choose, your excellency," he said. "It will not be possible for us to accede to your request immediately, but perhaps in a few days. . . . If you wish to remain on New Delphi, that is."

"Look, if you're concerned that I may not be able to pay your fees . . . ," the Count said on a note rising toward real anger.

"Georgi!" snapped his wife. "They said nothing of the sort. And if they want to check our bona fides, well, that's only common sense, no more than you'd do yourself before entering a card game with strangers. Not so?"

"It's nothing to do with yourself or your credit, Count Klimov," the Prior said calmly. "The Oracle isn't available to you or anyone else at present due to a matter of scientific concern. Since you're not in the Service, it might appear to be a matter of religious scruple. Either way, please accept my apologies."

"Father, perhaps we can show our guests the library?" Margarida said. "It's really the only part of the monastery that's present in the material plane. All the rest is spiritual."

She glanced at Daniel, then colored and looked at the floor of living rock. "I hope some day I'll be able to fully appreciate the marvelous spiritual world in which I'm permitted to live."

"Of course, child," the Prior said as he shuffled up the corridor. "You're young, dear. Enlightenment requires time; and I fear, looking back on my own youth, that it may require age as well. When one is young, no matter how deeply he may believe in the truth of the spirit the body has a certain insistence which the spirit cannot deny."

He looked at Daniel as they moved along together. "Perhaps you feel that also, Captain Leary?" he said.

"I'm afraid I'm unfitted to discuss religion, sir," Daniel said with seeming nonchalance. "I wonder, is the door by which we entered the monastery the only entrance there is?"

The Prior laughed. "Oh, goodness, no," he said. "How many entrances would you guess there were, Margarida?"

She trilled a laugh also. "I know of thirty-seven," she

said. "That's inside as well as outside the circle of the Tree. But the corridors run for scores of kilometers and we only use a fraction of them. In former times the Service was larger and there was also an extensive lay community on the northern rim."

"There've often been groups and individual hermits living within the Tree," the Prior said, sounding somewhat apologetic. "Apart from our Service, that is. There are hand-dug wells from ages before we have record. A sufficiently dedicated person can raise his or her own crops by carrying buckets up to where there's light. I suspect there are some such people now, drawn by a less structured form of the same impulse that brought me and Margarida."

He and Daniel led the group into a cavern. The corridors and refectory had been cut into the rock; the Tree formed only their ceilings and portions of the walls. It took Adele a moment to realize that this great room was entirely wood. Ages of humans, most of them barefoot acolytes, had worn the floor into troughs weaving toward the couch in the center.

"This is it!" the Count said in an insistent tone. "This is where you dream!"

"Yes," said the Prior. "After preparation that includes drinking an infusion brewed from the berries of the Tree, the querent sleeps here. The querent and the Tree become one during the night, and the querent rises with a full awareness—as full as a human mind can retain—of the questions he or she wanted answered."

"Part of the preparation involves focusing your mind properly before going to sleep," Margarida said. She smiled broadly at Daniel. "There are stories of querents rising with a certain understanding of how they should rearrange their reception room—but nothing about the political situation facing the planet they rule."

"I'd like to say that story was apocryphal," the Prior said with a faint smile. "It isn't, but that was an extreme example. We of the Service have been more careful in preparing the querents since that day, however."

Adele stopped listening to the discussion among the others present. Her eyes had finally penetrated the opposite side of the huge room. She walked toward it, guided by the floor the way wild beasts follow the paths their ancestors' hooves have hammered into the soil.

"Adele?" Daniel called. Then, insistently, "*Adele.*"

"The library's here, Daniel," she said. "I hadn't realized it was the same room as the incubation chamber."

The imagery in Adele's database suggested the two functions were physically separate. That was untrue and close enough to being a lie that Adele felt her anger blaze. There probably wasn't a conscious intention to deceive, but the photographer hadn't shown a sufficient concern to encompass the truth either.

The backs of a dozen consoles—all reasonably new and built either on Cinnabar or one of the advanced worlds of the Alliance—were set in a row so their blank backs formed crenellations between the stack area and the couch. Adele stepped between two of the machines and switched them on without thinking to ask permission. They came up promptly; she'd used virtually identical equipment in the past. A male acolyte working at the console on the far end glanced up, nodded, and returned to his display.

The hardcopy books were shelved in ranks which ran back to the dim reaches farther than Adele could follow without borrowing goggles from a spacer. The pedestals had been shaped from the wood of the Tree, but the shelves and their supports were of structural plastic tinted to match the natural ruddy gray.

The volumes were arranged by height and size; most had no spine title. Adele picked one at random, a Pre-Hiatus work on homiletics. It had been printed on Earth in the inconceivably distant past but at some point rebound in stiff, yellow-gray vellum. The book next to it was also very old, but it was printed—by letterpress!—in a script and language which she couldn't identify without the help of her handheld.

She started to draw the little unit out of her pocket, then remembered her surroundings. She turned and found the eyes of everybody in the large room—except the acolyte at the console—focused on her.

Adele's lips spread in a flat line that was as close to a smile as she could come when she was embarrassed. "Ah . . . ," she said. "I'm very sorry to have wandered off like this—"

She hadn't moved far physically, but her mind and soul had been in a different universe. It was a better universe, in her opinion, but she knew there were other viewpoints on the matter.

"—but, ah . . . this is a very interesting collection."

The Prior smiled affectionately at her. "Would you care to stay in the monastery, mistress, while your vessel is on New Delphi?" he asked. "I understand that our life here wouldn't be attractive to many of those living in the wider universe, but I think you're an exception. You can eat with us and I'll find you a cell. If you like, that is."

"Yes," said Adele. "I would like that very much. If . . . ?"

She looked at Daniel, now standing between the Prior and Margarida. His expression was momentarily grave, but he sounded affectionately cheerful as he said, "Yes, of course, Mundy. There hasn't been a great deal to attract your interests on this voyage. I'm glad we've finally made a landfall with more to offer you than it does those of us with less intellectual tastes."

Hogg snorted. "You can say that again," he said; but as he did so, he eyed Margarida sidelong.

"Shall I bring some kit for the two of us from the vessel, mistress?" Tovera said. She didn't speak loudly, but when she wanted to be heard—as now—everybody in the big room heard her.

Most of them probably understood the implications of what she was saying: Adele would be well protected. The Prior did, given the knowing smile he offered as he nodded first to Adele, then to Tovera.

"Yes, do that, Tovera," Adele said crisply. Then she turned back to the stacks, in part to avoid the eyes of the others. She'd never found it hard to sink into that better personal world in a library, after all.

The note in Daniel's pocket read:

> Beloved Daniel—
> I could withstand you, but I cannot withstand myself. There is an entrance two-thousand nine-hundred and twelve feet counterclockwise from the foot of your gangplank; it is known to no one living save myself and now you. If you come there at our midnight, I will be waiting.
> Please, beloved, destroy this note and never mention its contents whether you decide to come or stay. If anyone were to learn what I am doing, I would be expelled from the Service at the cost of my very soul. Please, if you are a gentleman—preserve the honor of one who has loved you from her first glimpse of your face.
>
> Margarida

✧   ✧   ✧

"Attention!" snapped Norton, the Tech 1 commanding the guards in the main hatch, when Daniel appeared from the companionway. She and two of her contingent hopped to their feet quickly, but the fourth—a Purser's clerk named Hilbride, dropped his sub-machine gun with a clatter more frightening than anything likely to come out of the darkness on this planet.

"Carry on, Norton," Daniel said as Hilbride skidded the dropped gun twice across the deck plating without managing to get control of it.

Daniel bent to pick the weapon up, clicking the safety on and handed it back. He'd burn a new asshole in whoever'd issued a gun to Hilbride without sufficiently explaining about the safety, but that was for the morning.

Now he said pleasantly, "Keep it switched off till you have a reason to shoot, spacer. And Norton—you might make sure he understands that. I don't want one of you to accidentally blow me in half when I come back from my little walk."

"God *help* me, sir!" Norton said, her face red and sweating. "Sir, it was my fault, but it won't happen again!"

Daniel nodded, acknowledging the apology without suggesting that the business was closed. "I can't sleep, so I'm going to walk for a few hours," he said. "I have my recall plate—"

He tapped his breast pocket, then his pistol holster.

"—and in case I'm attacked by a ravenous bark mite, I have this."

"Isn't Mr. Hogg going with you, sir?" Hilbride asked doubtfully. He held the sub-machine gun with the care worthy of a poisonous snake which had already bitten once.

"Mr. Hogg is playing poker with the Count," Daniel

said, smiling engagingly. He was breaking his own rules; he knew it and the guards knew it. But there was nobody present who'd stand up to the captain the way Hogg or Woetjans certainly would. "They're also drinking a bottle of what the Count calls Calvados and Hogg says is smooth applejack."

Everybody chuckled. Daniel touched his fingers to his brow in a friendly salute, then strode down the boarding bridge into the night. He wasn't wearing his helmet, but he slid his light-amplifying goggles over his eyes. Starlight brought the whorled wonder of the Tree into sharp relief. Oracle or not, it was a remarkable plant and a unique habitat—not least for the humans burrowing into its fabric like so many adoring beetles.

Grinning, Daniel began to whistle "Cruising Round Pleasaunce" and stopped in a moment's confusion. Margarida seemed a shy girl, even in the note she'd written. A song like that wasn't for the ears of a decent child like her.

He grinned still broader. Perhaps in the morning he'd teach it to her. . . .

Daniel kept his eyes on the Tree as he walked along its vast curve. He switched his goggles from light enhancement—which did a better job of showing the ground—to thermal imaging in order to pick up the higher body temperature of animal life.

He'd allowed himself plenty of leeway before local midnight, so occasionally he paused to examine some creature crawling on the bark. None of them were bigger than his little fingernail. According to the database all native species were wingless and multi-legged, but when he cued the goggles to caret movement he caught a few swoops from branch to branch, even after he'd filtered out fluttering leaves. Imported species, he supposed; like the humans on New Delphi.

He walked on more briskly. The wind among the gnarled branches formed a chorus as thin and cold as the stars singing.

Machines could have measured the distance for Daniel, but he chose instead to pace it—a countryman's skill he'd learned, like so much else, from Hogg while he was growing up on Bantry. 2,912 feet would be just around the curve of the tree from the *Princess Cecile*. That was fortunate, because Daniel knew that the guards in the main hatch were watching him if only because they had nothing better to do.

Margarida was an adult and anyway Lieutenant Daniel Leary wasn't her keeper, but though it wasn't his business to protect her honor, he *would* as a gentleman keep the bargain she'd offered: nobody would learn about the affair through Daniel's action or inadvertence. Instead of destroying the note, he'd hand it back so that she could be certain of its destruction.

This should be.... Daniel glanced over his shoulder as though looking up at the Tree's overhanging mass, a thing he'd done several times since he left the ship. The *Princess Cecile* was out of direct sight, as he'd expected. In a niche at the juncture of two separate trunks of the Tree was an arched doorway. In daylight it would've been invisible, but thermal imaging showed the panel to be minusculely warmer than the mass of living wood into which it was set.

Daniel removed the goggles and dropped them into a cargo pocket. He was wearing a utility uniform since anything else would've sent quite accurate rumors racing about the *Sissie*, but one didn't greet a potential lover looking like a creature peering up from the surface of a pond.

He knocked softly on the panel. A bar whispered; then the door opened outward, catching on blown sand.

Daniel quickly brushed the obstruction clear with the side of his boot.

"Daniel?" a voice whispered from the darkness.

Daniel stepped toward the blurred shadow in the doorway. "Ah, Margarida?" he said.

She threw herself into his arms, whispering, "Beloved!" before crushing her lips against his. He embraced her, noting that her robe slid smoothly over flesh with no sign of undergarments.

Margarida pulled her head back. "Come," she whispered, leading him inside and tugging the door to behind him. "There's a room here, nothing fancy but . . ."

They walked together down the narrow corridor, Daniel's left arm around Margarida's waist while her right hand toyed at his hairline. She was very warm and soft enough that the side of her body molded perfectly to his.

Something pricked at the back of Daniel's neck. *An insect?* he thought, frowning slightly.

His legs gave way. He was conscious, but everything around him happened behind a wall of glass. Margarida tried to hold him upright, but his weight bore her down until the dozens of robed legs scurried to help her. Arms lifted Daniel carefully.

The glass grew even thicker.

CHAPTER 22

Daniel was being carried; deep into the earth, he thought, but he wasn't sure whether he was confusing what was happening to his body with the slow trail his mind plowed down a slope of ice. He could see normally, but he was face down and couldn't turn his head for a view of anything but bare feet and the hems of robes.

He heard sounds, but his brain couldn't seem to connect them with the words he used to know. Once he managed to move his lips to mumble, "Tell Adele. They'll be worried about me. . . ."

The voices rose in volume; fingers touched his throat, then moved away. Another voice spoke reassuringly. Daniel kept going down.

There were no glowstrips. The companions of the men carrying him held lanterns whose bright white light seemed out of place here in the bowels of the tree. Hard shadows capered across the featureless walls. The rock-cut stairs turned and turned about at landings which seemed far apart. Several times Daniel felt the hands carrying him pass his weight off to others.

337

Feet moved ahead of him; metal squealed. They passed an iron door into a chamber. Daniel couldn't guess how large it was, but the lanterns didn't illuminate its full extent.

The air had a dry, vegetable odor. A long row of mummy-shaped bundles stood upright against a wall at right angles to the one in which the door was set. As Daniel's captors carried him past them, he suddenly realized that the bundles weren't balls of twine but rather tendrils twisting over and around themselves like those of a house plant in too small a pot. There were hundreds of the root clumps, perhaps more.

Daniel's captors spoke among themselves. Hands lifted his shoulders and set his feet on the earthen floor again. His legs supported him, though he'd have toppled onto his face without the others keeping him balanced.

Daniel could see his captors now, though the Prior was the only one he recognized. One of the robed figures moving at the edge of his vision might have been Margarida, but the light wasn't on her face. It puzzled him that he felt no emotion, but he supposed that was an effect of the drug that held his muscles catatonic.

An acolyte pulled a coiled rootlet toward Daniel and wrapped it around his forehead. The room's back wall was plant material, a vast plane of root plunging toward water flowing in the depths of the earth. His scalp prickled where the tree touched him. Fluid beaded on his skin, but he didn't know whether it was his own blood or sap dripping from the Tree.

Fingers reached into his breast pocket and came out with his recall plate. Instead of removing it, the acolyte bent Daniel's fingers around the plate so that he held it in both hands. Another man wound the tip of a second rootlet around Daniel's hands and wrists. The rootlet had a spongy tension, just enough to grip without either jerking free or pulling Daniel off his feet.

The hands released him. Daniel remained where he stood, held in place by the Tree. He could feel hair-fine cilia penetrating his skin; the contact was warm but not unpleasant. He'd thought the Tree might suck him dry for its own nourishment, but now he realized that the rootlets' purpose was to inject traces of the Tree's serum into his bloodstream.

The acolytes linked hands. The Prior murmured a prayer; the others responded by rote, their voices a sibilant echo in the great room. They walked out of Daniel's line of sight, returning to the long stairwell upward. The door closed with a clang, shutting off the beams of their lanterns.

In the cavern's unrelieved darkness, Daniel's mind began to shine with the light of all the universe.

Four spacers with sub-machine guns surrounded Adele at the console she'd taken for her own. They were angry and frustrated, as dangerous as live grenades. If they had a target or even the hint of a target, they'd blast it without the least compunction.

Adele knew exactly how they felt.

Nearby in the stacks an acolyte was making hand-written excerpts from a gardening book printed on Blaise a hundred and thirty years ago. Adele didn't know why or really care, but she'd checked to make sure of what the fellow was doing just in case it would help find Daniel.

It didn't, of course. Nothing thus far had helped. Possibly nothing would.

Woetjans and a group of spacers had gone off to the northern arc of the Tree. She and five of the others marched into the library looking tired, scruffy, and very angry.

"Nothing, ma'am!" the bosun snarled. "The Countess ferried forty of us in the aircar up the coordinates you give us, and we hiked back. We checked every nook and cranny on the map. There's no sign of the Captain and no sign of anydamnbody in the past hundred years."

They were treating Adele as though she were in charge now that Daniel was gone. As a result she was in charge. She wasn't sure she was a good choice for the task of locating Daniel, but she couldn't think of anyone better at the moment.

A squad of acolytes with static brooms entered from the corridor to sweep the large chamber. Adele grimaced at the use of charged pickups around the consoles, but if they were properly grounded there wouldn't be a problem. Windblown dust got everywhere in the complex, especially with so many angry Sissies stamping in and out paying scant attention to whether or not they were closing the outside doors.

"No sign?" Adele said, glancing around to see if the Prior was visible. No, not from where she sat at least. "Yesterday we were told that there were still hermits—"

One of the sweepers was the girl who'd accompanied the Prior yesterday. "Mistress!" Adele called. "Sister Margarida. Will you come here, please?"

Woetjans and two of the spacers guarding Adele—which Tovera, also present, had fortunately chosen to take as a joke rather than an insult—stepped toward the girl with one hand open to grab her and a weapon ready in the other in case she gave them an excuse to shoot. Instead the novice dropped her broom and came to Adele with her empty hands raised. One of the guards would've seized her arm anyway if Woetjans hadn't growled, "Don't be a bloody fool, Platt—she's coming."

"Mistress?" Margarida said. Her eyes were frank

and open. There was a degree of reserve as well, but the girl would have to be an imbecile not to know how very dangerous the situation was for her and all her fellows until Daniel was found.

"Yesterday you said that there were hermits living here apart from your community, did you not?" Adele said. She didn't raise her voice, but nobody looking at her would've been in doubt that she was angry.

"The Prior said that, mistress," Margarida said. "He may be right, but during my year in the Service I've wandered quite some distance in the Tree, farther than most acolytes do. *I* haven't seen individual hermits. Though they may have been hiding from me."

She offered a cautious smile. "The Prior is very old," she said. "Sometimes I think he remembers things from when he was young better than he does more recent events."

"I see," Adele said. She didn't trust the girl, but she was uncomfortably aware that her opinion might have been swayed by the fact that the novice had seemed to find Daniel attractive. "You may go back to your duties. Thank you for your help."

Margarida offered a bow, then picked up her broom and resumed cleaning. Several spacers glowered at her with expressions suggesting that they'd like to burn her alive. That wouldn't bring Daniel back, but it'd be a way of letting out frustration.

Adele returned to her display. She knew Woetjans was waiting for orders, but she had nothing to offer at the moment.

Adele had found seventeen maps in the monastery's database; she'd relayed them to the spacers making the physical search for Daniel. One of the maps, drawn a hundred and fifty standard years previous, purported to show all human habitations, past or present, within the Tree.

Woetjans' team had been searching the most distant, a warren burrowed into the northern edge of the Tree by a religious order not long after the Hiatus. The group only survived a generation or so, in contrast to the Service which the oracle had supported well into its third millennium by now.

None of the searches had found any sign of Daniel; and for the moment, Adele had run out of new places to look.

"Mistress?" prodded Woetjans in a desperate voice. "What do we do? He can't just have vanished into thin air."

"The books, the hardcopy here . . . ," Adele said, splaying the fingers of her left hand toward the extensive stack area. "Some of them contain descriptions of the Tree. I'm searching them in hope that there'll be something that isn't in the electronic files."

She paused and rubbed her eyes. "Nothing in the database is pre-Hiatus," she said, "though some of it is very old. Perhaps the books will tell me something, but I haven't found it yet."

Volumes she'd plucked from the stacks littered the floor beside and behind her. She hadn't bothered to reshelve them; the acolytes could do that after the *Princess Cecile* lifted from New Delphi. There were a hundred and thirty thousand books in the collection, according to the index. Most could easily be eliminated, but even so Adele had barely scratched the surface of the volumes that might possibly help.

Hilbride, one of the spacers who'd arrived with Woetjans, squatted for a closer look at the books Adele had gathered. He seemed to feel a personal involvement in Daniel's disappearance because he'd been one of the last people to talk with him when he left the ship.

"Mistress?" he said. Adele had always found him one

of the more literate Sissies. "How do you tell what books are where? They're not shelved in any order that I can see."

"No," Adele agreed, "only by height and thickness. But they're indexed—"

She gestured to the console she was using.

"—here, with the location." She focused on the next title her search program had highlighted. "*The Adventures of Captain Devereaux*," she quoted. "'An account of forty years of voyages as spacer and captain. Printed on Arslan in the tenth year of the third indiction of President Bella Gruen.'"

She closed her eyes for a moment to bring information into high mental relief. "That'd be roughly twenty-seven hundred years ago. According to the database, Devereaux once touched on New Delphi. Perhaps he'll say something interesting in his book, which is item thirty-one on the uppermost shelf of stack three-fourteen."

Adele grinned wryly at Hilbride. "If you'll go fetch it, we'll learn."

Hilbride glanced at a stack to see where the numbers were—at the top on either end—and started off, holding his sub-machine gun in both hands instead of carrying it slung. Woetjans looked even angrier than she had been. It struck Adele that if she'd given the bosun the command she gave Hilbride, Woetjans would have needed help to execute it.

The Prior entered the chamber on the arm of a young male acolyte. With him were the Klimovs and six spacers who'd been part of the the *Princess Cecile*'s anchor watch.

"What in bloody blue blazes are they doing here?" Woetjans growled. She started toward the newcomers. "If they think we're going to lift ship before we find the captain, they can bloody well think again!"

Adele got up and followed, in part to prevent the bosun from doing something they'd all regret. The Klimovs owned the *Princess Cecile*, and the courts of Cinnabar had a short way with mutineers—however sympathetic the judge might be to the cause of the crime.

"Mistress Mundy!" the Count called cheerfully. "The Prior here tells me that I'll be able to question the oracle after all! They're going to prepare me now, and tomorrow I'll know where the Earth Diamond is!"

He gestured to the couch. The touch of thousands of querents over millennia had blackened patches of the smooth wooden curves.

"Not without guards, you won't," Woetjans said. As soon as she knew that the Klimovs weren't going to demand something she didn't want to do, they returned to being "us" as opposed to "them," which was everybody on New Delphi who hadn't arrived aboard the *Princess Cecile*.

"Generally the querent is the only person in the room during incubation," the Prior said to Woetjans and Adele, "but we can screen the couch if you'd like. The querent should have a degree of privacy, but there's no need for anything that would interfere with your safety or continued work in the library."

"You got that right," Woetjans muttered, but even she seemed mollified.

"We're going to my study to begin the preparation, just down the corridor," the Prior said. He nodded to the guards. "These members of your crew are of course welcome."

"Yes, go ahead," Adele said because the spacers expected her to say something. She bowed to Klimov, hoping to wipe away the frown that'd appeared when he realized how completely his authority had been usurped in this crisis. "Good luck to you, your excellency."

The Prior, Klimov, and the train of guards shuffled toward a side door. Hilbride waited by the console, holding a rebound octavo volume in one hand and his gun in the other; he looked like a bizarre heraldic figure. Adele turned to him, then realized the Klimovna hadn't gone off with her husband.

"Mistress?" Adele said.

"Is there anything I can do to help you, Adele?" the Klimovna said.

Adele stared at her, considering the question. At last she said, "Thank you, Valentina, but I don't believe there's anything you can do. I appreciate the thought."

The Klimovna cleared her throat. "I wonder, Adele; do you believe in the power of prayer?"

Adele blinked. "No," she said. "No, I do not."

"Then perhaps I will pray," Valentina said with a sad smile. "So as not to duplicate someone else's effort, you see."

She turned and started back toward the door she'd entered by. The guards who'd accompanied her from the *Princess Cecile* had gone off with the Count and the Prior.

Woetjans stared at her back, then said, "Lamsoe and Griggs—tag along with her. It just might be she's got the best idea yet, so I'm damned if I want anything to happen to her."

Adele walked to the console and silently took the book from Hilbride; she'd set him to fetch further volumes while she searched this one for anything useful.

In her heart, she was glad for what Woetjans had said. She'd thought the same thing, but she was too much of a stiff-necked rationalist to say it.

CHAPTER 23

There was a man named Daniel Leary. The Tree was aware of him as it was aware of all the many billions of his species on many thousands of worlds.

The Tree knew.

Gas expanded and coalesced, forming suns and planets. The Tree was present because the mind of the Tree was omnipresent.

Slime formed in the warm seas of Earth and of innumerable other planets. It lived for a time, but as it started to spread vulcanism burned it back into its constituent elements. Life arose again, and this time a rain of cometary debris scoured the world clean. A third time, a fourth time, disaster following disaster; but eventually on Earth and many other worlds life survived. It covered the surface, then stepped across the reaches of space to other suitable environments.

Occasionally life form met life form. Interspecies conflict was rare because the needs and desires of alien races differed too greatly. Within species, however, rapid expansion gave opportunities for terrible wars and sometimes extinction when the extremities rebounded against themselves and the center.

Humanity avoided final oblivion, but by no more than a razor's edge. The thousand-year Hiatus from star travel could easily have become the eternal eclipse of the human race.

The Tree knew all things, but it cared about nothing.

Human fleets sailed between stars, threading in and out through the bubbles of the Matrix but returning to the sidereal universe except when catastrophe overtook them. The man named Daniel Leary had a feel for the Matrix, its currents and its pressures; but the Tree *was* the Matrix and all other existence, then and now and tomorrow.

On the planet men called New Delphi humans searched and struggled, their minds seething with anger and despair. The man named Daniel Leary felt their pain and would have washed it away had he been able to; but Daniel Leary no longer existed save as an idea in the Tree's awareness, the equivalent of the warmth of sun on leaves or the wind's eternal pressure on the multi-stemmed trunk.

A human asked a question; and the Tree knew. . . .

Adele awoke, momentarily angry that she'd been asleep. She jerked upright, rousing the spacers guarding her to full alertness. The watch had changed while she slept, but Hilbride slept curled on the floor at her feet.

The high-intensity lights in the stacks switched themselves on when a human being walked near, but they were all off now. Adele had been slumped over the console she was using, blurring the screen because her head lay over some of the holographic projectors.

Grimacing at her own weakness, she looked around. Tovera nodded with the slight smile she generally wore; the expression had as little humor in it as the similar curve of a cobra's lipless mouth. "Good morning, mistress," she said. "It's oh-six-fourteen by the ship's time."

"Have you gotten any sleep?" Adele said.

Tovera shrugged, her smile minusculely broader. "Enough," she replied; which didn't answer the question Adele asked but was responsive nonetheless. "I can function."

Tovera could function in any condition short of death, Adele presumed; and whatever killed her, as something doubtless would one day, had better not count her out for the sixty seconds or so a human brain retained enough oxygen to function.

Adele stood, noting the enormous clutter of books blocking access to several of the nearer consoles. An acolyte—the same man she'd noticed before—sat at the far end of the rank; he felt her eyes on him and turned to nod, then resumed his work.

Good God but she'd made a mess! And she wasn't any closer to finding Daniel than she'd been at the beginning of the night. Well, she wasn't dead yet, either.

Woetjans rose; she'd been sitting on a stack of books down the aisle. Adele winced when she saw the bosun's choice of a seat, but she didn't comment.

"Mistress," Woetjans said with a nod. The big woman looked a decade older than she had when the *Princess Cecile* landed. "I've been wondering what we do if, you know, he doesn't turn up."

The guards watched Adele in intent silence. Hilbride had awakened; he was poised to get up from the floor, but he didn't move while he waited for her answer.

"You go on, bosun," Adele said crisply. "As your duty requires. As you know."

But that didn't answer what Signals Officer Mundy would do. Adele wasn't sure of that answer herself. It was unlikely that her presence on New Delphi over the next years or decades would locate Daniel; but

perhaps it would make a difference . . . and perhaps that
was the decision she'd make.

For now, though, there were more volumes to
examine, at least a thousand of them. She looked at
the jumble of books she'd been through—carefully
enough? Had a crucial paragraph escaped in her haste
and fatigue?—and thought of the many-times greater
task still ahead. She sighed, stretched, and prepared
to return to it.

The Prior entered the chamber accompanied by
Valentina, half a dozen acolytes, and a pair of spacers. They walked toward the couch, hidden behind
drapes made by hanging gray robes from a frame of
plastic piping. The spacers guarding Count Klimov
watched with grim expressions.

"Let's join them," Adele said. There were grunts of
pleased agreement from the Sissies about her. An oracle
was a novelty in itself. Even if they were convinced
of the need to stand guard the way they'd been doing,
it was numbingly boring work.

Adele had another reason for her decision. If the
Count had gotten the answer to his question, he'd
probably want to leave New Delphi immediately. She
needed to be present to represent the Sissies, and to
represent herself.

The Prior was waiting; the girl Margarida supported
his arm. He bowed to Adele, then pulled open the
screen with his free hand; other acolytes set to removing the structure completely. Valentina walked to where
her husband lay, sleeping with his mouth part open.
Adele could hear the Count snoring softly.

"Speak quietly," the Prior directed her. "You can
touch him, but do so gently."

"Georgi?" Valentina said. She bent over the couch
and took the Count's hands in hers, chafing them
lightly. "Wake up, dear one. It's morning."

The Count opened his eyes. He started to lift his torso. His wife put her arm around him to help, but he seemed fit enough.

"I dreamed," he said in a tone of bright wonder. "I remember. *The Institutions, Book Ten, Caput Three.* But I don't know what it means."

"It's a book citation," Adele said. She stepped back to the console; she'd downloaded the index files to her handheld, but at the moment it was simpler to use the console already displaying the data rather than sitting on the floor with the little unit on her lap.

She scrolled, searched, and repeated the search. Twelve hits, titles including the word Institutions, and none of them likely to have any bearing on the Earth Diamond.

She looked at the Prior; he'd almost fallen when the Count spoke. Margarida was supporting his whole weight with an expression of terror.

"Sir," Adele said. "Where are *The Institutions* shelved?"

Her voice wasn't loud, no louder than the snick of the folding knife opening in Hogg's hand. He'd come in a moment ago, haggard from a day and night of searching on his own. Windblown grit clung to his hair and clothing.

"Mistress . . . ," the Prior said. His face was waxen. He nodded toward the Count but he didn't take his eyes from Adele. "Your excellency. There's been a mistake, I don't know how. We will refund your fee immediately, Count Klimov—"

"Where's the book, you fat whoreson!" Hogg shouted, grabbing the Prior's fine white hair and tilting his head slightly so that the point of the knife just pricked his throat beside a carotid artery.

Margarida screamed and tried to claw Hogg's eyes. Tovera—how had she moved so quickly?—clubbed the butt of her sub-machine gun across the girl's temple, dropping her where she stood. As if that were a signal, Sissies grabbed or knocked down the other acolytes present.

The man at the end console rose and started to run toward a doorway across the chamber. A spacer fired his stocked impeller, missing the fellow but blowing his console apart in a crash and shower of sparks. The running man screamed and threw himself to the floor.

"Cease fire!" Adele ordered, her ears ringing from the *Whack*! of the powerful weapon discharging in an enclosed space. Her own pistol was in her hand, pointing toward the ceiling till she had a better target. "You! Prior! Where are *The Institutions*?"

"I can't!" the Prior said, dangling from Hogg's grip in obvious pain and terror. "Only senior acolytes are permitted to read it, please!"

Hogg threw the man to the floor and squatted astride him. "I'll get it out of him, mistress," he said in a guttural voice. "You maybe want to look away for a bit."

"No," Adele said; and then, because Hogg had shifted his knife to the Prior's left eye, "*No*, Hogg! Not unless I can't find it myself!"

Until she spoke, she didn't have the faintest notion of how to make a quick search for a book not in the computerized index. Then, as the words came out, she did.

She sat down at the console. It used a virtual keyboard and light pen, familiar and adequate input devices if not the system Adele preferred. She called up the index by stack, then switched to graphical display and sorted each stack by number in groups of ten. By the time the first stack had run—ending in a group of seven titles, indexed from one to seven in sequence—she'd programmed the console to scroll through the remainder of the collection in order, allowing five seconds for each stack.

"Ma'am?" Hogg said. He sounded frightened, but he'd stepped away from the Prior and closed his knife again. Adele could see him from the corners of her eyes, but she kept her focus on the display.

"Give me five minutes, Hogg," Adele said. She understood how the servant felt, angry and desperate for something to *do*; ideally something that would help Daniel, but anyway something. "Maybe ten. You wouldn't learn anything faster than that your way, nothing you could be certain of."

Hogg grunted, but he didn't openly object. Two spacers held the Prior's arms; another stood with the muzzle of his impeller in the face of the girl still unconscious and drooling on the floor.

Rows of equal columns scrolled, paused, and vanished for the next stackful. Adele *did* believe in her way over Hogg's; but she knew Hogg's would work. The Prior—old and frail—might die before pain drove the words out, but there were plenty of younger, stronger acolytes. One of them would talk.

But Daniel wouldn't have wanted that. Oh, he'd have used torture if the safety of the Republic or his crew depended on it, but it would bother him; and it would bother him worse to know that an old man had died for him, that a pretty girl was now blind because for Daniel's sake battery acid had been dripped into her eyes.

Adele smiled faintly. If her method failed and she turned the business over to Hogg, she'd lie to Daniel about what had happened. That'd be easy enough; and what were a few eyeless faces to Adele Mundy, whose dreams already had so many visitors whom her shots had mutilated?

"I knew we could count on you, ma'am," Hogg said,

his voice calm again. "You'd never let the young master down."

He must have misinterpreted my smile, Adele thought. Then she thought, *Or perhaps he didn't.*

With that realization came the break, the rows of titles with one column shorter by a tenth than the rest. Adele froze the display, then said, "Stack Eighty-Seven, Title Forty . . . Two. Between *Pre-Hiatus Serials Catalogued at Las Primas Base,* and *A History of My Times,* by Vice-Admiral Beverly Coyne."

Hilbride, his sub-machine gun forgotten on a pile of culled volumes, started into the stacks. Woetjans would've joined him. If the bosun went, half the scores of Sissies in the chamber would've followed. Adele ordered, "Leave him be! Hilbride will get it."

All this needed was half a dozen semi-literates shredding the book in their struggle to be the one who brought it to her. . . .

To give the others something to occupy them, and partly because she was human and proud of what she'd accomplished, Adele went on conversationally, "We saw no books elsewhere in the monastery. Anything we did find would stick out like a sore thumb. Therefore the best place to hide a book is here in the library, a needle among a hundred thirty thousand other needles . . . but left out of the index."

She grinned with pride and satisfaction; Hilbride was coming back with a fat quarto volume held in both hands. "So I searched for a hole in the index. And found one."

"Here, mistress!" Hilbride said, handing Adele the book with the pride of a cat presenting its owner with a dead mouse. "What do we do now?"

Adele opened the volume with the care it deserved. It was covered with the same translucent vellum that had been used to rebind many of the other books in the collection. In this case the binding was probably original, and the work itself was a manuscript indited in a clear, bold hand that managed to be graceful without becoming ornate. She opened it, starting a quarter in from the back.

"I don't understand what this is about," the Klimovna said. "Georgi, it was the Earth Diamond you were seeking, was it not? Not Captain Leary."

Not the most politic thing to say in the present circumstances, Adele thought, but she continued paging forward in silence. With luck none of the Sissies would pick up on the remark.

"The Earth Diamond, of course," the Count said, frowning. "But I don't understand what the oracle meant. Surely the book is old, older than the time John Tsetzes fled with the diamond?"

"All I know . . . ," said Hogg. He'd walked away from Adele and stood looking down at the Prior's anguished face. "Is that this bird wouldn't be near so worried about the mistress reading his book if he didn't have something to hide. And the only thing we *know* is hidden around here is the master."

"*The Institutions*, the codex itself," said the Prior dully, "is almost three thousand years old. It's the bedrock of our Service, written by Senior Scientist Arlan Melzoff himself. Mistress Mundy, it is a sacred document. You must see that."

"Well, I tell you," Hogg said. "If the mistress don't find where the young master is by reading that thing, then I'm going to flay you alive and your friends can write another book on your skin. That may not find him either, but I'll feel better for doing it; and right now I got a ways better to feel."

"Amen to that," said Woetjans soberly.

"'We began the shaft in the Sanctum,'" Adele said, reading aloud as soon as she found the passage Klimov had cited on his return to consciousness. "'At first we used power tools, but some held doubts about their propriety. The Tree spoke through the majority of the order, so in accordance with the vote, the remainder of the shaft was dug by hand. At a depth of 512 feet the diggers entered the chamber in which as foretold subsidence had laid open the mind of the Tree.'"

She looked up without closing the book. She said, "The area marked as the Sanctum on the earliest maps is some three hundred yards northwest of here; that is, toward the decayed center of the Tree. Woetjans, I think we'll need digging equipment as well as cutting bars to remove wood that's in our way."

"Wait," said the Prior, spread-eagled on the floor. "I'll take you. And you'll want a quantity of saline solution as well."

"No!" cried Margarida, her right hand dabbing at the pressure cut on her scalp. "You mustn't—"

Hogg bent toward her, his blade bare in his hand. His face showed no more emotion than if he were preparing to wring the neck of a small animal for dinner.

"Hogg!" Adele shouted. "That's for Daniel to decide!"

Hogg turned and straightened. "Ma'am," he said in a trembling voice. "If the master comes back, he'll spare her for he's a gentle lad; and that's his right to do. But if he doesn't, then I'll have her heart out and this white-haired hypocrite's too—"

He kicked the Prior, not especially hard but enough to bruise regardless.

"—though you shoot me for it."

"If we don't get Daniel back unharmed, Hogg," Adele said as she rose from the console, "then *I* won't be defending them."

She looked at the men holding the Prior. "Let him up," she said. "As a matter of fact, carry him. He's going to lead us to the room this passage—" she waggled the book in her hands "—talks about."

"Is the captain there, mistress?" Woetjans said. She'd stuck a club of structural tubing through her belt; her right hand clenched and opened on the taped grip as she waited for an answer.

"Yes," said the Prior in a half-dead voice as the spacers dragged him upright. "Captain Leary is in the Chamber of the Tree. I'm taking you there because you'll cause less damage if I do."

They left the library and incubation chamber by one of the passages leading toward the center of the Tree. It was an odd procession, since none of the Sissies present intended to be left behind. That meant taking the dozen or more captured acolytes along as well, their arms wired behind their backs. They didn't protest, but occasionally a Sissie would kick one, for not moving faster or simply on general principles.

"You must understand," one of the older male acolytes said, "that this is greater than a single man."

Barnes punched him in the kidneys with the butt of his impeller. The man screamed and flopped forward.

"Guess it's greater than you, anyhow," Barnes growled. He and Dasi bent as if they'd practiced the maneuver. Each of the big men gripped the acolyte's elbows. They carried him with his feet and occasionally knees dragging, moaning softly.

"This is the original Sanctum," Adele said as they entered a moderate-sized room, this time set off the corridor instead being an expansion of it. There were no glowstrips in this section, but several of the spacers carried floodlamps. "Supposedly it's been abandoned."

Boxes and kitchen appliances, presumably nonfunctional, were piled in the center of the floor. Dug into the dead wood of one wall was a closet, empty but partly closed by a curtain.

"We been here before," said one of the men who'd been with Woetjans. "We searched it yesterday, right?"

"The door is in the back of the closet," the Prior said. "It slides to the left."

A spacer ripped the curtain down. Adele started to feel for a catch on the back wall of the closet.

Woetjans moved her aside, said, "Careful," and smashed the heel of her boot into it. Wood splintered, springing the panel free. Woetjans kicked again, sideways this time, and slid it open. Behind the panel, a set of stairs went downward.

Hogg led the way with a floodlamp in his left hand and an impeller slung muzzle-forward beneath his right arm. "Leave a couple of your boys up top, Woetjans," he called back. "Just in case our friends get ideas."

Several spacers muttered curses as they started down the long stairwell. Adele smiled coldly. Only those who'd been close enough to hear and understand the section from *The Institutions* would know how *really* long the stairs were, but they'd all have come anyway. The guards Woetjans picked for the stairhead complained bitterly that they weren't going to be part of the rescue party.

If it *was* a rescue party. . . .

Adele looked over her shoulder, past Tovera who was even more ghastly than usual in the hard shadows that the handlamps flung. Lamsoe and Claud carried the Prior with an arm over each of their shoulders. He had to move his feet to keep from stubbing his toes— neither Sissie was especially tall—but he wasn't supporting his own weight.

"Is Captain Leary all right?" Adele said.

"I don't know," said the Prior, his answer as blunt as the question had been. "Physically, he should be after so short a time. Mentally . . ."

He tried to shrug and couldn't, so he grimaced instead. "No one has ever been released before."

They continued down. Near the surface the treads were of wood. Pieces had been inset into the substance of the Tree when the original steps wore deeply concave. After the first landing the stairs were cut into stone, but even here plastic caps were sealed onto treads which had worn or crumbled.

"We should have waited," the Prior said. Adele looked back. She couldn't tell whether he was speaking to her or if he was just unburdening his conscience to the world at large. "He must not have been fully one with the Tree yet. He sent a message instead of merely being the Intercessor between the Tree and the querent. It was my fault."

"But where *is* the Earth Diamond?" called Count Klimov. He and his wife were close enough behind to hear the Prior's voice over the echoing susurrus which boots scraped on stair treads.

"I haven't any idea," the Prior said. "There's nothing on New Delphi except the Tree and the Service."

"Don't count on either of them being around after we lift from here," a motorman snarled. "I figure we could get a bloody good bonfire going if the *Sissie* hovers right over the woody part, right?"

An acolyte began to sob. The spacer holding his wired wrists raised her sub-machine gun for a blow, then lowered the weapon and growled, "You shoulda thought about that when you grabbed the Captain."

Adele didn't comment. There was no point in destroying the Tree; but if Daniel *wasn't* all right, she wasn't sure how strong a stand she'd take to prevent that happening.

"There's a door here," Hogg called, his voice echoing. Adele saw the rusted panel past him in the wavering light of his lamp. "Is it locked?"

"No," said the Prior. He sounded as though he were speaking from the depths of troubled sleep. "It pulls toward you."

Hogg paused; both his hands were full. The level surface at the bottom of the stairs was larger than the landings, but it still wouldn't hold more than half a dozen adults. If they didn't open the door quickly there was going to be a dangerous crush.

"I'll get it," Adele said, stepping past Hogg. She gripped the staple and pulled; the hinges squealed and fought her. In sudden fury, she jerked hard. Hogg strode in, his lamp held high and out to the side; she was immediately behind him, her pistol covering the right side of the room while Hogg's big weapon lay across his body to sweep the left.

They saw the mummies against the sidewall simultaneously. Adele took two steps down the line, then started running. She didn't know when the last time she'd run had been.

"Bloody hell!" Hogg shouted, turning to prod the Prior in the throat with his impeller. "Which one is he, you bastard? Which one?"

Daniel *had* to be at the far end. The line started at the door and continued without a gap. "Hogg, bring your knife!" Adele said, aware that her voice was shriller than usual.

"Don't cut it, use the saline solution!" the Prior wheezed. "The salt will make the roots release without damage. Please!"

Adele reached the last figure in the line. The nametape on the left breast of Daniel's uniform was visible, but swathes of hair-fine rootlets covered his head and hands. Adele felt dizzy; she bent forward, thinking for a moment that she might have to put her head between her legs to keep from fainting. Half a dozen Sissies ran up beside her.

"Bloody hell I won't use a knife!" Hogg said. He'd slung his impeller and held the winking blade in his right hand.

"No, it may be safer for Daniel!" Adele said, clear-headed again. She put a hand on Hogg's shoulder. She'd had a sudden horrific vision of the roots going into spasms that drove them into her friend's brain. How deep were they now?

"Mistress?" said Sun, handing Adele a condensing canteen. Because the crew had been searching the Tree and the dry wastes around it, they were wearing RCN dismount gear. "I dropped half a dozen salt tablets in it. Will that do?"

"Yes," Adele said, slipping the pistol into her pocket again. Hogg snatched off his bandanna and gave it to her. She slopped water over it, then applied the wet fabric to the roots covering Daniel's face.

For an instant, nothing happened; then she felt the plant writhe as though someone were pulling a piece of coarse brocade under the bandanna. A tangle of fine roots dropped away.

Daniel trembled; his eyes were closed and his face looked like that of a sleeping angel. Adele moved the bandanna higher up her friend's scalp and poured more saltwater over it.. The roots jerked away like hairs shriveling as they came too near an open flame. Daniel's hands opened; his recall plate clattered to the floor. He would've toppled onto his face if Hogg hadn't let go of the impeller and grabbed him.

Spacers and the Klimovs as well shouted amazed questions as they poured through the doorway. The echoes were odd. The cavern must stretch unguessably far into the distance like a gigantic organ pipe.

And how many strangers would have been kidnapped in the future, if the Sissies hadn't put an end to the business tonight?

Hogg knelt, lowering Daniel toward the floor. Adele sat cross-legged and cradled his head. Tiny red pimples spotted every inch or so of his bare skin.

"Did they kill the captain?" a Sissie cried. "Did the bastards kill him?"

Daniel opened his eyes. Adele waited, her face as still as the hard metal lines of the pistol in her pocket.

Daniel gave her a slow smile. "Hello, Adele," he said. "We don't have to go to Radiance to learn about the Alliance base after all. It's been complete for almost a month. Seven hours ago an Alliance fleet of eight destroyers, a heavy cruiser, and two battleships landed there."

CHAPTER 24

Daniel sat up very carefully because his euphoria disconnected him. All existence spun through his mind—only in flashes and sparkling, now, but that was still enough to lift him high above present existence.

He looked at those about him, his friends, his fellow humans—every soul of them, not only the Sissies and the Klimovs but also the robed acolytes. Their hands were wired and their expressions terrified, but they were Daniel's friends because their action had brought him to this exaltation. It was good he'd returned, though, because he had his duty.

Count Klimov bent to massage his right calf while looking at the long line of root-wrapped mummies, the hundreds of Intercessors of previous generations. "Will we never find the Earth Diamond, then?" he said to his wife, his tone peevish with disappointment and the pain of his leg muscles. *Which was nothing to what he'd be feeling after climbing back up those 815 steps*, the pragmatically human part of Daniel's mind noted.

"Your excellency?" Daniel said. Spacers were crowding about him; he looked through their legs to see the

Klimovs ten feet away. "I'll give you the Earth Diamond for a price."

The Count didn't hear him in the general bustle, and the surrounding Sissies didn't pay any attention to his words. Adele understood, though, and said sharply, "Back away from the captain! Give him room! Woetjans, give the captain room!"

"Right, move your asses back!" Woetjans shouted, jerked into action by Adele's command. When Lamsoe didn't straighten quickly enough, she grabbed him by the back of neck like a puppy and deposited him an arm's length away.

"Count Klimov!" Adele said. She didn't shout the way the bosun had, but nobody could ignore the note of aristocratic command in her crisp tones. "If you will come here, Captain Leary is offering to find the Earth Diamond for you."

"What?" said Klimov. "What do you—?"

He took an abrupt step toward Daniel. A muscle in Klimov's groin cramped; he toppled forward. Valentina grabbed her husband, but he would've hit the floor if Lamsoe—headed in the right direction because of Woetjans's shove—hadn't caught him.

Daniel blinked. During the instant his eyes were closed, the universe flared back into his mind with almost the same crystalline glory as he'd felt when it and he and the Tree were one. He opened his eyes, smiling on those around him and reveling in life and existence.

The recall plate had fallen to the floor when Daniel's hands opened; it lay between his legs. He picked it up and rubbed it between his palms. The physical connection with a familiar object was part of the process by which a human being became the Intercessor, the connection which translated between the Tree and each human querent.

The Count was speaking, but his words were merely variations on, "What do you mean?" Daniel found it a wonder to hear sounds again instead of *being* the vibrations himself.

"Count Klimov," he said; Klimov fell silent with his mouth open. "I need a vessel, your vessel. I'll trade you the Earth Diamond for the *Princess Cecile*, and I'll carry you and the Countess to Todos Santos. There you'll be able to take ship anywhere you wish. Back to Novy Sverdlovsk with your treasure, I would expect. Do you accept my offer?"

"He bloody well—" Hogg started to say, but Adele touched his lips with her right index finger. Hogg gulped back the remainder of the threat and grimaced contritely, first to Adele and then to the Count himself.

Klimov met Daniel's eyes. The smile appeared to bother him, but Daniel couldn't help it. Life in its profusion and in its detail was a wonderful thing, an entrancing thing.

"Captain Leary," the Count said, formal and far more impressive than he'd generally been since Daniel met him. "You know that I paid three hundred thousand florins for the *Princess Cecile*. She is a fine ship, no doubt, but the Earth Diamond is unique. There are those who would pay twenty times as much for it; I would pay so much if I were able to do so. Why do you make this offer?"

Klimov wasn't a fool. He knew there were hard men in the *Sissie*'s crew and that a whispered order from Daniel Leary might be the last anybody heard of two nobles from Novy Sverdlovsk. Even so, he didn't flinch.

In the recent past Daniel had known everything, been all things, and some memories of the things closest to his present life remained like dust-motes glinting in the sun. *This was the man who'd faced down*

*a peasant waving the bloody scythe with which he'd
killed his wife and her lover bare moments before*, he
thought; and smiled more broadly.

"There's no trick, your excellency," Daniel said. He
thought he could stand up now; perhaps in a moment
he'd try. "My nation, Cinnabar, has need of a ship.
Whereas money . . ."

He gurgled a laugh. "I've never needed more money
than what it took to buy the next round of drinks or
a lady's dinner," he said, noting the rueful agreement
in Hogg's expression. "Besides, the Earth Diamond
came from Novy Sverdlovsk; it should go back there."

Count Klimov bowed stiffly at the waist, then
straightened. "Captain Leary," he said, "I accept your
offer. I will sign whatever documents you desire."

He cleared his throat. "Now," he said. "When do you
expect to fulfill your part of the bargain?"

"Immediately," said Daniel. He tried to get up. He
could visualize every muscle fiber, every nerve cell, but
for a moment that conscious awareness replaced the
reflexes that should've brought action. He laughed again
as Hogg and Woetjans lifted him upright, worry carving
deep clefts in their faces.

"I'm all right," Daniel said. "I'm better than all right,
but it's like being drunk, that's all."

"I've bloody well seen you drunk, master," Hogg said
grimly, holding Daniel's left arm over his shoulders
as Woetjans supported the right. "You were never like
this!"

Daniel felt existence shrivel back down to a kernel
in his mind; his body worked normally again. "I'm all
right," he repeated, and to prove it he walked to the
mummy closest to where the Acolytes had placed him.
Hogg and Woetjans didn't let go, but they permitted
his legs to carry his weight.

Daniel opened his right hand. "Hogg," he said,

facing the shrouded, desiccated corpse of the man who had been interface between the Tree and humanity during the previous six decades. "Your knife, if you please."

Hogg snicked his blade open and slapped the hilt into Daniel's hand. He and Woetjans moved away. The scores of humans in the great chamber waited, only the whisper of their breath breaking the silence.

Daniel inserted the point at the mummy's bulging midsection and drew it down in a swift curve; the keen steel *tick*ed on the object beneath. The roots had dried when the Intercessor died; they were silk strong, but they didn't resist the edge.

He stepped back and closed the knife. "Your excellency," he said to Count Klimov. "If you'll reach in there, I think you'll find the Earth Diamond. My predecessor in this place was John Tsetzes."

"I never knew," the Prior whispered. He walked toward the mummy with the cautious determination of a very sick man. "We don't speak of the persons before they became Intercessor. The most recent elevation came before I joined the Service."

Daniel closed the knife and returned it to Hogg. The Klimovs knelt together, reaching into the husk that he'd sliced open. The dead roots scrunched to the side as the Klimovs babbled prayers of thanksgiving. They brought the diamond into open air for the first time in sixty years, holding it in both their hands.

Daniel remembered the blaze of white-hot suns; then he was back in a deep cavern, lighted by the Sissies' handlamps. The huge gem reflected and refracted the beams into a dazzle greater than the originals. Not only continents but the terrain features, rivers and lakes and mountain ranges, were etched on the globe's inner surface. They scattered the light into a thousand rainbows.

"Your excellency," Daniel said, "I hope our bargain suits you; for I can tell you, it suits me and the RCN very well indeed!"

Adele heard the corvette's klaxon, its sound muffled through the living walls of the tree. Her commo helmet said in Mr. Chewning's voice, *"Five to ship. We're about to clear sand out of the thrusters. Stay clear by fifty yards or you better be able to grow yourself a new hide. Five out."*

"You'll be gone before I'm elevated, Captain Leary," said the Prior, hunching slightly. Two husky male acolytes waited nearby to accompany him from the library and carry him down the long steps, just as Lamsoe and Claud had done earlier in the day. "Goodbye, then, and may good fortune attend your later endeavors as well."

He held *The Institutions* in both hands. Adele had scanned it to provide both herself and the Service with copies of the text, but the Prior would take the codex itself with him.

"Good day to you, sir," Daniel said, dipping his head in a cross between a nod and a bow. "I'm glad we could reach an accommodation that permits your Service to survive."

Adele noted with silent wonder the way Daniel verbally drew a glove over his iron fist. The present Prior would become the next Intercessor, and the same thing would happen at *his* death, then henceforth till time or the Service ended.

Daniel hadn't made an open threat when he addressed the Prior and his assembled acolytes, but they'd correctly understood what he meant when he said, "I will not permit the present situation to continue."

Intercessors lived longer than ordinary humans; the Tree was a wise and abstemious master. Much the same comparison could be made of pet cats and their feral cousins, Adele supposed. Pets generally seemed to be content, too. . . .

Most of the Sissies were aboard, making the ship ready for return to Todos Santos, but six armed spacers watched over Adele and Daniel so long as they were on the ground. From the guards' scowls and the way they held their weapons, they genuinely thought there might be trouble.

Adele didn't—the Service was completely cowed. But she carried her pistol and Hogg and Tovera watched the entrances on opposite sides of the long room; just in case—and at least for Hogg, in hope.

A waiting acolyte said harshly, "What happens to one man is of little account when balanced against the good of all humanity!"

His partner tried to shush him, a look of fear on his face. "Andre, it's been decided," the Prior said tiredly.

Adele looked at the acolyte. "Sir," she said, "you're welcome to make that choice regarding the worth of your own life. I wouldn't hesitate to make it regarding mine. But you will not make that choice for a friend of mine!"

Daniel looked at her and smiled. "No, they won't," he said. He turned again to the Prior and repeated, "Good day."

He strode toward the corridor leading most directly to the ship. Hogg and four of the guards walked with him.

Adele ran a fingertip over the vellum cover of *A Catalog of the Library of Barnard's World*, sighed, and followed her friend—but slowly. The library of Barnard's World, supposedly the finest collection of Terran books extant since the asteroids blasted Earth and humanity into the Hiatus, had burned three hundred years ago.

"Clear away, bitch!" one of Adele's escort snarled, brandishing his impeller. "Or take your chances on which end of this I use on you!"

Adele raised her head, recalled from a reverie in which young Adele Mundy grew up to become Director of the Academic Collections on Bryce, revered for her knowledge and the quiet assurance of her demeanor. The novice who'd lured Daniel into the trap, Margarida, waited in the corridor.

"Mistress?" the girl said to Adele. The right side of her head had been shaved so that the pressure cut from Tovera's sub-machine gun could be bandaged. "Might I walk with you?"

"Didn't I tell you?" the Sissie shouted, lifting his gun for a butt-stroke.

"Vincent!" Adele said. "If I wanted her dead, I'd have killed her!"

She took a deep breath, because part of her *did* want the girl dead; so very much that her arm trembled with the effort of not drawing her pistol. Tovera smirked, amused to watch a conscience in action. *Daniel wouldn't have to know. . . .*

"Yes, if you like," Adele said, her voice as calm as a pond in which a great carnivore waits. Did the girl think she was going to follow Daniel aboard the *Princess Cecile*? "To the boarding bridge and no farther."

Margarida fell in step. Without looking toward Adele she said, "The Service is a renounced community. You're aware of that, I suppose?"

"Yes," said Adele. "As soon as Daniel—"

She cleared her throat, then resumed, "When Captain Leary said this would be our next landfall, I read the histories of New Delphi which I had available. Quite a considerable amount of information, actually; though they omitted a few salient points."

"Yes," Margarida said, blushing a poisonous color in

the yellow-green light. "Now that you're leaving, I'm sure you'll see to it that the accounts are corrected. There'll be riots against the Lay Service, I suppose."

Adele looked at the woman in silence while one of the escorts unbarred the door to the outside. The wind curled in; tiny sand-grains gnawed Adele's face and hands.

"We'll certainly see to it that the wider universe learns the full truth of your operations here, yes," she said as she and Margarida started across the ridged sand toward the ship. "And people being people, there'll likely be a degree of anger at an institution for moral uplift which turns out to have practiced human sacrifice. So yes to the second part of your question also."

"It wasn't—" the girl said angrily, then blushed again and swallowed the remainder of her words. She was intelligent enough to realize that while Adele was being deliberately uncharitable, the description was within the bounds of truth.

"We see things differently, I know that," Margarida said, squeezing her arms against her torso. "I shouldn't have brought it up, I'm sorry."

She looked straight at Adele for the first time and went on, "Mistress, I wanted to ask you. . . ."

She paused, eyed the male spacers close ahead of them, and blushed. Then she continued, "I sent a note to Captain Leary as a trick so we could, well, take him for elevation. You know that?"

"To kidnap him," Adele said in a level voice. "Yes, I know that."

And I've allowed you to live because that's what Daniel wants, she added silently. *But don't push your luck.*

"Mistress," the girl blurted. "It was a trick. But I'm only twenty-three, I'm a *woman*. I haven't taken second orders yet, I'm still a novice, and I think . . . I think. . . ."

Margarida swallowed; she'd begun to cry. "Mistress," she said, "the Service does great good, unique good. I saw that on my own world, Regis, but it's the same on hundreds of worlds. Only I'm not sure I'm strong enough to be what I want to be. Mistress, what should I do? I *know* that you understand!"

Adele met her eyes, trying to compose a satisfactory answer; an answer that would satisfy either one of them.

"Sister Margarida," she said. She'd only hesitated a few seconds, but the chasm between them seemed far wider than that. "You believe I've renounced the world—" the euphemism twitched Adele's lips in a cold smile "—as you wish to do. That's not the case. I didn't have to surrender something that I didn't have in the first place."

The girl stared without comprehension. They might be speaking two different languages for all the communication they were effecting.

"Sister," Adele said, "I wish I could help you. I *can't*. I don't have either your faith or your desires. You'll have to decide for yourself what you do with your life."

She chuckled without humor. "That's true for all of us, of course."

They'd reached the catwalk. Most of the *Sissie*'s hatches were already closed, though the big port on the bridge remained open as well as the main hatch. The air had a burned smell, the residue of the recent trial of the plasma thrusters.

Adele stopped and put a hand on Margarida's shoulder, turning her so they were facing one another for the first time since they met outside the library. The escorting spacers were already on the boarding bridge. They faced about with worried expressions.

"Sister Margarida," Adele said more fiercely than she'd intended. "I can't tell you what to do, but I'll tell you what *I* did. Oh, not sex—that doesn't affect me, I told you that already; but the world in the larger sense does."

She gestured back toward the Tree. "Your library is interesting," she went on. "There are many unusual holdings and perhaps a few that're unique; but I've worked in collections that're easily a hundred times more extensive. I love them, I love the environment, and I could be back there now—but I'm not. I'm here in what's again an RCN warship with all that implies. I've killed many times, many *scores* of times since I put on this uniform—"

Her right thumb and index finger pinched the mottled fabric of the opposite sleeve of her utility uniform.

"—and I'll kill more people, I'm sure of it, until the day someone kills me as I'm also sure will happen. This is my choice, Sister, my *choice*: I chose the world!"

Adele dropped the girl's arm and strode up the boarding bridge. She didn't look back until she was in the access compartment and the main hatch had started to close.

Margarida was staring after her with a blank expression. Suddenly the girl turned on her heel and started back toward the Tree with determined strides.

CHAPTER 25

The *Princess Cecile* orbited Todos Santos, but so long as Adele had work to do she'd remained oblivious of the weightlessness. Now she set her console to complete the processing and looked over to the Klimovs in the bridge annex.

The Count seemed irritated; Valentina had a withdrawn, half-sad expression. Previously they'd been coddled during landing procedures; this time they were left to their own devices; they were no longer owners of the ship on which they travelled. Daniel was negotiating with the port inspectors, while Adele dealt with her own self-appointed task.

They don't really belong anywhere, Adele thought. *Their wealth gains them entrée to most societies, but they aren't really of those societies. Everyone else aboard the* Sissie *is part of the same family*.

"Your excellencies?" Adele said, speaking across the ten feet of open space instead of using the intercom. The ship while orbiting wasn't silent, but its systems didn't make the cacophonous racket they would when under power. "I'm providing you with a list of the ships

375

in San Juan Harbor with their values listed for tax purposes, the records of their captains where those are available, and the vessels' histories—again as available. The tax listings are relative, of course."

"But I don't see . . . ?" Klimov said, still frowning but now in confusion rather than pique. "What is this you're telling us?"

"You'll be buying or hiring a ship here, I presume," Adele said. From the look of comprehension on Valentina's face it was obvious that she already understood, but Adele continued for the husband, "I believe this information will make it easier for you to negotiate."

She cleared her throat. "I have an acquaintance— a relative, in fact—on Todos Santos. Under other circumstances I'd suggest that he use his good offices on your behalf, but the present emergency precludes that. Still, you should be able to find acceptable transportation home."

The *Princess Cecile* had dropped into normal space some four million miles from Todos Santos. Most astrogators merely hoped to make their initial reentry within the solar system for which they were aiming, though she knew Daniel had on occasion done even better. The first thing Adele did was to alert the Cinnabar exiles through their emergency net. She and Daniel had a meeting arranged in Adrian Purvis' mansion in three hours time or however much longer it took them to work through the landing formalities.

"We'll return to Cinnabar aboard a trader, I believe, and hire a Cinnabar ship to Novy Sverdlovsk," said the Count. "Without discussing in detail the curios we've collected."

He frowned and went on, "But Mistress Mundy, why is it that you went to this trouble for us? You've gathered information on more than a hundred ships, not so?"

Adele pursed her lips. A quick answer would've been, "It wasn't any trouble." That was true at least for her, but it wasn't really the answer.

"Your excellency," she said, "you've behaved like a gentleman during our contact on this voyage. The Mundys of Chatsworth have a reputation of giving as we receive, in good or ill."

"Adele, the relative you have here?" Valentina said. "That is how you rescued Georgi from the trouble when we first arrived, yes?"

"Yes, that's right," Adele said. "My cousin is one of a community of Cinnabar expatriates in the Cluster navy."

The port officials were closing their airsuits to return to their own ship. Adele had offered her resources to help with the bribe, now that the Klimovs were no longer the owners, but Daniel had assured her he could meet the requirements himself.

"And you will be visiting your relative and his colleagues when we land?" Valentina continued. "Because of the emergency you mention."

"Yes," said Adele, speaking even more carefully than she normally did. The Klimovna obviously knew more about the "Cinnabar expatriates" than Adele had told her. "Why do you ask?"

Valentina turned to the Count. "Georgi," she said, "we will loan them the aircar. They will want to make an impression, and they will be in haste because of the trouble. They should not have to hire the trashy common vehicles here."

"What?" the Count said. He shrugged. "Yes, of course. If you wish, my dear."

He rubbed his hands as he smiled quietly into the distance. "Our business will be here in the harbor anyway," he said. "And we're in haste as well. I don't even think I'll find a card game on this visit."

❖   ❖   ❖

Daniel preserved a pleasant smile and kept his right arm sprawled loosely on the top of the aircar's door, but doing that took more effort than facing the dragon with a clubbed gun had. It was easier to act in the face of oncoming disaster than to keep from acting. The aircar's speed and Barnes' white-knuckled grip on the control yoke were an oncoming disaster if Daniel had ever seen one.

"Perhaps we should put down in the street, Barnes," Daniel said, hoping that he sounded reassuringly positive. "The courtyard of Commander Purvis' palace isn't really made for landing—"

"Hang on!" shouted Barnes. He apparently wasn't listening. All things considered, Daniel supposed he wanted the driver to be completely focused on his job—given that even with full concentration he looked likely to make a real mess of it.

"You got *that* bloody right!" Hogg snarled from the far back where he sat alongside Dasi. "I swear t' God, master, I'm going to walk back if this don't break both my legs first!"

Daniel glanced over his shoulder with the instinct of an officer for the personnel under his command when things got tight. Adele and Tovera were in the middle seat. Tovera had a cool expression, while Adele was viewing something projected by her commo helmet. The image was a blur from Daniel's side.

"Adele, you'll want to hold—" Daniel said on a rising note. Tovera reached across her mistress and gripped the handrest, smiling at him.

To blazes with looking confident! Daniel braced his right arm against the dashboard and grabbed the bottom of the seat with his left. The aircar skimmed over the palace's facade, banked into a turn like a paperclip, and dropped into the middle of the courtyard. The screaming children managed to scatter in time, but a gout of bloody feathers as the car bounced showed that one of the chickens hadn't been so lucky.

Daniel held his mouth wide open so the shock didn't break his teeth on one another, but he came up hard against the seatbelt. When the car hit the second time, he found the cushions weren't up to the job of keeping the seat from trying to punch his spine through the base of his skull.

The car was still turning tightly, so this time it mowed down the poles supporting the clotheslines along the south face of the courtyard. When they finally halted, bright-colored garments festooned them like holiday bunting.

Barnes lifted an orange-and-yellow-striped tunic away from his face, then shut off the fans. He beamed at Daniel.

"Bloody *hell*, sir," he said cheerfully. "I was worried there for a minute, but I guess we come in all right after all!"

Daniel unlatched his door, untangled the set of baggy pantaloons that kept it from opening fully, and got out. "Some of the laundry's gotten into the fan intakes, Barnes," he said. "Remove it before we lift off, will you please? I've had enough excitement for the morning."

Adele took off the commo helmet and replaced it with the peaked cap that was normal headgear with the 2nd Class uniform she was wearing. She smiled faintly as she allowed Daniel to hand her out of the vehicle.

"Ordinary diplomats," she said, "would find a meeting like this one to be very stressful. Personally, I'm feeling quite relaxed now that I have my feet back on the ground. Perhaps we could offer a suggestion to the foreign service when we return to Cinnabar?"

"I don't know any diplomats well enough to dislike them that much," Daniel said, straightening his tunic. He felt good—buoyant, in fact. Surviving a ride like that was an exhilarating experience.

Whistling a snatch of "The Atlas Cluster Squadron," Daniel strode toward the staircase with Adele beside him. A tattooed female petty officer was in command of the guards. "Does your driver always land like that?" she said.

"Pretty much so," Daniel said nonchalantly as he started up the stairs. *Now orbiting off Thermidor we took aboard a shipwrecked whore. . . .*

"I'd like to say one gets used to it," said Adele over her shoulder. "But I haven't as yet, I'm afraid."

Commander Purvis ushered them into the loggia shaded by hand-carved screens. Admiral O'Quinn stood just within the doorway. Daniel had met them on the roof of the Anyo Nuevo the first time the *Princess Cecile* docked in San Juan, but he knew the other four officers present only by file imagery.

Adele had warned him, but great *God*! they looked terrible! If it weren't for the uniforms—flashy, locally-made versions of Dress Whites—Daniel wouldn't have connected them with the RCN or with any military organization.

"Admiral," Daniel said, saluting. He nodded to the others. "Fellow officers. I'm glad you were able to meet Officer Mundy and myself at such short notice. There isn't a great deal of margin, but the RCN is used to that—"

He felt the corners of his lips quiver in what was as much a snarl as a smile. When the time came he'd be calm; he knew that from past experience. Now, though, visualizing the battle ahead, he couldn't prevent the outward trembling of emotions older than the human portion of his brain. The Alliance might start the dance, but in the end the RCN would be calling the tune. . . .

"—and I think there's *enough* margin, if we act quickly."

"Act?" said Lieutenant Estaing, who was the least changed physically of any of them. "By cutting our throats, you mean, Leary? Because there's nothing else to do! Two battleships, *modern* battleships, a heavy cruiser, and a flotilla of destroyers. That's hopeless odds!"

Daniel crossed his hands behind his back and looked at Estaing. Not changed physically, but . . . and then again, from what Adele's records said about the man, maybe he was morally the same man he'd been before the mutiny, too.

"I don't believe it's that bad, Mr. Estaing," Daniel said calmly. "The Alliance squadron only arrived at Gehenna a week ago. They had an exceedingly difficult voyage from Pleasaunce. They'll be an additional month fitting out, and they won't be expecting an attack. I believe—"

"They won't be *facing* an attack either, Leary," said Admiral O'Quinn heavily. Daniel looked at him in amazement. The Admiral glowered for a moment, then grimaced and lowered his eyes to the floor. "Look, you're a young fellow, full of piss and vinegar—which is fine when you're young."

"We've been young too," said the grotesquely fat Lieutenant Tetrey. All the *Aristoxenos'* officers were holding goblets, but Tetrey was swigging hers between bites from a platter of glazed fruit slices. "That's why we're here now, at the back of nowhere."

"We have to face reality, Leary," O'Quinn said. "The truth is, I don't know that the *Zanie* could lift even if we took the full month you say the Alliance squadron will be refitting. She hasn't entered orbit in three

years, and it's seven since we last took her into the
Matrix. It's hopeless to imagine us engaging two
battleships!"

Daniel cleared his throat.

"I'm forgetting my manners," said Adrian Purvis.
"Here, Leary—and you, Cousin Adele. Won't you have
something to drink? Or eat, but these vintages are very
respectable."

"Try the red," said Admiral O'Quinn in a jolly voice.
"It's from my estate in the Dantas Mountains."

A pair of servants stepped forward with a carafe and
a silver-chased goblet, bowing low to Daniel. They wore
smarmy smiles.

Daniel waved his left hand before him, palm out in
a mixture of brusque refusal and disgust. "*No*," he said.
"No thank you."

He grimaced and—he could've stopped himself but
he didn't see any reason to—blurted, "For God's sake,
fellow officers, what are you talking about? I'm not
suggesting we fight a head-on battle with two battleships, even ships like these that've been configured for
a long voyage with reaction mass tanks replacing half
the missile stowage. We'll hit Gehenna unexpectedly
and catch the Alliance squadron on the ground."

Daniel gestured, lifting both hands as though he
were a preacher rousing his congregation. He'd
expected argument, doubts, and disagreement over
strategy. He was the most junior officer present; the
others had been of higher rank than he was now when
they fled the Three Circles Conspiracy. Of course they
weren't going to accept his proposed tactics immediately, especially since the others didn't have his recent
experience of knowing *everything* through the Tree.

What Daniel hadn't expected was the present willful apathy and determination to ignore a reality that
looked terrifyingly bleak. Admiral O'Quinn and his

officers planned to stick their heads in the sand and discuss vintages until the Alliance commander worked up his squadron and brought it here to rain down destruction on the Cluster—with the *Aristoxenos* the first target.

"One missile into each ship and they won't be able to lift without repairs," Daniel said cajolingly. "Even the battleships. And you can imagine how long it's going to take them to make repairs with only the Commonwealth's resources to draw on, right? With one stroke you'll have saved the Cluster, saved yourselves, and put the Republic of Cinnabar in your debt!"

"Well, Admiral, did you hear that generous offer?" Lieutenant Estaing said, his cheeks bright with drink and emotion. "We're to be given posthumous pardons."

He glared at Daniel, furious and frightened at the same time. "Except I suppose the pardons would be contingent on our succeeding," he continued with his voice rising, "and that's impossible. Impossible!"

"Mr. Estaing," Commander Purvis said sharply, "pray recall you're in my house and speaking to my guest."

Purvis turned to Daniel and coughed into his hand. "But the fact is, Leary," he continued, "that you just don't know what it's like here in the North. The *Zanie* isn't a warship any more, not with the sort of maintenance we've been able to do in a place like this. Oh, sure, we could probably see off a squadron of the flyboats the Commonwealth navy uses, but not real ships. Not a crack Alliance squadron. It just isn't in the cards."

"Fellow officers!" Daniel said, wondering if he sounded as desperate as he felt. "If you'll allow me to show you a simulation—"

Lieutenant Williams, the cadaverous Second Lieutenant, rose abruptly from the stool she was sitting on. Her goblet tipped in her hand. She was drinking gin, not wine. She opened her mouth with a stricken expression. Instead of speaking, she turned and vomited a gout of bile and liquor onto the rugs layered on the floor of the loggia.

Servants trotted over, whispering cheerfully among themselves. They shared space with the officers but remained apart, like the aviforms fluttering about the Governor's Palace. One held a basin of water; another had napkins draped over her arm. The rest rolled the stained rugs sideways with the skill of long experience and took them away.

Daniel turned slightly so that he could keep his eyes on O'Quinn but pretend not to see the retching Williams. "A simulation, as I say . . . ," he resumed.

Bodo Williams turned without rising. She'd given her face a wipe with a napkin that left it wet but not quite clean. "For God's sake, don't you understand?" she said. "There's no point in simulations, there's no point in anything! We can't fight battleships, we can't fight anybody! Just go away and leave us in peace for as long as we have left, can't you?"

Williams hugged her wasted chest and began to cry, though whether her pain was physical or mental was beyond deduction. Estaing stared at Daniel in silent fury; his goblet was only half-full but his hands trembled so badly that the contents were sloshing. The others kept their eyes averted, from one another as well as from Daniel and Adele.

"Fellow officers . . . ," Daniel said. He stopped there because he wasn't sure where to go from that opening.

He knew there had to be *some* way. He saw—well, saw the kernel—of a way to defeat the Alliance squadron. The *Aristoxenos'* officers didn't. They hadn't been the Tree, and also they weren't Daniel Leary who through luck, a crack crew, and perhaps something more, had won against long odds in the past.

All this Daniel understood, but he *didn't* understand RCN officers being unwilling to fight. The RCN had never lacked ignorant personnel and even downright stupid personnel, but no one imagined it was a haven for cowards. . . .

Adrian Purvis looked at O'Quinn, waiting for his superior to speak. Under the pressure of the commander's eyes, the Admiral said, "See here, Leary, I understand what you're trying to do, but you have to appreciate our situation. Helping out some Cinnabar spacers in a brawl here in San Juan, that's one thing, but now you're asking us to get involved in a war with the Alliance. When you were here before, Officer Mundy—"

He nodded to Adele, his expression sternly professional save for the nervous twitch at the corner of his left eye.

"—made it perfectly clear, insultingly clear I might have said, that the Republic had no use for us. Now you say it does? Well, I'm afraid it's too late!"

"Admiral O'Quinn," Daniel said. He was as calm as he'd be in battle, even a battle he knew he couldn't win. "You know that the first thing an Alliance squadron in support of the Commonwealth will do is to reduce the Cluster to submission. The *Aristoxenos*—"

"We don't know anything!" Adrian Purvis said. "We don't *know* that there's even an Alliance squadron on Gehenna. This is probably a trick by you and the Commonwealth to lead us into an ambush!"

Daniel looked at him. "Mr. Purvis," he said, "you have my word as a Leary of Bantry that the situation is as I've described it."

"Yes, and what's the word of a—" Purvis said.

Adele slapped him across the mouth with her right hand. It was a sharp sound, very like a pistol shot.

Daniel picked up a wine carafe. There wasn't much

chance of getting out if matters went the wrong way, though with Hogg and Tovera in the courtyard there was just a chance. If you were an RCN officer, you didn't stick your head in the sand and wait for death. . . .

Commander Purvis backed a step. He put his fingers to his mouth, then lowered them, his eyes fixed on Adele's. No one else moved.

Admiral O'Quinn said, "I don't believe there's anything more to accomplish here. I won't tell you your business, Leary, but I suggest you go back to Cinnabar and place the affair in the hands of the proper authorities. If they don't act or don't act quickly enough, well, that's not your fault."

"Cousin Adrian," Adele said in a voice which rang like a bell in the silence. "You are a disgrace to a family which has had more than its share of fools, but no cravens I was aware of until now."

"Fine!" Purvis said. "Since you insist, we'll settle this! My seconds will call on you in the morning."

Adele laughed. "Don't bother," she said. "My colleagues and I have matters of state to conduct. But I will say that the one regret I have about the *Princess Cecile* attacking the Alliance squadron alone is that I won't survive to cleanse the blot from the family honor with your blood!"

She turned on her heel and walked out. Daniel bowed to his host and followed. Halfway down the outside stairs he realized he was still holding the carafe; he handed it to the petty officer waiting at the bottom.

"Back to the *Sissie*, Barnes," Daniel called across the courtyard to those waiting with the concern in their eyes hooded. "And see if you can't get us up a hundred feet or so before you give us forward impulse, will you?"

"We *are* going to attack Gehenna ourselves, aren't we, Daniel?" Adele said in an undertone as she got into the car. "A force from Cinnabar can't possibly reach the North in time to save our traders from massacre."

"Yes, I rather think we are," said Daniel, smiling faintly as possibilities spun through his mind. If he could only grasp the right ones, in the right sequence. . . .

"But not directly," he continued. "The *Sissie* can't bull through the base's outer defenses the way a battleship might, so we're going by way of Morzanga."

CHAPTER 26

"All Alliance personnel!" Adele said. "This is RCS *Termagant*, ordering you in the name of Admiral Arnold Plumly to surrender or face extermination. War has been declared between the Republic of Cinnabar and the Alliance of Free Stars."

The Alliance castaways might have working sensors, and even a good telescope could distinguish between a corvette and a battleship in orbit. Daniel had decided that the *Princess Cecile* could pass for a light cruiser scouting for a powerful squadron, however. They were broadcasting the message on four different radio frequency bands which were or had been used by the *Goldenfels*. With luck, some of the castaways were monitoring the RF spectrum still, or at least were wearing their commo helmets. They must have hopes for rescue, after all.

"Gather without your weapons in the center of the native village near the wreck of the *Goldenfels*," Adele continued. "Keep clear of the wreck itself: we will vaporize it from orbit before we land on Morzanga to collect prisoners. Anybody who doesn't surrender will be killed."

The *Princess Cecile*'s low orbit whisked her over the horizon from the nameless village where the *Goldenfels* lay on its side. Adele broke the transmission and straightened in her couch to meet the eyes of the others on the bridge.

"I don't get it, sir," Sun said to Daniel in a troubled voice. "They must know that even if we really were a squadron big enough to rate an admiral commanding, we couldn't track 'em down in the bush. That'd take a regiment of ground troops with jungle training, not a couple hundred dismounted spacers. They're going to hide, not come traipsing out in the open to be thrown in a cage. Aren't they?"

Daniel rotated the command console so that he could smile at the gunner while still keeping an eye on the Plot Position Indicator which told him what was in the immediate neighborhood of Morzanga. At the moment nothing was, but that could change in a heartbeat.

"Quite right, Sun," Daniel said, grinning past him to acknowledge Adele at the Signals console. "They probably *will* run, most of them anyway. I suppose there'll be a few who prefer a Cinnabar prison hulk to living in the wilderness with a tribe of savages."

Adele's sensors picked up scatter from emitters on three of the four Alliance bands. The signals were low power and unintelligible over the horizon; all she knew for certain was that her transmissions had stirred the *Goldenfels*' castaways to talk among themselves.

"But my purpose is to get them away from the wreck itself," Daniel continued. "It's immaterial whether they hide in the jungle or stand in the middle of the village with their hands in the air. We'll be leaving them here when we lift off."

He looked at Adele again. "Officer Mundy, how many orbits should we make before going in? I want to be sure they've heard the warning."

"They're talking among themselves," Adele said. "I won't be able to tell what they're saying till we come over the horizon again, though, so perhaps you'll want to wait until I can pick up the content."

Daniel's sunny smile brightened the bare steel walls of the bridge. "Oh, I think we can assume that they're not setting up to defend the *Goldenfels* when they reasonably believe that we're going to blast it with plasma cannon or a nuke, don't you? And after all, we're in rather a hurry."

He switched to the intercom channel and continued, *"Ship, this is Six. We'll begin braking to land in seven minutes. This'll be another dry landing and there's at least a chance that there'll be some Alliance spacers popping small arms at us while we're coming in, so be ready for whatever happens. Six out."*

Daniel turned his attention to his console. Adele echoed it momentarily on her own in case she'd be called on to act shortly. She saw nothing for personal concern.

The command display kept the PPI on the upper left quadrant while the remainder was given over to engineering data—plasma thrusters, High Drive motors, machinery status, and the amount of reaction mass in each of the eight separate tanks. They'd topped off on Todos Santos—and had taken the time to lay in bulk provisions as well, since they'd been limited to on-board stores ever since the *Princess Cecile* left Tegeli.

"It could get pretty exciting clearing 'em out of a warren the size of the *Goldenfels*," Hogg commented, standing to the right of the bridge hatch while Tovera stood on the left. Strictly speaking they should've been strapped into their bunks during landing because they didn't have ship-handling duties—but it didn't really matter, and neither of the pair were people to whom folk spoke strictly.

"We haven't had any excitement for a long time," Tovera said. She gave Hogg a slow smile. "Too long, perhaps."

"There's that," he agreed, adjusting the bandolier which held reloads for his heavy impeller. "There is that."

Adele listened to the by-play as she made a final check of her own responsibilities. She didn't understand either Hogg or Tovera; but then, she didn't understand most people, herself included. At least you could predict with assurance what Hogg and Tovera would do in a given situation. If more people were like them, life would be simpler—albeit much more dangerous.

Daniel had planned the details of the operation with his officers on the brutal five-day voyage to Morzanga, all of it spent in the Matrix without the usual drops into sidereal space to check their position and to provide the crew with a brief taste of normality. Time was very short, especially if they ran into trouble here— and they were almost certain to run into trouble.

Adele's job was to update the imagery of the *Goldenfels* and the cannon-ripped country craft overturned in the jungle. The *Princess Cecile* had only made one pass in low orbit, but thanks to Mistress Sand the corvette's imaging equipment was of even higher quality than normal for an RCN warship.

She transferred the new visuals into a suspense file available to all the command group. Daniel and Pasternak were wholly involved in the landing, but she noticed that the officers in the Battle Direction Center opened the imagery at once. They were backup for the landing, but when Mr. Leary had the conn nobody else worried much.

"Ship, prepare for braking!" Daniel ordered. The thrusters roared to life, dropping the *Sissie* into the deeper atmosphere.

Adele pored over the visuals as they rocked and shuddered toward the ground. There were no differences she could see between these shots and the file images taken when the *Princess Cecile* lifted from Morzanga a matter of weeks, bare weeks, before. It certainly seemed longer than that. . . .

The jungle still covered the ancient wreck. That didn't prove that the *Goldenfels'* crew hadn't been working on her, but there was no sign they had. Of course if the Alliance spacers had already carried the High Drive motors to their own vessel, it'd save the Sissies some time.

That was unlikely, though. They probably didn't even know the older wreck existed.

"Prepare for landing!" Daniel ordered. *"Prepare for landing!"*

The thunder redoubled. The corvette bobbled like a ball in a waterspout, then touched: the stern outriggers feather-light, the bow an instant later and minusculely harder. Hatches started to open immediately.

"Laying down covering fire!" Sun announced. The cannon in the dorsal turret fired a burst of four high-intensity plasma discharges just short of the *Goldenfels*, which was on its side only a hundred meters from where the *Sissie'*d landed. The guns' directed thermonuclear explosions made the corvette ring like a struck anvil and dug fiery scoopfuls out of the earth. Fans of glass and blazing humus sprayed against the *Goldenfels'* hull.

Adele had a 360-degree panorama at the bottom of her display. She didn't see any Alliance spacers in it, but through the crash of plasma blanketing the RF spectrum she heard panicked squeals on the two frequencies the *Goldenfels* had used for short-range communication.

"Daniel, they're running!" she said into the two-way link. *Should she have used the general channel? And she should've called him Captain or Six or something else, but she was monitoring multiple simultaneous transmissions and that was bloody well enough to worry about!* "Everybody on radio's running for the jungle or telling other people to run."

Valves squealed open. Steam roared from the ground beneath the *Princess Cecile* as Mr. Pasternak dumped reaction mass to cool the plasma-heated soil. Heavily-armed Sissies leaped from the D Deck ports, staggering blindly toward the *Goldenfels* until they'd gotten far enough from the corvette to open their eyes again.

Daniel rose from his console and took the sub-machine gun Hogg handed him. He was already wearing his equipment belt from which now dangled several clusters of grenades as well as the holstered pistol. *"Mr. Chewning, you have the ship!"* he ordered as he started for the door. *"Six out."*

Adele had gotten up also. She was directly behind Daniel when he reached the companionway.

"You've got no business here!" Daniel shouted over his shoulder. "I need to see what condition the freighter's control room's in!"

"And I need to see their commo suite!" Adele replied tartly. "Which I suspect is more important to our accomplishing your intention than anything in the control room!"

Woetjans and fifty of the *Sissie*'s crew were dodging between the smoking craters the cannon had just blown. Daniel had brought the corvette down beside the *Goldenfels'* belly rather than her dorsal spine. Her ventral turret was still retracted, but the marooned crew had removed access plates on her underside. Ladders lashed together from saplings served them. Adele supposed that initially the crew had climbed out by ropes after antimatter detonations flipped the freighter onto her starboard side.

An Alliance spacer appeared at a hatch with a tarpaulin-wrapped bundle that seemed too heavy for her to handle easily. She dropped it to the ground fifteen feet below, then noticed the oncoming Sissies as she turned to put her feet on the ladder.

"Ship, don't shoot!" Daniel ordered. Adele had set one of the *Princess Cecile*'s main transmitters to rebroadcast low-powered signals from his helmet, but none of the boarding group seemed to be trigger-happy.

The Alliance spacer tried to change her mind, but she'd already committed to coming down. She lost her grip and swung out of the hatchway, hitting the ground not far from her bundle. She twitched but didn't try to get up.

The *Goldenfels* had mounted twelve High Drive motors on her underside. Normally the outriggers carrying the plasma thrusters would've been withdrawn against the hull before the vessel shifted to matter/antimatter annihilation. Since the ship had been in landing mode this time, the tops of the outriggers were slightly pitted—but only slightly, because the High Drive had failed almost instantly, melting not only the motors but portions of the surrounding hull plates as well.

Sissies climbed the steep ladders into the *Goldenfels* with their legs alone, leaving their hands free to point their weapons ahead of them. Nobody appeared to give them a target before they swarmed aboard the freighter. Most of the boarding party were riggers since the hullside crewmen were needed during landing. Rigging suits weighed more than the guns and munitions they were carrying now, and they were well-practiced in scrambling up antennas to clear balky winches and fouled cables.

Adele struggled to keep up with Daniel and Hogg as they pounded heavily across ground the *Princess Cecile* had burned bare the first time she landed on Tegeli. Running wasn't a skill she'd learned in youth, nor had poverty trained her in it. She wondered about navigating the corridors of a vessel lying on its side. She didn't suppose the spacers cared, since they were used to maneuvering in weightlessness where all directions were the same.

"Sir, there's some gone out the dorsal hatches!" a spacer called, using the alert channel instead of the general push that was full of pointless, excited chatter. *"They're getting away! They're getting away!"*

"Let 'em go, Raymond!" Daniel replied. Adele could've checked the transmitter number, but Daniel didn't have to. *"We want them to escape. Don't shoot! Don't—"*

A burst of shots rang from the *Goldenfels'* interior, multiplied by echoes into a pitched battle. A single pellet, a drop of crimson fire, zipped from what had been the entry hatch.

"—shoot!"

There were six ladders into the ship's belly. Barnes and Dasi waited at the bottom of the one which Daniel started climbing. Hogg followed him muttering curses, but Hogg cursed a great deal. He couldn't have really believed that Daniel was at any real risk with fifty Sissies ahead of him.

Adele reached for the ladder. The stringers were curving lengths of vine, woody and four inches in diameter, but the rungs were splits from straight sections of trunk; some oozed sap.

"We got you, mistress!" Dasi said. He took her right hand and led it over his shoulder as he turned his back to her. "Just hold tight."

"Woetjans told us t' wait, ma'am," Barnes said,

gripping her under the arms and lifting her to where her legs clamped instinctively around Dasi's waist. "Don't 'cha worry, they'll hold us!"

Dasi started up the ladder at what would've been a dead run on the level. Barnes followed, his hands planted in the seat of Adele's utilities to support at least half her weight. She was too shocked to be angry—not that her fulminating would've changed what anybody was doing.

And besides, Woetjans was right, as Adele realized when she allowed herself to think about what was happening. Signals Officer Mundy wasn't going to be much use to her captain if she lay sprawled at the foot of the ladder like that Alliance spacer.

The two riggers deposited Adele in the hold. The auxiliary power unit still operated so the *Goldenfels'* systems were live, but there'd never been many lights here in the freighter's belly. Three spacers wearing bits of Alliance uniform, and a red-haired native woman shivering with terror, lay on the deck with their hands on the backs of their necks. Lamsoe guarded them with a sour expression.

Crude steps gave access to the hatches into the compartment on the next deck; sets of companionways led on from there. Two of the armored tubes were close enough to what was now the deck that Adele didn't need help to follow Daniel and Hogg. Tovera brought up the rear.

They continued horizontally toward bridge level, crawling on the edges of the treads. Adele smiled faintly. She'd worked in stacks where access wasn't a great deal better, so she didn't have difficulty keeping up. The hatches at every deck were open. The corridors echoed with excited shouts, but there didn't seem to be fighting. Though the air-circulation equipment was working, the air smelled of wood smoke and human waste; neither the galley nor the heads would function with the ship at this angle, but some people had decided to make their homes in the vessel anyway.

Adele scrambled out onto A Deck. The riggers' airlock in the same compartment was open to the jungle beyond.

"Sir, we've got all the major spaces!" Woetjans said to Daniel. The bosun had stuck a pickup on a hatch coaming and flexed it to her helmet. That turned the ship's steel structure, otherwise a Faraday cage blocking helmet radio, into a giant antenna. "There wasn't any fighting, just one 'a the boys tripping with his finger on the trigger. No harm done, just some bits of slug in his butt that the medicomp'll get out no sweat."

She grinned in embarrassment. "Ricochet, you know."

"Get all the prisoners outside, Woetjans," Daniel said as he headed down the corridor bulkhead toward the bridge. "We'll have to build some sort of holding cage, I suppose. Dammit, I was hoping they'd all run but they just weren't organized enough!"

Adele checked the hatch of the Signals Room. It was closed and therefore automatically locked. She punched in the twelve-letter code she'd abstracted when Lieutenant Greiner allowed her to enter the *Goldenfels'* computer. The mechanism whined as hydraulic pumps lifted the armored panel open.

Adele climbed in, ducking so that her head cleared what was meant to be the left side of the hatch coaming. The air of the compartment had a lived-in smell. The now-deck was littered with things that'd flown from their proper locations when the freighter blasted itself onto its side.

Adele switched live the nearest console, the one

she'd used before. Rather than try to do more with a keyboard that'd now be vertical, she got out her handheld unit to synch it with the ship's system.

Bandeng, the tech whom she'd met, rose from where he'd been hiding behind the second console. He was aiming his pistol at her.

"By God, there is some justice!" he snarled. "Now, bitch, you're going to get me out of here or I'll blow your head off!"

"I'll be glad to get you out of the ship, Mr. Bandeng," Adele said. She wanted to put her little data unit away but she was afraid that might look threatening to a man who was obviously on the edge of blind terror. "Neither you nor your fellow crewmen are at any risk from us."

"You say!" Bandeng said. "You say! I know you can't carry prisoners on that sliver of a corvette. You're planning to shoot us all! In fact, maybe I'll—"

Adele felt rather than saw Tovera behind her. Bandeng's eyes shifted right to follow the movement. Six pellets from Tovera's sub-machine gun blew his face apart.

Bandeng convulsed backward, voiding his bowels. His pistol clacked off the ceiling and dropped. His heels were thumping a tattoo on the deck.

Adele turned. Her ears rang with the series of lightning-sharp *crack*s. The muzzle of Tovera's little sub-machine gun shimmered white. Ozone from the high-voltage discharge mingled with the stench of the dead man's feces.

Tovera smiled. "Shall I get a couple of the spacers to clear that out of here, mistress?" she said. She nodded to where Bandeng had ceased to spasm.

"Yes," Adele said. She seated herself on the deck with her data unit on her lap, and began to check the status of the *Goldenfels*' signals and code suites. Her work was critically important if the attack on Gehenna was to succeed.

And besides, if she managed to concentrate on her task as fully as she usually did, she would forget for the time the way Bandeng's right eye had splashed as the first pellet struck it.

"The truck's back again," Hogg shouted down from the dorsal hatch where he'd kept watch most of the four days they'd been on Morzanga. "Looks like Pasternak's come back with it."

Daniel glanced through the bridge port. The truck he'd bought in San Juan was trundling out of the jungle with the sixth and last of the High Drive motors they'd removed from the wreck of the country craft. The Chief Engineer and six of his team were aboard also, returning to their duties in the *Sissie's* power room.

The timing was perfect. There must be another twenty-odd personnel still in the jungle, but the truck could ferry them back at leisure. Six techs and the chief were the minimum required to move the corvette a very short distance under her own power.

Daniel smiled, because he was thinking and a smile was the default option to which his face returned when he didn't have conscious reason for another expression. Mr. Pasternak and six of his people in the Power Room, and Lieutenant Daniel Leary at the command console. . . .

He grinned more broadly. And Hogg, of course, because he didn't kid himself that he'd be able to convince Hogg to disembark for safety's sake.

The truck disappeared beneath the curve of the hull, but the remote camera Dorst had placed on their first visit still provided imagery of the burned-over meadow. The vehicle pulled up at the boarding ramp after very carefully negotiating the web of cables now linking the *Princess Cecile* and the *Goldenfels*.

The Power Room staff filed into the corvette while a rigger drove the truck to the edge of the clearing where the other motors had been off-loaded. The vehicle was stone-axe simple, although as imported machinery on Todos Santos it certainly hadn't been cheap. It was battery-powered with an open bed and cab, a bench seat, and four all-terrain tires. Most of the Sissies could drive it well enough—in contrast to an aircar—and it could carry far greater weights without risk. High Drive motors weighed the better part of a half ton apiece.

Tarps covered the motors that'd already been retrieved. That was probably a pointless concern, seeing that they'd spent the previous sixty years upended on the hull of the wreck, but Daniel didn't see any percentage in increasing the degree of risk even minusculely.

Woetjans came down from the hull wearing the boots and gauntlets from her rigging suit with her utility uniform. Her boots banged on the deck, making sure Daniel was aware of her presence before she entered the bridge. A dozen of her riggers had tramped through the airlock only minutes before, so her arrival wasn't a surprise.

"Good work, Woetjans," Daniel said. "I didn't expect you to finish the job for another day at least."

Woetjans scowled, loosening her gauntlets finger by finger before stripping them off. "Guess it'd be a waste of time asking if you're still going through with the damn fool notion," she said as she concentrated on the gloves.

"We have to go through with it, Woetjans," Daniel said, rephrasing his reply rather than accept her formation. "Short of bringing a dock ship out from Cinnabar, this is the only way we're going to get the *Goldenfels* back in working order. And we need the *Goldenfels*, you know."

"I don't know what we need," the bosun said. "I take your word for it, sure; but sir, she's *easy* three times our mass. If you lose a few cables, and you're *going* to lose a few cables, she'll settle back and it'll be the *Sissie* flipped over too. Or worse!"

"Six, this is the Power Room," Mr. Pasternak announced on the command channel. Pasternak was a humorless and ambitious man, neither of them an endearing trait; but he knew his business and didn't waste time. For those virtues Pasternak would have the option of serving in any vessel that Daniel commanded. *"The board's green. We're ready at this end any time you need power. Over."*

"Roger, Mr. Pasternak," Daniel said. "Break. Ship, this is Six. All personnel save the Power Room crew must disembark immediately. The Main Hatch will remain open for two, repeat two, minutes only. Get out and get clear, Sissies. Remember that these cables can part at both ends and fly God knows where, so don't trust being a hundred yards out. Six out."

Daniel called up a hull display on his console and began closing the ship. Plasma from the thrusters drifting in through the hatches wasn't a danger, but the risk of a line galling on a lifted cover was something else again. What he planned to do wouldn't be easy and might not be possible. He was covering all the bases he could.

Woetjans still stood by the console, a grim look on her face.

"Woetjans," Daniel snapped, "get your ass off this ship *now*. Do you hear me? You're no bloody use aboard and you just might manage to distract me. Now, I said!"

The bosun's face went blank in shock. She'd seen Daniel angry before, but not at her—and she was a spacer through and through, steeped in the chain of command. She'd been presuming on a relationship with Daniel that went beyond captain and warrant officer, but the snarled order slammed her back into RCN discipline.

"Aye aye, sir!" she blurted. She broke into a lumbering run as she left the bridge and started down the companionway. Hogg, who'd just come in by the airlock, stepped aside for her and gave Daniel a quizzical glance.

Daniel sighed. "I'm nervous about this, Hogg," he admitted. "I bit her head off. Though if me snapping at her saves her life, then I'll have one less thing on my conscience if this goes to Hell."

"Nothing's going to Hell," Hogg said equitably, sitting down on the gunner's couch. "Except maybe us after a lot more years."

He nodded toward the companionways and added, "Mistress Mundy'll be up pretty quick. She started over from the wreck when Pasternak arrived."

"Bloody Hell!" Daniel said. "She's got no business here. Any more than you do, Hogg!"

"I do have business here," Adele said calmly as she stepped out of the up companionway and walked onto the bridge. "I've set all the screens aboard the *Goldenfels* to feed through the signals board, which will transmit the images—"

She sat at her own console and brought up a display with over forty segments.

"—to me, for forwarding to you as required. You'll have a realtime display of what's going on aboard the *Goldenfels* as you right her."

Daniel stared at her. "Oh," he said. "Ah. Actually, that might be useful. I didn't realize it would be possible."

The best they could expect from this violent maneuver was straining of the *Goldenfels'* hull. If in fact the freighter started to come apart as it lifted— and the Sissies hadn't been able to check all her structural members without removing hull plates, a task for which they lacked both time and equipment—then the *Princess Cecile* would be involved in the wreck unless Daniel set her back down immediately. Internal imagery might give him warning that he wouldn't otherwise get.

"That's why you have me, captain," Adele said calmly. She clamped down her acceleration harness, then gave Daniel one of her wry smiles.

Daniel checked the time, then noticed something missing. He didn't like Tovera, but . . .

Aloud, frowning, he said, "Adele, where's Tovera?"

"She said she'd stay on the ground," Adele said without expression.

"She figures if the *Goldenfels'* crew's going to try anything, it'll be now," Hogg said, amplifying the simple statement. "She's got a point, and we figured one of us aboard was enough to take care of the ship's rats if they make a break from the hold."

"Yes, I suppose that's true," Daniel said. Hogg sounded vaguely regretful. *Well, we all learn we have to make choices in life.*

With a smile spreading across his face, Daniel checked his display. The eight thrusters showed green, ready to go, and the only opening was the main hatch.

"Ship, this is Six," he said, his finger touching the virtual keypad. "Closing ship."

He felt the vessel quiver. The main hatch was a thick steel plate. Even with the whole *Sissie* as an anchor for the hydraulic jacks swinging it down, closing the hatch moved the hull as well.

Whereas the *Goldenfels* was many times heavier than

the corvette. Well, they'd move her anyway; and with the help of luck and the good Lord, they wouldn't wreck both ships in the process.

"Lighting thrusters," Daniel said, starting the trickle of reaction mass into thruster throats where electrons were stripped off and the dense nuclei expelled violently.

The *Sissie* trembled again, this time getting a greasy, unbalanced feel. The present impulse was too little to lift the corvette's mass, but it unloaded the vessel enough to make it feel unstable.

Daniel grinned again. It was going to get a lot worse before it got better. If in fact it got better.

The display was still green. Oh, there were details that could become important—that's why six techs under Mr. Pasternak in the Power Room were watching the displays. Daniel had other things to attend to.

"Ship, I'm increasing thrust," he said. He opened the feed nozzles to 20%, then edged power up to 23% until the *Sissie* came off the ground. Daniel slid the corvette sideways until she started to tilt on her axis. He'd drawn taut the cables connecting her to the *Goldenfels*; now—

"Hang on, Sissies, here we go!" Daniel said as he opened the starboard thrusters another 3%, countering the pull of the freighter's mass. The two ships were knit together by a web of rigging cables, beryllium monocrystal of great tensile strength.

Great strength didn't mean infinite strength. The cables weren't meant to lift a starship, and no matter how skillful Daniel and Woetjans' riggers were, some cables would take more of the strain than their neighbors did.

Daniel increased power, another percent on the port thrusters, 2% to starboard and then another percent on Starboard 3. He couldn't have said why he'd fed more power to Starboard 3, couldn't even guess, but the corvette suddenly stabilized instead of skittering like a hog on ice.

"She's coming!" somebody shouted on the command channel. Somebody outside the ship, Chewning or Dorst, they were still on the net. *"She's—"*

And then the net was clear again, a quick jerk of Adele's control wands.

The wire-frame image of the freighter on Daniel's display was starting to tilt on her axis. A legend would've given the rotation in degrees, minutes and seconds if Daniel wanted it, but he didn't, he was controlling this by feel because there were too many variables to do it any other way.

A hair more power to the starboard thrusters, not to pull the *Goldenfels* but rather to skid the *Princess Cecile* sidewise to port. The freighter's rotation meant the cables attached to her dorsal masts had started to slacken. One had kinked and parted, a ringing crash like the sound of a plasma bolt striking the hull in vacuum.

"Come on, you fat bitch!" Daniel said, but he shouldn't've been swearing at the *Goldenfels*; they'd treat the freighter well and she'd be their friend. More power and the *Princess Cecile* slid measurably to port. The *Goldenfels* was coming, great God almighty she was coming, she was coming *over*, yes, by God she—

The freighter reached her balance point and hung. The *Princess Cecile* danced in a tethered hover, bobbing between the ground and ten feet in the air. Asymmetric strains made her porpoise as well, bow and stern rising and falling alternately. If the *Goldenfels* slipped back, her mass would flip the corvette into the ground on the other side of her unless the cables parted first; and they wouldn't, not all of them.

One of the *Goldenfels'* masts tore out of the hull

plating, jerked skyward on the pull of two cables. The freighter rotated another few degrees before her lifted outrigger rolled toward the ground at increasing speed. Maybe it was removing the mast's weight, maybe it was recoil from the shock of metal shearing; maybe it was luck.

Hogg cheered but Daniel didn't have time to. Instinct urged him to chop his throttles, but he'd thought the situation through over the past four days. He boosted power to his port thrusters, lifting that side against the inertia of the starboard thrusters. They were trying to spin the corvette onto her back now that the freighter's mass didn't anchor her through the taut cables.

The *Princess Cecile* rose twenty feet before Daniel got control, real control, and brought her into balance. He'd begun lowering her with her thrust reduced to 21% when the *Goldenfels'* outrigger hit the ground in a crash like the earth splitting.

The freighter bounced into the air again in a doughnut of yellow-gray dust swelling out around the hull, lifted by the shock rather than the touch of the steel outriggers. The compression wave buffeted the *Princess Cecile* but Daniel didn't overcompensate, just let the ship rise and fall; and, falling, kiss the ground to settle. They were twenty yards closer to the *Goldenfels* than they'd been when he lit the thrusters.

"Shutting down," he said by rote; and did so, cutting the feeds to the thrusters. In the hissing silence his ears still remembered the clash of the *Goldenfels* hitting, then hitting again. Bloody hell, they'd be lucky if they hadn't dismounted the fusion bottle in her Power Room. . . .

Daniel drew in a deep breath, then expanded his exterior display. The cables were a knotted tangle rather than the neat cat's cradle Woetjans and her riggers had strung; the outriggers lay across loops of them. They'd wind up leaving half the gear behind because they didn't have time to dig out each strand and coil it. . . .

Adele had cut in the external audio pickups. People were cheering. People were cheering Captain Leary.

Daniel slowly began to grin.

CHAPTER 27

Adele looked worn as she came around the end of the outrigger where Daniel stood looking up at the freighter's stern. Mr. Pasternak had left several minutes before to return to the *Goldenfels'* Power Room where he was rewiring the High Drive installation. Daniel had stayed to . . .

He grinned. He hadn't stayed for any particular reason beyond the fact that he was exhausted and nobody happened to be shouting at him right this moment, forcing his attention onto the next problem. If Adele was tired, she wasn't the only one. The past . . . seventeen days . . . had been very hard. Daniel felt obscurely pleased to have remembered the length of time they'd been here on Morzanga.

Adele followed the line of his gaze to the hull above. She frowned. "Are those cracks serious?" she said. Her lips pursed and she added, "That is, they are cracks, aren't they?"

"Yes, I'm afraid that my righting technique did more damage than the blast that threw her onto her side had in the first place," Daniel said, looking up again though he knew perfectly well what he was going to see. "Still, it couldn't be helped."

The outrigger struts were attached to the hull frames. They hadn't broken when the ship slammed down harder than the shock absorbers could compensate for, but they'd bent—and, bending, had buckled hull plates around the base of each strut. Straightening the plates would be a dockyard job and a major one at that.

"About thirty percent of the *Goldenfels'* spaces no longer hold air," he continued. "Fortunately the main passages are axial and airtight, so we can close off compartments and still have use of the ship from stem to stern. Since we're a skeleton crew, we don't need even as much volume as we have left."

He grinned. "We're a well-gnawed skeleton at that, I fear."

"She isn't the *Goldenfels*," Adele said absently as she knuckled her eyes. "That was her cover name. According to the bridge computer she's actually HSK2 *Atlantis*, an Alliance naval unit."

She looked at Daniel. "There's a separate bridge unit that isn't linked to the ship systems," she explained. "That's why I wasn't able to access it before when we. . . ."

She stuck her hand out, then turned it over to mime the way the freighter had flopped onto its side. The gesture was perfectly clear, but it amused Daniel to realize how very tired they must both be that they were unable to call up familiar words.

"Pasternak'll finish with the High Drive soon, probably within twenty-four hours," Daniel said, trying to swim through the fog that surrounded his mental processes. He really needed rest, and for the life of him he couldn't imagine when he was going to get it. The dilemma made him smile, albeit tiredly. "I really want to lift from here. There's hundreds of the *Goldenfels'* crew out there in the bush with impellers. I don't think they could successfully storm the ships, not with the plasma cannon constantly manned, but I expected constant sniping."

Adele cleared her throat. She seemed embarrassed.

Daniel gave her a sharp look; he was beginning to come out of his fog. "Go on, tell me," he said more sharply than he'd intended.

"Before Tovera entered my service," Adele said, looking out toward the jungle, "she worked for an officer of the Fifth Bureau, the Alliance security office which reports directly to Guarantor Porra."

"Go on," Daniel said. He hadn't known or particularly wanted to know the details, but the general outline wasn't a surprise. If Adele—and Hogg—trusted Tovera, that was enough for him.

"She has authentication codes that the Alliance signals officer would recognize, even if he isn't himself a member of the Fifth Bureau," Adele said. "Many of the castaways retain their commo helmets, so Tovera could contact them directly and expect her message to be spread throughout the body of the crew. She asked for my help because she wouldn't have been able to determine the correct frequencies herself."

"Ah," said Daniel. "Of course we'd have responded to snipers with the plasma cannon, but I was surprised that that implied threat had completely forestalled incidents. Tovera made the threat more personal, I gather?"

"She said that if a Cinnabar spacer was wounded, she'd kill a prisoner," Adele said. She swallowed and turned so that her eyes met Daniel's. "She said that if a Cinnabar spacer was killed, she would kill five prisoners. And she said that Captain Leary knew nothing of this: she was with the Fifth Bureau, and it wasn't for mere Fleet personnel to question the Guarantor's purposes."

She cleared her throat. "And I didn't stop her, Daniel."

"Stopping Tovera . . . ," Daniel said, "or Hogg, either one, isn't a process to enter into lightly. We have enough enemies in this business that I'm not going to turn down any help that's offered."

He rubbed his eyes but he shouldn't have, not for a moment yet, because when he was no longer looking at his immediate surroundings he caught a vision of what might have happened: Hogg holding a screaming prisoner by the hair—because Hogg was involved, had maybe planned the whole thing—and drawing his knife, he'd use his knife, across her throat.

"But I'm glad you didn't tell me before," Daniel continued, noticing the tremble in his voice, "because I would've tried to stop it."

He grinned, a harder expression than his usual.

"And given the good result it's apparently obtained," he said, "that would've been a pity."

Adele nodded. A team of technicians under Mr. Pasternak himself was adjusting the jury-rigged High Drive mounts in the bow. Probably to change the subject she said, "The ship those came from was much smaller than this one. Will these be able to lift us?"

"Well, lift isn't the question," Daniel said, walking forward a few steps so that they had a better view of the newly installed motors. "The plasma thrusters will do that, and they weren't damaged when the High Drive failed."

He grinned again. "Mr. Pasternak and I don't believe they were damaged. We'll see, of course. But the High Drive gives us our impulse in sidereal space. Since our progress in the Matrix is a function of that initial impulse, the present much-reduced output will delay our arrival at Radiance by more than I like."

Now that he was alert again, Daniel noticed shoots that'd risen from soil seared down several feet when the *Goldenfels'* High Drives failed. They were curling against the outrigger, inserting suckers into broken seams. And there was a colony of quarter-inch insect-oids living in the same outrigger! Goodness, where there was life, there was hope.

Not that there was a great deal of hope for those examples, particularly the tiny animals, unless they could breathe vacuum; but it was a good principle to keep in mind. To continue to keep in mind.

"I thought that the sails drove us in the Matrix," Adele said. Her eyes were on the gaping hole melted in the belly plates when a High Drive motor spewed antimatter into a normal atmosphere.

The damage was impressive enough to draw attention, that was for sure. Nickel-steel icicles hung down in a three-foot circle. A patch of pink structural plastic glued to the inner surface of the hull closed the hole. The patch was sturdier than it looked, but nobody, least of all Daniel Leary, would pretend to be happy with the situation.

"The sails only give us direction in the Matrix," Daniel explained, thinking as he spoke that if there'd been time, a cap of sheet metal for this crater and the eleven like it would've been a good investment against when they got into action. A plasma bolt would turn the plastic into a chemical explosive. . . . "We have only the momentum we start with when we enter other universes. The constants differ so that our apparent location in relation to the sidereal universe may change very quickly, but we can't add *real* velocity while we're in a bubble universe of our own."

He looked at Adele. "I don't mean to sound gloomy,"

he said. "If I didn't think the plan was workable, I wouldn't attempt it."

Adele looked amused. "Daniel," she said, "can you predict with certainty everything that's going to happen in the course of this operation?"

He drew back as though she'd slapped him. "No," he said in a reserved tone. "Of course I can't, not a fraction of the events. I hope to react properly, with the aid of a skilled crew. Granting that we'll be undermanned, of course."

"Since many of the events are unpredictable . . . ," Adele continued. Daniel could hear laughter bubbling under her words but for the life of him he couldn't understand why. "Then it's quite possible that most of them, maybe all of them, will turn out for the best, isn't it?"

"Well, yes," Daniel agreed. "That's of course what I'm hoping for, though I won't claim I expect matters to work out that way."

"Daniel," Adele said softly, "a person like you is never going to believe that a plan with so many variables is *certainly* unworkable. If the goal is important enough, you're going to attempt it. And every one of us in the crew is going to join you willingly because you're our captain."

She smiled, though the curve of mouth was as hard as a thruster nozzle. "And because you're Daniel Leary," she added.

Daniel laughed and linked arms with her. "Let's go back to the *Sissie*," he said. "I want to review the operation again with Mr. Chewning, and I'd like you to be there for the code briefing."

He began to whistle a snatch of "The Streets of Balshazzar," "*When I was a young man. . . .*"

But after all, while there's life there's hope.

❖   ❖   ❖

"It's first-rate equipment," Daniel said through his two-way link with Adele. *"No question about that—and Fleet Standard, too, not commercial crap. Well, not that Alliance commercial equipment is all bad. The trouble is that it's not what I'm familiar with. Do you find that also, Adele?"*

Adele pursed her lips, wondering how to respond. With the truth, she supposed; it was the choice she invariably made, and when speaking to Daniel there wouldn't be negative repercussions. Still, she could shade her answer. . . .

"Well, this is a new system to me, of course," she said, "but I've configured it to emulate my handheld. There was plenty of time for that. And, ah, thank you again for allowing me to use a station here on the bridge. I suppose it was for security that the, the Alliance kept the signals room separate, but I wouldn't be comfortable like that."

When Adele was working she was oblivious of everything going on around her—including, as she'd proved in the past, combat damage that made the *Princess Cecile* whip like a gavotting dancer. Nonetheless she preferred to be here on the open bridge instead of off in the signals compartment, even though most of her education and working hours had been in rooms and carrels where she was utterly alone.

She had a family, now, her fellow RCN spacers. She liked being with them, particularly when she was likely to die at any moment.

The *Goldenfels'* bridge was much larger than that of the *Princess Cecile*. A subordinate console was attached back-to-back with each primary position so that a junior specialist could echo the actions of the officer at each station. The exception was the command console, standing in solitary state in the center of the compartment.

There were bridge stations for a Navigator, a Third Lieutenant, and a commissioned Engineering Officer. None of those personnel existed in the *Princess Cecile's* crew, let alone the rump which Daniel had transferred with him to the *Goldenfels*. Adele was at the Navigator's console. She'd had no difficulty in patching the full capacity of the vessel's signals suite to it.

"*Six, this is Six-One,*" said Midshipman Vesey from the Battle Direction Center. She was using the command channel instead of a two-way pair, though that wouldn't have mattered to Adele, who routinely accessed all commo on the *Princess Cecile* and now on the *Goldenfels* as well. "*All personnel are present or accounted for. Over.*"

Under the circumstances that meant "present" since none of the personnel assigned to the *Goldenfels* were on leave, sick, or on detached duty. Vesey was following the form. That was proper at any time and inevitable now that the midshipman had become executive officer of a ship far larger than the corvette to which she'd signed on.

The *Goldenfels'* present crew was eighty-six personnel, which included seventeen formerly-Alliance riggers who'd asked to be taken on. Some had been captured when the *Princess Cecile* arrived, but ten had come out of the bush when they realized the situation. Spacers were by definition a transient lot. Even naval vessels ordinarily were crewed by people from a dozen independent planets, and the populations of some of the Alliance's client states were anything but pleased to serve Guarantor Porra.

Even so the freighter was undercrewed, but Daniel said the situation was satisfactory. It wouldn't be a long voyage, after all.

"*Thank you, Mistress Vesey,*" Daniel said. "*Break. Power room, report.*"

"*Power Room reporting all green,*" Pasternak replied. "*Anyway, there's nothing more I can do to turn this crippled pig into a starship. Four out.*"

"Roger, Mr. Pasternak," Daniel said. From where Adele sat she could see Daniel's fingers moving on his keyboard, shifting one display into the next. His face looked as calm as the statue of a saint. "*Break.* Princess Cecile, *this is Goldenfels Six. What is your condition, over?*"

Sun was at the gunnery station, leaving Dorst to handle the *Princess Cecile*'s plasma cannon. That wasn't a bad situation. The midshipman lacked Sun's experience, but he had a natural gift for weapons and—perhaps more important—had shown himself completely unflappable.

Chief Missileer Betts had remained aboard the *Princess Cecile*. Daniel would control the *Goldenfels'* missiles himself. The alternative would've required Chewning to act as the corvette's missileer, and all he knew how to do was rubberstamp the attack board's solutions—a near guarantee of failure. There was as much art to missile-slinging as there was to astrogation, Adele knew from listening to crewmen talk; and she knew also that Betts himself considered Daniel a master of that art.

Of course the *Princess Cecile* wouldn't be in a position where she needed her missiles if things went as planned, but the chance of *that* happening wasn't even worth a laugh. Thinking of the possibility of perfection, Adele chuckled.

"*Goldenfels Six, this is Sissie Six,*" said Mr. Chewning. He sounded earnest and a little nervous, like a small child presenting his class project. "*Sir, the* Princess Cecile *is ready to lift and proceed to the rendezvous location. Over.*"

Daniel had drafted the majority of the corvette's

riggers to his new command, but Chewning had the relatively simple task of taking the *Princess Cecile* to an orbit above an uninhabited—but marginally habitable—planet at roughly a day's voyage from Radiance. The *Sissie's* High Drive installation was undamaged, so even without Daniel's expertly-nuanced astrogation and Woetjans and her full team to execute the details, the *Princess Cecile* should be in position long before the *Goldenfels* arrived.

"*Roger, Sissie Six,*" Daniel said. "*I hope we'll see you again in approximately ten days. Good luck to you and your crew, Mr. Chewning. Goldenfels Six out.*"

"*Good luck and good hunting, sir!*" Chewning replied. "*Sissie Six out!*"

Daniel took a deep breath and shook himself in his harness. He saw Adele looking at him and gave her a thumbs-up, then returned his attention to his display.

"*Ship, this is Six,*" he said over the intercom. "*Prepare for lift-off. Lighting thrusters—*" his finger stabbed "*—now!*"

Adele leaned back in her acceleration couch as the plasma thrusters lit with a bone-deep growl. She wouldn't see solid ground again till the *Goldenfels* reached the Radiance system.

She grinned again. *If then*.

CHAPTER 28

Radiance was a bright spot in the panoramic starfield at the top of Daniel's display; Gehenna was a similar bead 30 degrees to clockwise along the ecliptic. Either could have passed for an unusually bright star to an inexpert eye, but Daniel would've picked out the planet and satellite by their slight proper motion during the ninety-seven minutes he'd been waiting for the picket boat to clear the *Goldenfels* to land.

The picket had just arrived, a 600-ton country craft whose antennas had been removed. Instead of making the vessel look sleeker Daniel found the result ugly and disfigured, like a man with cropped ears.

Though the picket was unarmed, its real duty was to act as trigger for the Planetary Defense Array orbiting not Radiance but rather its satellite Gehenna. If there'd been any doubts about there being an active base on Gehenna, the presence of a newly-installed Alliance minefield would've dispelled them. The Commonwealth homeworld itself was only incidentally covered by the array centered on the satellite, 730,000 miles from its primary.

"Four persons are boarding the scooter," Adele announced from her console. She was using her unaided voice across the stillness instead of speaking over the intercom; Daniel didn't know whether that was for security reasons—Adele was listening to low-power transmissions within the picket boat—or if she just preferred to talk normally when that was possible. "Three are Commonwealth personnel, a naval officer and two spacers. The fourth is Lieutenant Caravaggio of the Alliance Fleet, officially an advisor to the local authorities."

She coughed, keeping her eyes on her display instead of turning to look at her companions on the bridge as she spoke. "The guardship is named the *House of Peace*, but its crew and their control in the base on Gehenna refer to it as the *Outhouse*."

Daniel unlatched his shock harness, though he didn't get up from his couch just yet. "Sun," he said, "take your pipper off the picket boat. I don't want our friends to feel threatened when they board us in a few minutes."

"But sir!" Sun said. "What if they—"

"If you vaporize them, as I'm sure you could, Sun," Daniel said, "within ten seconds one of those mines is going to detonate and send a jet of charged particles through us. We both saw the result of that above Kostroma. Personally, I wouldn't find our lives a fair exchange for that orbiting dustbin."

The mines were thermonuclear weapons, each fitted with a simple magnetic lens. When the mine acquired a target, the device detonated and the lens in its last microsecond of existence directed a significant proportion of the blast toward that target. The mines were either triggered by command, or because a target had approached too close without the correct response to its interrogation code, or because the target violated some other parameter. Attacking the guardship would certainly be such a violation.

The gunner grimaced, but he immediately touched a control that made the targeting circles vanish from his display. "No sir," he said, "I guess I wouldn't either."

"They're leaving the guardship," Adele said. The scooter was a simple cage of struts and wire woven around a tank of reaction mass with a plasma thruster at either end. Daniel saw rainbow exhaust puff from the back. The image swelled rapidly at first, then burped plasma from the bow and slowed to a crawl.

Daniel rose from his couch. He wanted to give a final pep talk to the crew over the intercom, but Adele's concern for security stopped him. Instead he called in a voice that the score of spacers on the bridge and loitering in the corridor beyond could hear, "All right, Sissies. All we have to do is act like a gang of half-uniformed cutthroats who generally operate on their own. That shouldn't be much of a stretch, should it?"

Because the *Goldenfels*' cover was that of a freighter, her crew hadn't worn Alliance Fleet uniforms. Besides, on-duty clothing for spacers tended to be anything loose and drab no matter who they happened to be working for. The ship's present crew wore garments from both Alliance and RCN stores, along with a mixture of civilian garb from a score or more of planets which they'd visited in the course of their careers. In fact they looked exactly like the crew which Captain Bertram had commanded and were pretty similar to the crew of *any* vessel in either navy that wasn't either an admiral's flagship or otherwise cursed with officers who worshipped spit and polish.

Through the laughter, Daniel heard the clank of the scooter's electromagnets clamping to the hull, then lesser clinkings as the boarding party entered the airlock. He propelled himself into the forward transfer compartment which contained the companionways and airlock, waiting for the inner hatch to open.

Adele, still strapped into her couch, shook her head at the unthinking skill with which Daniel and the other spacers moved in freefall; he grinned boyishly at her. So far as he was concerned, that wasn't a patch on the way she navigated the thickets of information retrieval. It was all in what you were used to, he supposed.

The airlock opened. The Commonwealth officer and a spacer whose vacuum suit looked dangerously worn got out, followed by Caravaggio, the Alliance advisor Adele had warned about. He was a young fellow, no more than nineteen, with close-cropped black hair and a pugnacious expression.

Last through the lock was Woetjans, a hulking giant when her rigging suit doubled her apparent bulk. The boarding party must've left the remaining spacer on the hull to guard their scooter—a piece of mindless paranoia, so far as Daniel could see.

"HSK2 *Atlantis*, requesting permission to dock on Lorenz Base," Daniel said to Caravaggio, ignoring the Commonwealth officer who was nominally in charge. The latter was a man in his fifties with a sad expression and a drooping gray moustache, a considerable contrast from the bold red-and-silver patterns on his vacuum suit.

"Where's Captain Bertram?" Caravaggio said, his eyes narrowing. "And what the hell happened to you guys, anyway? You look like a wreck on the way to the scrapyard!"

"Bertram's dead," Daniel said, clipping his words and glaring at the Alliance lieutenant like he wanted to tear his throat out. Neither he nor Caravaggio was quite perpendicular—and they slanted in opposite directions. Daniel wasn't sure you could really be threatening when you looked like part of a comedy act, but he was trying.

"And as for what happened to the *Goldenfels*," he continued, "if you were cleared to know that you wouldn't have to ask. Give us the codes, sonny, and go back to wiping windshields for tips."

"Look, you!" the youth replied, flying hot before the situation really sunk in. When it did, he paused with his mouth open.

Daniel let his lip curl, which wasn't really an act. Though young, Caravaggio was older than Midshipman Dorst. Dorst would've kept his temper until he understood what was going on—though if he decided then that there was a problem, he'd proved himself in the past to be strong and determined when he went about finding solutions.

"Look," Caravaggio resumed in a less argumentative tone, "I have to report who you are. I mean, *whoever* you are, I have to report before they'll clear you through."

Daniel grunted. "I'm Kidd," he said. "I was the Third Lieutenant. Lieutenant Boster, he was the XO till the same problem as took off the Old Man."

In fact Lieutenant Kidd—whom they'd captured on Morzanga and released there with all the other Alliance spacers who hadn't signed on with the freighter's new management—was a lanky fellow who resembled Woetjans more than he did Daniel. Caravaggio and his superiors would very possibly have the *Goldenfels'* crew list, but it would be abnormally bad luck if the Alliance officer happened to know Kidd by sight.

The important thing was that Kidd and Daniel were about the same age. There was no way a twenty-three year old could pass for a senior officer of a vessel like the *Goldenfels*.

"And if you're wondering about Lieutenant Greiner," Daniel continued after a heartbeat pause to make sure his luck *hadn't* been abnormally bad, "don't, because

424   *David Drake*

he wasn't in the chain of command. If you take my meaning."

Caravaggio did and grimaced, though the Commonwealth official looked in puzzlement from his advisor to Daniel, then back again. The *Goldenfels* was a spy ship, and as such the signals officer was a specialist from a pool of officers other than those of the ordinary Fleet. Spies were folk whose business and associations made fighting officers steer clear of them, lest some of the muck stick.

Daniel smiled musingly. He understood how Caravaggio felt. If Adele weren't Adele, he'd feel much the same way about her.

"All right," said Caravaggio. "I'll feed the codes into your main computer, but be careful—once you enter the minefield, you have to follow the programmed course precisely. If you deviate by more than a few percent in course or speed, you're dead. There won't be a warning. The array's like a mousetrap: it doesn't think, it just acts."

"Thank you, Lieutenant," Daniel said calmly, as though the threat didn't concern him. "If I lose control of the ship that badly on landing, we'll auger in without needing a minefield to kill us. Follow me, if you will."

Daniel reached back for the hatch coaming, then pulled firmly to send himself into the bridge again. He gave himself just enough spin to rotate his body so that he faced forward when he reached his console and caught himself. Caravaggio kicked off a bulkhead and followed in a similarly slow, graceful flight.

Adele was concentrating on her own display, but Daniel smiled at the back of her head as he went past. The way spacers learned to maneuver in weightlessness *was* rather amazing when he thought about it, which he normally didn't, of course. Well, after all, you didn't normally think about walking on the ground either; but if you considered all the muscles that had to work just *so* to keep you from falling on your face, that was pretty remarkable also.

"Here, you can couple to the command console," Daniel said. He made a sweeping gesture with his right arm. "Or if you want to use another, be my guest. We're short-handed since the trouble, as you can see."

He gave Caravaggio a cynical smile. The *Goldenfels* was indeed short-handed. Daniel had thought about trying to conceal the fact by putting techs from the Power Room at the consoles. There were too many ways that could've gone wrong, though, so he'd decided to make a virtue of necessity and hint at the horrendous casualties which had also ripped open the freighter's belly.

Caravaggio looked grimly impressed as he seated himself on the couch. "No sir, the command console will be fine," he said, taking a data syringe from the pocket strapped to the left forearm of his vacuum suit. He pointed the syringe, a short tube with a pistol grip, into the console's input port and squirted the code into the ship's system.

When the telltale above the port winked green, Caravaggio stood and slipped the syringe back into its container. "There you go, Lieutenant Kidd," he said. "Your identification signal will change in a continuous keyed sequence which matches the interrogatories from the defense array. Just follow the program I've input and you'll be fine."

He pushed off toward the airlock where the Commonwealth personnel continued to wait in morose silence. Over his shoulder he called, "But for God's sake, don't abort your landing and try to lift again. You'll be blown to atoms before you've risen a thousand meters!"

"Thank you, Lieutenant," Daniel repeated, remaining where he was in the middle of the bridge.

With luck, Adele should be able to unravel and emulate the code Caravaggio had downloaded into the command console; she'd assured him the decryption suite of the *Goldenfels* was just as advanced as her own unit aboard the *Princess Cecile*. If she succeeded, then the defense array ceased to be a matter of concern.

If that codebreaking *didn't* work out, though, well . . . it wasn't going to prevent the *Goldenfels* from doing considerable damage to Lorenz Base. But it was very unlikely the *Goldenfels* and those aboard her would survive more than seconds following their initial slashing attack.

The *Goldenfels* was under weigh again. Vesey had the conn. Adele assumed that controlling the ship's descent into Lorenz Base was simpler than the chore Daniel had taken for his own: preparing to loose the full weight of their weaponry against the Alliance.

Adele was so sunk in her own work that she was aware of acceleration in the same fashion she was aware of breathing—mostly not at all. What a wealth—what a treasure house!—of information she was finding.

The ship's computer ground away at the code controlling the Planetary Defense Array. Starship computers had to be able to project courses through multiple bubble universes, each with varied space-time constants; no workable human encryption system could be more complex.

The algorithms necessary to attack encryption were quite different from those needed for astrogation, however. Adele had brought her software from the *Princess Cecile*. The system already aboard was configured specifically to the astrogation computer of the

Goldenfels, however, so she was using the installed version instead of her own.

She had nothing to add to the processing once she'd put it in hand, so she concentrated on Lorenz Base, dug into the surface of the moon which always faced Radiance. The installations were almost completely hidden, but by opening the files of the maintenance department—which weren't protected any more rigorously than the similar files of the Xenos city government were—Adele had retrieved complete schematics of the power, sewer, water, and air-handling systems of every portion of the base.

Some of it didn't mean anything to her—the huge overhead trackways could be for any purpose from food storage to missile transfer—but she was confident that Daniel could layer usage on her armature of facts. She was transferring the files to all members of the command group as she uncovered them, slugging them as to source and adding titles when possible.

It struck Adele almost absently that Lorenz Base was huge. It was built into the rim of an asteroid impact crater seven miles in diameter, the largest terrain feature on this side of Gehenna. On Radiance the crater was known as the Eye of Darkness, and many of the more devout inhabitants refused to do business on days when the Eye appeared to wink in the rising sun.

It was long after sundown on the portion of Radiance that now faced the moon. Adele didn't suppose what was about to happen in the Eye was bad news for those on the primary, but it would certainly look that way to anyone here on Gehenna.

While Mr. Pasternak was refitting the *Goldenfels* with High Drive motors from the wreck on Morzanga, Adele had taken the time to configure her console into the fashion she wanted it. Now she could control it directly with her wands instead of using her handheld unit as an interface.

Her fingers twitched, ripping data from banal files and reconnecting them in shapes that the people who'd entered the bits could never have imagined. By combining information from a score of service operations, most of them run by civilian contractors, she was creating the targeting data Daniel needed.

Lorenz Base's twenty-four hangars were dug into the crater's inner walls in groups of eight. Each hangar was 57 meters wide and 412 meters long if the power connections were flush with the walls. Two of the groupings were in the northwest and southwest quadrants; the third was to the east. There were 90 meters of rock between hangars in a group and 450 meters between the nearest members of the two western groupings.

"Adele, can you tell which ones are occupied?" said a voice through her console. *"Those hangars are big enough that any one could hold the whole destroyer flotilla. I don't want to waste time smashing empties unless I have to!"*

Adele was aware that it was Daniel speaking, though that didn't matter in her present frame of mind. Her task was simply to answer the question no matter who asked it; to retrieve the needed information in a form that the querent could use.

Power usage wasn't conclusive, but water was another matter. Water by the kiloliters was needed for washing, for drinking, and particularly for filling the reaction mass tanks of ships that'd been months in transit and avoiding landings for fear their movements might be reported. Hangars one through five in the southwest grouping showed a vast increase in water usage over the past fourteen days. There were frequent burps in flow to Hangar East One as well, but those were fairly consistent over the past three months.

"Here are the active hangars, sir," she said. "Sir" was a polite response to a querent, not a junior officer addressing her commander. She transferred to Daniel a schematic of the base overlaid with color-coded gradients based on water inflow. SW1-5 were bright red, E1 was yellow; the other eighteen positions ranged from violet to dark indigo.

"By God they are!" Daniel said. *"By God they are!"*

Adele drew a deep breath and relaxed. She had a realtime visual of Lorenz Base at the top of her display, but she hadn't taken time to look at it. Now she did.

The *Goldenfels* was slanting toward the crater at a steep angle from due west. Its jagged walls were ochre where sunlight touched them and sharp purple shadows where it did not: Gehenna had no atmosphere to blur the edges of light and not-light.

A few above-ground installations glinted, elevator heads and gun positions. Near the center of the crater floor was a slim naval vessel, one of the eight destroyers whose presence Daniel had foretold when he was released from the grip of the Tree on New Delphi.

Adele's console clucked an attention signal; she brought up the information which it thought she needed to have.

The console was correct. "The computer's solved the minefield code," Adele said as her wands moved in tight arcs, transmitting new orders to the node which controlled the defense array. "I'm setting the command node to reject all signals to attack the *Goldenfels*. I'll have it . . . there, we're clear."

"Roger that!" Daniel said. Then in an exultant voice he went on, "Ship, this is Six. Prepare to engage the enemy!"

CHAPTER 29

Daniel hadn't had enough time to do all the things he needed to do for an effective attack, so—*thank God and Adele!*—he made time now that it was safe to. He reached for the controls himself, shouting, "Ship, I'm taking the conn!"

He regretted treating Vesey with brusque discourtesy, since she'd been performing with her usual skill. Vesey's only flaw was that she couldn't read Daniel's mind—but that was critical now, because he couldn't explain to her the things that *had* to be done instantly. He'd apologize to her afterwards, if there was an afterwards.

Daniel rolled the thrusters up from the 40% power at which they were idling toward a landing to 95%, not quite normal maximum and certainly not through the gate into overload. He didn't need thrust quite that badly, and at the highest settings—even with the units properly warmed up as these were—there was always a risk of fracturing a nozzle and sending the ship into a dangerous oscillation.

Even so the shock of doubled power rang through the *Goldenfels* as though Daniel had driven her into the ground. Because they were coming in at a slant, the added thrust overcame forward inertia without being instantly sufficient to lift the vessel against the moon's gravity. Their angled course became vertical; the *Goldenfels* dropped toward the surface short of the crater's rim instead of inside it.

"*Goldenfels* to Base!" he shouted, hoping the adrenaline in his voice suggested panic instead of the blazing triumph he really felt. *It was going to work, by God it was!* "We have a problem! We have a problem!"

Heaven only knew what Lorenz Control thought when the incoming spy ship lurched toward the ground in a gush of expanding plasma. Their optical pickups would've shown the damage to the *Goldenfels*' underside, even through the mist of exhaust as she began braking toward them. The burp of rainbow fire was so great that it'd be natural to assume that her thrusters had exploded, but the very suddenness would make it hard for the base personnel to think *anything*.

The *Goldenfels* was configured as a spy ship and raider. Her gun armament was as powerful as that of a heavy cruiser of several times her displacement. She was intended to approach other vessels in sidereal space, posing as a merchantman. When she was close enough she'd unmask her batteries and blast away the other vessels' antennas and rigging, leaving them crippled.

The *Goldenfels* wasn't, however, expected to engage other warships in a normal action at long range. She had only two missile tubes, aligned to port and starboard, and the twenty missiles in her magazines were no more than the *Princess Cecile*, much smaller but a true warship, carried in RCN service. The missiles were for last-ditch defense when the raider was being run to ground; there was little chance that they would destroy an enemy, but they might force a more powerful adversary to maneuver violently and by so doing allow the *Goldenfels* to escape into the Matrix.

If Adele hadn't disabled the Planetary Defense Array, one of the mines would've ripped a sleet of ions into the *Goldenfels* as soon as she deviated from the pre-set course. The jet would vaporize a ten-foot hole in the ship, and if it passed through the Power Room the fusion bottle would go critical to finish the job.

The mines didn't detonate. Given time, somebody in Lorenz Control would begin wondering why they hadn't. Daniel had no intention of giving them that much time.

"Vesey, hold us in a hover!" he ordered, using the midshipman as though she were an extra pair of hands. "And on your *life* keep us below the rim of the crater! Break, Sun, clear your 15-cm guns and program them to take out the defensive installations when we rise above the rim again."

The turrets holding the 10-cm plasma cannon were extended to provide more space in the ship's interior. That was normal operating procedure; the guns were only retracted during entry into an atmosphere. The raider's four lateral twin installations were concealed, however. Approaching a secret base with those guns ready to fire would arouse comment and very likely a volley from the base defenses.

"Adele," Daniel continued, "send Sun a targeting template. Sun, keep the 4-inch guns—"

They were actually 10-cm guns, Fleet standard instead of RCN, but the distinction wasn't important just now.

"—under your control for targets of opportunity. Especially that destroyer! Out!"

As Daniel spoke, his fingers hammered the virtual keyboard to bring up the attack screen and to input data. This was going to be tricky, but with a little luck . . .

The shutters concealing the paired 15-cm guns shrieked open. The *Goldenfels'* hull had warped when the High Drive blew the vessel over on her side. Woetjans and her riggers had straightened the trackways as best they could with jacks and sledge hammers, but they hadn't even tried to do more than a quick and dirty job.

"*Template transferred,*" Adele said crisply. An icon at the top of Daniel's display pulsed to call attention to itself. As it did so, he realized that it'd been waiting for his notice for the past several minutes.

The *Goldenfels* porpoised as Vesey struggled to bring her under control. Daniel had dumped the thrusters back to 60% power as he handed over the ship, but it was already starting to rise. It continued to upward on momentum for several seconds; as it did so, Vesey almost inevitably overcorrected.

In response the *Goldenfels* plunged toward the surface, yo-yoing a thousand feet before the midshipman caught herself and the vessel. At last Vesey damped the drop into a slow shuddering climb while she cut thrust by one-percent increments.

"*Target programming complete!*" Sun reported. "*Sir, we're ready to go! We're ready!*"

"Mistress Vesey," Daniel ordered, "take us over the base at a thousand feet above the crater floor—"

The rim averaged 800 feet above the floor, but there were spikes sticking up 150 feet higher.

"—on a heading of three-four-nine degrees true, speed over ground eighteen feet per second. Over."

"*Roger,*" Vesey said. The *Goldenfels* had retained a slight forward motion from her earlier wobbling. Now she began to accelerate and slant upward. The outer rim of the crater had been a mile ahead of them. It swelled in the realtime display at the bottom of Daniel's attack board, itself a cat's cradle of vectors on which time was indicated by color coding.

The *Goldenfels* would cross the crater in a very nearly south-to-north direction. Daniel didn't have a choice because of the unusual lateral alignment of his missile tubes, but the situation was far from ideal. The direction the missile was pointing when it left the launcher didn't matter at the multi-thousand mile ranges of a space battle, but the *Goldenfels* would be firing her missiles point blank. They'd hit before they were able to course correct.

"Ship, we're crossing the rim in five seconds," Vesey warned. *"Now!"*

Sun had a clear line of sight with the forward 10-cm guns momentarily before any of the other weapons bore. He sent six plasma bolts into the dorsal 13-cm turret of the Alliance destroyer on the crater floor, preparing to lift off. His cannon syncopated one another, each firing as the other cooled for an instant. Then the loading mechanism injected another pellet of deuterium in a cradle that positioned it for the surrounding laser array. When the lasers tripped, they fused the deuterium and directed the blast down the bore as a slug of ions moving at the speed of light.

Gehenna had no atmosphere to disperse the bolts. They struck with full force, blasting holes in the steel and welding the remainder of the turret to the ring on which it turned. Blast-proof hatches aboard the destroyer would be closing automatically, preventing an explosive loss of pressure throughout the ship but also disrupting communication and traffic from one compartment to the next.

An instant later the forward 15-cm guns cleared the crater rim and opened fire according to the program Sun had set. The blasts jolted the *Goldenfels*, whipping her noticeably. *Bloody Hell! These guns were* way *too heavy for the ship!*

The *Goldenfels* was good sized, but her frames were

those of a freighter, not a warship. Seams started at
every shot, and when the rear turrets began to fire the
ship rattled like a tambourine.

But below where the bolts were hitting, flashes and
volcanic secondary eruptions brought down slabs of the
crater walls. Lorenz Base was defended by both plasma
and kinetic weapons—hypervelocity rockets and electromagnetic guns which accelerated slugs of a kilogram
and more. A starship could use its sails as one-time
protection against plasma bolts, but a heavy osmium
slug would pass through the molecule-thin fabric on
its way to punching similar holes in and out of a hull
of any conceivable thickness.

The raider's 15-cm guns were meant to be effective on targets thousands of miles distant. Now at barely
knife-range, their bolts turned the base defenses, their
shields, and tons of nearby rock into geysers of charged
gas. If the discharges shook the *Goldenfels* to bits, well,
that was a trade-off Daniel was willing to make.

The *Goldenfels'* tubes launched their first pair of
missiles, shaking the vessel even more violently than
the big guns did. Ships which carried missiles internally—some light vessels hung them on outside brack-
ets—had to expel them from the hull before the High
Drive ignited. The *Goldenfels* used the usual system
of heating water in a containment vessel, then voiding it into the missile tube as superheated steam to
hurl the missile from the ship. The violence required
to accelerate a multi-ton missile also had a significant
impact on the 4,000-ton ship on the other side of the
equation.

Judging from the footprint of the powered track, the
doors of these hangars were more than a meter thick.
Plasma bolts couldn't penetrate them. The missile from
the *Goldenfels'* starboard tube lit a few yards outboard
and curved toward Hangar E1 ahead of a line of

dazzling coruscance, the signature of matter/antimatter annihilation.

The angle on Daniel's display made him momentarily concerned that the missile's course would take it through the paired fire from Sun's dorsal and ventral turrets, raking the Alliance destroyer. It didn't, streaking on untouched till it slammed the hangar as a huge sledge.

The door, a sandwich of concrete within steel, buckled inward. Portions of the powdered core puffed out. Air jetted from the interior, touched the friction-heated facing metal, and exploded in a blaze as hot as an arc light.

The missile penetrated the hangar's interior. The remainder of the door valve hid the destruction it did within, but sparks from the hole sprayed hundreds of feet out onto the crater floor. Heaven knew what had been inside—probably the utility vessel the base used as a hack—but it wouldn't be of much use to the Alliance in the future.

The missile launched from the port tube dropped almost three hundred feet in splutters of radiance before its motor reached full output; one or both the High Drive feed lines had been clogged. Again, that wouldn't have been a problem at astronomical ranges, but here it meant that the missile didn't stabilize in time. It traced a sine curve fifty feet in amplitude until it struck the crater wall just above the door to Hangar SW1.

Rock shattered as the missile sprayed itself across the door and the face of the cliff. Antimatter still in the converter made a black flash which left behind a ragged pockmark.

The guns continued to hammer. The jolts from the 10-cm turrets were scarcely perceptible but the 15-cm weapons made the *Goldenfels* shudder violently.

Missiles were rolling from the magazine toward both launchers, but only the port tube bore on occupied hangars.

Reloading took a maddening seventy-five seconds, but there was no help for it. Missiles were massive items, dense as well as heavy, and they simply couldn't be flung around like footballs.

The *Goldenfels* slithered above the crater like a snake, twisted by the recoil of her lateral turrets. Her wreck and recovery at Morzanga had warped her frame, probably beyond even a major dockyard's ability to correct, but the pounding of these plasma cannon was beyond anything she'd have been able to take for long on the day she came from her builders. A belly plate fell off, winking with the reflection of the big guns.

Air-loss alarms were sounding; the crew already wore the light vacuum suits that were standard for emergency use, but Daniel knew from past experience that now some of the spacers would be locking down their faceplates. He didn't have time for that himself, nor was there need—yet.

The port-tube icon glowed green, then launched its missile automatically because Daniel hadn't countermanded the pre-programmed attack sequence. This round lit instantly, so close to the tube that Daniel could feel the bacon-frying sizzle of antimatter in the exhaust slaking its fury against the *Goldenfels'* hull.

The missile's course curved so slightly that it looked like a straight line on Daniel's display. It struck squarely in the center of the door to SW3, punching through. For an instant there was nothing more; then a blast blew the hangar door into the crater and a second blast spewed fire and debris as far as the wreck of the destroyer *Sun* was working over.

A wave of gas and plasma made the *Goldenfels* yaw to starboard. The 15-cm guns couldn't correct quickly enough and ripped bursts high and low, gouging the crater floor to starboard and the top of the cliffs to port. Daniel's harness caught him; the shock would otherwise have flung him out of the console.

Icons pulsed across the top of the command display like a tiara of rubies. A dozen compartments were open to vacuum. Daniel slammed down his faceshield; some of the air-tight doors had dropped into place but others were jammed in their tracks. You couldn't blame them. . . . The portside 15-cm turrets had stopped firing, and the channel carrying the reload missile to the port launcher had kinked when the missile leaped from its track and fell back.

"Belknap, get Launcher One reloaded!" Daniel ordered. "Woetjans, give him all the help he needs. I don't care what it takes to do it—rip a hole in the hull plating if you have to, but get me missiles again!"

Belknap, a Missileer 2d Class, was the highest ranking member of his specialty aboard the *Goldenfels*. It was his duty to handle the mechanics of the missiles while Daniel himself programmed their courses. Belknap had a pair of Missileer Threes under him, but what clearing the trackway required was brute force. The riggers were temporarily off duty, and they were *very* familiar with brute force.

Vesey'd fought the freighter steady again, then readjusted the course to the 349 degrees as Daniel had ordered—the blast had skewed them well to starboard. You don't expect a gust of wind on an airless satellite, particularly a white-hot squall sparkling with the hellfire of its creation.

They were three-quarters of the way across the broad crater, holding at 18 feet per second. That would've been perfect to finish the destruction of Lorenz Base in one pass if things had gone the way they were supposed to—

But they hadn't. Well, that wasn't a new experience in the RCN, and it wasn't an excuse for doing half what was required and running.

"Mistress Vesey," Daniel ordered, "bring us around if you will. We'll proceed on a reciprocal and finish the job."

Then, beaming a smile beneath his faceshield, Daniel added, "By God, Sissies, they'll talk about this one for as long as there's an RCN—and there'll be an RCN for as long as it can recruit spacers like you!"

They won't talk about us unless somebody survives to tell them! Adele thought tartly, but it wasn't her place to say that.

Besides, it wasn't true. There'd be Alliance survivors, and they'd tell the story. They'd use words like "fools" and "lucky," but it wasn't a story that could be hidden.

In truth, there hadn't been much luck involved in the business. Adele wasn't disposed to quarrel with "fools," though. Not that it mattered to her.

Everybody was jabbering on the intercom; Adele ignored the chatter except to make sure that none of the empty nonsense was getting to Daniel. She set the feeds so that all the crew could watch the external visuals if they had the time. They probably didn't—damage control should occupy everyone who wasn't directly involved in the battle—but it was part of her job.

Adele had access to all the traffic within Lorenz Base, because she'd used the *Goldenfels'* signals suite to convince Base Control that the ship's computer was its back-up installation. That pretty piece of work had given her a degree of satisfaction, but it wasn't as useful as she'd initially hoped. The Alliance personnel were babbling the same sort of inanities as the Sissies were, though theirs were tinged with panic.

Sun was shooting with both turrets, but thank

goodness the guns on the sides were silent. When they'd begun to fire, Adele had thought the *Goldenfels* was blowing up. When two or more of the cannon discharged simultaneously, her display lost resolution for an instant; each time it happened, she'd feared that her console itself would fail instead of just the hologram projectors losing alignment.

Adele wasn't afraid to die, but she was terrified of failing Daniel and the others who depended on her. Without access to her computer, she would fail.

She smiled coldly. There were other consoles, of course. And worst case, she could probably link her handheld unit to the ship's main transceiver and do a respectable job of providing the *Goldenfels'* officers with signals intelligence.

Tovera sat on the couch of the console coupled back-to-back with Adele's; it was meant for a junior to emulate the officer at the main unit. The junior would take over in event of battle damage to the electronics or the officer, either one.

Tovera hadn't brought the console live; she was simply using the couch as a seat while she waited for something that suited her talents. Those would be few and far between in an action of this sort, but she'd stepped over to snap a mask down over Adele's face when something massive hit the ship.

Daniel's console didn't have a subordinate station, so Hogg shared the couch with Tovera. He held a stocked impeller and locked his feet around the cantilevered support strut.

Adele couldn't imagine any present use for Hogg's big shoulder weapon, but it was his business if he wanted to hold it. Adele glimpsed his face occasionally between cascades of holographic data; his expression was alert and unconcerned. Tovera, as usual, looked like a smiling death mask.

The *Goldenfels* was either maneuvering violently or they'd been hit and were out of control. That wasn't Adele's business so she didn't bother learning which. She split her display, making the bottom half a visual of the base with radio emitters careted. There was a multi-frequency mast on the highest of the surrounding peaks which Adele hoped Sun would leave untouched: it was her point of entry into the systems of Lorenz Base.

Three figures ran across the crater floor, jabbering on FM. Just jabbering, not really to one another or to any purpose. They were airsuited survivors from the spluttering wreck of the destroyer, perhaps the only survivors, trying to get to cover in case their vessel's fusion bottle failed. They didn't matter. But—

The living rock into which the hangars were dug and the thick doors that closed them were completely impervious to RF radiation. The fact that Adele was getting strong signals from SW5 meant that the door was sliding open.

The *Goldenfels* launched another missile. The freighter was recrossing the base on the opposite heading; Daniel must be using the tube that hadn't been damaged earlier. He'd aimed it at SW4, the next target on his list. It was closed and therefore harmless, but SW5 was neither.

"Target!" Adele shouted. Here was where a better grasp of RCN communications etiquette would have been useful. She traced a scarlet highlight over the hangar door. At the small scale of her display she couldn't see a gap between the twin valves, but the radio signal couldn't lie. "Daniel, Sun, the hangar's open—"

For want of anything better to shoot at as the destroyer melted, Sun had been working over a maintenance bay on the crater floor between the southwest

and southeast groups of hangars. He began slewing his
guns as soon as Adele threw up the caret, but the sheer
mass of the armored batteries took time to move even
on frictionless magnetic gimbals. A 13-cm plasma bolt
spat from within the hangar to strike the *Goldenfels'*
dorsal turret squarely.

Adele thought the flash had blinded her, but that
was just the effect of the bridge's thin remaining
atmosphere fluorescing. Normal lighting returned, but
a sphere of ball lightning hung between Adele and the
back of Daniel's console. A mask of translucent blue
flicked off and on over its sullen yellow presence.
Sizzling, it rose at a walking pace till it vanished
through the ceiling.

The bolt's impact buckled the plating and frames
beneath the vaporized gun turret. The bridge hatch,
closed at the start of action, flew open as the bulkhead crumpled around it. The corridor's emergency
lighting looked flat because there was no atmosphere
to scatter it. Four Sissies ran toward the rupture with
a roll of sail fabric and adhesive guns to tack it over
the damage; returning air pressure would squeeze the
film into place until a longer-term fix was possible.

Which would require that the *Goldenfels* survive a
while longer, of course.

Adele had inset the command display onto a corner of her screen to be able to anticipate Daniel's
requests. As a result she knew that he'd shifted to a
gunnery board and taken manual control of the guns
in the side emplacements. They'd been silent since
they'd destroyed the targets Sun had set them. She
could see what Daniel *had* done, but for the life of
her Adele couldn't imagine how he'd shifted mental
and physical gears so quickly. It was like watching
Tovera shoot. . . .

The second bolt from the warship within the hangar

missed high by no more than the distance that the first had slammed the *Goldenfels* toward the ground. The turret, converted into a fireball of steel and iridium, had shoved the bow down. There wasn't a third bolt because Daniel was firing the guns on the *Goldenfels'* starboard side. They punished the ship herself, but when their bolts hit inside the hangar—

Adele's equipment told her that the radio transmissions were coming from three Alliance destroyers, the *Max Schultze*, *Richard Beitzen*, and *Paul Jacobi*. The information appeared automatically, in the sense that she'd set the system to provide names and schematic data whenever it correlated an identification transponder with a particular unit of the Alliance Fleet. Her console echoed the readout to Daniel and the Battle Direction Center.

It didn't have any effect on the battle, however, because of the arcing destruction the first two 15-cm bolts loosed within the hangar. The six that followed before forward motion carried the *Goldenfels* past the narrow opening were probably a waste of ammunition, since at least one fusion bottle had ruptured almost instantly.

A gush of radiance, ionized vapor instead of light, flashed from the hangar. This time it didn't blow the doors off. Instead the cliff face bulged upward, shot through by glowing gases, and shuddered down toward the crater floor. As it did so, the missile struck home in the center of SW 4. The explosions inside that hangar were just getting started when the avalanche flowed over the doors of both in a dance of rock and dust and the sparkling highlights of plasma that leaked through the cascade.

"Launcher One's reloaded, sir!" rasped a voice on the command channel, Woetjans speaking instead of Belknap. The rumble of the heavy missiles usually shook the ship unmistakably, but Adele hadn't noticed it this time.

"*Thank you, Woetjans,*" Daniel replied in a hoarse, breathy voice. "*Sun, cease fire. All personnel who don't have Power Room duties, put yourself under the bosun. Woetjans will take charge of damage control.*"

He paused, sucking in air with a gasp that his helmet microphone took for speech and transmitted. "*Mistress Vesey,*" Daniel resumed, "*get us out of here as quickly as you can, please. I'll plot us a course into the Matrix, but I'm not ready to do that right now.*"

The *Goldenfels* was accelerating hard, pushing Adele down on her couch. She remembered her first view of the raider, a halo of plasma thrusters blazing above the *Princess Cecile*. That was the view the survivors of Lorenz Base had of her now.

She glanced toward the command console. Daniel caught her eye, grinned, and raised a thumb in greeting.

His face sobered slightly and he resumed, "*Ship, this is Six. Spacers, an hour ago an Alliance squadron of two battleships, a heavy cruiser, and eight destroyers ruled the whole Galactic North. Because of your skill and courage, the elements of that squadron are either destroyed or so damaged that it'll take a year to dig out and refit the survivors. If the RCN can't get a proper force out here in a year to finish the job, then by God! you and I will come back and do it for them!*"

Daniel paused for the laughter he knew was sounding. Adele smiled faintly, wondering if she ought to cut Daniel back into the intercom channel so he could hear his crew's enthusiastic congratulations. On balance, no; he had more work to do, he'd said, plotting a course.

"*Fellow spacers,*" Daniel said, "*Fellow Sissies—God bless you, and God bless the RCN!*"

"*Sir!*" Vesey announced unexpectedly. "*A ship has*

*just returned to normal space 400,000 miles out.
They're querying Lorenz Base in code, over."*

Adele's face lost expression as she raised her couch
upright to make her work easier. They'd be switching
shortly to the High Drive, which in its present jury-
rigged state couldn't manage much more than one
gravity's acceleration anyway. Her wands quivered.

Sun, Belknap, Vesey and Pasternak were all speaking on the command channel. Daniel was not: he'd
brought up the navigation screen. The Plot Position
Indicator was inset into it.

Instead of speaking, Adele flashed a text message
at the bottom of every active display:

> THE SHIP WHICH HAS JUST APPEARED IS THE
> ALLIANCE HEAVY CRUISER *BLUECHER*, WHICH IS
> RETURNING TO LORENZ BASE AFTER A SHORT
> WORKUP CRUISE.

She didn't add any commentary to the flat statement.
It seemed obvious to her that though it'd take
the *Bluecher's* commander, Captain-of-Space Rafael
Semmes, a while to realize what had happened at the
base and to begin pursuing the *Goldenfels*, it would
be only a *little* while.

Daniel must have thought the same thing, because
he was working with the concentration of a demon on
plotting their escape into the Matrix.

CHAPTER 30

The *Goldenfels* was rigged for landing, her sails furled and her antennas telescoped and folded. Daniel's first thought was to drop into the Matrix immediately and set the sails there; many astrogators couldn't track another ship after it left sidereal space, and some wouldn't even try.

The Alliance had more than its share of able captains, however. If the *Bluecher* was commanded by one of them, the heavy cruiser would appear within seconds of when the *Goldenfels* shifted back into normal space the first time. Daniel found it wise to assume that his enemy was just as competent as he was.

"Woetjans, both watches," Daniel ordered. He hated to send riggers out while the ship was accelerating, but sometimes you don't have a choice. "Rig the maincourses of Dorsal A and Starboard A, both at 29 degrees starboard inclination. Move it, spacers!"

The riggers were spread through the ship doing damage control, but at least they were suited up. Woetjans would have the sails set within minutes, giving the *Goldenfels* maneuvering way from the moment it entered the Matrix. The *Bluecher* had Fleet-standard optical pickups, as good as those of the RCN, but nobody at 400,000 miles could tell an angle of twenty-nine degrees from thirty-one or twenty-seven. That was a wide enough variation that the heavy cruiser would have to quarter the region instead of landing directly on top of her wallowing prey, and only the very best astrogators could hope to follow a trail through the Matrix that was hours old.

There were pirate captains who managed the trick regularly, of course. It would've been child's play for Uncle Stacey, and Lieutenant Daniel Leary had managed it also. If the *Bluecher* had a commander of that quality, the *Goldenfels* wasn't going to escape—and she wasn't going to fight a successful battle against a heavy cruiser.

Daniel smiled as his fingers hammered additional calculations into his computer. Which didn't mean that they wouldn't fight. When he had leisure he'd check the status of the *Goldenfels'* weaponry, not that he expected to like what he learned.

Adele inserted another text at the bottom of his display:

> THE *BLUECHER*'S COMMANDER IS CAPT. RAFAEL
> SEMMES. DO YOU WISH DETAILS OF HIS SERVICE?

"Thank you, Adele," Daniel said on his two-way link. He continued to type; he wasn't familiar with this region. He'd studied the return to the rendezvous with the *Princess Cecile*, but he didn't want to head back directly in case they were pursued. "The identification is sufficient. I'm aware of the gentleman."

Now he was quite sure they'd be pursued. Daniel didn't remember the name of every Alliance officer he'd heard in passing, but when Oliver Semmes mentioned at the funeral that he and his brother Rafael had met

Uncle Stacey while they were serving under the great Captain Lorenz—that Daniel had remembered. Lorenz gave the officers under him the opportunity to become first-class astrogators—

And if they failed to do so, Lorenz railroaded them out of the Fleet. Rafael Semmes had survived.

Well, perhaps Daniel would get lucky with a missile. And the *Goldenfels* mounted heavy guns as well. Maybe there was a way.

A red legend flashed onto Daniel's display:

SA MAIN SET.

Adele had relayed the signal from Woetjans on the hull and highlighted it.

As soon as the dorsal sail was—

Another legend, this time a message from Pasternak:

REACTION MASS TANKS AT 47%. SWITCH TO HIGH DRIVE?

Adele must be filtering all his communications. It wasn't RCN policy, but it was the right thing now with Adele Mundy making the choices and not enough time to do half of what had to be done. . . .

Ordinarily a ship switched from plasma thrusters to its much more efficient High Drive as soon as it rose out of an atmosphere. Though Gehenna was a large satellite, its atmosphere was thin enough to be called hard vacuum for most purposes, but the limited power available from the jury-rigged High Drive and the present desperate need made Daniel hesitate.

Woetjans signalled DA MAIN SET.

"Ship, this is Six," Daniel said, shutting down the thrusters. "Prepare to enter the Matrix. Entering Matrix—"

He'd set the switches minutes ago, a lifetime ago; he'd set the switches as soon as the Alliance heavy cruiser dropped back into normal space. He pushed the EXECUTE button with the tips of two fingers, hard enough to have shoved a hatch closed. A virtual keyboard didn't care about pressure, but Daniel Leary wasn't a man for half measures.

"—now!"

Daniel felt the shudder of the vessel slipping into a bubble of normal space driving through space-times more alien than the heart of a sun. The sensation was by now long familiar, but it wasn't and probably would never become comfortable. The physicists said that nothing changed—the *Goldenfels* herself and the volume bounded by the tips of her antennas remained a part of the universe in which the vessel was built and her crew was born.

The physicists were wrong. A one-time passenger could have told them that, let alone veteran spacers with hundreds or thousands of hours in the Matrix. The ship might remain part of normal space, but something interpenetrated it. You could feel the difference, a scratchy sensation like wearing another man's skin beneath your own, and sometimes you saw things.

Once Daniel had seen a group of humans shambling down a corridor identical to that of the *Swiftsure*, the ship on which he was in training. They were naked and blank eyed. Behind them strolled a feathered biped with compound eyes; it stared at Daniel in shock and horror before vanishing with its charges as suddenly as an image tilts away in a mirror.

Sometimes you saw things that weren't real. Things that Daniel told himself couldn't ever have been real.

"Ship, this is Six," he said. His face had fallen into a mechanical smile at that memory—that *false* memory. When he realized, his expression turned into wry self-amusement. "I've programmed our course. I'm going onto the hull now to supervise the rig. In seven hours we'll drop back to take a star sighting, then proceed to rendezvous with the *Princess Cecile*. I estimate that'll take another eighteen and a half hours."

He took a deep breath, then added, "Sissies, there's a possibility that we're not done fighting just yet. You deserve a chance to rest, but we all know that life isn't fair. If things work out as they may despite my best efforts, I'm confident that Alliance cruiser will know it's been in a fight. Six out."

He'd check the armament, but not just now. . . .

Daniel started to get up from his couch; the shock harness still gripped him. He touched the release stud and rose again, smiling at himself. He was more tired—more wrung out—than he'd realized. Well, he'd get some rest when he could, but that wouldn't be till they took their star-sight in seven hours time . . . and maybe not even then.

"Mistress Vesey, you have the conn," Daniel said, walking toward the airlock. He wouldn't be on the hull long, so he wasn't going to bother donning a rigging suit.

The sailcloth patch in the corridor ceiling quivered; well, the Power Room crew could switch to damage control duties now that the ship was in the Matrix. Vesey would take care of that without being told.

He stepped into the airlock. Adele was with him. Daniel looked at her in surprise. *She* had no business out on the hull.

But to tell the truth, neither did he: Woetjans could handle the rigging without the captain on the hull to watch. Daniel's presence was a matter of moral support, that was all. And so was Adele's, of course.

Daniel beamed and nodded to her. He had a good team. The *Goldenfels* might be short handed, but she had the best crew she'd carried since commissioning, of that he was sure.

And if the *Bluecher* caught them, as the *Bluecher* might very well—it'd be just as he'd told his crew: when it was over, they'd know they'd been in a fight.

When Adele thought about it, this short run from Gehenna had been one of the most physically uncomfortable voyages she'd made. When she wasn't thinking about it, though—and she hadn't thought about it except fleetingly—the discomfort really hadn't made any difference. She'd been busy, assimilating the enormous lump of data she'd scooped from the systems of Lorenz Base when the Alliance forces were bypassing communications safeguards during battle.

Most of what she'd gathered wasn't obviously useful, but if Daniel ever wanted to know—for example—the name of the leading rigger on the *Bluecher*'s starboard watch, she'd have him the information in a few flicks of her wands. And you never knew what Daniel would need.

Rigging suits were designed for extended use, but most of the crew—Adele included—were in general duty airsuits instead. Fortunately the damage control parties had managed to keep pressure in one of the heads, though they'd had to jury-rig a sailcloth airlock to do so. And if they hadn't—

If they hadn't, worse things happen in wartime. That was one of the many RCN cliches Adele had come to understand were the basic underpinnings of any capable military force: the ability to look at situations and call them by their right names, but still to function.

Adele smiled as her wands moved, segregating files involving Alliance contacts with members of the Commonwealth government and bureaucracy. Mistress Sand would want to know that information, but she probably wouldn't want it spread about Cinnabar generally or even the whole RCN. Many times information was most effective when it wasn't used. The same was true of any other weapon.

"Ship, this is Six," Daniel said. He sounded alert, but his voice had an edge as ragged as that of hacksawed steel. "We'll be transferring to the Princess Cecile in orbit, Sissies. Our riggers will cross first and set lines, then the rest of us. Those who're less familiar with vacuum—"

Adele grimaced. She counted as "less familiar" and was awkward besides, but some of the Power Room crew had never been outside a ship above the atmosphere.

"—will be tied to more experienced personnel. Let me emphasize: we don't have a lot of time, which is why I'm making this transfer in orbit rather than on the ground as I'd intended and Mr. Chewning expects. But nobody gets left behind, Sissies. We've come this far, we don't leave anybody behind. Six out."

When she looked down the corridor, Adele saw a Tech Two from the Power Room marshalling the other six personnel from the port watch. The starboard watch was on duty, so these superfluous crewmen would be the first to follow the riggers across to the Princess Cecile.

"Six, this is Six-one," said Vesey on the command channel. "We're scheduled to return to normal space in one minute. Do you have any further orders for me, over?"

"Bring us toward the Princess Cecile on thrusters at one-gee acceleration, Mistress Vesey," Daniel said. His voice was getting back to normal, like a door that doesn't squeal as loudly after use knocks the rust off its hinges. "I'll take the conn for the final approach. When I do so, get yourself and your people up on the hull for transfer. Break."

Adele glanced over her shoulder toward Daniel. She couldn't see his face because of his rigging suit, but she could easily imagine the smile with which he contemplated the future. It struck her as odd that Daniel genuinely expected to succeed at whatever risky plan he embarked on, and that his belief in success rubbed off on everybody following him—even gloomy cynics like Signals Officer Adele Mundy.

That general, completely illogical, expectation was at least part of the reason why Daniel and those he commanded usually *did* win through—if not by the path he'd chosen, then by another path that opened for them because they'd kept their heads when all Hell was breaking loose.

"Ship, this is Six," Daniel said. "We're returning to normal space—"

Adele felt every atom of her body turn inside out. The experience was horrible, worse than any pain and almost as bad as what she felt when *leaving* sidereal space.

"—now!"

She had her work; that drew Adele back from disorientation at once. Occasionally she wondered how people who *didn't* lose themselves in their work managed; but part of her noted that they didn't manage very well, and the other part of her dismissed those people as being beneath a sensible person's concern.

There were various ways to find a starship orbiting an uninhabited planet like the one above which the *Goldenfels* reentered sidereal space. Because Adele was a signals officer, and because the *Goldenfels* was a spy ship outfitted with receivers just as sensitive as those Mistress Sand's people had installed on the *Princess Cecile*, she simply searched for RF sources.

Even with its main transmitter shut down, a starship is a bright emitter across the radio spectrum. Every electric motor and generator, every current-carrying wire, and even the half-watt transceivers in the crew's commo helmets, was a broadcaster as far as Adele's equipment was concerned.

She found a vessel just visible above the edge of the nameless, dun-colored planet, pinged its identification transponder with a modulated laser to make sure that it was the *Princess Cecile* and not an unpleasant surprise, and said over the command channel as she locked her laser communicator to follow its target, "Captain, this is signals. I have a channel open to the *Princess Cecile* if you'd like to talk to her. Over."

Sun turned at his console to stare at her, and she heard Vesey gasp in amazement. Tovera, seated on the other side of the holographic display, gave as broad a grin as Adele ever recalled seeing on her face.

Which was slightly embarrassing, because Adele had to admit that she'd intended precisely that result. She'd prepared her search protocols long before the *Goldenfels* came out of the Matrix. She'd executed them as quickly as possible, not because of the danger the ship was in but because she consciously and deliberately wanted to astound everybody with her competence.

"*Goldenfels* Six to RCS *Princess Cecile*," Daniel said, taking over the transmitter without wasting time responding to Adele's implicit boasting. "*Hold your orbit, Mr. Chewning, we'll match velocities with you in thirteen, I say again one-three, minutes. And Mr. Chewning—get your antennas raised. We'll be transferring personnel in vacuum rather than setting down, and I want to be able to get out of the region immediately upon accomplishing that.* Goldenfels *over.*"

Adele felt the ship shifting, flexing a little under push of the plasma thrusters. Ordinarily that was disquieting, but she found it oddly reassuring after the omnidirectional *pressure* of the Matrix.

There was what seemed to Adele an extremely long delay. She realized that though she'd—though her equipment had—driven a line of sight to the *Princess Cecile*, she had no idea of how far the corvette was from them nor in which direction it was orbiting. Had it gone behind . . . ? No, there it was, the signal source still highlighted on her display.

"Good God, sir!" came Chewning's voice. *"That is, Sissie Six to Goldenfels Six, we'll hold as ordered and get our antennas up. Ah, welcome back, sir. Sissie out."*

He was sending through a microwave transmitter, presumably because nobody on the *Princess Cecile* had been able to lock a laser on the *Goldenfels* to respond in that much more secure fashion. Adele pursed her lips; she'd do something about training as soon as she was back aboard the corvette.

There was a good deal of bustle behind her. The power room techs were going through the airlock to the hull.

Tovera had risen to her feet, wearing a sub-machine gun slung across her chest. Adele wondered whether she'd be able to use the weapon effectively while wearing an air suit and decided that, being Tovera, she probably would. Tovera was as soulless as a machine, but she had the virtues of a machine as well. The things she was programmed to do, she did superbly well regardless of circumstances.

Adele continued her work, dumping the information she'd gathered on the *Goldenfels* into the *Princess Cecile*'s computer. She'd only been able to review a fraction of it on the run from the Radiance system, but there'd be plenty of time for proper study when she was back aboard the *Princess Cecile*.

The corvette would be even more crowded than usual, she supposed, what with the former Alliance spacers added to the crew and a few Morzangan natives on the *Sissie* doing simple tasks. Well, that didn't matter.

"*Signals*," said the voice of brusque, calm Lieutenant Leary at the command console. "*A ship has just reentered sidereal space three hundred kay miles distant. Will you query her and determine who she really is, over?*"

When a ship moved between sidereal space and the Matrix, it caused a brief warping of space-time. The *Goldenfels'* sensors recognized and reported the distortion on the PPI, and probably on the attack and gunnery boards as well. It hadn't appeared on Adele's signals display till she imported it with a twitch of her wands.

Her face didn't have much expression, which she supposed was normal for her. The vessel's identification transponder said it was the freighter *Citoyen* out of Kostroma, but the locator beacon—which normally wouldn't be tripped unless the ship were crippled or derelict—said it was Alliance Fleet Ship *Bluecher*, as they'd feared and expected.

"It's the *Bluecher*," Adele said on the two-way link. If Daniel wanted the rest of the crew to know the situation, he'd tell them. Beneath her the thrusters changed note, cutting and then blipping several times before roaring at high output.

"*Citoyen*, this is the *Parsifal* out of Bryce," Adele announced calmly, using the main transmitter and her upper-class Bryce accent. "Have you met any other Alliance vessels? We were to rendezvous with the *Goldenfels* out of Pleasaunce. Over."

When the *Bluecher* pinged them, their identification transponder would announce that they were the *Parsifal*. If the *Bluecher*'s signals officer was as skilled as Captain Semmes obviously was and therefore knew how to trip the locator beacon, it would tell him the same thing. Obsessive behavior is a desirable trait in librarians—and spies.

The pause this time was one Adele expected. At last a female voice said, *"Freighter* Parsifal, *this is* Citoyen. *What is the ship in orbit with you? We can see there's a second ship. Answer immediately, over!"*

A text message from Daniel crawled across the bottom of Adele's display:

CAN YOU REMOTE FROM HELMETS SO WE LEAVE
SOONEST MOST URGENT

The letters were in puce, though how Daniel'd managed to do that was beyond Adele. It was clever of him to have picked up on text as a way of not interfering with critical radio traffic.

Adele made several adjustments to the communications system, using her wands to control the console. Her handheld unit was already stowed in a pouch attached to her equipment belt. She slipped the wands in their slots and said, *"Citoyen*, it looks like a derelict warship. Captain Vanness is aboard now, taking stock. He won't be able to reply until he's back aboard. We don't have suit radios. Over."

Certain that the hookup worked, she unlatched her shock harness. She would've floated away if Daniel hadn't grabbed her and propelled her toward the airlock. Hogg and Tovera sandwiched them, as usual. There was nobody else left on the *Goldenfels'* bridge or in the A Deck corridor.

Adele felt deaf and blind with only the clumsy helmet link to connect her with the outside world. She could shift between communication modes, but she wasn't in touch with *all* portions of the electro-optical spectrum simultaneously. At a time when she and her companions were within a heartbeat of destruction, she desperately wanted the connection as a security blanket. It gave her the hope that she *might* be able to do something to help.

Adele didn't try to control herself, simply allowed Daniel to muscle her through the hatches like a sack of grain. Weightless or not, her suited body was of respectable mass. He gripped the equipment belt in the middle of her back, then simply shoved and jerked. They moved as fast as the unburdened Hogg did in the lead.

The airlock was open, inner and outer hatches both, turning the chamber into a passage. That made sense since they were abandoning the *Goldenfels*, but it still shocked Adele's sense of rightness.

"Parsifal, *this is AFS* Bluecher," a male voice said abruptly. "*Shut down everything but your auxiliary power unit. Do not light your thrusters or High Drive. You will be destroyed if you do not obey these instructions to the letter. Do you understand, over?*"

This system's sun was a tiny dot in the black heavens but so brilliant that Adele's faceshield darkened automatically to save her retinas. The light turned the antennas and rigging into knife-edges where it struck them, but left them rifts in existence when they were in shadow unrelieved by the softening of an atmosphere. Adele had spent little time on the hull in normal space. Its appearance in the Matrix was a liquid, ever-changing thing far different from this harshness.

"Good God, *Bluecher!*" Adele said as Daniel dragged her to a line that she wouldn't have seen if he hadn't bent her arms around it the first time. "Have you gone mad? We're Alliance merchants, we're from Bryce! What do you mean by threatening us, over?"

There was the *Princess Cecile*! Adele assumed it was the *Princess Cecile*, at any rate, but she couldn't really make out the shape. The vessel was half-brilliant, half-darker than the space between worlds; there at least wide-spread atoms glowed with the energy of their creation. The ship was at least a quarter mile distant, though that too was hard to judge under the present light conditions.

Daniel clipped the end of a short safety cord to Adele's equipment belt; the other end was already secured to his own. Hogg was pulling himself toward the corvette, his legs crossed around the line connecting the two ships and his arms pulling him with long, powerful motions.

Daniel sailed past Adele, caught the line, and began doing the same. When he reached the ten-foot length of the safety cord, he jerked Adele along with him. She knitted her gloved fingers, making a loop of her arms, and tried not to brush the line as she wobbled after him.

"Parsifal, *don't worry about what I mean!*" snarled the signal from the heavy cruiser. "*Just do as you're told, or you'll be piecing the story together in Hell! Shut off all but minimal systems power until our pinnace boards you, or you'll take the consequences.* Bluecher *out!*"

Because there was no air resistance and they were fighting inertia rather than gravity, Daniel continued to accelerate himself and Adele as they neared the *Princess Cecile*. The corvette's masts were at full extension, spreading nobly in all four directions from her axis, but the furled sails gave her yards a fleshy, uncomfortable look.

Adele was echoing both sides of the discussion on Daniel's receiver, but he could speak only on intercom unless she unlocked his unit. She hadn't had time to explain what she was doing, but they didn't dare chance Daniel saying something that would unmask her deception. She'd apologize when they had the time, but the first priority was surviving the next few minutes.

"*Bluecher*," Adele said in feigned exasperation, "we'll obey you, but I won't lie and claim I understand. When Captain Vanness gets back you can take it up with him. *Parsifal* out."

She'd known a man named Vanness once. He hadn't shown much talent for library work but he'd tried his best, and his bloody murder was one of the scenes that came in the night to plague her. One of many scenes, by now; but she'd chosen the life.

She looked past Daniel's legs. They were really rocketing toward the corvette's hull now. What if they—

Hogg, just ahead of them, dived into a billowing length of sail fabric stretched between two stanchions. A pair of waiting riggers swung him out of the way.

Daniel twisted his body like a skilled gymnast despite the bulk of his rigging suit; his boots hit the left stanchion. He took up the shock by bending his knees, leaving the center of the fabric barrier for Adele.

She plowed into it face-first. She'd tried to get her arms out, but she'd misjudged the distance and was tumbling when she hit with an impact that jarred her head back unpleasantly. She'd be lucky if she got nothing worse than a headache from it.

"*Cast off!*" Daniel shouted over the intercom as hands grabbed Adele. Instead of clanking the weak permanent magnets in her bootsoles down onto the steel hull, two riggers held her between them as they followed Daniel. Adele was still tied to him, she realized, though she wasn't sure he remembered it. "*And Mr. Chewning, get under weigh now! Now!*"

"*Sir, they're launching!*" Chewning shouted, no longer sounding laboriously dull. "*They're launching missiles!*"

The line from the *Goldenfels* to the *Princess Cecile* was tied to a bitt near the *Sissie's* open dorsal airlock. Daniel dived into the chamber on top of Hogg, and the riggers carried Adele in just ahead of Tovera. As the outer lock began to cycle closed, she felt the jagged note of the High Drive motors starting up. Their vibration was at a much higher frequency than that of the plasma thrusters.

"All the more reason to get under weigh, Chewning," Daniel said in a cheerful voice. He grinned at Adele as he reached for the control to open the inner hatch. On their two-way link he added, *"While there's life, there's hope, eh, Adele?"*

She smiled back. He really did make the absurd seem possible. And so maybe it was.

CHAPTER 31

Daniel wished he had time to strip off his rigging suit, but the best he could do for the time being was to unlock his helmet and twist it to release as he threw himself down at the command console. A quick shuffle through the displays showed him that things were as well as could be expected: they were accelerating at 1.4 gravities, as much as the High Drive could manage when the corvette was so heavily loaded. Woetjans' riggers had begun setting the sails according to plan, now that the *Princess Cecile* was unmasked as fully operational.

The *Bluecher* had launched a spread of twelve missiles, a full salvo, which Daniel supposed he should take as flattering. Captain Semmes thought so well of the *Goldenfels'* commander that he was using all available force to crush what on the face of it was the crippled remnant of an initially weak opponent. Perhaps when all this was over, it would give Daniel a warm feeling; what he saw now was certain destruction accelerating toward them at 12 Gees.

Daniel punched a three-stroke combination into his

keyboard, triggering the complex program of commands he'd prepared aboard the *Goldenfels* before abandoning her. Missiles launched from both the freighter's tubes, and her thrusters lit at full power. The missile courses were vague approximations, but that wouldn't be certain to the *Bluecher* till they burned out.

He doubted that either of those things were going to befuddle Semmes, but they provided a few more factors on the Alliance commander's plate. Though Semmes seemed to have all the cards from where Daniel sat on the other side of the table, he knew that things would look different on the bridge of the *Bluecher*.

Betts had been alone on the *Sissie's* bridge until the regular crew arrived from the *Goldenfels*; Chewning and Dorst had been handling gunnery and command duties from their usual station in the Battle Center.

Sun, still wearing his airsuit, was at the gunnery console now, but the *Sissie's* four 4-inch plasma cannon couldn't significantly affect the oncoming missiles. There was no hope for escape save into the Matrix, and that was only a momentary bolthole. The corvette didn't have enough way on to get any significant distance from their present location, no matter how many times their relative velocity was multiplied.

"Ship, this is Six," Daniel said. "We're entering the Matrix—"

His left hand shut off the High Drive; his right thrust two fingers down hard to initiate the entry sequence. A complex charge built on the *Princess Cecile's* hull, acting both as pressure and a lubricant, forcing and allowing the vessel to slip from sidereal space into the complex of other space-times.

"—now."

To those aboard the *Princess Cecile*, it was as if time dragged on at an agonizing crawl during which the individual atoms of their beings turned inside out. In fact time was moving just as fast as it ever did, but within the bubble of special space-time movement slowed. The actual process of insertion into or extraction from the Matrix took anywhere from thirty seconds to a minute, depending on the energy gradients involved.

And it didn't affect the *Bluecher*'s missiles. Daniel had what was either a Matrix hallucination or a flashback to the time he was one with the Tree on New Delphi: the missiles launched on initially diverging courses which then curved back toward intersection; their twin High Drive motors reaching burn-out and shutting down as each round split into three segments, moving at .6 C and packing so much kinetic energy that a thermonuclear warhead would add complexity without increasing the effect of a hit; the segments crisscrossing the volume of space containing the *Goldenfels* and the *Princess Cecile*.

He'd hoped the *Goldenfels* would successfully make the transition into the Matrix where its track would at least be a distraction for Captain Semmes when he came hunting the *Sissie*. The freighter'd begun her programmed sequence at the same time as the corvette did, but the bigger vessel still wallowed in normal space when segments of two Alliance missiles plunged into her.

For an instant the *Goldenfels* looked like a barbell, untouched amidships but her bow and stern ionized by the impacts. Then the shockwaves met in the center and left nothing but an expanding fireball.

The vision faded, or the hallucination. Daniel blinked. For a moment he couldn't see the numbers cascading across his display as he ran course calculations.

A ship is merely a tool to be used, and if she breaks in use, well, that's part of life. Besides, the *Goldenfels* was an Alliance vessel, never formally taken into RCN service.

But for a short while Lieutenant Daniel Leary had commanded her. She'd served him and Cinnabar well during that time, and against all logic he regretted her loss. Though maybe it was only hallucination. . . .

Daniel took a deep breath. He'd seen/felt/imagined a segment of missile passing through the *Princess Cecile*, a quartering shot that struck on the starboard counter and passed out on the port bow. The missile and the corvette didn't exist in quite the same space-time simultaneously, but the almost-contact had made Daniel shiver for reasons that weren't entirely psychological.

He focused on his display. The astrogational computer had calculated where the *Princess Cecile* was in sidereal space. Daniel sighed. He'd entered the Matrix a good minute and a half sooner than he'd intended to. On a hunch, he supposed; and he'd been correct, that flashing missile would assuredly have vaporized the corvette if he'd been even a few seconds slower. Even so, the *Sissie* would have to return to the sidereal universe very soon to get up to useful velocities if they were to have any real hope of escape.

The truth was, Captain Semmes was as good as Daniel Leary was, and the *Bluecher* was far superior in all respects to the *Princess Cecile*. Daniel didn't really see how the contest was going to have a positive ending, but even the best commanders make mistakes. If Semmes made the first one, the *Sissie* could capitalize on it to escape. And if Daniel Leary made the mistake, well—

He grinned as he locked his helmet on again and rose from the console.

—it was hard to imagine that making their present situation worse. He supposed it was liberating, knowing that he wouldn't have to blame himself for a bad outcome. Of course he probably wouldn't have long for breast-beating anyway, given the velocities at which missiles travelled.

"Ship, this is Six," he said, starting for the airlock. "I'm going out to view the Matrix and adjust our plotted course from the hull. Mr. Chewning, you're in command of the ship, but I will be conning us through the semaphore system. Do you have any questions, over?"

Daniel wanted to rub his eyes, but it was too late—he'd closed his helmet. He was very tired, tired to the point that he felt disassociated from his body, but that wasn't a wholly bad thing. The Matrix seemed closer when his mind could float in it.

"Aye aye, sir," said Chewing, stolid and cheerful again. "Good hunting, over."

"What I'm hunting for, Mr. Chewning," Daniel said as he closed the airlock, "is a way out of this mess. Over."

"Roger, sir," said Chewning. "And I speak for all the crew when I say good hunting. Out."

Daniel heard general laughter as he shut off his intercom to go out on the hull. Then the only laughter remaining was his own.

The great danger of working on the hull of a ship in the Matrix was that you'd lose your grip and sail off into alien space-times, alone for eternity. It was the riggers' great fear, the one they'd only talk about when they were very drunk.

Adele walked across the hull with her left hand on the safety cord, her boots going *click-click-click* as the small magnets in the soles mated with the steel hull plating. She was careful because she was always careful doing things she wasn't very good at, but she wasn't especially afraid.

Death hadn't frightened Adele since the day she

learned her whole family had been executed. As for the manner of her death, the part that seemed to bother other people particularly—Adele had always felt apart from the people around her. The irony of becoming Adele Mundy, Bubble Universe, rather amused her. Not that she *wanted* that to happen.

Daniel stood at a semaphore platform between the first and second antennas of the dorsal row. The maincourses of both were furled, but the topsails and the sails above the topsails—Adele instinctively reached for her data unit to check the name, then remembered she didn't and didn't dare carry it here—stretched from the pressure of Casimir radiation bearing on them. Above, filling everything beyond the bubble of the *Princess Cecile* and the crew aboard her, was the pulsing, sullen, magnificence of the Matrix—of all worlds and all times, pressing in on the starship which had intruded on them for this brief instant.

Daniel's gauntleted fingers moved on the controls while his face remained turned to the patterns above. A rigger moved to the foremost mast and began to climb swiftly hand-over-hand. A latch had stuck or a cable was fouled; a human being was going aloft to free it so that another sail could billow out to match those Adele saw spreading at the peaks of the five masts behind it in the row.

She stepped forward, placing herself across the semaphore stand from Daniel; there he would see her but she'd remain out of his way. Catching the motion or perhaps feeling the tremble of her boots on the hull, he looked toward Adele and grinned through the heavy faceplate of his rigging suit.

Daniel motioned her forward, then touched his helmet to hers. Pointing toward the heavens with his right arm, he said, "There's a discontinuity there that we're following." His voice distant but very clear as it rang through the two helmets. "I don't suppose you see it . . . ?"

But obviously he hoped she did. Well, Adele thought she could make a librarian out of Daniel, but the chance of him making her an astrogator was something below the likelihood that she'd become Speaker of the Cinnabar Senate.

Nonetheless she looked upward, trying to follow the sweep of Daniel's arm. To her, looking into the Matrix was like staring at a well-stirred vanilla pudding—which was glowing brightly besides.

"I'm afraid I don't, Daniel," she said apologetically. It was something that mattered a great deal to him, and he doubtless regretted that it meant nothing whatever to her. "Is it a faster way home than, than another way would be?"

"Ah?" he said in puzzlement. "Oh, I see what you mean. It's a good passage at that, better in this direction than the other, to tell the truth. But what we're actually doing is retracing the route by which we came from Radiance to the rendezvous point. There we'll reenter normal space for the first time, build up speed, and then strike for Todos Santos."

He paused, eyeing the quivering splendor for a moment in silence. Then he bent into contact with Adele again and went on, "I'm hoping that Captain Semmes will lose our new course in our backtrail. There's so much traffic into Radiance that only God Himself could follow us on a cold track outbound."

He coughed and added, "And God, of course, is on the side of Cinnabar."

"Of course," Adele said without emphasis. She assumed Daniel was joking—while religion wasn't an acceptable subject of conversation in the RCN, she'd certainly never known him to visit a temple—but his assurance of the *rightness* of the RCN was at least very close to religious faith. Daniel was a sophisticated man in many respects, but there were parts of him that were frankly childish.

Of course, if the God Adele didn't believe in had provided the RCN with commanders like Daniel Leary, then he was correct in his faith.

"What I'd really like to do would be to load reaction mass on Radiance," he continued, "but at this point I don't trust the Commonwealth government to accept the story that the *Sissie* is a private yacht."

He chuckled; Adele heard the sound as a distant grunting.

"Though in fact that's just what we are, you know."

As Daniel talked, he continued to watch the Matrix. He made a slight adjustment at the semaphore. Adele didn't see any change in the sails from where she stood, but the glowing pudding overhead began slowly to rotate around the corvette's axis, a motion distinct from the streaks which seemed to move longitudinally.

"Will we be all right?" Adele asked. She hoped she didn't sound frightened; she wasn't, after all, she was just curious. What happened if they ran out of reaction mass?

"Oh, heavens, yes," Daniel said. "Only we're down to 58%, which means we'll have to make at least one landfall before we reach Todos Santos."

He coughed and continued, speaking with a degree of reserve, "Chewning did a fine job, a very professional job, but instead of orbiting at the rendezvous point, he kept the power on to maintain artificial gravity. He's experienced, but he'd never seen action before. I don't think I sufficiently emphasized to him that in war the only things you can count on are the ones you hold in your hand."

"Daniel?" Adele said. He'd brought it up himself,

noting that the *Sissie* was a private yacht. "Have you considered what will happen if the Commonwealth government lodges a formal complaint? We're not at war with the Alliance, not officially, and very likely there were Commonwealth citizens killed at Lorenz Base also."

This wasn't something she wanted to talk about, but she felt she had to. There were no secrets within a starship, especially a small ship like the *Princess Cecile* carrying thirty-odd crew in addition to her Table of Organization. Out here on the hull, though, no one could overhear what she had to say.

"Yes," said Daniel. "That what we did was technically piracy, you mean?"

He snorted, then went on, "Call a spade a spade—it *was* piracy, of course. I thought about the fact that the *Goldenfels* rather than a Cinnabar-registered ship made the attack, but the story'll get out after we dock. Assuming matters go as we hope they will in the Radiance system and afterwards, of course, so that we do get back."

Daniel looked at the heavens, reached for the semaphore control, and brought his hand back without touching it. He leaned his helmet against hers and said, "Adele, I never had the stomach for politics, but Speaker Leary's son isn't going to grow up without knowing how the game's played. I understand very well that the best result so far as the government of Cinnabar is concerned would be if the *Princess Cecile* vanished without a trace and the attack on Lorenz Base remained a mystery. Guarantor Porra would be more than happy to suppress the news, I'm sure. But . . ."

He turned his face upward again, though this time Adele was by no means sure it was anything within the Matrix that Daniel was focusing on. Touching her helmet again, he said, "Adele, every soul aboard the

Princess Cecile trusts me to get them home. I don't know that I'm going to succeed—our trick of backtracking wouldn't have fooled me, and I don't expect it'll fool Captain Semmes either. But I owe the Sissies more than I owe Cinnabar, and by God! if I fail them, it won't be for want of trying."

"No," said Adele. "Nobody who knows you would imagine anything else, Daniel."

And just maybe, God *was* on the side of Cinnabar.

CHAPTER 32

"—*now!*" said Daniel's voice over the general channel, and everything except the interior of Adele's mind blurred in what had become a familiarly horrible fashion. Transition was worse than travel in the Matrix, and that was uncomfortable enough.

Adele thought for a moment about the times in her life when she hadn't been uncomfortable. There'd been many of them, long periods in fact, but they all involved her being lost in her studies or her work. It was difficult to work while the starship was in transition, but perhaps she ought to try harder in the future.

The *Princess Cecile* had been three days on the voyage from the rendezvous point—Salmson Catalog 115A3 but otherwise unnamed—to Radiance, a distance the *Goldenfels* had covered in a little over a day. The difference was the ship's velocity at the time they entered the Matrix. They could've dropped back into normal space to increase speed once they'd gotten clear of the *Bluecher*—Dorst had asked about the possibility—but Daniel had preferred to take the longer, less exposed route.

As Adele knew from their private conversations, Daniel didn't believe they _had_ gotten clear of the _Bluecher_. While the _Princess Cecile_ was in the Matrix, she couldn't be touched by an enemy who, no matter how skillful, was literally in another universe.

The sidereal universe returned as though somebody'd rolled back the rug covering Adele's existence. Things were brighter, sharper, and the communications display came alive with RF emitters. Adele had purpose again, so she was content.

They'd reentered normal space 250,000 miles from Radiance and almost three times as far from Gehenna, on the sunward side of its primary. There were thirty-seven vessels in what Adele had set as her immediate coverage area, a sphere with a million-mile diameter centered between Radiance and the moon. Many of the ships were orbiting Radiance at a lower level, preparing to land or to light their High Drives before entering the Matrix. Those were the normal traffic of a busy commercial port.

Another of the ships was the _Bluecher_, orbiting Gehenna within the Planetary Defense Array.

"Unidentified ship exiting Matrix," said a male voice transmitting from the cruiser on microwave. _"This is AFS_ Bluecher. _Identify yourself immediately or we'll destroy you, over."_

"Daniel," said Adele, clipping the syllables short as her wands arranged the other thirty-six vessels by type at the edge of her display. "They're calling on tight-beam, that means they were watching us return to normal space."

Ten of the ships orbiting Radiance were elements of the Commonwealth fleet. They were 600-ton vessels no different from those trading and raiding all over the Galactic North save that their crews were paid—indifferently—by the State, and that they were armed

with batteries of short-range rockets. No Commonwealth warship had been aloft when the *Goldenfels*
attacked Lorenz Base four days earlier. That disaster
had obviously convinced the Commonwealth government to lock its barn door, now that the horses had
been stolen.

"*Roger,*" said Daniel imperturbably. "*And targeting
us, no doubt. They'll have visual identification shortly,
but stall them if you can, over.*"

Adele opened her mouth to reply to the *Bluecher*
and froze. *Good God, would they be able to recognize her voice?* She switched her transmission to the
upper sideband so that the compression would conceal her voice to most ears—and said, "*Bluecher*, this
is AFS *Nymphe*, Lieutenant Archimbault commanding. Admiral Raeder sent us ahead to make sure
Lorenz Base is prepared to take his squadron in thirty
hours time, over."

If the *Bluecher* had them under optical observation,
they couldn't pass for a country craft—Adele's first
choice—nor even a merchant vessel from the Alliance
or one of the neutral worlds outside the two power
blocks. The *Princess Cecile's* slim lines and the suit of
sails that required a large crew to work marked her
as a warship beyond question. The only option was to
pretend to be an Alliance warship.

"*Nymphe, shut down your High Drive,*" the voice
ordered after a delay greater than the considerable
distance separating the vessels explained. He didn't
make any comment about the fact the "*Nymphe*"—
a real sloop in the Fleet list, one of a series of false
identities Adele had ready for emergencies—was
responding on a single sideband in the 20-meter
range. "*Our cutter will board you after you've fallen
into orbit, over.*"

The *Bluecher* must have a very skilled team on its

sensors to've been able to spot the distortion of the *Sissie's* imminent arrival. Still, they seemed to be fooled—

"*Sir, they're launching!*" Sun shouted over the command net.

Daniel's hands moved. The thrusters and High Drive lit together, braking the *Princess Cecile* more fiercely than Adele had ever before felt.

"*Mr. Betts, fire one!*" Daniel shouted as he fought the throttles into balance. The solid *CLANG* of a slug of vaporized reaction mass ejecting the 30-ton missile rang through the *Buzz!* and *Burr!* of the power units. "*Fire two!*"

Adele didn't have leisure to call up a realtime display, but the relative positions of the ships on her signals board indicated that the *Princess Cecile* was diving toward Radiance. She was confident Daniel knew what he was doing, and regardless she had enough things on her plate to occupy her.

The emitter of the laser communicator was formed by fifteen separate light guides. They could operate in unison, in bundles, or as individual lenses sending an ultra-tight-beam message in fifteen simultaneous directions.

Adele split the emitter to target the ten Commonwealth warships and said, "Peacock Throne—" the call sign of the control station in the Palace of Delegates below "—to all Commonwealth vessels. The Alliance of Free Stars is launching a surprise attack on the Commonwealth. Destroy the cruiser *Bluecher* at all costs! It's preparing to launch missiles into the spaceport and palace. Destroy the cruiser at once!"

She was scrambling her message according to the Commonwealth naval code for the month. The automated response from the receiving units indicated that three of the ships didn't have the code loaded, so she looped her signal alternating scrambled and clear. *Idiots! Couldn't anybody do his job?*

Sun's bow guns hammered, trying to turn an oncoming missile by blasting material off one side to nudge the remainder in the opposite direction. It was impossible to destroy a solid, multi-ton projectile, but with luck and sufficient time the plasma cannon might redirect it. The range here was probably too short for even that.

"Holy God our savior!" cried somebody who must've been watching imagery of the battle. Almost with the words, a vibrating *Whang!* heeled the *Princess Cecile* violently to starboard. A missile had severed an antenna or mainspar, thick steel tubing whose structural strength couldn't withstand the impact of a projectile accelerated to an appreciable fraction of the speed of light.

The *Sissie* launched two more missiles in succession, rocking with the recoil of each. Adele had studied the data on their opponent while she was providing it to the command group. The heavy cruiser mounted twelve missile tubes and had a hundred and twenty reloads in its magazines. The details would mean more to Daniel than they did to her, but it would be obvious to a child that a straight-up slugging match between a cruiser and a corvette with only half her normal twenty missiles could end only one way. "Bluecher, *what in God's name are you doing!"* Adele screamed into the sideband transmitter. "Admiral Raeder will feed you to the antimatter converters, you idiots! Stop shooting!"

She didn't expect her feigned panic would convince the *Bluecher* to cease fire, but it might. She wondered how the *Bluecher* had unmasked them. Probably they'd gotten a solid visual identification and had acted on it; Captain Semmes was obviously a decisive captain as well as a skillful one.

Adele focused a microwave on one of the net of communications satellites orbiting Radiance. She linked to channels for the Commonwealth navy and government, and also to The Word of God, the state-run civilian broadcasting system. "Alliance warships are attacking Commonwealth vessels!" she said. "Launch all ships immediately or they'll be destroyed on the ground! The cruiser *Bluecher* is attacking Commonwealth vessels!"

The confusion of additional scores of vessels milling above Radiance would make the *Bluecher*'s calculations more difficult. It might not help much, but it'd help; and anyway, it was something for Adele to do while the *Princess Cecile* maneuvered violently.

Other people could put their faith in God, but Adele would get along with belief in the things she could touch:

Semmes was skillful, but he wasn't as good as Daniel Leary.

The *Bluecher*'s spacers weren't as good as the Sissies.

And whoever Semmes had for a signals officer couldn't match Adele Mundy.

"Alliance warships are attacking the Commonwealth!" she cried as she felt two more missiles slam from their tubes. The plasma cannons' firing drummed through the hull, and a heavy shove twisted the corvette as something ripped away part of her sails.

"Launch all ships immediately to engage the cruiser *Bluecher*!"

The *Sissie*'s antennas were raised, so Daniel couldn't land on Radiance even if he'd been ready to kill the riggers on the hull. Buffeting on the way through the atmosphere was rough even with the antennas and yards telescoped and the sails furled about them. The best that'd happen if the ship came down with her antennas at full extension was that everything would wrench off. If by some miracle it didn't, they still couldn't set down on the ventral row.

Woetjans had both watches out, ready to instantly adjust the sails however Daniel wanted them. She'd figured that they wouldn't want to stay in the Radiance system any longer than they had to, once Daniel had calculated the best escape route based on what he saw when they came out of the Matrix. This would've been their first star sighting since they'd fled Salmson 115A3.

The bosun was correct about them not having much time, but unfortunately they had even less time than that. The *Bluecher* was so close and so alert that the corvette had no chance whatever of returning to the Matrix before a salvo of missiles arrived.

But if Radiance wasn't a bolthole, at least it was big enough to stop Alliance missiles and direct observation. Daniel was diving toward the planet as the only chance the *Princess Cecile* had of surviving the next five minutes. After that—well, first get the five minutes.

"Betts, fire at will!" Daniel shouted over the command push as he tried to do three things at once. It'd be tempting to conserve the *Princess Cecile*'s slight stock of missiles, but unless they managed to screw up the *Bluecher*'s plans, the corvette would shortly take a direct hit that'd vaporize the missile magazine along with everything else.

Not even the coolest officer likes to see hostile missiles streaking across his attack board toward him. The slight chance of disconcerting the cruiser's command group was worth all the "what if?" fairy gold of saving rounds for later.

Daniel had programmed the first two missiles, but the rest Betts would have to aim. It was his job, after all, and he was perfectly able—he wouldn't have been aboard the *Princess Cecile* at this time if he weren't. He couldn't read Daniel's mind, though. In a perfect universe the *Sissie*'s missile launches and maneuvers would be parts of a choreographed whole.

Well, in a perfect universe the *Sissie* wouldn't have been trapped by a heavy cruiser commanded by a man who'd get Daniel's vote for Best Captain in the Alliance Fleet. And if it came to that, a perfect universe wouldn't need warships and fighting officers to command them. Daniel'd play the hand he'd been dealt.

There was only so much he could do. Semmes hadn't expected his prey to dive for the planet, but his twelve-missile salvo had allowed him to hedge his bets. Space might be infinite, but in human terms a corvette covered a considerable volume of it with her antennas extended seventy feet from the hull in all directions.

Daniel's Plot Position Indicator was three-dimensional and multi-colored. The incoming missile tracks were blue with their predicted continuations in purple. A purple trace appeared to intersect with the yellow line of the *Princess Cecile*'s course. Daniel expanded that tiny segment till the corvette's 230-foot length filled the width of the display. The purple line was still there, merely a thread even at the larger scale.

Bloody Hell, it was going to—

Daniel couldn't *add* power, so he shut off the thrusters instead. The High Drive took thirty seconds to build or collapse, so he didn't bother with it. The effect of reduced braking was to move the *Sissie* slightly higher above Radiance and slightly forward of the path the astrogational computer had predicted.

The incoming missile segment slipped beneath her hull. If they'd been lucky it would've missed entirely, but it clipped Antenna Ventral B. The impact converted twenty feet of the mast to vapor which shredded the sails of VA and VC. Expanding gases rang the hull like a steel drum.

Daniel lit the thrusters again, knowing he was stressing the corvette beyond what her frames were meant to bear. He loved the *Princess Cecile* as much as a man could love a machine, but if she got her crew clear of this and back to Cinnabar then they could scrap her. *Pray God, just get the Sissies back to Cinnabar!*

Daniel reverted to a standard PPI. Instinct showed him the opportunity that the software couldn't have computed. He throttled the thrusters back to 70%, a slight but calculable reduction. The *Bluecher*'s sensors noticed the change and fed it into the attack computer. Three seconds later, the cruiser launched another salvo of missiles.

Missiles under power could follow a curving course. The *Princess Cecile* was ducking into the ballistic shadow of Radiance, but the cruiser's attack computer could send missiles into her predicted position even though there was no line of sight between the *Bluecher* and her prey.

"Chewning, get the riggers inside!" Daniel ordered, wishing he'd thought to say that before they lost people—almost certainly—on Ventral B. The riggers were of no use outside as things were. If the *Sissie* escaped into the Matrix they could go out again, but they weren't going to attempt to enter the Matrix while the *Bluecher* followed.

The cruiser had waited in an unpowered orbit so she was slow getting under weigh, but the acceleration of her missiles meant the launching vessel's speed didn't matter. The *Sissie* could keep Radiance between her and the *Bluecher* for the time being, but she couldn't get away; and when the cruiser got moving, the corvette couldn't hide either.

Daniel watched the PPI as an incoming missile's

curving track changed from purple to blue—then stopped abruptly when it intersected a Commonwealth warship. Daniel had factored in the other vessels, but the Alliance missileer had not. The victim bloomed as a varicolored fireball, not only superheated metal but the propellant and warheads of its rockets.

Another Commonwealth ship launched three salvos of forty-eight rockets apiece at the *Bluecher*. The range was too great for the primitive Commonwealth fire control computer, but the sheafs of tiny projectiles caused three more of the country craft to launch also. As soon as they'd emptied their external rocket racks, they dived for the surface of Radiance.

Daniel continued maneuvering to keep the planet between the *Princess Cecile* and the cruiser. He was dropping deeper into the gravity well also so that Radiance subtended a broader arc. It was a temporary expedient at best, since they were only ten thousand miles above the surface. That was a considerable altitude under most circumstances but a matter of minutes when it's your lifeline.

He'd expected to lose realtime imagery of the *Bluecher* as soon as he put the *Sissie* behind the planet, but there was no gap in coverage after all: the cruiser continued to be visible as a blur in the midst of ionized exhaust. Adele was importing a signal, probably from Lorenz Base. Commonwealth observation satellites were unlikely to be this clear if they even existed. How had she been able to do that?

But thank God she had!

Semmes had been accelerating on High Drive, but he cut in his plasma thrusters when the *Bluecher* became the target of hundreds of unguided rockets. Daniel judged his enemy's new course and adjusted the *Sissie* to stay in the planet's shadow in this deadly game of hide and seek.

Three Commonwealth ships unloaded their rockets at the cruiser, then two more. Great heavens, Daniel hadn't imagined a reaction anything like this when he tricked the *Bluecher* into destroying a country craft! He hadn't imagined the Commonwealth vessels *could* react that quickly even if they'd wanted to. It was as if they'd been waiting for an excuse to launch on an allied vessel!

More ships were rising from Radiance. Daniel couldn't tell whether they were civilian or more naval units; the only external difference was the bundles of rockets on naval vessels, easily overlooked among the folded rigging. Captain Semmes must not have been able to tell either, for the *Bluecher* suddenly opened fire on them with her 15-cm plasma cannon.

Daniel supposed Semmes was simply trying to discourage another irritating rocket volley, because nobody'd expect serious results from plasma cannon at a range of several hundred thousand miles. The guns were for defensive purposes, to deflect incoming missiles which couldn't be dodged. The country craft were so fragile, however, that the concentrated hammering of six cannon—only three of the cruiser's turrets bore on the target—caused the victim to stagger and curl back into the atmosphere.

A handful of Commonwealth rockets suddenly detonated against the *Bluecher*. The cruiser's image sparkled like a butterfly's wing shaking off scales. The rockets' small fragmentation warheads were meant to destroy an enemy vessel's masts and rigging so that it couldn't escape—or pursue, depending on who was pirate and who was prey during a given engagement. They wouldn't seriously damage the hull of a country craft, let alone the thick plates of an Alliance heavy cruiser.

But nobody likes to be shot at, to have the steel around him ring with slamming explosions followed by the sizzle of fragments that ricocheted among the rigging. Maybe it was for that reason that the *Bluecher*'s gunnery officer began ripping another rising Commonwealth ship instead of turning the concentrated fire of his cannon on a projectile from the *Princess Cecile* as he should've done.

The segment hit a stowed dorsal antenna, erupting in a white-hot spray like the tail of a comet nearing the sun. The damage wasn't serious, but everybody aboard the *Bluecher* knew that it could've been: that a course different by a matter of meters would've gutted the cruiser and left her adrift for the salvage teams.

The *Princess Cecile* now had at least a prayer of succeeding. The cruiser'd launched another salvo after vaporizing the Commonwealth ship, but those missiles had missed by several miles. Daniel resumed acceleration with both powerplants as soon as he'd put the *Sissie* behind Radiance. Semmes' missileer didn't have the direct observation of the *Princess Cecile* that Daniel—thanks to Adele—did of the *Bluecher*.

"*Six, there's a heavy vessel reentering sidereal space out-orbit of Radiance, over,*" said Vesey. She'd focused on her duties, watching the sensor board while the battle raged around her. Many officers with more experience wouldn't have been able to do that.

But it didn't matter now: the *Princess Cecile* would be clear or destroyed before the new opponent got sufficiently organized to take a hand. The description "heavy vessel" was based on the amount of distortion Vesey's instruments recorded as the newcomer reinserted itself into normal space-time. There hadn't been another cruiser in the Alliance squadron, so that probably meant one of the battleships had also been working up when the *Goldenfels* destroyed the vessels hangared at Lorenz Base.

"Ship, this is Six," Daniel said as his fingers pounded a new set of instructions into his virtual keyboard. "We will be entering the Matrix—"

His display flashed with orange letters each the size of his extended hand:

BREAK BREAK BREAK

"*RCS* Aristoxenos, *this is RCS* Princess Cecile," said Adele's voice over the announcement channel. "*We have a target for you, Admiral O'Quinn—an Alliance cruiser. All other vessels are friendly. I repeat, all vessels except the Alliance cruiser are friendly.* Princess Cecile *over.*"

Daniel felt the rocking clunk of the *Sissie*'s last two missiles sliding into the tubes, ready to launch. "Mr. Betts, cease fire!" he ordered, instinctively placing a lockout on the attack console. "Prepare attack solutions for the *Aristoxenos* and transmit them to her soonest. I don't trust their computers or their people either one, but the good Lord knows I'm glad to have their company, out!"

Betts had been doing a fine job, but he might not see the sudden necessity of holding the *Sissie*'s final rounds in reserve. Daniel would explain the situation when he had a moment, but the first priority was to prevent the Chief Missileer from spending what might otherwise become an opportunity to mousetrap the Alliance cruiser.

Adele was in conversation with the *Aristoxenos*. She'd cut Daniel into the channel but he was too busy controlling the *Princess Cecile* to worry about what they were saying.

The *Bluecher* had swung from its predicted course and shut down its thrusters when the missile grazed it. Daniel had to fight the *Sissie* back into Radiance's cone of shadow. As a practical matter, that meant dipping closer to the planet; they were already deep enough that the upper stratosphere created minuscule but noticeable drag. The corvette wasn't safe until the last Alliance projectile was headed harmlessly out of the system, and even then there was the problem of landing with what might be unnoticed damage.

The cruiser had stopped launching missiles with the fourth salvo. She was accelerating at 1.5 g, probably the best she could manage under the High Drive alone, along the course Semmes had set while he was preparing to winkle the *Princess Cecile* out of concealment. It would take her past Radiance on the down-orbit side—and, probably the major factor now—away from the *Aristoxenos*.

Semmes doesn't know what's happening, Daniel realized. He must be pretty sure the newcomer wasn't a friend, but he couldn't be certain she was an enemy either. Having managed to get into combat with his Commonwealth allies, he'd be especially cautious not to repeat the mistake with—

The *Aristoxenos* launched four missiles at the *Bluecher*. One of them described a tight arc. It was headed back toward the battleship when one or both High Drive motors failed and the missile disintegrated into a sphere of molten droplets.

The *Bluecher* responded with a salvo split between the *Aristoxenos* and the *Princess Cecile*. The cruiser was extending its antennas. A large piece drifted away, the spar damaged by the *Sissie's* missile, cast off or broken off by the acceleration.

The battleship had thirty-six missile tubes: thirty-one launched at the *Bluecher*. The thirty-second tube exploded, a blue-white cancer against the vessel's bow which took fifteen seconds to burn down. Daniel keyed in his final corrections, waited a heartbeat for a green icon to indicate the attack computer concurred, and launched the *Sissie*'s remaining two missiles.

He boosted thrust from the High Drive. The *Sissie* was far more nimble, now; even the half-magazine of missiles she'd carried on this voyage weighed in aggregate a quarter of the corvette's empty weight. The six missiles the *Bluecher*'d just launched blindly at them weren't a serious threat. The cruiser's missileer would've been smarter to direct the entire salvo at the battleship for which he had full course and speed information.

Daniel brought the *Princess Cecile* out from behind Radiance, adjusting their course to a line nearly reciprocal to that of the *Bluecher*. He touched a port-side plasma thruster, then countered the thrust instantly with a blip from starboard, rolling the ship 30 degrees on her axis so that her dorsal and ventral turrets both bore on the cruiser.

"Sun," he ordered, "dust 'em up! I want to give them something to think about besides their proper jobs!"

"Roger, roger!" the gunner said delightedly, swinging his guns to take advantage of the unexpected target. There was no practical reason to fire 4-inch plasma cannon at a cruiser over a quarter million miles away; the *Bluecher*'s own 15-cm weapons couldn't have done serious harm to the corvette at this distance. The psychological effect of plasma bolts—though only sprays at this range—flash-heating the cruiser's hull might cause somebody to make a mistake, though, the way the Commonwealth rocket salvoes had distracted a gunnery officer who should've been worrying about an incoming missile.

The ventral turret rubbed hard enough to send a squeal trembling through the whole vessel. It was supposed to be free-floating above the turret ring on magnetic repulsion. Given the strains the corvette had been taking Daniel supposed they ought to be thankful it rotated at all.

The *Princess Cecile* could probably escape while the cruiser was occupied with its new enemy, but the possibility barely crossed Daniel's mind like the chance of landing on Radiance. Neither was a real option: the latter because the corvette wasn't rigged for landing, the former because Daniel Leary was an RCN officer and the RCN didn't run from fights. Even mutineers remembered that, apparently, once they'd had a chance to reflect.

The *Aristoxenos'* antennas were extended with sails spread on many of them. O'Quinn hadn't taken the time—or perhaps had the crew—to clear the ship for action before entering sidereal space for what must've been meant as an attack on Lorenz Base. The *Aristoxenos* could've made a quick pass from outside the Planetary Defense Array, launched a salvo of missiles at the hangars, and then—if things worked out— escaped back into the Matrix before the Alliance survivors could respond.

It was a perfectly good plan, basically what Daniel had intended when he went to Todos Santos; though if the expatriate spacers had agreed then, they'd have had Adele's signals skill to make the task easier and a great deal more safe.

Daniel had to admit that it'd taken the *Aristoxenos* over a month to reach the Radiance system, though. Were it not for the *Sissie's* earlier attack, that would probably have been too late.

Not that he was complaining at the way matters had developed. Neither "easy" nor "safe" was a watchword of the RCN; victory, however, was.

As the *Bluecher's* half-salvo neared the *Aristoxenos*, the battleship's 8-inch plasma cannon began to fire from two turrets which the ship's own rigging didn't mask.

A double-pulse caught one of the missiles before it'd separated into segments, converting it into a sphere of glowing gas spreading at the rate of a nuclear explosion. Other bolts vaporized segments with such violence that their destruction buffeted the remaining parts of their clusters off course.

An 8-inch turret blew up with a white flash. A portion of the laser array that compressed the tritium pellet hadn't tripped, but the other lenses were sufficient to detonate the charge with only the gun's iridium breech to confine it. The blast sculpted a divot from the battleship's belly and sheared off two antennas of the ventral row.

That cleared a line for the other belly turret, which immediately began to fire. Battleships had independent targeting, and the turret captains were apparently tracking even though they couldn't fire until the targets appeared beyond the ship's rigging. None of the cruiser's missiles made it through the sledging defensive fire, though one segment vaporized close enough to its target that a pair of topgallants ripped away when the *Aristoxenos* slid through the still-expanding cloud.

The weight of the *Aristoxenos'* missiles was beyond the ability of any defensive battery to withstand, even that of another battleship. Semmes reacted in the only fashion that even hinted survival, slamming High Drive and plasma thrusters both to full power at right angles to the incoming salvo. The *Bluecher's* frame warped visibly at the overload, but the acceleration took her almost out of the cone of predicted missile tracks.

The cruiser's eight big plasma cannon concentrated on the segments at the near edge, that ones that were still potentially dangerous. Bolt for bolt the 15-cm guns had only half the punch of the battleship's 8-inchers, but the *Bluecher* was cleared for action and her gunners were at a high state of training. The guns' hammering reduced parts of the multi-ton missile segments into gas whose escape drove the remainder off at angles harmless to the cruiser.

Daniel knew precisely what acceleration the cruiser could manage in an emergency because he'd seen the *Bluecher* react to avoid the Commonwealth rockets. He predicted the direction of that acceleration by the angle he'd have chosen if he captained the *Bluecher* and the battleship was launching at him. The *Princess Cecile*'s last pair of missiles stabbed in unnoticed till the cruiser's starboard turret desperately engaged a second before impact.

A segment struck the *Bluecher*'s bow as a cloud of gas still so dense that it crushed hull plating and carried away the leading dorsal, starboard and ventral antennas. Microseconds later another segment hit the stern squarely. The release of kinetic energy engulfed the last twenty meters of the vessel in a fireball which left only vacuum behind when it dissipated.

The *Bluecher* had been about to launch missiles when she was hit. Several left their tubes but tumbled; the computer which should've updated their courses until burn-out instead spasmed when the cruiser whipped sideways.

"Sissie Six to flagship," Daniel said, adding the alert channel so that the corvette's crew could listen to his transmission. They'd earned it, the good Lord knew! "Admiral, I suggest we cease fire until you offer the *Bluecher* a chance to surrender. Her captain is named Semmes, and I won't willingly participate in the murder of a man so able. *Sissie* over."

"Sir?" said Betts, turning toward Daniel but speaking over the command channel. The bridge was too noisy for unaided voice. *"The battleship* has *to cease fire. The conveyors from her magazines to the launch tubes are all frozen. They just had what was in the tubes when they lifted from Todos Santos."*

"*Sissie Six, this is Zanie Six,*" said Admiral O'Quinn's voice, wheezing noticeably. Both ships had visual capacity, but standard operating procedure in the RCN was voice only. In a battle, bandwidth could become too valuable a commodity to waste on frills. "*You take their surrender, Leary. You knocked her out.*"

O'Quinn snorted and went on, "*Your missileer even launched our missiles, though I'm damned if I know how he got control of our system. I didn't think that was possible! Over.*"

Ah. Daniel hadn't thought it was possible either, but obviously Adele had known better. Apparently she hadn't been wasting her time while the *Princess Cecile* was moored adjacent to the battleship in San Juan harbor. That explained why the salvo had come so quickly. Daniel had expected minutes to pass before the *Aristoxenos* was ready to launch, even with Betts transferring solutions to the battleship's attack board.

"Admiral," Daniel said, "the *Princess Cecile* was only a target before your very welcome arrival. If you'll take the credit for the victory which you've certainly earned, it'll make my job easier when I talk to people back in Xenos about what the Republic owes you. As I most certainly will, over."

There was a pause greater than transmission lag before O'Quinn responded, "*By God, Leary, if I'd had half the respect for your father that I do for you, we wouldn't be in this place now. Break. AFS Bluecher, this is Admiral O'Quinn, RCN. Do you surrender, or would you prefer to provide the target practice which I'll admit my crew could use, over?*"

Over the intercom alone Daniel said, "Personally, fellow Sissies, I'm just as glad they *are* here now."

Adele let the cheers sound over the general push, though they almost drowned out the mumbled words of Captain Semmes surrendering unconditionally.

CHAPTER 33

"Ship," said Daniel, "this is Six. We'll be extracting from the Matrix above Todos Santos in a few minutes."

Adele shielded him from the chatter on the intercom, but because of the *Sissie's* internal hush at this point in a voyage he heard spacers shouting, "Yee-haw!" and "Booze and women!" followed a moment later by Maginnes calling, "You can keep the women—this time I want a pretty little boy who's hung like a pony!"

Maginnes was a rigger, waiting in her suit at the airlock with the rest of the starboard watch in case Woetjans and the port watch unexpectedly needed help lowering the minimal sail set with which the corvette had made this last leg of the run. Daniel thought of her, a squat stump of a woman with a face like a pug dog, and the pretty boy she wanted. But Maginnes was a spacer with money in her pocket, and she'd get whatever she wanted until the money ran out.

"Now listen, Sissies," Daniel said, smiling in the knowledge that though he commanded this crew, they were his family as surely as he was part of theirs. "When we left Todos Santos we were on friendly terms with everybody except some folks from Pleasaunce. Those folks aren't around any more."

He paused for laughter.

"But a lot can change in a month," he continued. "Just ask the garrison of Lorenz Base about that if you don't believe me."

More laughter. They'd been through a lot this voyage. The Sissies never doubted that Daniel was captain, but this was a good time for him to remind them that he was *their* captain, the man who wouldn't send them any place he wouldn't go himself.

"There may have been political changes here," he said. He ignored the cries about wogs. "And there may well be an Alliance ship in port, in which case we won't stay any longer than it takes me to input the course data I've already prepared."

They'd have been safer if they'd remained in company with the *Aristoxenos*. Alliance warships might be willing to disregard the Cluster government long enough to overwhelm an RCN corvette, but not in front of a Cluster battleship. Though seriously battered by the strains of the Matrix and explosive failures in her own armaments, the *Zanie* remained an impressive sight.

Daniel had come alone because the *Aristoxenos* had only six High Drive motors functioning out of the original forty-eight. Her systems rated a complement of nearly a thousand, but her present crew was two hundred and fifty former RCN crewmen, supplemented by an equal number of their retainers who didn't have any experience off-planet. The Ten Star Cluster had no lack of experienced spacers, but only a handful of them had been willing to sign on with the decayed battleship. Not even those few would've boarded if they'd been told the details of a plan they'd have found insane.

The *Aristoxenos* had been lucky to arrive off Radiance as quickly as she did, and it'd take her longer to get home. The *Princess Cecile* would've added a minimum of nine days to her voyage if she'd returned to Todos Santos with the battleship.

"We've taken enough chances this voyage, Sissies," Daniel said. "I don't want to put us through more."

"*Six, this is Five,*" Chewning announced in an apologetic voice from the Battle Direction Center. "*We'll be reentering normal space in—one minute. Over.*"

"Roger, Mr. Chewning," Daniel said. "Break. Ship, prepare to return to sidereal space—"

He pressed the control.

"—now!"

The *Princess Cecile* shuddered into sidereal space like a fish swimming through transparent glycerine instead of water. Daniel wasn't really worried about what would happen over Todos Santos unless colossal bad luck brought them out of the Matrix within spitting distance of an Alliance warship.

Nobody should be looking for them here. People would notice the corvette's arrival and some might have hostile intentions, but Daniel had full confidence in Adele's ability to identify a problem in time for the *Sissie* to escape. They'd refilled their tanks of reaction mass on an uninhabited world a day out from here. They could make it to Cinnabar on their present load if they had to, though it'd mean short rations by the time they arrived.

Present reality returned with a crystalline suddenness that turned all the previous time in the Matrix into half-remembered nightmare. It wasn't really bad while you were in it, but when you came out you had a sticky itchiness on your soul like the way your skin felt after swimming in salt water.

The *Princess Cecile* was 80,000 miles above Todos

Santos. The PPI was full of ships. To Daniel's momentary horror, a voice over a laser communicator—which proved that the *Sissie* had not only been noticed but but that she'd been located with as much precision as fire control would require—said, "*RCS* Melampus *to unidentified vessel. Identify yourself immediately, over.*"

In the lower right-hand corner of Daniel's display appeared a box of text in red outline from Adele:

> THIRTEEN COUNTRY CRAFT
> RCS MELAMPUS DIANA SEAHORSE CLYDE
> KAPILA

There were details of size, armament, and Table of Organization crew strength, but Daniel knew all that or knew it well enough for his purposes. The first four Cinnabar vessels were destroyers; the *Kapila* was a battleship which'd been in Harbor Three when the *Princess Cecile* lifted as the Klimovs' private yacht.

"*Melampus*, this is starship *Princess Cecile*, out of Xenos with a former RCN crew aboard," Daniel said. He was careful *not* to claim to be a naval vessel, as he'd done without hesitation when signaling anybody else. "We arrived to take on supplies for the run home, but finding you here I'd like to report to somebody on your commander's staff if that's possible. *Sissie* over."

There was a pause. Daniel turned to his gunner. Calling across the bridge because he didn't want to risk accidentally transmitting to ships whose missileers were ready to launch, Daniel said, "Sun, lock your guns *now*. We can't afford a mistake. These people might be sorry to have killed us when they figure things out, but they're *not* going to miss!"

"*Princess Cecile, is Lieutenant Leary your captain, over?*" the destroyer said at last.

Daniel heard the 4-inch turrets clack into the fore-and-aft position that kept them from shifting when the vessel was under power. He pursed his lips, then said, "Roger, *Melampus*, this is former Lieutenant Leary. Ah, *Melampus*? We're on a ballistic course, waiting for direction as to how we should proceed. Over."

After a longer pause, a different voice—Adele's text crawl read FROM RCS KAPILA—said, "*Princess Cecile, this is Movement Control. You're to land in Berth A-12, San Juan Harbor, immediately. A vehicle will be waiting to transport Lieutenant Leary and Signals Officer Mundy to the RCN Ground Detachment Head-quarters. Do you understand, over?*"

"Movement Control," Daniel said, frowning but trying hard to keep his voice neutral, "do we need clearance by the Cluster authorities also, over?"

"*Princess Cecile, there are no Cluster authorities any more as regards space travel,*" the voice from the *Kapila* said. "*This is RCN territory, mister. Carry out your orders! Over.*"

Daniel met Adele's eyes across the bridge. She was nodding and wore what was for her a broad grin.

"Roger that, Movement Control," Daniel said. "*Sissie* out."

He looked at his display. The Battle Direction Center—which probably meant Vesey, as Chewning simply wasn't quick enough to have done it—offered a landing solution that would bring them down at San Juan in an orbit and a half.

Daniel grinned. "Mr. Chewning?" he said. "Do you feel comfortable about landing us this time, over?"

"*Yes sir,*" said Chewning. "*I mean, it's pretty straight, isn't it, sir? I mean, it looks pretty straight to me. Over.*"

"And to me as well, Chewning," Daniel said, releasing his shock harness. "You have the conn. Break.

Officer Mundy, I know we ought to be strapped in for
a landing, but you and I need to get into our Dress
Whites soonest, and that means getting started now.
Six out."

The main hatch lowered with a wheezy sigh, swirling
in the air of the Todos Santos. Hot steam had boiled
from harbor water mixed with garbage and lubricants,
and it was shot through with ozone.

Adele smiled. She'd come to associate that complex
of odors with safe landings. Smelling it again gave her
a feeling of nostalgic warmth.

Riggers were mooring the *Princess Cecile* bow and
stern. Here in the entry compartment, a team of ship-
side spacers under a petty officer tilted the gangplank
out by hand and let it clang to the quay instead of
bothering with the hydraulic extender. Two of them ran
across and tied the shore end off to bitts. The horizon rose and fell gently as the corvette rocked on waves
she'd created when she landed.

Through the dissipating steam Adele could see an all-
terrain ground vehicle, a bug of a body supported on
four huge knitted-wire wheels, waiting on the quay. The
front bench was open except for a roll cage mounting
an automatic impeller, but the back was enclosed; the
fenders bore stenciled Cinnabar markings.

"Ready, master?" said Hogg, resplendent in pantaloons, a ruffed shirt, and a broad silk sash, in contrasting colors. He didn't carry a weapon openly—they were
going to meet Cinnabar officials, not the benighted
locals, after all. Except Adele knew the term in Hogg's
mind was closer to "fucking wogs."

Tovera was in an off-white pants suit. It sounded
conspicuous, but the creamy fabric didn't glow even
in bright sunshine and in the shade looked like a
splotched wall. She carried her attaché case for no

better reason than Daniel checked the set of his saucer hat: it was what you did when you left the ship.

"Yes, I think we are," Daniel said, grinning at Adele. Hogg swaggered down the gangplank in a mixture of pride and truculence.

They'd done great things in the North, but that was in the past; now they must deal with the present. The ordinary machinery of the RCN was concerned with the way things were accomplished as well as what the things were. Hogg, for all his blustering countryman's appearance, had a sophisticated awareness of the distinction: he'd have been hanged long since if he hadn't.

Daniel strode toward the quay ahead of Adele as befit his rank. Tovera was last of all, the secretary too commonplace to notice—especially with Hogg in front to draw attention. The two made a good team, as good as Daniel and Adele did in their different fashion.

Tovera understood the risks of doing the right thing the wrong way as clearly as Adele did, but neither of them cared enough about their own lives for that to matter. Daniel, on the other hand, loved life and pleasure as much as any other soul aboard the *Princess Cecile*. If all went well he'd be relaxing tonight just as his spacers did, with enough liquor to float the corvette and one or more air-headed bimbos to share it with him.

But if Daniel knew with absolute certainty that doing the right and necessary thing would cause him to be executed by his own government, he'd do what he thought was right and necessary. Hogg would be beside him, muttering that the master was a damned fool, and all the Sissies would be following.

The car's driver got out as soon as Adele and Daniel started across the gangplank. At their approach he opened the door to the rear compartment.

Hogg turned and raised an eyebrow toward Daniel.

The driver said, "Why don't you servants ride up front with me, eh?"

"Why don't you button your lip till we hear what the master wants, eh, boy?" Hogg said. His tone was pleasant enough despite the words.

Adele glanced into the back of the vehicle. Cushioned seats faced one another in pairs; Lieutenant Wilsing sat in the middle, bending forward to look at them.

"Come on up front with me, Hogg," Tovera said in an unusually loud voice for her. "I've met the gentleman. Mistress Mundy can handle any trouble that he causes."

Daniel nodded smilingly to Hogg, then handed Adele into the seat and went around to the other side himself. The car started off as soon as he closed the door behind him. The tires made a ringing hum on the pavement.

"Captain," Adele said, "this is Lieutenant Wilsing. You may remember him from when the *Princess Cecile* was fitting out in Harbor One."

Adele had sent a coded report to the *Kapila* when she found a receiver to handshake with hers. She hadn't been certain until then that Mistress Sand's organization was participating in this operation, but she wasn't at all surprised that it was. This was clearly more than an RCN initiative.

"Yes, I do," Daniel said in a distant tone that showed he not only remembered, he understood. "Good morning, Wilsing."

"I'm an aide to Captain Carnolets, who's head of the RCN Ground Detachment here," Wilsing explained. "We've only been here two days, so matters are still being sorted out. Count Klimov arrived in Xenos on a Cinnabar freighter from Todos Santos, telling of how you'd located an Alliance squadron on Radiance. The

Count had recovered the Earth Diamond here in the North, which proved he couldn't be entirely a crackpot."

Wilsing spread his hands with a supercilious smile. "Admiral Anston took the report seriously enough to scrape together a squadron to set up a base on Todos Santos," he said. "And a civilian advisor—"

Mistress Sand, obviously.

"—convinced some important Senators that there should be an advisory mission to help Governor Sakama through the present difficult situation. He retains control of the Ten Star Cluster, of course, but well, we couldn't have the Alliance setting up a base here as well as on Radiance, could we?"

"The Alliance squadron's been pretty well scotched," Daniel said. He cleared his throat. "The base on Gehenna's still usable, though, most of it. It's something Admiral Keith will need to deal with. Ah, that is, I assume the Admiral will want to prevent the Alliance from reoccupying the base."

"Scotched?" Wilsing repeated in a rising tone that filled Adele with a mixture of embarrassment and fury. "Well, my goodness. If that's true, it's very fortunate. There was a good deal of concern as to how the *Kapila* was going to perform against two modern Alliance battleships. She'd been relegated to guardship duties, you know."

"The lieutenant's statement is quite true," Adele said. "As one would expect of anything said by a Leary of Bantry, of course."

Wilsing's tongue touched the corner of his mouth. "Of course," he said. "I—"

"And as for concern, Wilsing," Daniel said, smiling but with a muscle at the back of his jaw jumping, "I doubt it was shared by any *real* RCN officer. The day an RCN battleship can't see off a couple wogs, I'll join the priesthood. Eh, Mundy?"

"You'd look remarkably silly in robes, Captain," Adele said with a hard smile for Wilsing's benefit. "But I doubt either of us will live to see that happen."

The vehicle slowed to a halt, its tires singing on a descending note. A section of street was closed off with razor ribbon and concrete barriers, guarded at each end by an armored vehicle mounting a plasma cannon and a squad of the Land Forces of the Republic.

Wilsing nodded with a fixed smile. "The Ground Detachment has been granted these buildings by Governor Sakama," he said. "We'll walk from here, if you don't mind."

Daniel laughed and got out the door Hogg opened for him. "Well, Mundy," he said. "It looks better than some of the places we've been together, doesn't it?"

Arm in arm, and with their servants, they followed the discomfited Lieutenant Wilsing through the narrow entrance to the headquarters of the new government of the Ten Star Cluster.

CHAPTER 34

Ground Detachment Headquarters was a palace like that of her cousin Adrian, and it certainly hadn't been abandoned before the Cinnabar squadron arrived a few days ago. Somebody'd been touching up the frescoes on the ceiling of the entrance hall. The scaffolding remained, but work had stopped.

Adele wondered who the owners had been and what they'd done to lose their home abruptly. They'd very likely lost their heads as well, which made her think of the Three Circles Conspiracy.

"Adele?" Daniel said. She came alert, feeling a hot itch shudder momentarily just under her skin. A clerk of some kind was waiting expectantly for Daniel to go off with him, but Daniel was watching her with concern. "I'm to meet with a board, they say."

"Sorry," Adele said. The smile on her lips didn't belong to her; nothing belonged to her, she'd died half a lifetime ago when she heard of her family's massacre. "I was daydreaming."

"If you'll come with me, mistress," Lieutenant Wilsing said, "Captain Carnolets is waiting."

He sounded concerned but no longer slickly supercilious. Adele's smile became real. Wilsing had learned something during the ride here. And she wasn't dead. She belonged to the RCN and to the *Princess Cecile*; and she belonged to herself again, because she had the respect of men and women whom she herself respected.

"Good luck with your board, Captain," she said, nodding to Daniel. She had no idea what he was getting into; she simply hadn't had time to search records here. "I can provide any documentation you need, of course."

"Thank you, Mundy," Daniel said. "And the best of luck to you as well. RCN forever, eh?"

The clerk led him and Hogg past the guard of a ground floor room. Wilsing, seeing that she was ready to follow him, took Adele in the other direction and up three flights of stairs. Tovera followed silently.

Adele heard voices and the sound of office machines in the rooms they passed, but the suite at the top of a corner tower was silent. A male secretary met Adele at the door. He bowed her in and remained outside with Wilsing and Tovera as he closed the door.

The room was covered in overlaid rugs, a meter wide and three meters long, which must have come with the palace. The desk was crackle-finished metal with a smooth enameled top—straight RCN issue. It was large, but only because three identical modules had been dovetailed together.

The man behind the desk was typing into a keypad while watching a holographic display. Simultaneously he spoke into a pickup with active sound cancelling: Adele saw his lips move, but she couldn't hear anything but the hum of the display as she walked toward the desk. The man nodded her to a puffy cushioned chair, part of the original furnishings, while continuing to speak silently.

Adele brought out her handheld and searched the map database to learn who'd owned the property before the RCN moved in. In part she was interested in the answer, not that it was likely to mean anything to her; but it was also true that she didn't care to twiddle her thumbs while somebody else carried on with his own business. Carnolets was the military governor here, that was obvious; but she was Mundy of Chatsworth.

Captain Carnolets was a tall, broad-shouldered man who'd stayed in shape despite being in his late sixties or older. He wore a 1st Class dress uniform with a considerable number of medal ribbons on both breasts. Adele wasn't expert in such things, but the varying size of the ribbons suggested to her that many of them were from foreign governments rather than the Republic itself.

This palace was still listed as the property of Duchess Ayesha Ramos, a member of the Governor's Inner Council. Presumably the Duchess had given the wrong advice recently, or perhaps Governor Sakama had simply needed a scapegoat to take the blame for something when an RCN squadron arrived.

Adele glanced hard-faced about the room, taking in the statues in alcoves and the geometrical parquet of the ceiling. While it lasted, life had been pleasant for Duchess Ramos. Lucius Mundy might well have said the same thing.

"All right, Mundy," Carnolets said, switching off his display to look across the desk at her unveiled. His expression probably seemed intimidating to many of those he interviewed. "Your report made interesting reading."

Adele shrugged. After you've faced 15-cm plasma cannon, a scowling human holds few terrors. "Gathering the information was interesting also," she said. "Now that I've had time to digest the experience, that is. While it was going on I didn't feel much of anything."

Carnolets frowned, then broke into a smile and slapped the desk ringingly. "Bernis Sand said you don't look like much but not to be fooled," he said. "That's right, isn't it?"

"I don't know Mistress Sand as well as you appear to, Captain," Adele said, "but I'd be willing to take her word on most things."

Carnolets nodded. "Aye," he said, "and so would anybody who matters in the Senate. That's why the Republic's as healthy as it is, a lot of folks say. *I* say it."

Adele nodded without speaking, waiting for the captain to come to the point. There *was* a point, she felt certain, or he wouldn't be representing Mistress Sand.

Carnolets drummed on his desk with the index and middle fingers of his right hand. "All right, Mundy, I've got your report, but it's not the same as being there. Give me—give us—your assessment of the Alliance threat remaining on Gehenna. Nobody's looking to take your job if you're wrong."

Adele gave Carnolets a smile similar to that she'd bestowed on Lieutenant Wilsing in the car. "With respect, Captain," she said, "my *job* is signals officer of the *Princess Cecile*. If Mistress Sand chooses to relieve me of any tasks I perform for her as a citizen of the Republic, she's welcome to do so."

She coughed into her hand. She understood why Sand used uniformed personnel for liaison duties, but it was awkward. Most naval officers weren't fools, not really, but they were narrow and they thought in narrow tracks. Even as a child Adele Mundy hadn't run on a track that a man like Carnolets could recognize, though she was simple enough in all truth.

"As for Lorenz Base," she continued, "the two

battleships are probably reparable but not quickly. Perhaps as many as four destroyers survived, possibly undamaged. Though it's equally likely that all were destroyed."

She smiled at a memory. "The heavy cruiser was destroyed," she said. "Of that I'm sure."

"What're the chances of Alliance reinforcements, then?" Carnolets asked.

Adele shrugged. "The base wasn't expecting any," she said. "I've made a sufficient study of the material I abstracted from their files to determine that, and we interviewed officers from the *Bluecher* before we set them on a habitable world."

Carnolets brought up his display again and resumed typing. "Good," he said. "Excellent. I'll recommend Keith follow up his advantage even though things here in the Cluster aren't completely settled yet. You did a fine job, Mundy, a *fine* job."

"I'm fortunate to be part of the crew of the most efficient vessel in the RCN, Captain," Adele said. Suddenly, shockingly, she felt tears start into her eyes. Trying to control her stammer she went on. "Even when she's not technically in the RCN any more. God *damn* it!"

The last was to herself in a savage whisper, furious at her weakness. The tone if not the words penetrated Carnolets' abstraction. He looked at Adele in puzzlement and said, "Is there anything else you need to mention, Mundy? If not . . . ?"

"There's another matter, yes," Adele said. The emotion remaining was a much harder thing than the love and pride that had briefly overwhelmed her. She grinned in her heart: love and pride had briefly *unmanned* her. "There's the matter of the crew of the *Aristoxenos*. They were in great measure responsible for the success of the operation. It's time that they're restored to Cinnabar citizenship."

"You have a cousin in that lot, I believe?" Carnolets said, glaring at her through his holographic display.

"My cousin Adrian Purvis was killed aboard the *Aristoxenos* when a missile exploded in its tube during the recent action, if that's what you mean," Adele said. Her voice was controlled, but her expression made the man across the desk shut down his display again. "If you mean anything else, say it."

"I beg your pardon, Mistress Mundy," Carnolets said. "I misspoke. No one viewing your record could imagine that you'd put family purposes ahead of the needs of the Republic."

He stood and bowed to her, then sat down and continued, "As for the mutineers—the RCN doesn't play politics. I won't pretend to have sympathy for officers who forget that rule. On the other hand, it's been a long time; and besides, Bernis asked me—"

He stopped and corrected himself with embarrassment that showed his contrition better than the prevous words had, "Mistress Sand *ordered* me, I should rather say, to show you every consideration should we meet. I suppose this request falls into that category."

Carnolets raised a finger of apology and brought up his display again. He made a short series of keystrokes, then shut down.

"There," he said, beaming at her. "I've enlisted the surviving officers and crew of the *Aristoxenos* as the Ground Detachment Naval Militia, with pay of one florin a year and full Cinnabar citizenship. That'll protect them from the locals if they stay here, and it'll let them go home if they prefer. Satisfactory?"

Adele rose. "That's quite satisfactory, Captain," she said. "Thank you. I'll leave you to your important work, but of course I'll be available if you have further need of me before the *Princess Cecile* lifts."

She walked to the door over the thick, yielding rugs.

And when will we lift, and where to? But one thing at a time, and this had been a very great thing.

This had been the end of the Three Circles Conspiracy.

The rating led Daniel and Hogg to a door just around the corner from the entrance hall. He tapped twice on the panel, then lowered the tilting-bar latch and called through the crack, "Mr. Leary's here, Commander."

"Then send him bloody in!" a voice growled from inside. The rating swung the door open and nodded to Daniel.

In the center of the room was a long table topped with colored marble. The frames of the chairs along either side were carved and gilded with green satin upholstery. The high ceiling had gilt decorations, and the walls were papered in a scintillant peacock-tail pattern up to a frieze of mythological scenes.

Oddly enough, the RCN-standard filing cabinets and the four data consoles under the mirror the far side of the room made the original furnishings look out of place, not the other way around. Ratings were working at the consoles.

Across the table from Daniel sat three RCN officers—a commander in the center, a female lieutenant to his right, both in 2nd Class uniforms; and a grizzled man to his left in utilities so worn and stained that his rank wasn't visible. He was probably a lieutenant also, commissioned from warrant rank for his technical abilities. The lieutenants had hand-held units on the speckled marble before them, and the engineer was sunk in his display.

"Sit down, Leary," the Commander said, gesturing at the chairs on Daniel's side of the table. "We just got the data twenty minutes ago. Not the way things ought to be run, of course, but needs must when the Devil drives, eh?"

Daniel seated himself gingerly. Hogg stood against the wall behind him, looking grimly expectant. The chairs were just as uncomfortable as Daniel'd expected. The seat tried to throw him into a back so deep it'd be extremely difficult for him to leap up suddenly.

He wouldn't really have to, but his body had been trained by tens of millions of years of pre-human existence to categorize all threats in terms of physical responses: fight or flight. The chair wasn't suited to either, and the situation *was* threatening.

"Ah, Commander . . . ?" Daniel said. The president of the board wasn't anybody he recognized, and his name-tape was half-hidden. It was Brit-something, Britton or Britling, but it wouldn't do to guess wrong. "Should I have defense counsel present?"

"Don't be an idiot, Leary," the president said, spreading three sheets of hardcopy before him. When he moved, Daniel saw that his name was actually Britten. "We're the survey board, sitting on the *Princess Cecile*. The Senate authorized Admiral Keith to buy vessels to supplement his squadron. As you can imagine, we left in a hell of a hurry, a *hell* of a hurry."

"Your corvette's a godsend," said the female lieutenant, Feininger unless a trick of the light made Daniel misread her name. "Worked up and with a trained crew."

"We'll need to draft some of that crew, of course," Britten said, shuffling more hardcopy onto the table with a disgusted look on his face. "Sorry, Leary, but that's how it is. Needs of the service, you know."

"Ah," said Daniel, organizing his thoughts to deal with a situation very different from the one he'd expected. "Sir, I suppose we could lose twenty personnel without struggling too badly, but you must recall that we had casualties in action with Alliance vessels."

And so they had, seven riggers dead when the *Bluecher's* missile cleared a section of the hull with a bubble of white-hot gas. The *Sissie* and *Goldenfels* together had shipped forty extra personnel, Alliance deserters and Morzangan natives who hadn't fully understood what they were getting into, though.

"Twenty?" said Lieutenant Feininger. "Don't be daft. You'll send thirty trained spacers to the *Kapila* and thank God we need a corvette for long-range scouting even more than we need the other eighty souls in your crew!"

"Sirs?" Daniel said. They didn't seem terribly interested in him, but there were things he needed to get out. "I should mention that nothing that happened at Lorenz Base, that is in the Radiance system, involved a Cinnabar ship—no ship that had ever been in RCN service, that is. And the action off Salmson 115 began with an unprovoked attack by an Alliance cruiser, so *Princess Cecile* had every legal right to reply. Technically."

Commander Britten looked up in exasperation. "Technicalities be damned, Leary!" he said. "Are you an officer or a bloody lawyer? This is war or the next thing to it! I don't want to hear you blathering about bloody legal bullshit. D'ye understand me?"

"Yessir," said Daniel, sitting very stiff on the edge of this *damned* soft chair.

"They were on the verge of declaring war when we lifted from Harbor Three, Leary," Lieutenant Feininger said. "Speaker Leary was blaggarding Legislator Jarre up one side and down the other in front of the whole Senate. We signed the armistice on the basis of *status quo ante*, and here the Alliance was shifting a squadron to Radiance where they bloody well *hadn't* been at the beginning of the last war."

"Speaker Leary . . . ," Britten said as a new thought crossed his mind. He frowned. "Related to you, Leary?"

"I suppose so," Daniel said. "We're not social acquaintances, if that's what you mean."

That was literally true: he and Corder Leary hadn't spoken in seven years, and their last interview had been of the sort that would've ended with pistols at dawn if they hadn't been father and son.

Daniel preferred that the relationship not come up when he was talking to fellow officers. In order to prevent misapprehensions, he'd have to say a great deal more about his personal life than he or any other gentleman wanted to do.

Feininger leaned toward Britten and whispered into his ear, her eyes on Daniel. Britten grunted and said, "Right, I'd forget my head if it weren't screwed on. There's too bloody much work to do in a year, and they're giving us two weeks!"

He lifted the attaché case on the floor behind him and slammed it down on the sheets already on the table. He lifted the lid, rooted through the contents, and came out with a document on parchment with ribbons and red wax seal.

"There you go, Leary," he said, handing the document across the table. "We've got a bale of blank commissions as you might imagine, but Admiral Anston himself signed one for you. You reverted to active duty. . . ."

Britten turned the document around to read the date.

"Seventeen days ago, I make it. When you get back to your command, be sure to swear your crew in, will you?"

"I, ah . . . ," Daniel said. His mouth was dry. "Yes sir."

"What condition's the spars and rigging, eh, Leary?"

asked the engineering officer. His nametape was illegible, bleached by the chemicals which had failed to clean some of the stains out of the fabric. "Your log says you lost three antennas in action."

"Ah, yessir," Daniel said. "And we expended a quantity of cables in circumstances that prevented their recovery. But we were able to replace all missing spars, sails, and rigging from the *Bluecher* before we dropped the wreck onto Gehenna."

The engineer nodded, then turned to Britten and said, "Beggars can't be choosers, Commander, but it seems to me she'd be a good choice regardless. She was surveyed at a million four-seven-five as a prize two years ago, and I see no reason to court a writ when we get back home by offering less now."

"Lieutenant Feininger?" Britten said, looking to his right. She nodded.

He pulled a form out of his briefcase, scribbled down figures, and signed it before handing it to the engineering officer to sign. "Done!"

"Now understand, Mr. Leary . . . ," Feininger said as she signed in turn. "We don't carry specie. This is a draft on the Treasury, but that doesn't mean money in your pocket until God knows how many faceless clerks on Xenos countersign the proper documents. You'll be waiting years to see money, likely, unless you go to a discounter."

"I've had experience with prize money, Lieutenant," Daniel said, piqued at the lecture but aware that it was well-meant. Most officers *didn't* have experience with prize money. "That raises a question, if you don't mind. Is it permissible for me to divide this money among my crew in shares as if it *were* prize money?"

"She's *not* a prize," said the engineering officer. "You didn't capture the *Princess Cecile*, you bought her. That's what the bill of sale says, anyway. Doesn't it?"

"Yes, but . . . ," Daniel said; and stopped, because he wasn't sure how to go on.

Commander Britten snorted. "You can do any bloody fool thing you want with your money, Leary—that's what spacers do, generally, piss their money away like bloody fools. But you don't need to give away three-quarters of what's all yours."

He waved his hand. "Go on, get out of here," he said. "God knows you're not the only thing we have to deal with this afternoon."

"With respect, Commander . . . ," Daniel said, rising to his feet. The document giving him close to a million and a half florins shivered in his hands. There'd be electronic equivalents, but the document had a physical reality that took his breath away. "I believe I do need to divide the money. The Learys of Bantry have done hard things over the years, but nobody ever accused us of cheating our retainers."

Hogg, standing unnaturally stiff in a failed attempt to give himself dignity, threw the door open. Daniel stepped out. Adele was coming toward them down the hall.

Daniel drew in a deep breath and looked again at the draft to make sure it really said what he believed it did. He opened his mouth to say, "Adele, the most amazing thing has happened!"

But Adele, smiling like a happy child, was already saying, "Daniel, I have wonderful news!"

DAVID DRAKE RULES!

Hammer's Slammers:

The Tank Lords	87794-1 ◆ $6.99	☐
Caught in the Crossfire	87882-4 ◆ $6.99	☐
The Butcher's Bill	57773-5 ◆ $6.99	☐
The Sharp End	87632-5 ◆ $7.99	☐
Cross the Stars	57821-9 ◆ $6.99	☐
Paying the Piper (HC)	7434-3547-8 ◆ $24.00	☐

RCN series:

With the Lightnings	57818-9 ◆ $6.99	☐
Lt. Leary, Commanding (HC)	57875-8 ◆ $24.00	☐
Lt. Leary, Commanding (PB)	31992-2 ◆ $7.99	☐

The Belisarius series with Eric Flint:

An Oblique Approach	87865-4 ◆ $6.99	☐
In the Heart of Darkness	87885-9 ◆ $6.99	☐
Destiny's Shield	57872-3 ◆ $6.99	☐
Fortune's Stroke (HC)	57871-5 ◆ $24.00	☐
The Tide of Victory (HC)	31996-5 ◆ $22.00	☐
The Tide of Victory (PB)	7434-3565-6 ◆ $7.99	☐

The General series with S.M. Stirling:

The Forge	72037-6 ◆ $5.99	☐
The Chosen	87724-0 ◆ $6.99	☐
The Reformer	57860-X ◆ $6.99	☐
The Tyrant	0-7434-7150-4 ◆ $7.99	☐

Independent Novels and Collections:

The Dragon Lord (fantasy)	87890-5 ◆ $6.99	☐
Birds of Prey	57790-5 ◆ $6.99	☐

• BOLO: The Future of War •

• •

What is a Bolo? The symbol of brute force, intransient defiance, and adamantine will. But on a deeper level, the Bolo is the Lancelot of the future, the perfect knight, *sans peur et sans reproche*. With plated armor, a laser canon, an electronic brain, and wheels.

• •